TO LOVE A DARK LORD

Jillian didn't know what made her do it, but suddenly she found herself lifting up on her tiptoes to kiss Duncan. As her lips brushed his, she slid her hand around his neck. The scent of him was intoxicating . . . the taste of him pure magic.

"Jilly," he whispered against her mouth, his resonant voice sending shivers of pleasure through her body. No one had ever spoken her name as Duncan did.

"Yes," she heard herself murmur as she parted her lips, a sudden sense of urgency in her kiss.

Duncan kissed the pulse of her throat, murmuring words in some foreign tongue. Jillian couldn't breathe. She couldn't think. She knew she shouldn't be responding with such wantonness, but she couldn't help herself. She rested her hands on Duncan's shoulders, leaning against him, marveling at the sen sations he created. How was it that he knew instinctively how to touch her?

"Jilly . . ."

"I can't see anything in this blackness," she whispered. "I just want to touch your face."

Jillian could feel his gaze intent on her as she slowly pushed back the veil and then let it flutter to the floor. She brushed her palm against the cheek she had never seen.

With light fingertips, she explored his flesh. She let her hand slide down his face to rest on his muscular shoulder. She caressed the sinewy muscles in awe of his strength.

"It's time," she told him, knowing her voice trembled with a blend of emotions. "It's time to make me your wife . . ."

Books by Colleen Faulkner

FORBIDDEN CARESS
RAGING DESIRE
SNOW FIRE
TRAITOR'S CARESS
PASSION'S SAVAGE MOON
TEMPTATION'S TENDER KISS
LOVE'S SWEET BOUNTY
PATRIOT'S PASSION
SAVAGE SURRENDER
SWEET DECEPTION
FLAMES OF LOVE
FOREVER HIS
CAPTIVE
O'BRIAN'S BRIDE
DESTINED TO BE MINE

Published by Zebra Books

DESTINED TO BE MINE

COLLEEN FAULKNER

ZEBRA BOOKS
KENSINGTON PUBLISHING CORP.

ZEBRA BOOKS are published by

Kensington Publishing Corp.
850 Third Avenue
New York, NY 10022

First Printing: May, 1996
10 9 8 7 6 5 4 3 2 1

Printed in the United States of America

This one's for Lori Darlin'. Thanks.

Prologue

Somewhere in the Maryland Wilderness
American Colonies, Spring 1646

Tsitsho of the Bear Clan of the Mohawk crouched low behind an inkberry bush at the edge of the hardwood forest, his hand resting on the hilt of his war hatchet. Cautiously, he surveyed his surroundings. He heard the call of a whippoorwill and the sound of swaying tree limbs. He smelled the scent of a scurrying squirrel, and of the white men in the cabin in the midst of the clearing.

He watched the smoke rise from the stone chimney and knew that it was soft pine they burned. Somewhere a hen clucked.

Tsitsho guessed a family lived inside the cabin. Outside he saw evidence of a woman and children—clothing hanging to dry on a rope strung between two trees, a leather ball left abandoned near the chiseled stone steps of the single room cabin. A family, yes, that was good. It was what he'd been looking for.

Suddenly the cabin door swung open and a bearded man stepped out into the morning sunshine. He wore boots and white men's cloth leggings; his chest was bare. He leaned his musket against the oak-hewn wall behind him and stretched, raising his arms over his head.

Tsitsho felt his heart pounding beneath his breast. Out

of habit, he touched the mark on his left cheek, eyeing the white man.

This was what he had come for. This was why he had walked hundreds of miles. This was what he had risked his life for time and time again. This was why he had killed his brother.

But Tsitsho was no coward, so he rose, stepping out of the shadows of the morning forest.

Immediately the man in the beard gave a cry of alarm, reaching for his musket.

"Yahten!" Tsitsho called, raising his hands. "Do not shoot." The English words tasted strange on his tongue. "I mean you no harm."

The white man aimed the musket, staring at Tsitsho's colorfully tattooed chest, evident beneath the sleeveless, quilled leather vest. Tsitsho watched the white man as he took in his appearance—his loincloth and porcupine-quilled moccasins, his hair shaved in a scalplock, the mark on his face. Tsitsho knew the man was judging him. He knew the white man feared him, and he knew that he was justified in that fear.

"What do you want, you scurvy redskin?"

Tsitsho shook his head, his blue-eyed gaze meeting the white man's. "No. I am no Mohawk. I am English. A captive." He was surprised by how quickly the English words came back to him. How many years had it been since he'd heard or spoken them? Six? Seven?

The man took a step closer, squinting in the bright morning sun. "God above," he swore. "You've got blue eyes. Who are you?"

Tsitsho let his broad hands fall to his sides. By his calculation he was only eighteen years old, and yet at this moment he felt as if he'd lived five-score years . . . ten. Painful memories flashed through his head—the Mohawk attack on his English family, his mother's screams, the torture, the slow acceptance. He felt the weight of his dying infant son in his arms, and he remembered the acrid stench of his wife's funeral pyre.

Slowly Tsitsho lifted his gaze. "My . . . my name is Duncan. I am Duncan Roderick, the Earl of Cleaves."

One

London, England
August 1661

Taking her sister's hand, Jillian slipped through the glass-paned double doors into the peaceful sanctuary of the overgrown garden. "Gemini!" she swore. "There's as much confusion in that house as at a Gypsy fair."

"We're supposed to be supervising the unpacking of the silver plate," Beatrice protested weakly, glancing over her shoulder as she was led away. The sound of a splitting wooden crate, crashing silver, and the shrill voice of their mother could be heard through the open windows. "We shouldn't disobey. Mother will be frightfully angry."

Jillian's laughter rose, filling the hot, humid air as she directed her sister over the flagstones that drew them past the blackberry bushes, broken and leaning, and deeper into the unkempt garden. "Can you believe we're finally in London?" she asked. "I was beginning to fear Father was going to keep us hidden in the country until kingdom come!"

The Hollingsworths had just arrived in the city from their country home in Sussex. A full year had passed since the throne had been restored to Charles II, and finally Jillian's father had agreed it was safe to bring his family to their home on the Strand. The house had not been occupied, except by caretakers, in two and a half decades. After the death of Cromwell, Lord Hollingsworth, a Royalist, had insisted upon keeping his family in the country until he was certain the Stuart government was stable again. The Hollingsworths had returned for the fall season of parties and suppers, to visit relatives, and to see their eldest daughter, Beatrice, finally wed.

Jillian dragged her sister down the path, ducking beneath low-hanging branches and vines grown wild with years of neglect. The garden was filled with the heady, sweet scent of blooming flowers and the humming, chirping sounds of insect song. "Father said the new gardener had the Chinese goldfish delivered this morning. Don't you want to see them?" Jillian arched one brow, her freckled face beaming with excitement.

"No, no I really do believe it's best we follow Mother's bidding. I—"

"Oh, stop your bellow-weathering, Bea. It's time you started making your own decisions. In a few short months you'll be a married woman yourself, with your own properties and a husband to order about!"

Beatrice blushed, covering her mouth with her delicate palm. "I can't believe it, Jillian. After all these years, he's really coming for me. I'm going to be a countess!"

The two sisters walked to the stone fish pool and sat down at the water's edge. Jillian peered into the fresh blue-green water in search of the exotic fish. "Fiddle! They must be hiding." She dipped her fingers into the cool, inviting water. "I knew he'd come for you. Father said he was waiting for his call to the judicial courts before he returned to England for you. Now that he's been declared the true heir and his title has been returned, he's finally in a position to wed you properly. God's teeth, Bea. You wouldn't want to marry a penniless Colonial, would you?"

Beatrice studied her younger sister's face. "It's true enough I'm anxious to be out from under our parents' feet and a woman of my own right. Heaven help me, I'm nearly twenty-eight, but what if what Cousin Elizabeth says is true? What if he is a he-devil with a forked tail?" Superstitiously, she lowered her voice, as if mere mention of the beast could conjure him up. "What if he is scarred so horribly that he truly must wear a mask?"

Jillian pulled a thick strand of her own bright-red hair off her shoulder and tucked it into her mouth thoughtfully. "Gossip! It spreads like summer fire in the meadow! A man in a mask, indeed!" She touched her sister's arm lightly. "Father met him at Whitehall Palace only a week ago. You don't think the man could have hidden a forked tail in his breeches, do you?"

"Elizabeth said all of London is calling him the Colonial Devil," Beatrice whispered, her hazel eyes still wide with fright. "They say he has the eyes of glowing coals and the hair of a wretched ghoul."

Jillian dragged her hand through the fish pond, watching the water part and the lily pads sway. "We'll meet him tomorrow and see for ourselves, won't we?" But when she saw the frightened look on her sister's face, she reached out to take Bea's smaller hand in her own. "Ignore such prattle. Elizabeth is a liar; everyone knows it. She's just green with jealousy because you're marrying an earl and she's only marrying an earl's son. By the time Toddy Burke inherits, Elizabeth will be toothless and bald."

Despite her fears, Beatrice couldn't resist a chuckle. "Oh, Jillian. I don't know what I'll do without you when I must go to America with my husband. I'll miss you terribly!"

On impulse, Jillian slipped off her kidskin slippers and began to roll down her hose. "Nonsense, once Jacob and I are wed, we'll come, too. There's nothing for us here. We'll live in a parsonage within riding distance." She spun around, lifting her apple-green taffeta petticoat above her calves. "I always wanted to see the American Colonies with their red savages anyway."

"Jillian! Father said he would hear no more of the parson's son." She looked this way and that, fearing someone might be eavesdropping in the deserted garden.

Jillian lowered her feet into the cool water and gave a sigh of delight. "I'll have Jacob, I will, and Father won't stop me. We'll elope if we have to."

Beatrice wrapped her arms around her own waist in fear. "Don't say that; please don't say that, Jilly. Promise me you won't do anything foolish. Promise me you won't ruin our family name by marrying below your station."

"I'll promise no such thing. I always told you that when I married, it would be for love." She lowered her feet deeper into the water, leaning over to peer into the stone pond. "Where *are* those goldfish? Father paid nearly ten pounds for the lot of them. For that sum, I vow, you would think they'd be big enough to see!"

Beatrice giggled. "Jillian, you'll be in that pond in a moment. Put your slippers on. Someone will see you and tell Father!"

Jillian gave a wave of her hand, dismissing the thought. "It feels wonderful." She lifted her long mane of curly red hair off her prickly warm neck. "Want to try?"

Beatrice shook her head.

"It's so cool, I just might climb all the way in and take a swim." She leaned over, still searching for the fish. "I'd find the little buggers then!"

Beatrice giggled. "You wouldn't!"

Jillian threw a mischievous glance over her shoulder in her sister's direction. She was standing on the shallow side of the pond, her abundant taffeta skirting pulled up around her knees. "Was that a dare I heard?"

Beatrice broke into nervous laughter. "No. No, it wasn't. It wasn't a dare!"

"Sounded like a dare to me . . ." Jillian sang, already beginning to unfasten the pearl buttons that ran the length of her gown. "You should know better. You know I can't resist a dare."

Beatrice jumped up from the stone wall, throwing her hands into the air. "Jillian! Please. I was only teasing! Have you lost what little sense you ever had? Someone will see you!"

"Who, pray tell?" Unfastening the last of the tiny buttons, she pulled the gown over her head. "Every maid and footman are busy hauling crates," she insisted through the stiff folds of the gown. "Mother, Father, and the sisters are all occupied with unpacking. I'll just take a quick dip, and no one will be the wiser." Finally her head appeared through the skirting of the gown. "Catch!"

Beatrice gave a little squeal as she dove to keep the hem of the new gown out of the fishpond. "You've really gone too far this time, Jilly," she hissed at her sister, who had begun to wade into the deeper water. "You know what Father said. He said he'd send you back to Aunt Prudence in the country if you didn't act like the lady you were born to be."

"He won't send me back because he's trying to keep Jacob and me apart. Not that it will do any good, because Jacob is coming for me." She unhooked her busk and tossed it through the air, discarding it along with her gown.

Jillian heard her sister give another little squeak as she lowered herself into the pond. "There's one! I see one of the goldfish!" she cried, laughing. "Oh, Bea. You should come in, too. They're so beautiful."

Jillian turned her back to her sister, pushing her wet linen smock aside where it floated in the cool, clean water. Twice she tried to catch one of the fat, bright goldfish the size of her palm, but both times they managed to slip through her fingers. She was just about to turn and head back for the pool's edge when she heard her sister give a strangled cry of fright.

"Bea? Bea, what—"

Jillian knew her jaw must have dropped as she spun around, and for a moment she felt her heart flutter beneath her breast. "My heavens," she murmured.

There in the neglected garden, standing not six paces from the fish pond, was a giant of a man . . . a man with a purple veil covering the left side of his face . . . a man of threatening masculinity.

Beatrice stumbled backward a step, the gown and busk bundled in her arms.

"It's all right," Jillian assured her sister as she waded quickly toward the pool's edge. In her rush, she made no attempt to cover her nearly naked form, draped in the wet, transparent linen of her smock. Although her sister was nearly six years her senior, Jillian had always felt it was her responsibility to look after Bea, ever since they were children in their nursery.

"Can . . . can I help you, my lord?" Jillian managed, knowing full well this must be her sister's betrothed. Who else would be wearing a scarf to cover his face? So the tales were true, she thought, wondering impulsively if she should be looking for his forked tail.

But the man did not smile like the devil. Or perhaps he did, for Jillian's great-grandmother had always said Satan would not come to her with a forked tail breathing fire and shouting obscenities, but as a handsome man with a come-hither smile and words as sweet as clover honey.

Instinctively Jillian put herself between the stranger and Beatrice. Beatrice was now making little mewing sounds, too frightened even to move. Surely she, too, realized who this man was.

"Well," Jillian demanded of the gentleman, for he surely was a gentleman by his dress. "Why are you here in this private garden? You've scared the lady half to death!"

His lazy smile made her forget the purple scarf that obscured one side of his face. He was robed fashionably in a rich burgundy doublet and wore wide-legged breeches with a short brown periwig and a plumed cavalier's hat dyed the same shade of red. Around his waist was strapped a fine sword. What she could see of his face was suntanned and ruggedly handsome. Earl or not, here was no milksop dandy of the King's court, this man of her sister's. His unobstructed eye was the color of the morning sky, so piercing that he seemed to see through Jillian to her very soul.

"I must ask your business, here, my lord," she repeated, her voice true and clear, "because you're trespassing."

He swept off his hat and bowed as if they were the Queen's maids of honor, keeping eye contact with her. "The baron is expecting me, madame. I am Lord Duncan Roderick, Earl of Cleaves, your servant." He raised an eyebrow, his voice mocking her as he returned his hat to his head. "And might you, by my good fortune, be Beatrice Hollingsworth?"

Bea, standing behind Jillian, sucked in a strangled breath.

Jillian shivered in her wet shift, not because of a chill, but because the earl looked at her with an expression she'd never known. He frightened her, yet intrigued her at the same time, and for a moment she forgot that he was her sister's intended. For the briefest second she contemplated what it would be like to be this man's bride.

Suddenly she crossed her arms over her breasts, trying to cover her unclothed form. "No, no, my lord I'm not," she snapped tartly. "A sister." She didn't know what made her answer so rudely, perhaps because she did find him so attractive, even with his obvious deformity. She frowned, angry that her sister's betrothed would be so ill-mannered, angry because she knew this man was not a good match for Beatrice. The poor girl had to be distracted with fear. How could Father have betrothed her dear Bea to such a brute of a man?

Jillian made eye contact with the earl once more. "Now if you'll excuse us, my lord . . ." she murmured, beginning to back up, still positioned between him and her sister. She reached behind her back to take Beatrice's trembling hand and then turned and ran, pulling her sister behind her.

* * *

Duncan stood on the path of the disordered garden a full minute, chuckling to himself. What good luck to find a half-naked woman in Hollingsworth's garden, what poor luck she wasn't his intended wife. He was instantly attracted to the chit with her flaming red hair, nutmeg eyes, and rosy breasts. Now a woman like that—she wouldn't be difficult to bed and get with his heir.

Duncan sighed. He knew he might as well get on with the call. He'd been too long in putting it off already. He had promised Lord Hollingsworth last week that he would come by and meet the daughter he'd been betrothed to since he was a boy. It was time he had a wife, and his duty to his dead father kept him to this promise. Besides, Hollingsworth owed the Rodericks a considerable sum of money. That matter needed to be discussed as well.

Duncan followed the path along which the two women had fled, through the garden, through the open door, into a sunny dining parlor. Boxes and crates were stacked everywhere with footmen and maids running in circles. Duncan stood there a moment, unnoticed, then cleared his throat.

A young girl looked up from where she leaned into a slatted crate and gave a frightened squeal.

"Your master," Duncan ordered, well used to such reactions and bored by them. "Tell him the Earl of Cleaves has arrived."

The servant backed out of the parlor, bumping into a portrait against the wall as she made her way out the door. "Yes, m'lord," she cried, trying to upright the painting of someone's sour-faced grandfather. "Right away, m'lord."

Not a minute later, Lord Hollingsworth and his wife came hustling into the disorganized parlor.

"Your lordship, let me offer my apologies for not being about to greet you at the door!" Hollingsworth bowed. "I hadn't been informed you'd arrived. Such a chore organizing a place that's not been occupied in twenty-five years and dealing with a household of females with vapors. You understand?"

Duncan bowed gracefully and nodded, trying to be polite. "I understand entirely, sir."

Lady Hollingsworth tapped her husband's arm with a painted fan.

"Goodness, my apologies again." Lord Hollingsworth took a lace handkerchief from his ruffled sleeve and wiped his wide forehead, beaded with perspiration. "My wife, sir, Lady Hollingsworth. Lord Roderick, the Earl of Cleaves, my dearest."

Lady Hollingsworth, a plump woman with sleek hair dyed the color of eggplant, curtsied. "Your servant, my lord. What a pleasure it is to finally meet you," she bubbled.

Duncan bowed again, this time with irritation. He was convinced that if only the English would give up this absurd notion of introducing and being introduced, they'd gain a full score of years to their lifetime. "Your servant, madame."

She rose, red-faced, clasping her hands so that her breasts rose above her pink silk bodice. "Would you care for a refreshment, my Lord?"

"No, no thank you. I'm expected elsewhere shortly."

"Surely you're staying for supper?" She nudged her husband.

Hollingsworth gave a start, flustered. "Indeed, indeed, sir, you would honor us with your presence."

"The kitchen is a mess, but I've just hired the most wonderful cook," her ladyship prattled. "He's just arrived from France. There'll be fresh goose with the most exquisite raspberry jelly."

Duncan lifted his hand, wishing he were anywhere but here. Even an Iroquois red-ant hill was beginning to look inviting. "I assure you I cannot stay."

The Hollingsworths then lapsed into a weighty silence, standing in the dining parlor, a rolled tapestry separating them from Duncan. They were obviously trying not to stare at the purple veil he wore, but were doing a poor job of it.

Finally Duncan, completely losing his patience, spoke up. "You'll recall I've come but to meet your daughter and sign the necessary agreement." He cleared his throat. "I haven't much time."

Lady Hollingsworth raised her hands to her purple hair. "Heavens, yes. My apologies, your lordship, for my ill manners." Then she spun on feet surely too small for her ample frame and fled the parlor.

This time Duncan made no attempt at polite conversation with Hollingsworth. Instead, he crossed the room to where three works of art rested along the wall, having just been removed from their crates. He studied first one painting, then the next with great concentration. Reaching the third, he crossed his arms over his chest with a sigh of approval. "Ah, a Botticelli."

"A collector, are you, your lordship?" Hollingsworth was wiping his damp brow again, obviously relieved to have something to speak of.

"No. Only an admirer."

The sound of feminine footsteps in the hallway immediately caught Duncan's attention. His betrothed was approaching. Finally he would have a look at his dear lady-wife-to-be.

But Duncan took his time in turning to greet her, giving himself a moment to fantasize. He couldn't help but wonder what she would look like. Would she be short and plump like her mother? Or would she be like her young sister? Would she have hair the color of autumn leaves and a rich, deep, sensual voice? Would she be a cold fish a man had to drink himself half silly to bed, or would she have a body he would crave to touch.

Duncan frowned. With the luck he carried, he guessed she'd have yellow buck teeth and a hairy wart growing from her chin. He turned to greet her.

She had neither.

But just the same, Duncan was immediately disappointed. His betrothed was none other than the cowering woman of the garden. She was small with tawny hair and a pert mouth. She reminded him of his mother . . .

"Your lordship, this is my daughter, Beatrice Mary."

The woman dipped low into a subservient curtsy, obviously frightened out of her wits.

Duncan bowed, a bad taste in his mouth. Now that he had gotten a closer look at her, he suddenly felt ill. "Your servant, madame."

"Yours, sir," she responded, her voice barely above a whisper.

Duncan watched her as she lifted her small, trembling hand to brush her neckline.

This wasn't going to work, damn it.

Duncan knew he was expected to marry this Hollingsworth. It was his duty. The Rodericks and the Hollingsworths had betrothed their children as infants before the war. Duncan owed this to his deceased father. It was the right thing to do. . . . Yet how could he marry a woman who looked so much like his bitch mother?

Immediately the thought of the redhead in the garden flashed through his head, replacing hazy images of his dear lady-mother, Constance. Duncan recalled the silhouette of the redhead's rounded breasts pressing against the wet linen of her smock. He had been able to see her pale areolas through the transparent undergarment. Her pink nipples had taunted him, teased him . . .

Duncan looked up at Hollingsworth, scowling with displeasure. "You have other daughters?" He did not look at Beatrice again, though he could hear her hyperventilating.

"Yes . . . yes, I do." Hollingsworth's voice trembled. "Beatrice is the . . . the eldest."

"I want to see them."

Hollingsworth looked up with rounded eyes, his mouth gaping open to show a recent abscess. "My . . . my lord?"

Duncan raised his hand beneath the purple veil and wiped his mouth. "Humor me," he stated flatly. "I want to see her sisters." *If I must marry a Hollingsworth,* he reasoned, *why not the best of the lot?* "Now."

Two

Duncan stood in the baron's dining parlor, his hands on his hips, trying to control his irritation. "I asked to see your daughters, sir."

"These . . . these are my daughters." Hollingsworth gestured weakly toward Beatrice and her three sisters, who all stood in a line before Duncan, their eyes downcast.

Duncan frowned. The four women were all similar in appearance with honey-blond hair and comely enough faces, but she was not among them. "These are *all* your daughters, sir?"

Hollingsworth glanced uneasily at his wife, who fluttered near the doorway. "Your lordship?"

"It's a simple question!" Duncan came toward the man. "Are these all your daughters or not? I saw a young woman in the garden." He turned to address Beatrice, who had looked up when Duncan had raised his voice. She immediately lowered her gaze to the floor again. "The woman in the garden with you." He touched his periwig. "Red hair, very wet." His mouth twitched into a smile, but it was gone as quickly as it had come. "She said she was your sister. What is she, some bastard relation?"

Beatrice's lower lip trembled. She seemed unwilling or unable to meet her betrothed's gaze. "N—n—no, your lordship. She's as legitimate as I. That—that was J—Jillian, sir."

Duncan crossed his arms over his chest. "So where the hell is she?" He glared at the baron. "I asked to see all the daughters, sir. It's the least you can do, considering the *circumstances* of your debt."

Hollingsworth glanced at his wife, his face reddening.

The baroness looked at Duncan, at her husband, then back at Duncan again. "Our—our daughter Jillian is indisposed at the moment, your lordship. She—she had an accident. She—"

Duncan had had his fill of civility. He wanted to see the red-haired chit, and he wanted to see her now. "I will see her."

Lady Hollingsworth gave her husband a nudge. He looked at Duncan. She prodded him again. "Surely," the baron stumbled, "I don't see why—"

"Do you wish me to leave and consider this matter at an end? I can have my goldsmith send you a list of your debts, sir." Duncan raised an eyebrow. "Would thirty days' grace be acceptable before you pay in full?"

Hollingsworth's eyes widened. Both men knew that to repay Duncan with interest, it would take practically every pound the Baron possessed. Both men knew a daughter was not worth a man's ruination. "I—I don't understand, your lordship."

"I think you do."

The baron turned to his wife. "Get her."

She lifted her brows meaningfully. "She's wet, sir. I sent her to her chamber. She's not dressed properly."

"I don't care." Duncan clenched his teeth. "Bring her down stark naked if it pleases you, madame, but I want to see her and see her now."

"He doesn't care." Hollingsworth nodded weakly, almost as fearful of his wife as he was of Duncan. "You heard his lordship. Get her—now."

After a moment's hesitation, Lady Hollingsworth lifted her pink skirts and hurried from the room, leaving her husband and their four daughters to stare at the mysterious earl.

Duncan turned his back on them, returning to study the

paintings he had looked at earlier. He knew he was behaving irrationally. He was betrothed to the meek Beatrice. Why couldn't he just accept the fact as most other men did? He knew he should marry her, get her with his child, and then return to the Maryland Colony and his mistress as he intended. Beatrice would truly be but a small annoyance.

But somewhere in the back of his mind, he heard his mother's cold voice. The truth was, he didn't know if he could sleep with Beatrice when she reminded him so much of Constance; and after all, the whole point of this marrying fiasco was to get a son, wasn't it?

The baroness appeared in the dining parlor a few moments later with the redhead from the garden in tow. *Jillian, wasn't that what they had said her name was?* He liked the sound of it.

Jillian took a place beside her sister Beatrice; but while the other four young women all stared at the floor, Jillian looked him straight in the eye.

She wore a pale-blue silk dressing gown; her feet were bare. Her wild, red mass of hair, still damp and curling at her temples, fell over her shoulders.

A virgin sacrifice, Duncan mused.

The baroness clasped her hands. "M—my daughter Jillian, your lordship."

Duncan made a slight bow.

Jillian barely paid him due honor. She was staring at him as if he'd just called her to the gallows.

"Not caught a chill have you, madame?"

He saw her cheeks color, and he chuckled. So even if the chit were swimming in the fishpond, she had some sense of decorum.

Duncan turned to the baroness, suddenly feeling much better. He almost smiled as he spoke. "Tell me, madame, do you have trouble in lying-in?"

Her brow furrowed in a most unattractive way. "Your lordship?"

He raised a hand. "Birthing? Have you trouble? I see you have no sons."

The baroness glanced at her husband, then back at Duncan, her tone softer . . . apologetic. "We were not so blessed."

"Stillbirths?"

"O—one— a daughter, too. But pardon me your lordship if I ask why—"

"You want me to marry your daughter, don't you?" he went on impatiently.

"Well, yes. Of course. It's all been arranged."

"Well, I want children, madame. Isn't it true that a daughter follows in her mother's footsteps? I want to be certain she's healthy enough to produce an heir."

The baroness glanced at her eldest daughter. "Well, of course she's healthy, your lordship. Beatrice rarely faints and never gets the ague."

Duncan turned to face the Hollingsworth daughters. They were all staring at their slippers, obviously frightened or disgusted by his appearance. Perhaps a little of both. Even his dear betrothed kept her gaze lowered. But not Jillian. She was looking at him as if she wanted to sink a dagger into his heart, that or challenge him to a duel.

Duncan was amused, which pleased him. So little amused him. He touched his veil lightly. "Does this frighten you, madame?" he questioned Jillian.

She shrugged. "No, your lordship. I fear nothing but God and my own willful ways. I'm merely curious."

Duncan did not smile, but he liked her response. He liked the tone of her voice and the fact that she was willing to stand up to him. Few *men* were. There was something about his size, the way he carried himself, the confidence of his speech, that intimidated most, and Duncan tended to use that to his advantage.

He tucked his hands behind his back and walked the length of the parlor, passing each young woman one by one, his footsteps echoing off the plastered dome ceiling overhead. Slowly he turned and retraced his steps, knowing the Hollingsworth family waited. "All right," he finally declared. "I will marry your daughter, my lord. But this one." He stopped before Jillian.

Beatrice gave a strangled cry.

The sisters all sucked in a great breath of air in unison.

Jillian stared coldly.

"Heavens! Heavens!" The baroness threw up her hands. "Impossible. Morton! Tell his lordship that's impossible. The agreement was signed for Beatrice. Jillian is younger. She must wait her turn in line to be married. He must marry Beatrice!"

The baron took his ever-present handkerchief from his sleeve and began to mop his brow. "Im—impossible, sir. The agreement was made for you and our eldest daughter," he repeated after his wife.

Jillian crossed her arms over her pert, young breasts. "I won't marry him," she declared to anyone who would listen. "I won't marry Beatrice's betrothed. I won't marry anyone but Jacob."

"She can't marry him," Lady Hollingsworth wailed. "Tell him, Morton. Tell his lordship."

The baron groaned. He spoke to his wife as if Duncan weren't standing not three paces from them. "But he says he wants Jillian, not Beatrice. He—"

Duncan's mouth twitched in a smile. The room was suddenly in an uproar. The sisters were all talking at once. The baron and his wife were arguing hotly. Beatrice sniffed, tears running down her cheeks. Only Jillian stood in the middle of the madness utterly unaffected. Yes, this young woman would do; she'd do nicely.

After a moment of the infernal noise, Duncan raised his hands. "Ladies, ladies!" he boomed. "Sir . . ."

Suddenly the room was quiet and Duncan was in complete control again, precisely the way he liked it. "Sir, I beg you consider my proposition wisely," he addressed the baron. "My father made the agreement with you that I would marry your eldest daughter. Give me the girl I wish, and I will absolve you of your entire debt to the Roderick family." He shrugged his broad shoulders. "Nothing has changed here, sir, except that I wish to marry not that one," he pointed to Beatrice, "but that one." Duncan indicated Jillian with a casual wave.

"Father." Jillian looked to the baron, her dark gaze piercing. "I will not marry my sister's betrothed. You can't do this to Bea! Not for money!"

The baron glanced at Duncan in obvious distress.

"Come, come, sir, have a backbone. It's your right to marry your daughters as you see fit." Duncan spread his hands. "I'm obviously a qualified suitor; and sir, quite frankly, you need this union."

"But Beatrice—"

"I don't mean to be disrespectful, sir, but the truth is that I will not have her. It's nothing personal, only that she reminds of someone I do not wish to be reminded of. I want the redhead." He did not look at her. "Jillian shall be my bride."

The baron wrung his hands, glancing at his wife, then back at Duncan. "Could . . . could we discuss this further?"

Duncan lifted the watch that hung on a chain at his waist and checked the time. "No, sir, we cannot. As I stated earlier, I have an engagement. Make your decision here and now and let the matter be done."

"No, Father!"

"Morton, you have to look to your responsibility to your entire family," the baroness said swiftly. "Jillian is not your only daughter. You've the others to consider. How will you find them suitable husbands with nary a pound to your name?"

The baron looked at Jillian. The girl had crossed her arms

over her chest, thrusting her lower lip out. He turned back to Duncan. "I suppose that will do, your lordship."

Jillian blanched. "Father . . ."

Beatrice broke into new tears.

The other sisters again began to talk at once.

Duncan smiled, pleased with himself, pleased to have this affair over with. Now he could attend a supper of a friend he'd known from Oxford and not be bothered with this matter again tonight.

The baroness waved her hands, shooing her daughters, including Beatrice, from the room. Only Jillian remained. She stood between her distraught parents, staring at Duncan, her anger plain on her lovely young face.

"I'd like to speak with my betrothed alone for a moment, if you don't mind, sir," Duncan said, amused by the chit's boldness.

The baron looked at his wife.

"It's not generally done—"

"Now," Duncan said.

"But, I suppose that will be all right," the baroness rattled, "considering the fact that you'll soon be wed . . ."

The baron and the baroness were already backing out of the room. "We—we'll prepare the papers, sir," Lord Hollingsworth said. "It will take but a minute to replace Beatrice's name with Jillian's. I'll have it ready in my office momentarily."

Jillian watched her mother and father retreat from the dining parlor. *Cowards,* she thought. *You didn't want to do it, but you let him bully you. You sacrificed me for the sake of your cash box; but worse, you sacrificed Beatrice.*

The earl stood before her, watching her with a lazy amusement, an amusement that made her want to strike that smirk from his scarred face. It was obvious that she meant nothing to him, that Bea meant nothing to him. He didn't care that he had just ruined two women's lives. . . . After all, they were just women, weren't they?

"I take it you don't approve of me as a husband," the earl said after a long moment of silence and stares.

"You were betrothed to Beatrice," Jillian answered flatly. "She waited a long time for you. All those years when my parents thought you were dead, then while your estate and title were returned. Bea should have been wed long ago, but she waited for you."

"Another suitor will come along."

"Perhaps, perhaps not. She's beyond marrying age, and you well know it." She watched him as he turned from her and walked to the open doors that led to the garden. "So why me?" she asked after a moment, her curiosity getting the best of her. "Why me and not Beatrice?"

"She was afraid of me."

Jillian gave a little laugh, but she was not amused. "And why wouldn't she be, with you wearing that veil across your face and bellowing!"

He turned in the doorway to face her. "You weren't afraid of me."

The truth was, Jillian did fear him. She feared his angry voice, his bullying. She feared what was beneath the scarf. But mostly she feared her immediate reaction to him. She feared her damp palms, the flutter in her stomach, her shortness of breath.

Jillian wrapped her arms around her waist, hugging herself, as if she could ward off his piercing gaze, knowing she couldn't. "He can't make me marry you."

Duncan broke into a grin. "Ah, but he can. It's a father's right."

"What about my right?" she exploded, taking a step toward him. "What about my right to marry a man I love, a man who will cherish me?"

The grin subsided. "You have no rights. As your father, the baron will decide what is best for you. As your husband, I will then decide what is best for you."

He made eye contact, and Jillian shivered. "Bastard," she murmured.

Again, he was smiling. "What makes you think I won't cherish you? You don't know me. You don't know my ways. I'll make a better husband than you could choose for yourself, I would venture."

"I've seen enough to know we are ill-suited. You bullied my father. You hurt my sister."

"Your father should not have allowed me to bully him. When we have daughters, *dear,* no one will force me to marry them to anyone I do not choose. As for your sister, I'm sorry if I offended her, but it would have been wrong to take her as my wife, feeling as I do about her."

Jillian didn't know what to say. She was stuck. She knew it. He knew it. And he was right, of course.

English law gave her father and later her husband the right to control her as each saw fit. She had no rights by English law, only the rights her father or her husband gave her. She stared at the man standing before her, his face covered by a purple veil. She would only have what rights this man—this devil—chose to extend her.

"I won't marry you," she stated between clenched, even, white teeth. For now she was even more frightened than before. This man wanted control. She could see it in his gaze. She could hear it in his voice. He wanted to control her.

"I won't marry you," she repeated with more conviction. "I'll run away. You'll never find me!"

Something snapped in Duncan's mind and suddenly he was transported back in time. He barely heard Jillian's last words, and the memories came rushing back out of the blackness . . .

It was the smells that still clung to him after all these years, tearing at him with claws of numbing terror. . . . The acrid scent of the burning house, the sweet, nauseating odor of spilled blood. There had been the aroma of apples and cinnamon still fresh in the air from an apple pie left to cool on a sideboard.

Duncan remembered the sounds of the dying livestock and the screams of his little sister. From beneath the trestle table, he had been unable to distinguish between the two after a while.

Duncan thrust out his hand in stark fear. *Don't leave me. Don't leave me,* his mind screamed.

"My lord, are you quite all right?"

Jillian's voice tore him from the memory. He looked down, his mouth dry, to see his own extended hand. He lowered it, embarrassed, and glanced up to see her staring at him, her face suddenly filled with concern.

"Are you ill, sir? Should I call my father?"

"Don't be ridiculous," he snapped, angry at himself for allowing his mind to wander. He grabbed her wrist roughly. "Let us go to your father and have these documents signed. You'll be residing at my home until the wedding takes place." He ushered her through the doorway. "So you see, dear Jillian, you will not be leaving me after all."

Three

The judgment was made so swiftly that Jillian didn't have time to react; she didn't have time to think. The earl refused to discuss his impulsive decision to imprison her in his family home until the wedding could take place. He insisted her father send her by coach before dusk to Breckenridge House. There she would be chaperoned by his paternal grandmother. The baron had no choice but to comply or see the betrothal agreement annulled and his debt called. The man known as the Colonial Devil signed her betrothal agreement and then was gone.

There was a whirlwind of repacking as Jillian stood in the corner of the bedchamber she was to have shared with Beatrice. Her sister stood beside her, her face ashen, tears streaking her cheeks.

"I cannot believe he's going to take you away from us," Beatrice whispered, holding her sister's hand tightly in her own.

Jillian watched as her mother and a handmaid wrestled her new forest-green ball gown into a trunk. "I'm so sorry," she murmured. "I didn't mean to take your husband, Bea; I swear by all that's holy, I didn't."

Beatrice looked at her sister, her eyes filled with sadness, disappointment. "I know you didn't. It can't be helped. But my tears are not for the loss of a husband, but for fear for you. What they said was true, Jilly. The man is a beast."

The terror Jillian saw in Beatrice's face made her forget

her own fears for the moment. "Afraid for me? Don't be such a ninny! It's an act you know." She gave a wave of her hand, hoping her sister didn't see its tremor. "He only shouts and stomps for the drama of it all. The man belongs on stage at the king's theater." She made herself smile. "I'm not afraid of him; truly I'm not, Bea. It's just that I don't want to marry him." She lowered her voice. "Jacob is my true love. I can't marry the earl and run off to the American Colonies. I won't."

"Too late. You heard Father. The decision's been made." Bea's lower lip trembled. "But, oh dear, I don't want you to go. I don't want you to leave me."

Jillian thought her sister's statement silly. What was the difference if it were Jillian or Beatrice who married the earl? Surely Bea must have realized that once she was the man's wife, she would have left her father's home. The sisters' parting had always been inevitable. The only difference now was that it was Jillian who would be leaving the family first.

But Jillian didn't speak her mind; instead she plucked one of her curls thoughtfully. She wasn't ready to succumb to the idea of marrying the veiled earl; but she knew that, at this point, she would be better to play along until she decided how she would handle the matter. "The earl said I could bring one maid with me to see to my needs." She looked at her sister, the thought of getting the best of Duncan even in a small matter rather appealing. "Would you come with me, Bea? Just until I'm wed? Just until I've gotten used to a strange house, the earl, his dowager-grandmother?"

Beatrice brought her hands to her pale cheeks. "Oh, I couldn't. Father would never . . . the earl would never—"

"Just think, we could be together a little longer." Jillian took her sister's hand in hers. "Oh, please Bea, for me? Will you do it?"

Beatrice looked into her sister's eyes in obvious quandary. "I don't know. I . . ."

"Perhaps the earl might be able to find you another husband," Jillian cajoled. "He's a very rich, influential man; surely he has unmarried acquaintances."

"Oh, Jilly . . ."

"Please," Jillian begged sincerely. The truth of the matter was that she needed her sister. What if she couldn't find a way to be with Jacob? She needed Bea if she was going to manage a devil-husband.

"All right," Beatrice breathed. "I'll go, but just until the wedding." She squeezed her sister's hand and whispered. "And you have to tell Father . . ."

"You did what?" Lord William Galloway raised a jack of ale to his numb lips. The sounds of the dockside tavern filled the air; ivory dice clattered across scarred wooden tables; a Fleet Street whore laughed; a mangy dog in the alley behind the tavern barked. The place smelled of rotting timber, the salty sea, and piss.

Galloway preferred to drink in ladies' salons, but this was where Duncan liked to sup and gamble. He said that it was in sweaty ordinaries like this that he felt most comfortable.

Duncan cocked his mug, wondering if he'd made a mistake in telling his friend. But hell, he was going to marry her. Sooner or later Galloway would know he had a wife. "I said I signed the betrothal agreement. I marry the Hollingsworth chit come All Saints Day."

Galloway gave a low whistle, slapping his ale jack on the table. He was a short, stout man with a ruddy face and an honest disposition. "By the King's cod! You really did it, didn't you? Damn if I didn't lose ten pounds to Bretton. I bet him you'd back out." He leaned across the table, wiping his wet mouth with the back of his hand. "So what's she like, dear Beatrice? An ancient, poxed hag with warts on her nose?"

Duncan smiled to himself as he lifted his ale jack and

sipped the pungent brew. "No, she's a redhead with dark eyes. Her name's Jillian."

Galloway squinted in the dim, smoky light of the public room. "I thought you said last night she was called Beatrice Mary. You said she sounded like she belonged in a nunnery." He guffawed.

Duncan set his jack on the edge of the table. "I didn't like the one called Beatrice." He shrugged. "So I took one of the other daughters. 'Twas no great event. One woman is much like another when the light is out, is she not?"

Galloway continued to stare across the table, making Duncan uncomfortable. Will Galloway was a privateer. He also owned land adjacent to Duncan's Maryland acreage and had been a friend for many years. He was a good man, though he drank too much. And he knew Duncan well, too well.

"Christ, if I didn't know better, I'd say you were smitten with her," Galloway teased. "How old is she? Ten? Twelve?"

Duncan picked a bit of bread off his pewter plate and tossed it at Galloway, striking him on the cheekbone. "No. She's well of marrying age."

"But young?"

"Aye, young," Duncan conceded, beginning to wish he'd not brought the matter up at all.

"And pretty?"

Duncan's gaze met Galloway's, the veil over his one eye casting a strange light across his friend's flushed face. "Pretty enough that if you so much as speak to her, I'll cut off your gonads, pickle them, and send them to your mother."

Galloway laughed heartily, slapping his palm on the table, making the pewter plates rattle. "A man smitten with his intended! By the King's cod, you're as out of fashion as a farthingale in a Stuart's drawing room! Tell me, has she other sisters?"

Duncan frowned. "She does, several, but you'll get no introduction from me. You're liable to give the poor girl a disease." He shuffled a deck of dog-eared cards and began to deal. "So, are you in for a hand or are you just going to sit there, laughing like the jackass that you are?"

"I'm in, I'm in. I've got to come up with the coin to pay for this lousy meal, don't I?" He reached for the cards Duncan dealt him. "But tell me, did you wear that ridiculous scarf of yours to meet her?"

"I did."

Galloway snickered. "And the wench still agreed to wed you? I've got to see this paragon for myself!"

"She's staying with me. Atar should be getting her settled now. So come sup with us tomorrow evening. Nine on the hour, and try to come sober, will you, Will?"

Galloway lifted a thick eyebrow. "At Breckenridge House? Me? You certain your grandmother will let me past the front stoop?"

Duncan fanned out his cards in his hand. "Bring her sweets. She can be bribed. Now will you play your card?"

The closer the coach grew to Breckenridge House, the more nervous Jillian became. Inside her leather gloves, she could feel her palms growing damp. Perspiration beaded above her upper lip. Beside her, Beatrice sat rigidly, staring at the empty coach bench across from them. The vehicle rocked to and fro as it made its way toward Aldersgate Street just outside the city gates. There, Breckenridge House had been home to the Rodericks since before the civil wars.

Jillian peered out the window as the coach swung left and rolled up a drive through an iron gate hanging askew. Her first view of the home disappointed her. Breckenridge House was a three-story, ivy-walled brick structure that had obviously been left unkept for many years. Glass panes were shattered, bricks crumbling at the sills, ivy growing wildly over some windows. Shutters hung sadly, some open, some closed, and the roof was missing a good many shingles. The drive was bumpy, littered with branches left from the last summer thunderstorm.

"Uds lud," Jillian swore, disguising her apprehension with sarcasm. "For a rich man, he doesn't keep his place well, does he?"

Beatrice made no response but to stare through the small window and nod.

When the coach rocked to a halt in front of the great, looming house, Jillian leapt off the leather seat and threw open the door. The footman barely made it with a wooden step before Jillian alighted from the coach. "Looks like a lair, doesn't it?" she asked her sister, staring up at the vast, crumbling house in the last of the summer's light.

Beatrice grasped her sister's arm. "Do—do you think *he's* here?" she managed, her hand trembling.

"I hope not. Carry my bags in," she called to the footmen and driver. Then she lifted the skirts of her simple cotton-and-chintz traveling gown and started immediately for the front door.

Jillian had to take care in climbing the old steps because the stones were loose in the places where the mortar had cracked. Without hesitation, she drew back the iron knocker with the head of a wild boar and let it fall. Impatiently, she did it again.

When the door yawned open, Jillian peered into the semi-darkness of the candlelit entryway. "Jillian Hollingsworth," she announced to the tall, stocky black man dressed in a short red coat, dark breeches, and worn shoes. She pushed past the servant. "Your master is expecting me."

The black man took a step back, allowing Beatrice to follow her sister inside. "Yes, he is expecting you, but he is not available." The man's English was as impeccable as his red coat.

The hallway was cool with a high plastered ceiling and Italian-marble floor tile. Portraits of stiff-collared old men lined the papered walls with ancient muskets and swords, floor to ceiling.

"Your apartments are already prepared, madame. I can show you the way." He took another step back, indicating with a silky black hand that she should go up the staircase.

"Excellent." Jillian tugged off her kidskin gloves. Duncan thought he was in control? She would show him control. "This is my sister, Beatrice. She'll need a bedchamber adjoining mine. She'll be staying with us as well."

The servant bowed. "As you wish. My name is Atar. I am the master's retainer. Whatever you wish, madame, I will see to."

Just then Jillian heard the sound of male footsteps approaching on the marble floor. Her heart gave an involuntary trip. Was it *himself* come to greet her? She turned toward the sound, poised.

But out of the darkness appeared not the massive hulk of her husband-to-be, but a slender man in a tasteless lime-green doublet with a great many gold garnitures and matching leather heels. "Good evening," he called. Once in the circle of candlelight, he offered a leg and bowed formally. "That will be all, Atar. Scurry along. I'll see that the lady is settled in." He waved his hand in dismissal.

But the African didn't budge. "Atar," the man in the hideous doublet repeated. "I said, you are dismissed."

After a moment, the servant retreated into the darkness of the corridor beyond the circle of hallway light and the man in the coat returned his attention to Jillian. "Allow me to introduce myself. I am Algernon Roderick, cousin to your host and, I understand, your husband-to-be."

Jillian dipped a curtsy, offering her hand as was customary; but when his lips touched her bare skin, she withdrew, uncomfortable with the cousin's gesture. Something wasn't right about this man. Her distaste for him was immediate. "Your servant, sir. And this is my sister, Beatrice. She's come to stay with me for a short while."

The two paid honors as was appropriate, then Beatrice stepped back behind her sister again.

"I must apologize for my cousin's poor behavior." Algernon lifted his hands in an effeminate way. It was obvious the man was taking great care to imitate the young fops of the Court. Jillian had heard this was all the mode, but he came off as a fool, especially in comparison to Duncan's rugged masculinity.

Jillian gave a half smile. Despite her unwillingness to marry Duncan, she would not air her dirty linens. She would not publicly speak harshly of the man she might be forced to marry. She was too smart not to realize how disastrous such an error could be. If she were made to marry the earl, he would have utter control over her life. He would dictate where she went, what she wore, what she ate. He had a right as her husband to bathe her in the luxury he was capable of or to lock her in a solitary tower until her death.

"That's quite all right," Jillian responded to the cousin smoothly. "I wasn't expecting his lordship . . . Duncan." She didn't know why she used his Christian name with such familiarity. It was improper that an engaged couple use their first names until after they were wed. But there was something about the way Algernon stared at her that made her uncomfortable. There was something about the tone of his voice that made her want to seek the protection of Duncan's name.

Out of the corner of her eye, Jillian noticed a silhouette in the shadows. It was Duncan's man, Atar. So he didn't trust the cousin either . . .

Jillian turned to the footman. "If you could show us to our apartments . . ."

"Nonsense," the cousin interrupted before the footman could act. "I'll see you there myself. See to the ladies' bags," he instructed the footman. Then he offered his arm to Jillian. "Madame?"

Jillian had little choice but to take his arm and allow him

to lead her down the dark hallway and up the monstrous, curving grand staircase. Beatrice hurried behind.

Despite the poor condition of the exterior of Breckenridge House and the poor upkeep of the hallways, Jillian found her apartments satisfactory. The dark walnut furniture was old and heavy with massive legs, but adequate. Though the wall paint was dingy, the bed-linens and draperies had been cleaned and the room well aired. To Jillian's surprise, there were vases of garden flowers here and there about the bedchamber, filling the otherwise dull room with color and sweet fragrance.

"This will be your bedchamber. Your sister can sleep in the small room through those doors." He indicated to the left with a sweep of his hand. "But do let me show you the other rooms."

"That won't be necessary." Just inside the doorway, Jillian halted. She had no intention of permitting Algernon inside, despite his pressing her. "My sister and I are fatigued. It's been a dreadfully long day." She stepped back to allow a footman and Duncan's servant, Atar, to carry her and her sister's trunks inside. "There'll be plenty of time for exploration on the morrow."

The men left the luggage beside the massive walnut bed and made a fast exit.

Jillian stood with her hand on the doorknob. "So good night to you and thank you. No doubt we shall see you tomorrow, Mr. Roderick."

"No doubt." Algernon smiled, clearly annoyed that he hadn't been invited in. "Good night then." He bowed. "Your servant, madame."

She dipped a hasty curtsy. "Your servant, sir." She closed the door and leaned against it with a sigh. She eyed her sister, not wanting to speak of the cousin for fear he was still behind the door. She rolled her eyes dramatically.

But Beatrice had walked to the far side of the room and

was staring at the dark glass of one window. "At least there are no bars," she said softly.

Always one to make the best of a situation, Jillian shrugged, tossing her gloves and reticule onto the bed as she passed it. "Creepy, isn't it? But it could be fun investigating the household. Perhaps the earl has some relative walled up in the cellar."

Thc look on Beatrice's face made Jillian regret what she had said. "Oh, I'm sorry. I was just teasing." She looped her arm around her sister's waist and gave her a hug. "You must be tired. Let's find your bed and get you settled in for the night."

With a nod, Beatrice allowed Jillian to lead her into the adjoining chamber. The room must have been meant for a personal maid because it was much smaller than Jillian's bedchamber, but it was acceptable with a rope bed and clean linens.

Though used to having maids to aid them, Jillian and Beatrice managed to undress and redress in nightclothes. An hour later, Beatrice was asleep in her bed and Jillian was left alone.

Jillian climbed into the poster bed that was to be her own and pulled a soft linen sheet over her thin, silk sleeping gown. Suddenly she felt alone and just a little frightened. She had been fine as long as she had been caring for Bea; but left alone to think, she came face to face with the reality of her situation.

Jillian didn't want to be here. She didn't want to marry the earl. She knotted the bed-linen in her fist in frustration. She wanted to marry Jacob! *Jacob, dear Jacob.* He didn't even know where she was now. She would have to get a letter to him.

A sudden knock at the door startled Jillian. *Heavens, was it that Algernon again?* Before she had time to respond, the door swung open.

Instinctively, Jillian pushed back against her pillow, raising the sheet higher over her sleeping gown. Then she relaxed. The bedchamber was dim, lit only by a few candles, but even in the darkness she could see it was the earl and not his cousin.

"What the hell do you think you're doing?" he bellowed.

Jillian had had perfect intentions to treat Duncan sweetly the next time she encountered him. After all, couldn't a man be better manipulated with honey than venom? But all thought of lady-like behavior was gone from her head the moment she heard his tone of voice.

"What the hell am *I* doing?" She threw back the coverlet and slid her bare feet over the side of the bed. "What the hell are *you* doing?"

Four

Jillian padded barefoot across the bedchamber floor. "You insisted that I come here immediately, and then you're not here to receive me. You told my father I would be well chaperoned. There's no chaperone! There's no one but a few servants—" She swayed her head. "—and *dear cousin Algernon.*"

"I didn't think it necessary that I be here to receive you. My man Atar was to see to your needs. As for your chaperone, my grandmother took ill with the summer ague and turned in early. She wanted to stay up and wait for you, but I insisted you were a woman capable of seeing herself in. Now—" He held up his index finger. "—tell me why you brought *her* with you."

Jillian lifted a feathery eyebrow. "Whom?"

"I am not in the mood for gaming. You know very well of whom I speak. Your sister."

He was dressed casually now. He appeared as if he had settled in his apartment for the evening, then been roused by some well-intentioned servant. Or perhaps it was Cousin Algernon who had tattled on her.

Gone were Duncan's sword and sword case, as well as the coat and feathered cavalier's hat. He wore a pair of dark breeches and a soft white shirt with long, full sleeves. The fashionable heeled slippers had been replaced with black, knee-high boots. Even his periwig had been removed so that she could see his hair, a rich chestnut brown pulled back in a Colonial queue. The purple scarf looked as if it had been added as an afterthought, set slightly askew so that she could see his entire, sensuous mouth.

Jillian crossed her arms over her breasts, realizing the sleeping gown she wore was inappropriate to receive in. She was suddenly uncomfortable, with him standing there, so frighteningly attractive, and her nearly unclothed. "You—you said I could bring a woman with me."

"A maid."

"I brought my sister."

"A maid." He shook his fist. "I said you could bring your own personal maid. I did not say—"

Jillian brought her finger to her lips as if scolding a small child. "I beg you, sir, lower your voice or she'll hear you." Her eyes narrowed. "Haven't you harmed her enough for one day?"

"And you don't think it will hurt her seeing the two of us together? Blast it, Jillian! I will not have the woman I was supposed to marry moping about my household whilst I try to woo my wife!"

"I want my sister here." Jillian set her jaw. "You made me come here against my will. You and Father are trying to marry me against my will. I should at least be able to have my sister with me for comfort."

"She goes home tomorrow come first light."

Jillian stared at the man's veiled face. "No."

"You should have asked me. This is my house. You will be my wife. You should have gained my permission to bring her here."

Jillian lowered her antagonistic gaze. This was not the way to get what she wanted from him. She couldn't meet every word he spoke with a challenge. He now had complete control over her life. She knew it; he knew it. If she expected him to give in a little, she knew she would have to do the same. "Please," she said softly. "I beg you, my lord, don't send my sister away."

There was an awkward silence in the dark bedchamber. Jillian could hear his breathing, the rhythm increased by their argument. Surely he must have heard her own heart pounding. Despite what she pretended, she was afraid of him and his raw masculinity. She was apprehensive of this house, of the cousin, even of the grandmother. She truly did need Bea. Bea made her strong.

"All right."

Jillian looked up, thinking she had misunderstood him. "Pardon, sir?"

"I said, all right," he repeated gruffly. "You may have your sister here as long as I am no part to sniveling. She may stay until the wedding." He raised that finger again. "But no longer."

Jillian was confused. The man made no sense. One moment he was shouting and shaking his fist, the next moment he was gentle and soft-spoken. She was intrigued by the look on his face. She wondered what made him tick. What really was beneath that purple scarf? "What made you change your mind?" she questioned.

"You asked. I am a simple man, Jillian, with simple needs. Respect me and my wishes, and I will respect you and yours."

She nodded, looking down at her bare toes peeking from beneath her gown. "And what of my wish not to wed you? Will you respect that?" Slowly, she lifted her gaze to meet his intense one.

"That is not negotiable. Your father and I have made the decision for you."

"And I'm supposed to pretend I'm pleased?"

"You're supposed to accept your lot in life and make the best of it." He turned for the door. "Like the rest of us."

Jillian watched him go, her emotions in a jumble. She was angry with this man, hurt by his cold words, frightened by his intense gaze. And yet, at the same time, something drew her to him. She had felt it even in the garden. There was a sexual attraction there she couldn't deny, but it was something more than that. Something about Duncan made her want to draw him to her breast, to stroke his hair, to somehow comfort him, for surely he was in dire need of comfort.

"And what is yours?" Jillian asked, taking a hesitant step toward him.

He turned in the doorway, the shadows crossing his face so that the scarf went unnoticed. For an instant Jillian tried to imagine what he would look like without the scarf, with the deformity beneath it. Was it truly so hideous?

"Madame?"

"Your lot in life. I'm asking you what it is you must accept as your lot."

He caught the doorknob in his hand. "Good night to you, madame."

Then he was gone, leaving Jillian to stand in the middle of the dark bedchamber, alone, frightened, and just a little intrigued by the man who claimed he would soon call her wife.

Jillian dressed carefully the following morning, for a message had come from Duncan's grandmother. She had invited both Jillian and Beatrice to share the morning meal with her. *Precisely nine o'clock, in the garden* were the instructions brought by a handsome, young footman.

So Beatrice and Jillian hustled about their new apartments, washing, dressing, putting up each other's hair. Beatrice said little as she helped her sister get ready to meet the dowager, but Jillian talked continually.

It was what she did when she was nervous . . . or happy . . . or sad. Talking was what her father told Jillian she did best. He had once said that Jillian could talk the ear off a cattleman or King Charles himself, and charm them both.

Jillian stood before a walnut-framed mirror studying her

reflection. She had dressed in a day gown of rich azure blue with full three-quarter sleeves and an appropriate lace décolletage. She wore her sapphire earbobs with the matching necklace. Though she had only a few good pieces, she was fond of her jewelry. Lastly, she had Beatrice sweep most of her hair up in a handful of azure ribbons, leaving a few red tendrils of hair to fall at her face.

Jillian turned in front of the mirror. Would Duncan find her attractive? Then she wondered why she cared. . . . If she had any sense, she'd cut her hair short and jagged and cover her head with ashes. She could tell Duncan she was in mourning for her beloved. *The earl would not be anxious to marry a demented woman, would he?*

"You look lovely," Beatrice whispered, resting her hands on her sister's shoulders, staring wistfully into the mirror at their reflections side by side. Bea had dressed in a utilitarian brown gown with ecru lace. The dress was new and fashionable, but not particularly becoming.

"Something's still not right," Jillian said, studying herself critically. "I look like a father's daughter, not a man's intended.

Impulsively, Jillian picked a paring knife up off a side table where it had been left with a bowl of fresh fruit. With a couple quick slices of the knife, she trimmed the long hair that fell forward until it framed her face with curls. "There," she cried triumphantly. "Now I'm all the mode. Just like the woman we saw at the 'Change."

Beatrice covered her mouth with her hand with a sharp intake of her breath. "Jilly! Mother said that woman was a paramour!"

"She was pretty, though, wasn't she?" Jillian walked away from the mirror, giving her sister an impish grin. "Shall we go?"

Jillian and Beatrice came down the grand staircase just as a dusty case clock on the landing struck nine. By the light of the morning, Jillian could see that the old house was in even greater need of repair than she'd thought last night. Though the house had certainly been grand once upon a time, it sadly lacked upkeep. The ceilings were cracked so that dust filtered down through the air. Some of the portraits on the walls hung askew because their nails had loosened in the crumbling wall-plaster. Many of the stair steps were marred from lack of oiling, and the banister was in desperate need of a good scrubbing.

Jillian reached the bottom of the staircase. "God's teeth, if this is the state of ruin he keeps his grandmother in, what do you think he intends for me in the Colonies? A savage hut?"

Beatrice clung to her sister's arm. "In all fairness, sister," she whispered as if the portraits might hear, "the earl has only recently come into his entitlement. Father said it was the cousin who kept the dowager these many years."

"Whose side are you on?" Jillian frowned. "Well, something will have to be done about this." She ran a finger over a mahogany chair rail and showed her sister the thick dust. "I'll not live in this state, and the earl ought to be ashamed of himself for leaving a feeble old woman in such decay."

The footman who had brought the dowager's message appeared in a doorway. "This way," he called, bowing as the two woman passed him.

Then he led the sisters through a maze of dark hallways and rooms, each one in a sadder stage of dilapidation than the last, until finally they walked out through a glass door and into the sunshine of the garden.

As poorly as the house was cared for, Jillian was shocked by how beautiful the garden was. Copied after an ancient Roman garden, it was finer than any Jillian had ever seen. Though she could only identify a few of the leafy plants and expertly pruned trees, it didn't take a botanist to appreciate what must have taken many years to build. From there on the stone landing, Jillian could see that the garden stretched on for what seemed an eternity, with chiseled Roman statues and stone benches for meditation. Somewhere beyond, she heard water falling.

The feeble old dowager was not what Jillian had expected either. Out of nowhere appeared a woman, old, but by no means feeble.

The Dowager Roderick approached Jillian and Beatrice with a bucket full of dirt in one hand and a trowel in the other. She was a tall, slender woman dressed in flowing Turkish robes with a turban around her head. And though her face was well wrinkled by time, tumbling from beneath the turban was hair as bright red as Jillian's own.

"You must be Jillian," the dowager said, coming straight toward her. She put down her bucket and trowel. "No offense meant, dear," she told Beatrice, "but I know what my grandson likes." She offered her dirty-gloved hands to Jillian, and Jillian accepted them with a warm smile.

"I am Daphne Roderick." She squeezed Jillian's hands with conviction.

The older woman's laughing eyes told Jillian she had nothing to fear. If she were to have one friend in the household, she knew it would be the dowager.

"I'm pleased to meet you, madame." Jillian swept a deep curtsy.

Beatrice curtsied behind her.

"Madame? Goodness, you're going to give me great-granddaughters. Call me Daphne, and I'll call you Jillian." She looped her arm through Jillian's as if they were the best of friends. "Let's eat. I'm starving, aren't you?"

The dowager lead Jillian down a pathway. Beatrice followed behind.

"It's well time Duncan married," the elderly woman rattled on. "A man needs a good woman to straighten out his head. Heavens! He's as mad as those Colonial savages, wearing that ridiculous scarf over his face!"

Jillian wanted to ask about the scarf, and she was

tempted, but she thought better of the idea. She *would* ask the dowager, but later.

They entered a small clearing where a table had been set with polished silver. Another handsome young footman pulled a chair out for the dowager.

"Thank you, Charlie." She winked at him as she handed him her gloves.

Jillian tried not to gape at the dowager, flirting openly with her servant, but she couldn't help herself. She'd never met a woman like Daphne Roderick before.

"Sit, sit, sit, ladies." Daphne spread her arms, and the footman jumped to help first Jillian, then Beatrice into their seats.

The dowager immediately began to uncover steaming platters of blood sausage, egg pie, and baked apples. The scents that rose from the plates were heavenly. "And you must be the sister he turned down." She addressed Beatrice.

Bea lowered her gaze to her plate, and Jillian slipped her hand beneath the table to squeeze Bea's.

Instinctively, Jillian took up for her sister. "It was really rather awkward, madame—"

"Daphne." The dowager served herself a healthy slice of egg pie and blood sausage. "I told you to call me Daphne, Jillian."

"Daphne—"

"Stuff and nonsense, Jillian. Let her answer for herself." The dowager stabbed a piece of sausage with her knife and pushed it into her mouth. "Was it awkward, dear? Are you upset that your sister has taken your husband? You don't look upset."

Jillian watched Beatrice as she struggled to find her voice.

"I . . . truthfully madame, I have to agree with the earl. I . . . he—he and Jillian are much better suited."

"Bea!" Jillian protested.

"Hush, child, and eat." The dowager pushed the serving

dish of egg toward Jillian. "Your sister's attempting to converse."

Beatrice glanced up meekly. "It's—it's true that we were betrothed, but his lordship chose Jilly instead." She twisted her hands in her lap. "I think it's what's best."

"He didn't suit you then?"

Beatrice squirmed. "No, no he didn't, madame."

"Too loud." Daphne speared another bit of sausage. "Too moody, too arrogant."

"Y—yes."

The dowager smiled. "Well, then, good for you."

Beatrice stared quizzically. "Madame?"

The old woman shrugged. "Don't look at it as if you were turned away. You turned him away, the arrogant bastard. Good riddance, I'd say. Someone better suited to you will come along. Trust me. A woman my age knows."

"Thank you, madame."

"Please, it's Daphne to you."

Beatrice smiled just a little.

The dowager waved her knife at Jillian. "Now, what of you, granddaughter? Are you pleased with the turn of events? My grandson is handsome and wealthy. He's quite a catch for a girl from a family like yours."

Jillian scooped a small bit of the pie onto her plate and pushed the serving dish toward Beatrice. She knew she should have been offended by the woman's reference to her family, but she wasn't. "In all honesty, ma—Daphne, I am not."

"Good. I like honesty in a woman. Most females aren't honest. That's why I've never had much use for them. Now tell me, why don't you want to marry my grandson? You'd make handsome children, males and females, you know."

Jillian reached for the bread. "I had someone else in mind to wed."

"You were betrothed?"

"No." She looked at the dowager, who was chewing

heartily on a fresh bit of bread. "My father doesn't approve, but I love him."

Daphne sighed. "Pity." Then her voice changed to one of practicality again. "But I agree with your sister. She's a wise girl. Perceptive. I may even find her a husband myself." She pointed with her knife. "You and Duncan are as well suited as peas in a pod." She grinned, showing remarkably perfect teeth for a woman her age. "That or flint and steel." She nodded, buttering her bread. "I approve. I approve wholeheartedly of the union. You have my permission to wed. Should my grandson grace us with his presence, I'll give him my blessing as well."

Jillian set down her knife. "But you don't understand. I don't want to marry him."

The dowager grimaced. "You think I wanted to marry Duncan's grandfather? Good heavens!" She made a sound like a horse. "I had a simpleton cousin chosen. We'd already shared kisses. We were certain we were madly in love."

Jillian knew she blushed; she could feel the warmth in her cheeks. She and her dear Jacob had exchanged kisses in the church courtyard just last May Day.

The dowager shrugged. "But my father knew better. The earl, God rest his soul, knew better. I despised my husband at first, but I came to care for him a great deal . . ." She smiled the smile of a woman who had truly loved. "With all my heart." She reached for the serving platter of egg and sausage again. "And you will come to love Duncan in time. Trust me."

Jillian folded her napkin on her lap, unsure of what to say. Of course she couldn't come to love the Earl of Cleaves. She was in love with Jacob. But it seemed pointless to argue. Instead, Jillian chose to change the subject. She reached for a bowl of fresh chopped fruit. "Your garden is so beautiful that I'm surprised by the state of the house." There. The dowager wanted honesty? Honest she would be. "The staircase is dangerous. I fear you might injure yourself."

"Oh, blather! You think I walk up those steps to my apartment myself?" She hooked her thumb, which sparkled with a ruby ring. "What do you think I have Charlie here for? The boy carries me."

Jillian must have had such a ridiculous look on her face for the dowager began to laugh. She reached out with one wrinkled, bejeweled hand and covered Jillian's hand with hers. "I was teasing, sweet. You don't think I would waste such a fine young man's strength on such nonsense, do you?" She released Jillian's hand and pushed the bread toward her. "Eat, child, you're thin. It will take a great deal of energy to manage your husband."

"Do you mind if I ask why the house hasn't been cared for?"

"Not in the least." She wiped the corners of her mouth with a white damask napkin. "It's Algernon." She leaned forward, lowering her voice. "The boy always was a niggard."

"He's withheld funds to repair the family estate?" Jillian was shocked.

Daphne shrugged. "It hasn't mattered much, dear. I have my garden and my footmen. An old woman such as myself has little need for furnished salons."

Jillian dropped her napkin onto the table. "Well, Duncan now has control of the family funds, does he not?"

The dowager sipped coffee. "I suppose he does, doesn't he?"

Jillian pushed her chair away from the garden table. "Then he needs to make amends." She rose. "It's not right that a woman of your rank should be living in the ruins of that house. Duncan will—"

"Duncan will what?" came a deep, masculine voice as Duncan appeared on the stone pathway between two great boxwoods.

Five

Jillian took half a step back. *God's teeth, she hadn't expected him to appear through the bushes!* "G—good morning, sir," she stammered. "W—we were just having breakfast with your grandmother."

"And speaking of me when I wasn't here to defend myself. Typical female," he intoned sarcastically. He nodded to Beatrice and then walked over to his grandmother. "Good morning."

Daphne chuckled. "Same to you."

He turned to address Jillian. "Would you walk with me in the garden, *dear?* I'd like to speak with you."

Jillian touched her head, stalling for time. Her talk was bold when Duncan was nowhere to be seen, but now that he was here, she wasn't certain just how brave she was. She didn't want to walk alone in the garden with him. She wanted to stay here with the women where she felt safe. "My hat, sir. The sun is strong. I'll just run up—"

Duncan took her arm, giving her no choice in the matter. "Come, come, we won't be long. I promise you I'll not permit the sun to harm your delicate skin."

"Grandmother." He nodded again. "Beatrice."

Beatrice gave him a half smile, nodding in return, and then Duncan led Jillian off down the garden path he'd come.

The two walked side by side for a good distance, down the winding stone path, past a tiny waterfall, through the trees and flowering shrubs. Duncan did not, however, release her arm, and Jillian was all too conscious of his touch.

Only after they were out earshot of Beatrice and the dowager did Duncan finally speak. "I don't appreciate you talking about me behind my back," he stated flatly. "You and I are going to be man and wife. We'll be a contingent—you and I against the world, Jillian. I'll have no backstabbing by my spouse. I thought you of better breeding than that. Smarter, too."

"I wasn't talking about you."

"I heard my name. It was your voice."

Jillian stopped on the path, pulling her arm from his. It was too difficult to speak to him while touching him. Now that they stood a safe distance apart, she could think more clearly. "We were talking about the house. You ought to be ashamed, letting your grandmother live like this."

He raised his voice. "What are you talking about?"

"Don't shout at me!"

He lowered his voice a few decibels. "My grandmother wants for nothing. She has her servants, her exotic organgery. These gardens are as beautiful as any I've seen in the world."

"They are beautiful, but I'm talking about the house."

"The house?" He looked at her with the one eye she could see. He shrugged. "So it's in need of a little plaster, a dab of paint."

"A little plaster! The blessed house is falling down around her!"

"You understand the previous situation. Cousin Algernon had both the title and the monies until they were granted to me. He's been living here these years and caring for our grandmother. It is he who has let the house deteriorate."

"Fine." She dropped her hands to her hips, made angry by the thought that Algernon had neglected the house so. She couldn't help but wonder if the dowager had been neglected in the same manner. "But now you have the money. It's your duty to restore your family home—"

"All right."

"—What must people think? Have you no sense of honor? Don't you want to see your grandmother well cared for at her age? It's dangerous for her to live like this. The stairs are cracked; there's plaster falling from the ceiling, there's—"

"I said *all right.*" He was smiling at her now, the corner of his mouth that she could see was turned up.

Jillian ceased her prattle, realizing she'd overdone it again. "What did you say?"

He was still smiling as he reached out and caught a stray lock of hair that curled at her temple. "I said, *all right,* Jilly. The house does need repairs, and I have been remiss in not beginning the work immediately. I simply haven't had time to deal with the matter. I'm a very busy man."

Jillian held her breath as his hand brushed her cheek.

"So, you deal with it," he went on. "Hire the workers. Have done what you see fit. Atar will escort you wherever you need to go. He's here to be of assistance to you when I don't need him. Send the bills to my goldsmith."

Jillian stared at Duncan. He had let his hand fall to his side, but her face still felt warm where he'd touched her. It had been an innocent enough gesture, and yet it had seemed so sensual to her . . . perhaps because they were strangers.

"You want *me*—" She touched her chest lightly. "—to oversee the repairs of your family's estate?"

"You *are* going to be the head of my home, as my wife, are you not? I assume you have been trained in such matters." He lifted his hand in a bored gesture. "So take care of it."

Now she was truly perplexed. "You want me to spend your money? Without your prior approval?"

"I just gave you my approval."

"But there's a great deal of work to be done—more than you might realize. It could be costly."

"Now that my father's estates have been returned to me, I've more than enough money for my tobacco plantation in the Colonies. I can certainly spare a few hundred pounds so that my grandmother and wife can live more comfortably."

Jillian smiled at him, the irritation she had felt only a moment before dissipating. "You're not what you seem to be, are you?" she asked softly. She watched his face change, wishing she could see what it was that he hid beneath his scarf. Today it was blue.

"I don't know what you speak of."

She took a step closer to him, her hand itching to touch the veil. Would he let her lift it? "You're loud and demanding. You try to push people away from you, and yet . . . yet your heart is kind."

"Female nonsense," he scoffed. But when she took a step closer, he didn't back away. He seemed to be as intrigued by her as she was by him.

Jillian raised her hand. "Could I see?" she asked him. "What's behind the veil?"

He touched the veil himself, shying from her. "No. Why would you want to?"

"It can't be so horrible."

"You don't know what horrible is, Jilly. You're too young, too sweet, too innocent."

"You think I'm a child."

"In some ways, you are."

"But not so much a child that you don't want to wed and bed me."

The smile appeared again. "Touché."

She raised her hand again, and he stepped back. "You're being absurd," she accused, letting her hand fall. "You expect me to marry you not knowing what you look like."

"Perhaps."

She chuckled. "And in our bed?" Of course she had no intention of sharing a bed with the man, because she had no intention of marrying him; but she couldn't resist asking. "Do you intend to wear that ridiculous thing to bed as well?"

"Perhaps."

Jillian shook her head. "You want me to be afraid of you, don't you? Well, I'm not. If you want to scare me, you'll have to try a different tack." She turned on her heels and started back up the path the way they had come. "I'll start work on the house immediately," she called over her shoulder. "I'll have to take your coach into the city, of course. I hope you can manage on horseback."

"Wait, I'm not done with you!" he shouted after her. "I've invited a friend to sup with us tonight. I'll expect you at nine in the dining parlor."

Jillian waved over her head in acknowledgment as she turned the corner, pleased with herself on how she had managed the Colonial Devil. Just as she disappeared from his sight, she heard him mutter to himself, *"Chit . . ."*

Jillian smiled.

Jillian spent a busy day finding men to begin the initial work on the house. She was so occupied with making appointments for the following days that she barely had time to think of Duncan. It wasn't until she returned to her apartments in the early evening that she finally had a moment to contemplate her encounter with him that morning.

She sat on a low stool before the mirror while Beatrice stood behind her, dressing her hair for supper. "Tell me something," Jillian said thoughtfully. "Do you think he's handsome, the earl, I mean?"

Beatrice's forehead crinkled. "Handsome? With that veil that covers his face?"

"Forget the veil." Jillian closed her eyes. "Imagine how he looks without it."

"One of the chambermaids told me only this afternoon

that he was terribly burned as a child. The servants say those are the scars he hides."

Jillian opened her eyes, frowning.

"Remember Lucy Madden, Mother's cousin from Yorkshire?" Bea continued. "She wore a veil after she had the smallpox."

"A man can't get the pox on only one side of his face." Jillian folded her arms in her lap. "It must be something else."

Beatrice pulled a thick hank of curly hair off Jillian's shoulders and began to pin it high on the back of her head. She held silver pins in her mouth so that her speech was garbled. "Father said there was rumor at Court that he had been captured by Indians in the American Colonies. That's where he was all those years he was missing. Maybe they burned him."

"We don't even know if that's true, the Indian tale. All we know is that he and his family disappeared and that they were killed, all but Duncan. It could have been a shipwreck, or the plague, for all we know."

Beatrice stuck the last pin into Jillian's coiffure with satisfaction. "So ask him, sister. A woman has a right to know her husband's background before she weds him."

Jillian leapt up, her petticoat bunched in her fists. "I told you earlier, I'm not marrying him."

Beatrice stood back to admire her sister in her handsome forest-green gown and sparkling emerald earbobs. "You certainly act like you're going to marry him. Ordering him about. Spending his money. Making changes in the house."

"The dowager deserves better care. The house is in need of the work; and if he's not going to do it, I shall." She reached out to touch a purple flowering branch left in a vase beside her bed. "I assure you, I have no intentions of becoming the Countess of Cleaves. The repairs are but a way to occupy my time until Jacob can come for me." She took the fan her sister offered and started for the door.

"Jacob!" Beatrice hissed, following Jillian. "Father forbade you to contact him! You're the earl's betrothed now! No decent woman would approach a man after her betrothal agreement had been signed."

"Jacob doesn't know where I am. I have to send him a message. He'll be worried sick when I haven't written."

Beatrice picked up her basket of stitching. Though she'd been invited to dine, she'd begged out, pleading a headache, and would remain alone in the apartments the remainder of the evening. "I'll have no part of such deceit, I warn you, Jilly. I'll not be a messenger for such illicit behavior."

Jillian stopped at the door, swinging around so that her abundant petticoats swirled at her feet. "You're not being terribly supportive."

"You should marry the earl." Beatrice crossed her arms with such conviction that it startled Jillian.

"You didn't want to marry him after you saw him, why should I?"

"I'd have married him if Father had bid me to." Beatrice let her gaze drift to the floor. "If his lordship had wanted me."

"Oh, Bea." Jillian's voice softened as she came toward her sister. "I'm sorry that this has turned into such a spoiled brew, truly I am. But I'll find you a husband; I swear I will. Jacob and I will run away and be married, and then you can come with me."

"Such talk is nonsense. You'll marry the earl just as Father has arranged." Beatrice gave her sister a push toward the door. "And you'll be happy with him, I'll wager, scars and all. The two of you are cut from the same cloth, even the dowager says so."

"That's a ridiculous notion!" Jillian swung open the door. "Don't wait up for me. I imagine I'll be late."

"Good night," Beatrice said softly. "You look lovely tonight, sister. I'm certain you'll charm *him*."

Jillian wrinkled her nose at her sister as she swept out of the bedchamber, thinking such a statement unworthy of a reply.

* * *

"Ah, you must be Duncan's betrothed."

Jillian had barely reached the salon door when a stout fellow in his mid-thirties wearing a rich burgundy coat and breeches approached her. He gave a low whistle. "But you're a gnashing beauty."

Jillian lifted her petticoats in a curtsy. "I fear you have the unfair advantage, sir. You know me, yet I don't know you."

The man bowed formally. "That scoundrel, Duncan. I suspect he didn't tell you of me for fear you and I would run off and be wed before he could make it to the dining table. I'm Will Galloway. Your servant, madame." He took her hand, making an event of kissing it.

"Jillian Hollingsworth. Your servant, sir."

"I don't know where Duncan is. He ordered me to be prompt, and now he's not here." Will swung an arm gracefully. "So, the pox on him." He took her hand and led her into the salon. "I'd rather talk with you than grump head, anyway. You're a plain sight prettier, and more even tempered, I'll wager."

"Don't be so certain of that," came Duncan's voice as he appeared out of the darkness of the hallway.

"Duncan! I was hoping the lady would agree to elope with me before you made it to supper. Now you've dashed my plans to hell and back."

Jillian couldn't help but laugh at Will Galloway's easy banter. He, for one, seemed unintimidated by the earl.

Duncan brushed past his friend, removing Jillian's arm from Will's and wrapping it around his own. "A drink before we dine?"

"Yes, thank you." She threw an apologetic smile in his direction. "White Rhenish, if you please, sir."

Will followed them into the salon. "Duncan, don't tell

me you're so impressed by that new title of yours that you insist your betrothed call you *sir.*"

Duncan looked at Atar, who stood quietly, as he always did, waiting to follow his bidding. As usual, he was dressed in his pressed red coat and, by contrast, hole-riddled shoes. "Refreshment for us all, Atar. White Rhenish for the lady, something sturdier for Galloway and me."

It was a strange relationship between Duncan and his servant, Jillian thought. Atar was at his master's beck and call, dawn until midnight. He saw to his every personal need, and yet there seemed to be no bond between them, no intimate relationship. Atar remained as cool and aloof as Duncan at all times. Perhaps that was what made them a good pair.

Duncan took the glass of white wine Atar poured for Jillian and offered it to her himself. He had dressed for dinner in a dark-green coat and gold breeches with a gold-garnitured sword case. "Did I invite you here?" he questioned Will good-naturedly. "I don't recall doing so."

"You did, indeed. Only last night."

Duncan offered Jillian the glass of sweet white wine. "I can't imagine why. Refresh my memory, will you?"

"Why?" Will reached for the glass Atar offered. "Why, to meet your betrothed, of course."

Duncan shook his head, serving himself a healthy portion of brandywine. "So, where was my head?"

"In your cups, no doubt." Will winked at Jillian.

"I know you can't behave properly. Why do I invite you anywhere?" Duncan threw up his hand. "So, go with you. Surely you're expected in some lady or gentleman's drawing room tonight?"

Jillian watched the two men exchange their nonsense. The longer she knew Duncan, the more complex he seemed to become. She could tell from the tone of the two men's voices that they respected each other. They were not just acquaintances, but friends, good friends. The idea that the earl could have a true friend spoke of his character.

"I have no other engagements tonight, thank you." Will took a drink of his brandy. "I'm yours, the lady's, and Grandmother's for the evening." He glanced about. "Tell me, where is the blessed dowager? I expected she'd be awaiting me."

"When I told her you were coming, she took to her bed. She'll not be joining us."

"Took to her bed with one of her footmen, is more likely." Will peeked around the corner to where a dining table had been set. "So, tell me, are we eating, or are we not, because I'm famished."

Duncan turned to Jillian. "Please accept my apologies, madame, for the rude supper guest. I should have known better than to invite him. He's not used to respectable women."

Jillian smiled at her betrothed. "Will is welcome at any table I'm seated at."

"Oh, he is, is he?" Duncan lifted an eyebrow with amusement. "Well, come then and serve as my hostess, will you?"

Will followed them into the dining parlor. "You two don't sound like you're going to be wed in two months time. You sound more like—"

"Good evening, madame, sirs." Algernon appeared in the doorway behind them, dressed for the evening. Tonight he wore canary yellow coat and breeches with lime-green, looped ribbons. "I hope I'm not intruding."

Duncan frowned. "Jillian, Will, and I are just sitting down to dine. Care to join us, cousin?" There was little attempt at persuasion in his voice.

Jillian stood near Duncan, alert to the tension in the room. She noticed that Will had wandered to the open window, barely acknowledging Algernon's arrival.

"No, I fear I cannot." Algernon glanced at Will's back and gave an obligatory smile. "I've other plans. I'm expected in a lady's drawing room shortly; and if I'm not on time, she's sure to be vexed. I just wanted to ask our dear

Jillian if her apartments were comfortable." He turned to her. "Is there anything you or your sister have need of?"

"No. The rooms are quite satisfactory."

"Algernon," Duncan said sharply. "If my betrothed has need of anything, I'm certain I can see to it myself."

"Yes, well—" He smoothed his thin mustache with his thumb and forefinger. "—we all know how busy you can be, don't we?" He backed out of the room. "Your servant, madame, *my lords.*"

A silence fell upon the room as Algernon made his exit.

Will came away from the window, his glass empty. "I don't know why you didn't kick that little eel out on his ass when you had the opportunity, Duncan. He's always slithering about, eavesdropping."

Duncan sighed. "We've been through this before, Will. First the monies and title were his, then they weren't. I feel bad for him."

"But not bad enough to hand the earldom back to him."

"No. It is rightfully mine. My father was the eldest son. But to offer my cousin a home and a small allowance is the least I can do."

"The man is trouble, I warn you. You can see it in his little reptile eyes. And saints in hell, his taste in clothing is appalling."

Duncan frowned, pulling out a chair for Jillian at the square, mahogany dining table. "Enough of such talk. Shall we dine?"

The remainder of the evening went smoothly. Mostly Jillian sat and listened to the two men banter, joining in on occasion. They talked of politics, of the Dutch, and of the price of Colonial imports.

Truthfully, she enjoyed the evening more than she had anticipated. For the first time in her life she was included in male conversation, and she found it stimulating. All these years her father and male relatives had never been interested in her thoughts, only in what she looked like. Come to think of it, not even Jacob had ever cared to discuss anything of substance with her.

Before Jillian realized how late it was, Will was excusing himself for the evening and Duncan was escorting her up the dark, dilapidated grand staircase. At her door, she paused, wanting to say something, but not knowing what.

"I . . . enjoyed the evening. I like Will. He's quite charming."

Duncan stood close enough to her that she could feel the warmth of his body so near to hers. "I'm glad that you like him. We've been through a great deal, the two of us. He's a good friend."

Jillian looked up at Duncan, sensing he, too, felt awkward. Candlelight from the sconce on the wall cast shadows across his veiled face. He was staring at her intently.

"I told Grandmother what you were doing with the house. I think she's pleased. She likes you."

"And I like her.

He chuckled. "Once you get used to her bluntness."

She laughed softly with him. "I suppose you're right. Her garden is beautiful. I admire her dedication and her thoughtfulness."

"Her thoughtfulness?"

"Why, yes. She's left fresh flowers in my room yesterday and today. They make it seem more like home. I'll have to be sure to thank her."

He smiled at her, and again, she couldn't help but wonder what was under the green veil he wore. But for some reason it didn't seem that important tonight. She put her hand on the doorknob behind her, wondering if he were going to attempt to kiss her. Jacob never got her alone that he didn't. "Well, good night, Duncan."

"Good night, Jillian."

To her surprise, he made no attempt to touch her, but turned on his heels and disappeared down the dark hallway.

And to her surprise, she was just a little disappointed . . .

* * *

Algernon rolled onto his back with a satisfied groan, both arms stretched out to accommodate his young lovers. "Christ, you two wear me out," he murmured in the darkness of the tapestry bed curtains. "Have you a little wine for my throat, dear heart?"

"Aye. Anything for you." Mary slipped from his arm and bounced up, parting the heavy curtains. A breath of fresh air filled the dark bed space, chasing away the musky scent of their exploits.

Algernon caressed her tight, pale buttocks as she left his bed. The bed curtains fell, and again he was left in darkness.

"I'm so pleased the two of you could meet me tonight," he told the lover cradled in his arm. "I've had a blessed lousy day. The creditors are hounding me and that damned parsimonious cousin of mine refuses to give me an advance on my year's pittance." He scratched his hairy groin with a yawn. "I'll be lucky if I'm not in Newgate come Candlemas Eve."

"I'll visit you if you are."

Algernon brushed his lips against his partner's. "You're sweet. That's why I like you. You're not only discreet, but a dear."

His lover drew a hand low across Algernon's belly. "That's not why I like you . . ."

Algernon chuckled. "Did I tell you about my cousin's betrothed?"

"No," came the soft, sensual voice.

"Comely little bitch. Innocent as an autumn's snow. He's got her locked up in the house for fear she'll lose her maidenhead before he can take it." Algernon chuckled. "I must admit it's tempting." He stared up at the mirror overhead. In the darkness of the bed curtains he could barely make out the silhouette of their two bodies twisted in the sheets.

"I'm going to take the monies and the title back, you know."

"I know. I'm counting on it."

Algernon ran his fingers through his own short-cropped brown hair. "Perhaps I should take her, too. An earl needs a wife. She's from a good family, the Hollingsworths. She could bring an heir of dignity to the Roderick name." He turned over onto his side. "It's rightfully mine, you know. The monies. The title. It should have been mine. It was always mine."

"I know. You told me."

The curtains parted, and lamplight sprang across the bed. Mary drew herself inside, a wine goblet between her delicate fingers. The curtains fell, leaving the lovers in darkness again.

"Here you are."

She offered the wine, and Algernon sipped from the goblet still in her hands. When a little of the Rhenish dribbled down his chin, Robert sat up.

"Here, let me get that for you." His tongue flicked out, catching the drop, and Algernon sighed with pleasure at the feel of the young man's warm tongue on his flesh.

"Yes, I'm definitely glad you two could make it," Algernon mused softly as he laid back on the heaped goose-down pillows. Already Mary and Robert were touching him the way they knew he liked to be touched. "Perhaps dear Jillian might want to join us one day," he whispered. "Perhaps one day soon . . ."

Six

Jillian stood on a ladder in the front hallway, her hands on her hips. "No, the right corner must be lifted," she ordered one of the workman. She groaned as the picture of Duncan's grandfather shifted perilously some ten feet off the floor. "If you drop that," she warned the hired man on the scaffold, "I'll have your head in a basket!"

The days were slipping through Jillian's fingers like the falling leaves in the dowager's garden. September had come and gone; and before Jillian realized it, October was upon the city of London and her marriage to the earl loomed ahead.

Jillian kept herself busy overseeing the work on Breckenridge, so busy that she had little time to think of Duncan. She saw him only three or four times a week, and then, almost always in a formal setting. Once, he took her to a bearbaiting, another time to Hyde Park to see the Birdcage Walk where there were exotic birds from Peru, China, and even the Indies. But wherever they went, they were accompanied by friends of his, and Beatrice always went along as chaperone, so there was little time for private talk.

Twice Will Galloway came to sup with them, and Jillian enjoyed those evenings immensely. She told herself that she found the suppers pleasurable because of Will and his antics, but the truth was that she enjoyed Duncan's company even more. She liked to listen to his voice as he talked and laughed with Will. She liked to watch him, imagining what he would look like without the veil, without the scars that must be beneath it.

"Good, good," Jillian called to the workman. "That's nearly perfect. Now fetch the next one. Yes, the woman with the large ears." She pointed to the row of family portraits leaning against the wall. Now that the walls of the entryway to the house had been replastered and painted, she was having all the portraits returned to their places of honor in the gallery. Next, the weapons would be returned to their proper locations.

"Heavens! What are you doing on that ladder, child?" The dowager appeared from behind a canvas drop meant to protect the other rooms from the dust of the sanded plaster. Beatrice trailed behind her.

Jillian gripped the ladder and came down the rungs. "I wanted to be certain this dolt lined the portraits up straight. I had to get higher to see." She smoothed her wrinkled, dusty gown as she crossed the hallway toward Daphne and Beatrice. "Did you have a pleasant walk in the orangery? I understand the lime trees are blossoming."

"Indeed they are." Daphne hurrumphed. "No thanks to that blasted gardener of mine. I have instructed Simeon again and again on how to prune a lime, and still he mutilates my trees."

Jillian had to smile. The dowager was dressed this morning in a bright pink gown with a décolletage so low that the garment must surely have been meant for a woman fifty years younger, yet on Daphne it was becoming. Jillian had learned a great deal about the dowager in the last few weeks, certainly more than she'd learned about Duncan.

Jillian had quickly discovered that there was a reason why all of the dowager's servants were young, virile males. Once Jillian had gotten beyond the shock of the idea, she found it quite titillating. For despite the dowager's age, somewhere in her early eighties, her sexual appetite had not waned. Daphne Roderick had a full staff of young men who not only cooked for her, brought her meals, and helped her in the garden, but served as bed partners as well.

"I was just walking Daphne upstairs for her nap," Beatrice said, eyeing her sister. "A *letter* has come for you. Will you take it here or shall I leave it in your apartments?"

Jillian wrinkled her nose. Why in heavens was her sister behaving so oddly? What did she mean by that tone of voice? Then Jillian realized who the letter must have come from.

Jacob. He'd written to her again.

"I'm done here." Jillian put her hand out. "See Daphne to her apartments and I'll take the letter."

"God's breath, girls. I don't need an escort to my bed." She lowered her voice. "Unless it's one of those boys painting that wall." She gave a wink.

Beatrice's eyes grew round, aghast. For though she had become as much a companion to Daphne as to Jillian, she did not share Jillian's liberal view of the old woman's idiosyncrasy. More than once Beatrice had lectured Daphne on passages in the Bible concerning adultery. The dowager, luckily, had not been offended, but rather amused.

Daphne threw back her head, filling the chamber with rich laughter as she parted the canvas drops and headed up the staircase.

Jillian thrust out her hand again. "Give me the letter."

Beatrice tucked her hand behind her back. "This is the place to end it, Jilly," she whispered, turning on her heels.

Jillian followed her sister out of the front hall and down a dark hallway. "Give me my letter!"

"I'll respond for you. I'll simply tell Jacob that you'll be marrying the earl."

Jillian crossed her arms angrily over her chest.

"Oh, come on, Jilly. You like the earl, admit it. I see the way you look at him." She reached out and seized her sister's hand. "I see the way he looks at you. Heavens, Jilly, the man's already half in love with you."

Jillian smiled. "Do you think so? He certainly doesn't act it."

Beatrice let go of her sister's hand. "You have no future with Jacob Brentwood. He's a boy, and this is a man who is willing to wed you. Use your head, Jilly. You're not in love with the parson's son. You're only in love with the idea of love."

Jillian bit down on her lower lip. Beatrice understood her all too well. The truth was that Jillian thought less and less about Jacob each day, and more about Duncan. It was Duncan's face she saw when she closed her eyes. In her fantasies, it was Duncan who swept her into his arms and kissed her with passion. Of course it was all a fabrication. Duncan had not even attempted to kiss her yet.

Jillian looked up at her sister. "Even if I've decided to follow my father's wishes, I should answer Jacob's letter. I owe him that."

"You mean you'll marry the earl?" Beatrice leaned against the wall behind her with a smile. "I think it's the right thing to do, Jilly. I think you'll be happy."

Jillian's brow creased. "Happy?" She took the letter from her sister's hand. "You think I'll be happy with the man who was your betrothed?"

Beatrice lowered her gaze, studying the uneven floorboards. The carpenters had not reached the rooms in the east wing yet. "It would never have worked, he and I. I'm too weak a female, but you, Jilly—" She looked up. "You could make him happy. You could heal whatever it is that hurts him, whatever it is that makes him so gruff and demanding."

Jillian toyed with the letter from one man while thinking of another. Did Beatrice speak the truth? Jillian realized that it was unrealistic to think she and Jacob could elope and live happily the rest of their days. Where would they live? How would they feed their children? But would it be possible with the earl? Could she convince him to pull aside his veil? Could she reach him? Could she make him care for her? The thought made her cheeks grow warm. Jillian didn't know how it had happened, but she knew she was infatuated with her betrothed. What an amusing thought.

Slowly Jillian opened the wax seal on the letter and read it.

"What does he say?" Beatrice asked, keeping her voice low.

"He wants me to meet him." She folded the letter carefully. "In an ordinary in Haymarket near the Park. This afternoon. He's waiting for me now."

Beatrice watched her sister's face in the shadows with care. "Will you meet him?"

"I would be a coward if I didn't."

"No. You would be saving him the pain and a great deal of trouble, should the earl discover the meeting. Heavens, Jilly. The earl could demand a duel. It would be his right. Jacob could die."

Jillian exhaled slowly. "It seems cruel to just send him a note. I feel badly. I was the one that initiated the contact after I arrived here. I told him that I wanted to see him."

"And do you . . . now?"

"No," Jillian whispered. "Not really. He and I weren't much alike. It was just that he paid some attention to me."

"And that he was forbidden?" Beatrice added.

Jillian felt childish. "I suppose so."

Beatrice reached out and took the letter from Jillian's hand. "I'll go for you," she said softly. "I'll tell him that you will obey your father's wishes and marry the earl."

Jillian lifted her gaze. "You really think he cares for me—Duncan? He pays me so little attention. I barely see him and yet we live in the same house."

"He's a busy man, Jilly. Just wait until you set sail for the Colonies, then he'll have time for you."

The thought of taking a ship far across the sea with a man she barely knew was more than Jillian wanted to consider at that moment. But the prospect of being Duncan's wife suddenly excited her. It had been a slow transformation. She wasn't certain when she had gone from disliking Duncan to liking him, she only knew that she had.

"No." Jillian looked up. "I will marry Duncan, but I have to tell Jacob in person. It's only right."

Beatrice stared at her sister. "You're determined, aren't you?

"Yes."

Beatrice threw her arms around Jillian and gave her a quick hug, pressing Jacob's letter into her hand. "Then be careful, will you?" She studied her sister's face. "And if anyone asks for you while you're gone, I'll say you went into town to chastise the plasterers."

"Thank you." For a moment Jillian stood in the semidarkness of the hall, watching Beatrice disappear. Jillian had made a decision that would affect her the rest of her life: She was going to marry Duncan Roderick and become the Countess of Cleaves. She was going to learn to love him, and make him love her back. That was her commitment.

With a smile on her face, Jillian went down the hall. If that were her decision, then today she would turn over a new leaf. She would tell Jacob goodbye and then she would set her mind on Duncan. If Duncan didn't have time for her, he would have to make time. She would demand it. And she'd start by inviting him to sup with her tonight after she met with Jacob. She would have the servants prepare a meal and serve it in the garden in the moonlight. She would be so charming that the earl would find her irresistible.

With that thought, Jillian hurried down the hallway. She turned the corner, striking something hard . . . someone. "Oh! I'm sorry!" She looked up to see Algernon. Out of the corner of her eye, she saw Atar going in the opposite direction and disappearing around the corner.

Heavens, she thought with irritation. *Not him.* She tried to avoid Algernon in the house whenever possible, but it seemed as if he sought her out, always cornering her in the dark, alone.

"Are you all right, dear?" Algernon clasped her shoulders unnecessarily, as if she needed to be steadied.

"I'm fine. Thank you." She took a step back, pushing his hands away. He was dressed in another one of his ridiculous costumes, this one pink and red with high-heeled pink shoes and a cavalier's hat with a pink feather. "I—I apologize for my clumsiness. I didn't hear you coming." She couldn't help but wonder how much of her and Beatrice's conversation he'd heard.

He stood in front of her, blocking the hallway. "I haven't seen you in days, dear; how are you? I hope my brute of a cousin hasn't been treating you too harshly."

Jillian bristled. It seemed that at every turn Algernon tried to get Jillian to cast disfavor on Duncan. But she wasn't falling for it.

She smiled a smile without warmth. "Actually, he's been quite delightful. I'm anxious to be wed."

Algernon threw back his head in laughter. "Delightful? That ghastly, scarred son of a sorry bitch." His laughter subsided. "Come now, dear, you can tell Algernon the truth." He took a step closer to her, backing Jillian against the warped chair rail. "He's cruel to you, isn't he?"

"No!"

"He rants and he raves, calling you foul names. He fondles you, trying to force you to do what no decent woman would."

Jillian almost laughed at the absurdity. "Certainly not!"

Algernon reached out, grasping her arm before she could dodge him. "You can tell me," he whispered, a line of sweat beading above his upper lip, "because I can help you."

Jillian gritted her teeth. For a small man, he was quite strong. "Let go of me," she insisted.

"It's not rightfully his, you know." He leaned closer until she could smell the anchovies on his breath. "The title. It's mine and it will be reverted. It's only a matter of time. The court will hear my case, and I will have the earldom again."

"Let go of me," Jillian hissed, trying to twist her arm from his grip. "You're hurting me, Algernon."

He pulled her closer to him until her breasts brushed the ruffled collar of his red doublet. "You could agree to marry me now, you know. I would have you. And then you could still be the countess."

"Marry you?" Jillian wrinkled her face in disgust. "I wouldn't marry you, not for a duchy, not to be Queen of all bloody England." With a hard jerk, she snapped her arm from his grasp and, giving him a shove, darted behind him. "You stay away from me," she warned angrily, backing down the hallway. "Do you hear me? You stay away or I'll tell Duncan, and then you'll be out on your ear! It's only the goodness of his heart that keeps food in your belly, and you know it!"

Algernon leered at her. "How dare you speak to me that way, you ungrateful jade!" His face reddened with fury as he shouted down the hallway after her. "I was offering to save you from that animal! I was offering to give you the life you deserve, and you ridicule me!" He wiped the spittle from the corner of his mouth with the back of his hand. "You've made a grave error, dear Jillian," he whispered now, and became all the more menacing. "Grave. I'm not a man to make an enemy of."

"Stay away from me!" Jillian shouted down the hall. "And take your idle threats elsewhere!" Then she spun around and hurried down the hallway back toward the front entryway.

"Stinking jackanape," she muttered. He'd frightened her. The man was unstable. Jillian half-considered telling Duncan what had happened, but he wouldn't have anywhere to go. She knew Duncan would kick him out of the house—if he didn't kill him first.

* * *

Duncan stood in the front hallway to Breckenridge House, a smile of bemusement on his face. There were six workmen busy hanging armaments and portraits of his late ancestors on the freshly plastered and painted walls. The floor beneath him had been sanded, the warped boards replaced, and the chairs in the receiving area had been recovered in a rich azure damask. The room was imposing, as a proper English entryway should be, and it was all due to the work of his busy bee, Jillian.

Duncan had to give the chit credit. He had, on impulse, granted her permission to do the repairs. As Atar reported, she had taken on the assignment with enthusiasm. He had thought it would occupy her mind and take one matter off his. But he surely had not expected her to oversee such a superior job. He hadn't expected her to spend so much damned money either.

"Steady there!" one of the workman called as a scaffold shifted overhead. "Watch it, Jimmy!"

Suddenly the floor of the scaffold tipped. Duncan reacted by lifting his arms above his head to catch whatever was falling. A musket with a bayonet fell into Duncan's hands. "Ouch! Damnation!" he called as the bayonet sliced his palm. "You'd best be more careful or you'll cut off your damned heads with one of these!" He handed the musket back up to the sheepish worker and turned on his heels, pressing his palm to mouth.

"Heavens!" Jillian appeared between two parted canvas drops. "Are you all right, Duncan?" She came across the floor, her heels tapping on the freshly sanded boards.

"I'm fine. A scratch, nothing more."

"Let me see." She took his hand, leading him through the canvas drops to the window on the far side where they were in better light. "It's bleeding, Duncan." She lifted her white cotton apron to touch the superficial wound tenderly.

Duncan couldn't resist a smile. His betrothed was dressed in old clothing with a housekeeper's mobcap pulled over her head, her curly red hair spilling out. Her face was smudged with dirt, her bodice wrinkled. She was utterly appealing.

"I've been wounded in battle, madame. I can assure you I will not bleed to death." But he made no attempt to pull his hand from her grasp. He liked standing so close to her, for though he could hear the workmen, he and Jillian were completely isolated by the close proximity of the canvas drops. She was so near that he could smell the sweet scent of her skin. He could almost taste her lips.

Jillian looked up at him, still cradling his larger hand in hers. She smiled shyly. "What is it? Why do you watch me so intently?"

"I was thinking to myself how beautiful you are." Duncan didn't consider himself a courtier. He never knew what females wanted him to do, to say. He was only speaking the truth.

She was still staring at him, clearly surprised by his words. And why shouldn't she be? He'd barely spoken two words to her in the last week.

"Are you trying to court me, sir?"

"No." He encircled her in his arms. "Trying to kiss you, I think."

And then he did. Before she could open her mouth to retort, he kissed those soft, rosy lips. And to Duncan's surprise, she did not pull away. She kissed him back, the corner of his purple veil resting on her smooth, pale cheek.

"Jillian," he whispered against her mouth. "You're as sweet as a morning rain." Still, she didn't resist, so he kissed her again, this time pressing his mouth harder against hers, his tongue slipping out to taste her.

Duncan felt her hands settle on his shoulders. He could have sworn he heard her moan softly. Their tongues touched hesitantly, and then suddenly he was deep in her mouth, exploring.

When Duncan withdrew, his breath coming ragged, he stared into Jillian's cinnamon-brown eyes. She was not in the least bit put off by his veil. She looked as if she had enjoyed the kiss as much as he had.

"I don't know what to say." She spoke softly, her gaze averting to a speck on the window.

Duncan traced the line of her jaw with his fingertip. "There's nothing you must say. You're going to be my wife, Jilly, very soon. This is what husband and wife do."

"Do they enjoy each other's kisses this much?" She lifted her gaze to meet his, her eyes sparkling. Then she touched her fingers to the place he had just kissed. "I had thought that out of mode."

Duncan let his hands slide over her shoulders, down her arms. He was pleased with himself, with Jillian. This wouldn't be so bad after all—having a wife. It might even be pleasurable.

"Out of mode, perhaps," he answered, "but certainly quite enjoyable for us both, don't you think?"

She was resting her hands on his chest now. He could feel her warmth through his muslin shirt. Damnation, but he was attracted to her, more than he had realized. "We could get married now," he whispered. "The banns have been read. It could be done tonight." Duncan didn't know what made him say it; it just came out of his mouth in a husky whisper.

"Marry you tonight?" Her voice trembled. "You're not serious?"

He took her hand, not knowing what had come over him. Suddenly all he could think of was carrying Jillian off to his bed chamber, stripping off her dusty clothes, making love to her on the bed's counterpane in the last rays of sunlight. "I am serious. Say it and it will be done."

She smiled, lowering her gaze again. She was so close that he could feel her breath on his cheek. "No. Not tonight, Duncan. Let's wait. It will only be another fortnight." She looked up at him and he knew that in her heart that she did not see the veil, but rather the man beneath it. "And that will give us both something to look forward to."

Duncan hesitated, wrestling between his good sense and his desire for her. He would not take her without being wed, he had vowed that before he had brought her to the house. That was one of the reasons he had been avoiding her. He hadn't wanted to be tempted by his attraction to her. But now that he had kissed her, and knew that she was willing, he feared his own lack of control.

"All right," he said softly, releasing her. The way she smiled at him made his chest tight. "I can wait if you insist."

She was still smiling as she passed between the canvas drops back into the hallway. Duncan was still smiling when he made his way through the hallway and back to his office. For the first time in ages, he hummed to himself as he walked, remembering a bittersweet lovesong he'd sung to his dying son such a long, long time ago.

Seven

Jillian alighted from the coach in front of The Three Rings on one of the side streets in Haymarket close to the Park. Though it was dusk, the street was alive with activity. The air smelled of raw sewage, smoked meat, and unwashed bodies, city scents she had not yet become accustomed to.

A dairy maid walked by, pushing a cart, making a last call for her fresh goat's milk before she left the city for the day. A man stood on the corner, a monkey on his shoulder, playing a pipe while the chimp danced and an audience pitched coppers into a cup. Swaggering men passed in groups, some students, others gentlemen, all bound for a light supper and heavy drink, no doubt.

Accepting her footman's hand, Jillian stepped down and crossed over the sewer that ran the length of the congested street. "That will be all, Marston," she ordered, putting her vizard in place so that her identity would be masked. She wanted no one to recognize her, for if one of Duncan's friends saw her, she'd have a difficult explanation to make.

The footman glanced at the carved sign swinging overhead, bearing three rings of painted gold. "You don't want me to go with you, mistress? The master's man, he said to stick with ye."

"Where I go is my business and no one else's. Atar is a servant like you. He has no right to be giving instructions, except by direct order of the earl." She looked directly into the middle-aged man's eyes. "So if you seek *comfortable retirement* in my household, I'd suggest you look in another direction and begin to pay less attention to Atar and more to me. Do you understand what I'm saying?"

"Aye."

She slipped her hands into her kidskin gloves in a businesslike manner. "Good. Now, have the driver pull the coach around there, near the side of the ordinary, and wait for me. I won't be but five minutes."

"Yes, ma'am." He ducked his head and disappeared around the far side of the crested coach.

With a sigh of resignation, Jillian made her way into the ordinary, a gathering place where men dined, drank, and talked of politics and war. It was not unusual for a woman to frequent such an establishment, but it was odd that she was unaccompanied. No doubt, anyone who saw her would assume she was a lady on an assignation with a gentleman.

Jillian stared through the slits in her vizard, held on by a button between her teeth. Where the devil was Jacob? She scanned the room. Several gentleman had looked up, noticing her arrival. She lifted her chin with an air, making clear she was no wealthy widow looking for companionship.

"Excuse me, madame, might I aid you?"

Jillian looked down to see a portly man in workingman's clothes with an apron tied around his waist. The proprietor, she guessed.

"I—I'm seeking a gentleman."

"Might you be Jill?" he questioned, taking note of her dress.

Jill. That was what Jacob called her, though she had never cared for it. "Perhaps." She looked at him through the black vizard. "Why do you ask?"

The proprietor lowered his voice, his gaze darting across the room. "The gentleman you seek," he said secretively, "awaits on the street behind. I am to escort you, if you would allow me the honor."

Jillian glanced around the smoky public room. She didn't

know that she liked the idea of going anywhere with a man she didn't know. London City was not a safe place for unchaperoned country women. But what was she to do? She'd come this far; she'd see her decision through. Once this was over, once she said goodbye to Jacob, then she could concentrate on her relationship with Duncan.

"All right," she murmured, holding her mask with her hand so she could speak. "But hurry. I'm expected elsewhere shortly."

So the proprietor led her between the trestle tables, through the public, out a swinging door, past the kitchen that smelled of burning potatoes, and through another doorway that led outside.

"This way," he called and then pointed. "There."

Jillian immediately recognized Jacob standing beside a dogcart. She lowered her vizard. "Thank you, sir," she said to the proprietor, fishing a coin from the silk bag on her waist. "I appreciate your discretion." Then she lifted her damask skirts and picked her way through the refuse that littered the ground. She stepped over a rotting cabbage.

"Jill! Oh, Jill!" The moment Jacob spotted her, he came running. "Oh, my love, my love!"

Jillian allowed him to hug her; but when he tried to press a kiss to her mouth, she turned so that he touched only her cheek. After the kisses she and Duncan had shared, the surprising ardor, she knew that Jacob's would never satisfy her again. Perhaps she was fickle, but in comparison to Duncan, Jacob was barely noticeable.

"I'm so glad you managed to get away," he declared passionately. "I feared I'd have to come to Breckenridge House and take you by force. I've not met the Colonial Devil myself, but word has spread even to the country of his bizarre ways."

Jillian took a step back, uncomfortable with Jacob's touch. She was Duncan's now. His kiss had branded her. "Don't you know me better than that? I'm free to come and go as

I please. The earl is a decent man. It's nothing but foul rumors you hear."

He took her gloved hand, looking into her eyes. "I can't believe it's you. I can't believe that finally we can be together. I left, you know." He dropped his hands to his hips proudly. He was wearing an ill-fitting black suit of cheap damask. "Father said I couldn't come to London, but I came anyway. I came for you, Jill."

Jillian looked at Jacob, wondering what could possibly have attracted her to him in the first place. He was a thin man her own age, with hollow cheeks and sandy hair. He was not unattractive, but reminded her much of a scarecrow in a yeoman's field. Now when she saw a man, any man, it was the massively broad-shouldered Earl of Cleaves that she compared him to.

"That's why I came, Jacob. I have to talk to you." She made herself look at him, despite how blessedly guilty she felt. "I came to talk to you about us. About you and me."

"What about us? We're to be married. Tonight. We'll have a clergy perform the ceremony, and then we can take care of the legal matter afterward. Oh, Jill." His pale-blue eyes shone. "I can't tell you how I've missed, how I've dreamed . . . dreamed," he added shyly, *"of being your husband in every manner."*

Jillian gave a sigh. He was talking of bedding her, of course. She deserved this; she knew she deserved it. This was her punishment for having been so childish, so capricious. It was her penance for thinking she wanted to marry this milksop. "Jacob, listen to me," she said sternly. "Listen to what I'm saying."

He peered into her face. "What dear heart, what do you say?"

"I say I cannot marry you. I say, I will obey my father's wishes and, come All Saints Day, marry the Earl of Cleaves."

Jacob took her arm. "No, no dearest. You don't have to

marry him. I'll take care of you." He started to lead her toward the two-man dogcart. "I swear I will."

Jillian pushed at him, giving a little laugh, though she saw nothing amusing about her situation. "Jacob, I'm serious. I cannot go with you. I can't marry you." She took a deep breath. "I don't want to marry you." *There! She'd said it. She'd admitted not only to Jacob, but to herself.*

But Jacob wasn't listening. Despite her own considerable strength, his was overpowering. Her sweet, yielding Jacob was suddenly out of control, forcing her into the cart!

"Don't worry, dear heart," he said. "I'll take you to a place where the bastard can't find you. We'll leave the country; we'll—"

"Jacob!" she protested. "Let go of me!" She still couldn't believe this was happening. She didn't want to make a scene, or hurt him any further, but damned if she wanted him to carry her off! "I'm not going with you," she repeated firmly. "I'm not going with you." But he grabbed her by her waist and forced her onto the narrow leather seat even as she struggled.

Jillian fully intended to jump out of the cart. This was all so ridiculous! Gentle, mild-mannered Jacob trying to kidnap her! Surely he was jesting. Surely he wouldn't carry off what was considered the Earl of Cleaves' property! But before Jillian could find her footing beneath her tangle of petticoats, Jacob pushed onto the seat beside her and took up the reins.

"Jacob!" she shouted, suddenly afraid, not for herself, but for him. "Let me—"

Her words were lost to the sound of splintering wood as the back door to the ordinary swung open with such force that the door ripped off its hinges.

Jillian immediately recognized the guilty party. "Duncan!" she cried, whirling back around. *Sweet Jesus, it was Duncan.* He would kill Jacob! She had to stop Jacob. But before she could get out another word, Jacob slapped the reins on the horse's back and the dogcart sped off.

"Come back here you futtering footpad! Bring her back! Bring her back or, so help me, I'll eat your liver!" boomed Duncan.

"Stop!" Jillian screamed, grabbing his arm as the cart rocked precariously up on one wheel as they turned the corner in the alley. "You've got to stop this madness! He'll kill you, for God's sake!"

"I don't care!" Jacob insisted passionately. "I'll give my life for yours! I won't let him take you. I won't let him hurt you!"

Now Jillian was scared. The dogcart was swaying wildly as Jacob careened down one side street and whipped onto another. She'd lost sight of Duncan, but she guessed he was not far behind.

"Look out!" she cried as the cart headed straight for a gaggle of geese waddling down the center of the road.

The gooseboy gave a cry of fright, waving his staff frantically in the air. Some geese ran; others attempted to take flight with their clipped wings. White feathers filled the air like those from a torn pillow.

Jillian wrapped her arms around Jacob's neck, partly to keep from being thrown from the vehicle, but also to try to get his attention. She'd never seen him like this, so determined, so out of control.

"Jacob," she begged. "Stop the cart. Stop the cart and put me out. The earl will kill you. I swear by all that's holy, he'll run you through."

Jacob shook his head with single-minded determination. "You don't have to marry him. They can't make you. I'll take you. I'll be your husband."

Out of the corner of her eye she spotted Duncan on horseback coming around a street corner up ahead. He was headed straight for them.

"Jacob! Jacob, listen to me! I want to marry him. Do you

hear me? I don't want to hurt you, but I want to marry Duncan."

After a moment, Jacob loosened the reins in his hand and the careening dogcart slowed. Duncan was still headed directly for them.

"You want to marry him?" Jacob said, as if in a daze. "But I thought you wanted to marry me."

"I'm sorry. I'm so sorry." She took his hand in hers. The cart had almost stopped now. "I didn't mean to hurt you. This is just a more suitable marriage. Your father is right. Mine is right. You and I wouldn't be good for each other. We're too different. Our families are too different."

Jillian saw a blur as Duncan dismounted from his white horse and came charging toward the dogcart. "Get down from there, you cur!" he shouted, swinging his broad fist

"Duncan, please—" But before Jillian could finish her sentence, Duncan had grabbed Jacob by the collar of his poorly made coat and was dragging him down off the seat.

"Sir, sir, there's been a misunderstanding," Jacob gurgled.

"Duncan, I beg you, listen to me!" Jillian leaped out of the cart, hauling her petticoats up to her calves to run after them.

"How dare you! How dare you!" Duncan bellowed.

A crowd was beginning to gather. The gooseboy was there, his flock forgotten for the moment. Two gentlemen traveling in a hired hackney stopped to gawk. Shopkeepers stuck their noses out their doors; ragged children appeared from the shadows of the alleys.

"Duncan, please don't kill him!" Jillian cried, throwing herself against his back, wrapping her arms around his waist.

"Don't kill your lover?"

"No, no it wasn't like that. It never was."

"You were leaving me!" Duncan swung around, still holding onto Jacob's coat. The half of his face left uncovered by the veil was bright red. She had never seen him so furious. She had never seen anyone so furious. "You were leaving me to go with him."

"No." She touched the sleeve of Duncan's doublet, half fearing he would strike her. "I came to tell him I was going to marry you. I came to tell him that I wanted you and not him."

"Liar." He was panting heavily.

"No. No, it's true." Jillian wanted him to believe her, but she didn't want to put any more blame on Jacob than necessary. "There was just a misunderstanding."

Duncan gritted his teeth, seeming now to be attempting to control his rage. "That's one hell of a misunderstanding." He gave Jacob a shake, and the young man cowered. "Carrying off a man's betrothed . . ."

Jacob was visibly trembling. "I—I—"

"Shut up. Don't open your mouth again," Duncan spat. Then he let go of Jacob, shoving him onto the filthy street. "I'd challenge you to a duel, but I don't fight children."

Then he swung around, turning his back on Jacob to face Jillian.

Jillian knew she had to be shaking. She would have taken a step back if it hadn't been for the crowd pressing closer.

"Come here." His voice reverberated in the still evening air.

Jillian couldn't bring herself to take the step. "I said I was sorry. I was trying to make amends with Jacob before you and I wed."

"He's the boy your father spoke of?"

She nodded. "We had intended to run off and be wed before—"

He stared at her, unyielding. *"Before I came along and futtered your plans?"*

"Yes . . . no . . ." She hung her head not knowing what to say, knowing she couldn't possibly make this right now.

Duncan stood for a moment as if trying to make some decision. Jacob still lay on the ground behind him, afraid to get up, no doubt. Jillian could only stand, frozen, wondering what Duncan was thinking. Would he send her home to her father in shame? Would he humiliate her by calling in a physician to exam her and determine whether or not she was still a virgin?

Jillian made herself take a step toward Duncan, not wanting to share her words with the greedy gawkers. "I assure you, sir," she said softly, "I did not compromise myself or your good name. What is rightfully my husband's is still fully intact."

Duncan scowled. "You betrayed me."

She shook her head violently, her own anger rising "I didn't; and if you would only listen to me, you would see that. I made a mistake and I was trying to fix it. I wanted to come to our marriage with the matter settled. For some reason which now eludes me, I thought I owed it to you!"

Duncan's arm snaked, out and he caught her elbow.

"Ouch."

He gave her a little jerk. It didn't hurt. Her father had certainly handled her more severely, but something went off in Jillian's head. Before she had time to think, to consider the consequences, she reached out and struck Duncan hard across the face. As her hand ricocheted back, it caught on the purple gauze of his veil, tearing it away.

A sound of shock rose from the crowd.

Jillian lifted her head quickly in horror and struck her cheekbone hard against Duncan's elbow. "Duncan, oh, God, I'm sorry—" By the time she lifted her head, he had returned the veil to its proper place, his face a mask without emotion. She had seen nothing of his scarred face, but apparently the crowd had.

"Duncan," she whispered, her cheek and eye stinging with pain. "I'm sorry. Let me—" She reached to touch his face, but he pushed her hand away. "Let's go," he said beneath his breath.

Jillian followed him without another word. She didn't look

back at Jacob, not even when Duncan mounted his horse and lifted her with his powerful arms onto the saddle in front of him. She looked up at Duncan, seated in his lap, sidesaddled as she was. "Please don't take me home, my lord. I haven't shamed you. Don't return me to my father . . . please."

Duncan swung the massive steed around and sunk his heels into its flanks. The horse leaped into the air, throwing Jillian against Duncan's broad chest.

"Where are you taking me?" she whispered, wishing she had been in the crowd that saw his face, wishing she understood the pain that she knew went deep. "Tell me," she pleaded, fighting tears.

"To the cathedral," he stated without a fleck of emotion in his voice. "We will be married tonight."

Eight

Jillian stood near the window in her white, silk nightdress, cradling a glass of rhenish. It was her second and, most likely, not her last. She drank from the fine Italian crystal, her jaw set.

Never in her life had Jillian been so humiliated. The Earl of Cleaves had neither called a physician nor returned her to her father. Instead, he had carted her from one place of worship to the next, all over London Town, until he had found a clergyman willing to marry them. Jillian had worn no wedding dress. There had been no band of gold to place on her finger. There were no wedding guests, no feast, no toast to the bride and groom. The only witnesses to the blessed event had been an old man and his wife, servants of the church. They had stood witness at the altar with a broom and a polishing cloth in their hands—not exactly the wedding Jillian had dreamed of.

She took a sip of the white wine, enjoying the warmth it created as it trickled down her throat. Breckenridge House was quiet, save for the sound of the patter of the rain on the slate roof. The servants had been turned away for the night so that the newly wed couple might have their privacy.

Jillian had only a moment with Beatrice when she arrived home with the earl. Because it was raining, Duncan had said Beatrice might spend the night and take the news of her sister's marriage home to their father in the morning. But Beatrice's belongings had been moved to another set of apartments in the far wing, leaving Jillian alone for her wedding night. Alone except for him.

Jillian glanced over her shoulder, her anger barely in check. There he sat, the Earl of Cleaves, on his wedding night, doing his correspondence. It was nearly midnight, and he was still writing, adding insult to injury. First, he had dragged her into that church to be married against her will; and now, he ignored her.

Jillian drained her glass and moved to pour herself another.

"Going to drink yourself into a stupor, are you?" came Duncan's voice, thick with caustic sarcasm.

It had been so long since he had spoken, that he startled her. Jillian went on pouring her wine, but her heart was pounding in her chest. "It's cold tonight. I should have called for a fire."

"Should I build one?" He asked it as if nothing had happened today—not the near-kidnapping by the parson's son, not the incident with his veil, not even the wedding.

Jillian set down her glass. She didn't want the wine. She didn't want to hear Duncan's voice so distant and cordial that it grated on her nerves. She wanted him to holler, to stomp his feet, to break glass. She wanted him to tell her what was under the veil. She wanted him to show her.

"No," she responded with an equal coolness. "The fire won't be necessary. I'm going to bed."

He did not look up from his writing; nor did he even lift his quill. "I'll be with you shortly."

Jillian stood beside the bed, her arms crossed over her breasts. "Son of a bitch," she muttered beneath her breath.

"What did you say?"

She whirled around to vent her frustration. "I said, *you son of a bitch*. You might as well sit there all night, because you're not going to lay a hand on me! Have you lost your head? Why, I wouldn't lie with you at this moment if you were the last futtering man on this godforsaken earth!"

Ah, Finally she'd gotten his attention.

He glanced up. "Come, come, madame," he said, talking to her as if she were her mother, or perhaps even a woman at the 'Change. "Don't tell me we are going to play these virginal games. You know what my right as your husband is. I will be quick, I promise you." He lifted his hand as if to swear by his name. "It'll be over in a matter of minutes."

Jillian was so angry now, so frustrated by Duncan's indifference, that she had to wipe at the tears in her eyes. She didn't understand what was happening. She had thought Duncan cared for her, at least a little. Why else would he have kissed her the way he had this afternoon?

She looked away, not wanting him to see her foolish tears. Didn't he understand? She didn't want him to discuss the matter of his husbandly rights with her. She knew what his rights were. What she wanted was what every bride wanted: She wanted him to woo her, to make love to her, to treat her as a man treats his wife on their first night together.

She turned to look at him, lifting her chin with determination. "I'll not give you my leave. You can rape me if you wish, sir, but you'll not have me otherwise."

He rose from his chair. He had removed his doublet and hose and wore only a pair of breeches and a soft cotton shirt. His hair fell loose about his shoulders with the veil in its usual place. "You are being infantile, ridiculous."

"Ridiculous? Ridiculous?" she stammered. "Look who's being ridiculous!" She pointed an accusing finger. "You force me into a wedding tonight without even a family member to witness it, and you think you're going to roll me like some stray bitch-hound?" She pressed her fists hard into the mattress, leaning forward. "God's teeth! What makes you think I would want to bed a man wearing a scarf over his head?"

Duncan lifted his hand to touch the veil lightly. His attitude changed in an instant. "What do you want of me?" he asked softly.

Jillian took a moment to answer. What a paradox Duncan was. This was the man she cared for. This was the voice she recognized, the voice she wanted to comfort. "I want to make this marriage more than an arrangement between families. I want you to care for me."

"I do care for you, Jillian. If I didn't, I'd not have married you tonight."

She shook her head, watching him in the shadows of the candlelight. "How can you say that? You don't know me, Duncan. You don't know what I like to eat, what I read. You don't know the name of my kitten that died when I was eight."

Duncan ran a hand through his hair. "Why must women make everything so difficult?"

"Why must men insist everything be so simple?" She took a step toward him. "All I'm saying is that now that we're wed, I think we should make the best of the matter. We're going to be together the rest of our born days, Duncan. Don't you think we ought to attempt to—"

"What? Love each other? Please don't tell me you expect me to fall in love with you."

His words hurt. "No," she answered softly, looking down. "Don't be silly. I just think we need to get along."

Duncan reached out and touched the bruised place beneath her eye. It had happened in their struggle on the street. "Does it hurt?" he asked.

"No." She watched him. "I'm sorry for what happened today. I didn't mean to embarrass you in public." She felt her breath catch.

He was watching her with a most intense gaze. "No harm done," he answered. "I knew no one on that street. It will be nothing more than fuel to feed the fire of gossip in this damned city."

She couldn't tear her gaze from him. She couldn't stop thinking about that veil and what lay behind it. "Would you take off the veil, here in the privacy of our bed chamber,

Duncan? It would be the best way to begin this marriage anew. Would you do it for me?"

"No."

Jillian turned away, hurt again by his words. "Then good night." She walked to the massive bed and climbed beneath the counterpane. Without as much as glancing at him, she rolled onto her side and closed her eyes. She didn't know what to expect. Would he rape her as was his legal right?

But after a long, frightening silence, she heard his footsteps crossing the room. The chair at the small desk scraped wood on wood as he eased into it. When next she opened her eyes, the room was dark and she was alone on her wedding night.

"You did *what?"*

Duncan tipped back the glass and drained it. "I married the chit."

"When?"

"Tonight, at St. John's."

"You son of a poxed whore! And you didn't invite me?"

"We didn't invite anyone," Duncan answered grumpily. Then, he added, "She tried to leave me, Will. She tried to run away with some pale-faced boy."

"Jillian?" Will poured Duncan another drink. The two of them were sitting in the dark in the parlor of Will's apartment. Will wore nothing but a silk dressing gown, for it was well after midnight. "You must not have it right. Jillian is mad for you."

Duncan set down his glass. He really wasn't in a drinking mood. What was wrong with him? He should have been at Breckenridge now, in bed with his lovely young wife. Why had he left the house in a thunderstorm to come here? He knew Will had a young lady waiting in the bedchamber. This was his problem, not Will's. Will couldn't help with this one.

"So are you going to tell me why you're here and not

there?" Will asked, stretching his legs out before him and tipping back a glass of brandy.

Duncan ran his hand over his face. He had removed his veil with his hat. Both lay on the floor at his feet. "She said she'd not lie with me."

Will chuckled.

Duncan glanced up, his stare grim. "I see no humor in the matter. I've never raped a woman. It's bad medicine. And I'd certainly not rape my lady-wife."

Will chuckled again and then attempted to cover the sound with a sip of brandy. "Just out of curiosity, friend, why won't she sleep with you? Did you show her the size of your cod? Perhaps she'd be willing then."

Duncan frowned, refusing to be baited by the jest. "She says I don't know her. Something about what she likes to eat, the name of some damned cat." He looked up. "You know, female crap."

"Did you show her your face?"

Duncan didn't understand. How was it that Will was always able to cut to the crux of the matter? "No."

"Is that a problem for her?"

"Yes."

"So show her your pretty smile and charm her a little. Don't just tell her to drop on all fours. That's not what women like, Duncan." Will rose, tightening the silk tie on his robe. "Sing to her, bring her flowers, better yet, jewels. Take her riding, take her to a play to show off her jewels. Ask her the damned cat's name. For sweet Christ's sake, seduce her, Duncan."

"Seduce her?"

"Yes, you addlepate. You want to get her with child, don't you? Well, the only way that's going to happen is if you lie with her. Play her game. I warrant you it will move much faster than yours."

Duncan sighed. "I don't know. I'm not up to it. I haven't time to play the gallant like you. I have work that has to be done before I set sail for Maryland."

"The hell you haven't time for her. Make the time." Will leaned on the mantel of the cold fireplace. "You'd like her, I think . . . if you'd just get to know her."

Duncan looked up. "You sound sure of yourself."

"I am." Will picked up Duncan's hat and veil and tossed them to him. "You might surprise yourself if you give it a chance. You might just fall in love with the little minx."

Duncan dropped the veil over his face and adjusted it. Such a comment didn't even deserve a retort. "I'm sorry for disturbing you and your *companion.*" Duncan eyed the hallway that led to will's bedchamber.

"It's nothing."

"I imagine she'd say the same." Duncan chuckled at his own joke. "Well, thanks for the drink."

Will held open the door for him, slapping him on the back as he went by. "So, when can I come bearing wedding gifts? I'll deliver only to the bride in person and supper must be provided."

"You'll come when you're invited," Duncan snapped. Then he was down the dark hallway and gone.

Jillian stood at the window of Duncan's vacant office, surveying the need for fresh paint. Behind her, she heard footsteps. She did not turn because she knew who it was.

Duncan shuffled his feet in the doorway. "What are you doing?" There was a definite lack of hostility in his voice. He was attempting to be nice and doing a fine job of it.

"Trying to decide if I'm going to have the walls painted lime or tangerine." She turned to face him, unsmiling. She, Beatrice, and the dowager had dined alone this morning. This was the first time she'd seen him since last night. She didn't want to let him off too easily. "Which would you prefer, my lord?"

He looked up at the paneled wall that framed the window looking out into his mother's garden. "I was thinking both.

Lime here—" He pointed to one wall. "—and here." He gestured with the other hand. "And the tangerine on the other two walls. What do you think, madame wife? Would it suit me?"

Jillian couldn't resist the hint of a smile. "Not at all. Your cousin, mayhap, but not you. Black would be more appropriate for you, I should think."

It was his turn to smile. He looked away and then back at her. He was dressed handsomely today in a black doublet and fawn-colored breeches. By the simple cut of the cloth and the hat he held in his hand, he appeared to be headed for the docks where two of his merchant ships had only recently come into port from the American Colonies. "It's good to see that you have a sense of humor. I should think we shall both need one if we are to make this marriage a comfortable one."

Jillian bit down on her lower lip. Was he trying to apologize? Was he saying they would start anew? Why was it that men had to always be so cryptic with their emotions? Why couldn't he just come out and say he was sorry?

She picked up the paint samples from his neat desk and turned to face the paneled wall again. "Apology accepted."

"Pardon?"

She glanced over her shoulder. "Your apology is accepted, my lord." She went on without skipping a beat. "I know you said my sister must go, but can she stay just another few days? She's been invaluable to me with the work being done here."

Jillian heard him chuckle.

"You're a clever minx, Jilly. I'll offer you that."

She turned around, this time giving him her best smile. When Duncan spoke to her like that, he made her shiver with warmth. A man like this, a woman could fall in love with.

"I don't mean to be clever, sir. It's only that I want my

sister near me. And your lady-grandmother has become so fond of her. She'll not want to see her go either."

Duncan nodded, feigning gruffness. "All right, she can stay another few days, but keep her out of my way."

Jillian bobbed a curtsy. "Thank you, sir."

"But . . ." He held up one finger, seeming to be enjoying their banter as much as she was. "I have one request."

Jillian dropped her hands to her curved hips. She had dressed carefully this morning in a forest-green woolen gown that accentuated the color of her hair. "If you think I'm going to let you kiss me, you're wrong."

He threw back his head in laughter. "A kiss, is that what you were thinking?"

A kiss? God above, what had possessed her to say such a thing?

He took a step closer, and Jillian began to feel like a lamb being stalked by a lion.

"No, actually," he said softly, "I wanted to tell you we'd be attending a small party at Whitehall tonight. The king has requested our presence. He wants to see the new Countess of Cleaves. Word travels fast through the city, doesn't it?"

"The king!" She brought her hands to her cheeks. "I can't call on the king. What have I to wear?"

Duncan took a step closer, chuckling. "I'm sure you'll come up with something. And now that you mention that kiss, I think I'll take one . . . *wife*." He crooked a finger bidding her come closer.

Jillian meant only to give him a brotherly peck on the cheek, but when her lips touched his smooth-shaven skin, he moved his head. His mouth touched hers and immediately a spark arced between them. He smelled of shaving soap and maleness. Jillian couldn't help herself. Without thought, her hands raised, only to lower on his broad shoulders. She parted her lips to taste him, to be tasted. Her pulse leapt. Her heart pounded in her chest.

"Jilly, Jilly," he whispered, his arm encircling her waist. He brushed his lips against her cheek, then the lobe of her ear, tickling her, his warm breath making her shudder with anticipation. "I am sorry for being such a brute last night. It was wrong of me. And I'm sorry for my accusations concerning the boy."

Jillian pulled back so that she could look into his face. Cautiously, she lifted her left hand so that she could touch his cheek. Only the purple veil was between her hand and his scars, which seemed to have no texture through the material. "So we begin again," she answered.

"You mean you'll let me come to your bed tonight?"

She smiled, slipping her hand into his. "I mean I'll accompany you to Whitehall tonight, and promise nothing more."

With a smirk, he gave a squeeze to her hand and broke away. "I'm expected at the docks, but will be home in the early evening. I'll have the coach ready by eight." He gave a mock bow at the doorway. "So until tonight, madame, your servant."

Jillian curtsied, nearly giddy with his touch. This was what she had imagined it would be like. This was how she had imagined he would fall in love with her. "Your servant, my lord."

Jillian heard his footsteps in the hall and then another's. As she turned to go back to the paint selection, she heard Duncan's voice. He was speaking to Algernon. Though she couldn't hear their words, she could hear the two pitches of their voice, Algernon's being higher than Duncan's. After a few moments of talk, the sounds died away.

Jillian walked around Duncan's orderly desk whistling to herself. That man could be so utterly charming when he wanted to be, couldn't he? *That man . . . why he was her husband!*

Jillian was so preoccupied with her thoughts that she

didn't hear any footsteps. All she heard was someone close the door behind her.

She swung around, laughter still in her voice. "Duncan, I thought—" She stopped mid-sentence. It was Algernon. Her smile fell. "Oh, it's you." She turned her attention back to the wood paneling around the window.

"I cannot believe you did this behind my back."

She could smell the ale on him from where she stood. "What are you talking about?"

"You know full well what I speak of!" His words were noticeably slurred. "Marrying him." He came around the desk toward her, his face contorted in anger. "Didn't I warn you it wasn't advisable? Didn't I tell you I wanted you for myself?"

"You need to go, Algernon. You're intoxicated. Duncan will be back momentarily."

"He will not." Algernon took a step closer, and Jillian walked around the leather-upholstered chair, putting it between them. "The earl has gone to the docks to see his precious ships." Algernon's voice was thick with resentment. "He'll not be back for hours."

Jillian gave up pretending to concentrate on the task at hand. She tossed the paint samples onto the desk. "I'm busy. What is it you want?"

"Now, now, dearest Jill. We must talk."

She refused to meet his gaze. "Please leave."

He put his hands on the arm of Duncan's leather chair, leaning in toward her. "You can have this two ways, Jill-*y*. You can make it easy on yourself or difficult. But once the land and title have been restored to me, I can promise you I'll remember who my friends were. Duncan will be out on his ear." He stood up again. "Pity you married the cold fish." He shrugged his shoulders. "But I'll let you stay in the house just the same." He raised one plucked eyebrow. "In return, of course, for certain *feminine favors*."

The tone of his voice made her shiver despite the sunshine pouring in through the window. Suddenly, she was afraid. "I've been patient with you up until now. I haven't told Duncan what you've been saying, what you're doing."

"Doing?"

She gave the chair a push toward him, angry that he could frighten her this way. Algernon couldn't harm her. She knew that. This was just a fantasy of his, having the monies and title returned. He was drunk, and that was why he was making such ridiculous statements. He would never be the Earl of Cleaves again. She knew it. He knew it. This was just the raving of a jealous, inebriated man. "You've been following me, listening to my conversations." She pointed an accusing finger, a thought suddenly dawning on her. "Why I'd wager you told Duncan where I went yesterday."

"I did no such thing."

Before Jillian realized what he was doing, he reached out and brushed his knuckles against the swell of her breasts.

Jillian reacted without thinking, bringing her hand up to slap him hard across the face.

Algernon's hand flew to his mouth and tears welled in his eyes. "You hit me," he wailed, suddenly sounding more like boy than a man. He looked at his hand spotted with red. "You made me bleed."

"Duncan will do worse. Now, leave me and don't bother me again. I'm warning you, I'll tell him and then you'll be gone. There'll be no allowance, Algernon. No money. No roof over your head. No money—no drink, no cards, no Fleet Street whores." She pointed to the door. "So save yourself while you have the chance."

Algernon stood there for a moment, unsteady on his pink-and-blue high heels, nursing his cut lip with a lace handkerchief.

Jillian held her breath. She had feared this confrontation for weeks. And now she had surely made an enemy.

To her relief, Algernon backed down. He shook his head

as he walked toward the door blotting his mouth. "You've made a mistake, Jillian." He hiccuped. "A terrible mistake."

There was a sudden rap at the door, then it swung open. Jillian was relieved to see Atar's solemn face. He glared at Algernon. "Could I be of assistance, madame?"

Jillian looked at Algernon. She didn't know how much Atar had heard. "No," she said after a moment. "Algernon was just leaving."

The manservant and Duncan's cousin exchanged looks.

"I was just going," Algernon said, sulking.

Jillian waited until Algernon had left the room. Now she wasn't certain how to handle Atar. He was her husband's manservant. Surely he passed information onto the earl about what occurred in his household. She cleared her throat. "I don't know what you heard, Atar, but—"

"It is not my duty to hear, only to follow my master's bidding. I am here to serve you as well as the Earl of Cleaves."

She smiled. "Good. Excellent. It's just that I don't want my husband to be inconvenienced by such trivial matters."

"Is there anything else, madame?"

She looked at the man's broad, black face, thankful to have him as an ally. "No. No, that will be all. Thank you."

Atar left the room without a sound.

Nine

The two sisters walked along the garden walk, hand in hand, Beatrice, silent as she often was, leaving Jillian to her thoughts. The London air had grown cool in the last few days. Leaves had fallen from the trees overhead, littering their path with bright golds and deep reds.

Soon the rains would come, and then the snow and another winter would be upon them. Jillian wondered when she and Duncan would set sail for the Colonies. Not until spring she guessed . . . she hoped. For though she knew it was inevitable she would have to leave Beatrice behind, she wasn't ready, not yet, when matters were so unsettled between her and Duncan.

Jillian swung her sister's hand casually as they walked. Two weeks she and Duncan had been legally wed, yet she still didn't feel like his wife. He had made a deliberate effort to be kind to her. He had brought her gifts: a rich green-velvet cloth, embroidered with silken thread from China; an old book found in a London shop he thought would interest her; a gold bracelet studded with tiny emeralds said to have been brought up in a treasure chest from the depths of the sea. Duncan was attentive, amusing, and utterly charming.

He had taken her to Whitehall to meet the king, to a play at the theater, even sailing on the Thames. But the best aspect of his courting, for surely he was courting her, was that he had made no attempt to demand his husbandly rights. He had left their intimacy up to her, moving at a pace she set. They held hands; they kissed; he touched her with the familiarity of a husband, but not intimately. He was waiting for her, and she was beginning to think that she was almost ready . . . if it were not for the veil.

That veil Duncan wore over his face to hide his scars still lay between him and Jillian. He proclaimed it was of no importance, but she insisted it was. If he could hide his face from her, what else did he hide? In many ways Jillian felt she had gotten to know Duncan in this fortnight, but in many ways he was still the stranger she had encountered in her father's garden. He had learned much about her, but somehow managed to tell her nothing of himself. When she questioned him, when she tried to discover what truth there was to the rumors that abounded in London, he grew dark humored and ruminating. Because Jillian didn't want to spoil their progress, she had not pushed him. She longed to share the intimacy of husband and wife with him; she burned for it when he was near, but his secrecy kept her from giving into her desires.

"Jilly . . ." Beatrice's voice broke Jillian from her reverie.

"What is it, sister?" She squeezed Beatrice's hand, thankful she had her during this trying time.

"Jilly, I think it's time I went home to Father's house."

Jillian stopped on the path, turning to face her. "Go? You can't go. You can't leave me here with him, alone."

Beatrice did not meet her sister's gaze, but instead concentrated on a wren fluttering in the lilac bush just off the path. "Perhaps that is what you need. No man . . . no man wants the woman he was once betrothed to in his newlywed house. I . . ." She sighed. "I'm afraid I'm interfering."

"Why would you say that?" Jillian caught Beatrice's hand, forcing her to face her.

"It—it's no secret in the household that he doesn't sleep with you, Jilly."

"Oh, that." Jillian let her sister's hand fall. "Atar watches my every move. He knows more about Duncan's habits than Duncan does. I suppose the servants gossip."

"Some."

Jillian glanced at her sister with errant determination. "Well, it's no one's business but our own. I barely know the man. I have a right . . . no, *we* have a right to take our time with this!"

"I'm sorry." Beatrice stared at her shoes. "I didn't mean to upset you. It's simply that I was afraid it was my fault. He said I was to go home. He keeps saying I should go home, but you keep me here."

"Oh, heavens, don't you know Duncan well enough by now to know that he growls simply for the sake of hearing himself?" She caught her sister's chin with her hand. "Bea, if he really wanted you to leave Breckenridge, you'd have gone from here that first night."

Beatrice sighed. "I suppose you're right."

"I am right." She tugged on her sister's hand. "I want you with me. I need you. You know I'm not comfortable with Algernon creeping about the house the way he does and Duncan forever down at the docks or attending to his shipping business."

Beatrice dropped one hand to her hip, lowering her voice as if she feared Algernon might be sneaking about the hedges. "I can't believe you've not told Duncan, Jilly. You have to tell him."

Jillian started down the path again, snatching a late-blooming chrysanthemum as she passed by. "Don't start on me again. You know why I've not said anything. If I tell Duncan, he'll kick Algernon out of the house."

"He shouldn't be here."

"And who will care for the dowager besides hired servants when Duncan and I have gone to America?" She spun around on the path, walking backward. "Tell me that."

Beatrice shook her head, pulling her brown wrap tighter around her shoulders. "That's not up to you. She's Duncan's grandmother. That's his duty. But your duty, as wife to the earl, is to tell him what happens in his household."

Jillian gave an exasperated sigh as she turned face-forward again. "Algernon is also Daphne's grandson, and he's harmless."

"You hope. You pray."

"He wouldn't hurt me. He wouldn't dare." She thought grimly of what had happened when she struck him. Algernon had crumbled. "He hasn't the bullocks."

Beatrice covered her mouth with her pale hand, shocked by her sister's bold talk. "Jilly!"

Jillian chuckled, amused by how easily her sister was offended. Jillian guessed she herself had been spending too much time in the company of Duncan and Will, that was where her boldness was coming from. "I don't want to talk about this anymore, Bea." She tucked the white flower behind her ear. "The subject is closed. Now, come on, let's go see that horse the dowager wants us to. You know how annoyed she gets when she has to wait on anyone." Jillian smiled at her sister.

After a moment, Beatrice smiled back. "All right, but promise me you'll think about talking to Duncan." She hurried to catch up. "Promise me if Algernon bothers you again you'll tell your husband."

"I promise! I promise!" They turned the corner around a Roman pillar, and the estate's great barn loomed ahead.

"Ladies!" The dowager waved when she saw them, motioning to them. "Come, come, while the groom is still leading him." The dowager was dressed in a burgundy riding gown of the latest French fashion, with a skirt, and a coat identical to a man's riding coat. Her cocked hat, set perfectly on her dyed red head, was ornamented with a burgundy feather. "Good afternoon." She smiled as the girls approached. "I've been waiting for you." She pointed, turning to watch the groom lead the roan horse by them. "Isn't he a handsome sight?"

Jillian wondered if Duncan's grandmother meant the horse or the groom, but she didn't dare ask. "Aye," she answered, watching the horse go by. "And so calm. You've done a superb job with him, Daphne."

"Stuff and nonsense! I've done nothing but give him a little time and a little lead line." She eyed Jillian speculatively. "The horse was sorely treated by its last master. What he needed was understanding, and *patience.*"

Jillian wasn't certain, but she got the impression the dowager was not just talking about the gelding. She was talking about Duncan, too, wasn't she?

"Sometimes situations are not as they appear," the dowager went on. "But these matters can be settled."

Jillian exhaled. "Duncan and I are all right, Daphne. We're simply taking time to get to know each other."

The dowager watched as the gelding walked by again. "Well, I must say, in my day, a bride and groom slept together, but then what am I but an old woman? What do I know, but of soft porridge and aching bones?"

Jillian caught Beatrice's eye and smiled. "Don't worry about us. Duncan and I will settle our differences in due time."

"I want great-grandchildren. I'm not getting younger, you know."

Jillian stroked the old woman's arm. Jillian knew the dowager well enough to realize that, despite her gruffness, she wished them good will and happiness. "There will be children, God willing."

The dowager tapped her silver-tipped cane on a flagstone, thoughtful. "I wish you had known him when he was a child, before he went to those Colonies, before he changed."

"What was he like? He won't talk about himself or his past."

The elder woman smiled, her head surely full of dusty memories. "He was a smart lad. Curious, always laughing . . ."

Jillian could have guessed the intelligence, the curiosity, for she surely saw that was a part of him now—but laughter?

"Indeed," the dowager continued with a chuckle. "I'll never forget him, that Christmas morning. He couldn't have been more than three years, barely into his breeches. His father gave him a rocking horse." She reached out, closing her eyes, stroking the toy she imagined in her head. "It was made of sleek mahogany." She inhaled deeply. "It smelled of freshly oiled wood." She opened her eyes, smiling. "That boy rode that horse straight through until evening. He even made his father carry it up to his trundle so the horse could sleep beside him."

Jillian smiled at the thought of young Duncan being so carefree and couldn't help wondering where that boy had gone. What terrible events that the dowager would only hint at had occurred in the Colonies? What had changed him, and how could she help him? "I wish I could have seen him like that," Jillian told Duncan's grandmother. She watched the gelding go by. "I wonder what happened to that rocking horse."

"I imagine the old thing is still in the attic with his cradle."

"Is it?" Jillian had a thought. "Do you think I could find it up there?"

The old woman shrugged her shoulders. "Imagine you could, if you had a mind to." She turned to look at both sisters. "So who's going riding with me? Bea? Shall we put a little rose to those pale cheeks?" She squeezed her hand with good humor.

Beatrice shrank back. "Oh, madame, I'd rather not. You know I'm not terribly fond of horses."

"I'll go," Jillian piped in. "Do you mind waiting whilst I change? I've a mind for a little fresh air and wind."

"I'll wait for you, granddaughter." The dowager shooed the women with a gloved hand. "But you'll have to hurry. The Countess of Shrewsbury is expecting Beatrice and me at six." She began to walk away, headed toward the stables. "I fear we'll have to hear about her ague again, but at least her cakes are sweet and her footman sweeter." She gave a wink over her shoulder.

Jillian was still chuckling to herself when she and Beatrice entered the house. Hand in hand, they went up the grand staircase, now partially blocked by skeletal scaffolding.

At Jillian's bedchamber door, the sisters parted. "I'm going to see that the dowager's gown is pressed for this evening. You know how she likes to show off in front of Shrewsbury," Beatrice told Jillian. "Enjoy your ride."

Beatrice had just turned to go when Jillian heard a sound in her bedchamber. *Odd,* she thought. The room had already been cleaned thoroughly this morning. What need would there be for a servant to be in her apartments?

Beatrice must have seen the perplexed look on her sister's face, because she stopped midway down the hall. "What is it?" she asked softly. "Something wrong?"

Jillian pointed to her closed door. "There's someone in there," she mouthed.

"Duncan?"

Jillian made a face. Beatrice knew Duncan wasn't sleeping with her. Apparently everyone in the household knew, probably everyone in London. "No. He went to the docks early this morning," she whispered. "He said he'd join me for supper tonight."

The two sisters' gazes met. Jillian knew Beatrice was thinking what she was thinking. *Algernon.* Would he dare, with his grandmother on the property?

Beatrice came to Jillian, taking her arm and whispering. "Just come to my chamber with me. I'll send a servant for something. That will scare him off."

Jillian stared at the closed panel door. Algernon didn't have a right to make her afraid like this. She'd not stand for it, she thought stubbornly.

When Jillian reached for the doorknob, Beatrice tried to

grab her hand, but it was too late. "What do you think you're doing?" Jillian demanded as the door swung open.

To the women's surprise, they were met by Duncan's sheepish face.

"Duncan?"

"Jillian?"

Jillian touched her breast lightly. Her heart was pounding. "It's just Duncan," she told Beatrice with a breath of relief.

Beatrice was already backing out of the doorway, her face red with embarrassment. "Good day, my lord," she called making a fast exit.

"Whom were you expecting?" Duncan asked. "Is there something wrong? The two of you are acting damned odd. Odder than normal."

Now Jillian felt silly. She closed the door behind her. "It—it was nothing. Just . . ." She dug for a tiny lie. This wasn't the time to discuss Algernon. It wasn't the place. Besides, he'd not bothered her in days. She'd not even seen him. "I suspected one of the serving girls has been sneaking into my room to snitch my perfume. I only thought to catch her in the act and teach her a lesson."

He nodded his head, but seemed unconvinced.

Jillian's brow crinkled. "What are you doing here anyway?" *In my chamber,* she wanted to add. He'd not even attempted to set foot inside since their disastrous wedding night. "I thought you'd gone to the wharfs." She glanced behind him. He seemed to be hiding something on the side table beside the fireplace. "Duncan?"

"I . . ."

She walked toward him craning her neck. Behind him on the cherry table lay a bundle of freshly picked flowers, surely the last in the dowager's fall garden. "Duncan?" She looked at him. "You were doing this? You've been putting the flowers in my room?" She knotted her fingers together, smiling. "I've always thought it was the servants. I thought your grandmother sent them up. She didn't deny it when I thanked her."

Jillian could have sworn she saw Duncan's cheek blush. "It's nothing. I . . ." He was struggling for words, something Jillian found touching. "I only wanted to make you feel more at home." He turned and stuffed the flowers unceremoniously into the empty vase. "It was really nothing."

Jillian walked up behind her husband and took his arm, gently turning him until he faced her. "Thank you, Duncan. It was very thoughtful."

He looked down at her. "Just flowers, Jilly."

She threaded her fingers through his. "Just flowers," she mimicked. Then she raised up on her toes and pressed a bold kiss to his mouth. "Just flowers," she whispered. "And just a very sweet gesture." Then she leaned over the table and took a deep breath, inhaling the sweet scent of the late blooms.

Duncan suddenly seemed flustered. "I—I came back for some records." He started moving toward the door, going on faster than before. "I had said I'd return home in time to sup with you, but I fear I won't make it. I've business with my goldsmith and then I'm to meet with a group of merchants. They've a shipping venture to discuss."

"It's all right." She smiled, pleased with him, pleased with herself. She was making progress with this masked man. It was slow and they had setbacks, but she was truly beginning to believe that she could make a life with the Earl of Cleaves, even a happy one. "I'll see you for breakfast."

He had reached the door. "Good. Excellent. And . . . and tomorrow afternoon, we'll go with Will to the bearbaiting if you'd like."

She wrinkled her nose. "I'd rather see a play. *Cleopatra* is playing at the King's theater. Your grandmother said she enjoyed it."

"Fine. Good. Until tomorrow, then."

And before Jillian could say another word, Duncan had hurried out of her chamber, closing the door behind him.

Duncan reached the staircase before he grabbed the rail and closed his eyes. He could feel his heart pounding, his palms cold and sweaty. He couldn't get any air, as if a Huron had his hand on his neck, squeezing his life's breath out of him.

Duncan squeezed his eyes tighter, trying to blank out the memories. He didn't know what set them off. He didn't know why he couldn't control them . . .

Suddenly Duncan's head was filled with the sound of laughter . . . his sister's laughter. Sally . . . Sally . . .

Then he saw her.

She was running through the field of wildflowers, her baby honey-blond hair rippling down her back. Duncan was pretending he couldn't run as fast as his little sister. It was her favorite game.

Then the scene changed and Duncan was standing alone in the field, his hands useless at his sides. He couldn't scream. He couldn't move. He was paralyzed by his terror. At his feet lay sweet Sally, a bloody mass where the four-year-old's face had been. Where was her hair? Where was the blond hair that a moment before had blown in the summer breeze?

Then, as quickly as it had come, the waking nightmare was gone.

Duncan felt the tears on his cheeks and wiped at them with the back of his hand. Cautiously, he raised his head to look in one direction and then the other. The staircase was empty, the hall behind him empty. Getting his bearings, he started down the steps again, feeling like an ass. That was how he always felt when this happened. Out of control. He needed to work, to concentrate on getting his ships loaded. As soon as his wife was pregnant, he would set sail. There was so much work to be done on his plantation in the Maryland Colony that he wouldn't have the time for this nonsense there. There the visions would leave him. There he'd finally have some peace.

Late in the evening, when Beatrice and the dowager had turned in for the night, Jillian lay in her bed trying to read a book of sonnets Duncan had brought her. She liked the poetry, but for some reason tonight she couldn't concentrate.

She had been very pleased to discover that it was Duncan who had been bringing her the flowers ever since the first day she'd come to his home. That was tangible proof that he cared for her, wasn't it?

But that wasn't enough. Jillian knew that it was up to her to bridge the gap between them. She had to be the one to convince him to lower his veil, both literally and figuratively.

She thought of the young boy the dowager had spoken of today, and then an idea came to her.

Jillian rose from her bed and covered her sleeping gown with a flowing silk night rail Duncan had given her. He said it had come in on one of his boats from the Orient. She slipped her feet into a pair of mules. Then, taking a candlestick off the fireplace mantel, she crept out of her room. The hallway was dark and empty, of course. Duncan still wasn't home. With Algernon gone on another one of his reported binges of drinking and whoring and the servants having turned in for the night, Jillian was completely alone in this wing of the house.

Swallowing against her childish fears of the dark, Jillian went down the hallway to the end and opened the small paneled door. A narrow staircase loomed before her. This led to the rambling attic that ran the full length and width of Breckenridge House. The dowager had taken Jillian and Beatrice up one afternoon to see it. The attic was a maze of rooms cluttered with centuries of cast-off furniture, portraits, and clothing. Each section led into another, attic extensions built as additions to the main house were added through the years.

Even in the light of day, Jillian had found the attic eerie. The ghosts of years past had seemed to her to hover in the dust motes. It occurred to Jillian, as she stood at the bottom of the steps, that perhaps she should wait until daylight to go up alone; but up there, somewhere, was the rocking horse. Up there, in the darkness, she told herself, was a piece of Duncan she didn't know.

"What a silly goose," she said aloud, chuckling. "Ghosts, indeed!" And her voice comforted her, chasing away her silly fears. She was a grown woman, married, for heaven's sake. By right, this was her house. And she certainly wasn't afraid to walk about it at night.

Hiking up her silk robe, Jillian ascended the steep staircase, raising the candlestick to light her way. At the top of the stairs, she turned right with confidence. She remembered a small room in this direction where she'd seen crates of books and piles of children's old toys. Perhaps there she would find Duncan's rocking horse.

Now that Jillian was in the attic, she really wasn't afraid. Actually, the low-ceilinged rooms seemed rather friendly, reminding her of the attic at her father's country home where she and her sisters had grown up. This attic smelled the same. There was something about that telltale scent of warped floorboards, musty books, and rodent droppings that gave her a sense of continuity. Perhaps someday her own son or daughter would traipse through this attic in search of a lost childhood memory.

Jillian ducked her head to avoid a low rafter and rounded an old leather trunk, walking into a smaller room. She knew she was close now. She recognized a torn portrait of some great-uncle left leaning against a three-legged chair.

It was when she stepped down into the next room that she heard a sound that made her turn on the balls of her feet. What was it?

A mouse? A rat?

She stood for a moment, holding her breath, listening . . .

Then she heard it again.

Footsteps?

A chill ran up her spine. "Hallo? Someone there?" she called.

Nothing now . . . not even the footsteps.

But Jillian knew someone was there. She knew it. "Algernon!" she shouted.

No answer.

Then, after a long moment of eerie silence, she heard the footsteps again. This time there was no mistaking them.

A chill crept up Jillian's spine. This had been stupid, coming up here alone in the dark. How could she have been so foolish? What if Algernon tried to attack her? He had threatened her, hadn't he? Even if she screamed, who would hear her now?

Staring into the darkness in the direction she'd come from, Jillian put out her candle with her fingertips. It was all she could think to do.

Instantly, she was surrounded by velvety blackness. He had almost reached her now. He carried no light, but she knew he was there. She could hear him breathing.

Ten

Jillian held her breath, inching her way backwards. She prayed that in the darkness he wouldn't see her . . . wouldn't hear her heart pounding.

"Who's there!"

The male voice, coming from so near, startled Jillian so that she flinched. She recognized the voice immediately, but it wasn't Algernon's. She gripped the candlestick tightly in her fingers. "D—Duncan?"

"Jillian?"

She exhaled with relief. "Oh, you scared me." She reached out in the darkness to him, her heart still thumping beneath her breast. Her hand met with the solid wall of his chest.

"What the hell are you doing up here in the dark, Jillian? Why are you calling for Algernon?" But even as he spoke the angry words, he was pulling her into his arms to comfort her.

"It's silly," she said, resting her cheek on the linen of his shirt. The gesture came so naturally. He smelled of tobacco, of wet leather, and of unbridled masculinity. "Never mind."

"Never mind, hell! Something or someone spooked you. You're standing here in the dark, shaking all over."

"My candle went out, was all." She offered the candlestick lamely. "I don't know how you found your way here in the dark."

"I played in this attic on rainy days as a child. I know every room as well as I know the back of my hand." He stroked her hair, still holding her against his solid frame. "So, tell me, wife. Has Algernon been trouble? I want the truth."

She looked up at him in the darkness. And though she could see nothing more than the silhouette of his face and the veil, she knew he was watching her. "It—it's been nothing I couldn't handle."

"The yellow bastard. I'll skin him."

She reached up to brush his shoulder with her hand, still unwilling to let Duncan release her from his embrace. "That was exactly why I didn't say anything. He's harmless, truly."

"Then why were you afraid?" He caught her chin with his callused fingertips.

Jillian didn't know what made her do it, but suddenly she found herself lifting up on her tiptoes to kiss him. As her lips brushed his, she slid her hand around his neck. The scent of him was intoxicating . . . the taste of him pure magic.

As she pressed her lips against his, Jillian felt Duncan hesitate, but only for a fleeting moment. Perhaps he didn't hesitate at all . . .

The candlestick fell from her hand and rolled away.

"Jilly . . ." he whispered against her mouth, his resonant voice sending shivers of pleasure through her body.

No one had ever spoken her name as Duncan did.

"Yes," she heard herself murmur as she parted her lips, a sudden sense of urgency in her kiss.

He thrust his tongue into her mouth, bringing his broad hand up to cup her breast. No man had ever touched her this way before, and yet it seemed as natural to her as drawing breath.

Jillian heard herself moan softly, thinking to herself that she shouldn't respond so boldly. What would her husband think? But, oh, his unhurried caress was exquisite.

Duncan kissed the pulse of her throat, murmuring words in some foreign tongue. Oddly, it didn't matter to her that she didn't understand what he said. Endearments were the same in any language, weren't they?

Jillian, heady with his touch, felt herself sway in Duncan's arms. When he slipped his hand beneath the silky nightgown, she heard herself make a sound that was born of relief and pleasure.

She felt her nipple grow taut beneath the caress of his callused thumb.

Jillian couldn't breathe. She couldn't think. She knew she shouldn't be responding with such wantonness, but she couldn't help herself. Her blood was rushing hot in her veins, pooling in a heat between her thighs.

So this was desire. This was what women died and men fought for. It was for this searing lust that ancient treasures were lost and kingdoms seized.

Jillian rested her hands on Duncan's shoulders, leaning against him, marveling at the sensations he created. How was it that he knew instinctively how to touch her?

In the darkness, she looked up at him. This man was her husband. It occurred to her that she would live with him until death separated them, and yet she barely knew him. Hesitantly, she touched the veil that covered the left side of his face. "Duncan," she whispered.

"Jilly . . ."

He was not denying her. But what emotion did she hear in his voice? Pain? Fear?

"I can't see anything in this blackness," she whispered. "I just want to touch your face."

Jillian could feel his gaze intent on her as she slowly pushed back the veil. Did he wait for her to turn away in disgust? Did he really think she would care about the scars, no matter how severe they were?

His hand was still on her breast as she took the veil and let it flutter to the dusty floor. Then she brushed her palm against the cheek she had never seen.

With light fingertips, she explored his flesh. He was clean

shaven. That did not surprise her. What did surprise her was that no matter how she searched, she could feel no scars.

But this was not the time to question Duncan. Somehow, here in the darkness, her husband had found a way to meet her halfway. Here in the blackness, he could cast out his demons and reach out to her as he had not been able to reach out to her before.

She let her hand slide down his face to rest on his muscular shoulder. She caressed the sinewy muscles in awe of his strength. "It's time," she told him, knowing her voice trembled with a blend of emotions. "Make me your wife."

His mouth met hers again, this time with all the pent-up passion of their relationship waylaid too long. Jillian barely realized they had moved, yet she found herself on the floor, exchanging kiss for kiss, trapped beneath Duncan's hard, warm body.

He was touching her now—her arms, her legs, her waist. Through the silk of the gown and robe, his fingers burned hot on her flesh.

When he parted the bodice of the sleeping gown and lowered his mouth to her breast, she arched her back, meeting him halfway. She heard herself moan aloud, fascinated by her own awakening desires. He was speaking softly to her, encouraging her. His voice surrounded her, enveloping her, just as his touch did. Her entire body was alive and pulsing with the feel of his hands, his mouth.

He tugged gently with his teeth on her hard, pink nipple, and she cried out in pleasure. When he slipped his hand over her flat belly to the apex between her thighs, she could think of nothing but the ache inside and her need to feel him there.

"Jilly, my sweet Jilly," he murmured. "I've wanted to touch you like this since that day in the garden. I had to have you. You had to be mine."

Jillian couldn't breathe. She couldn't think. Duncan slid

his hand up beneath the hem of the gown and all she could do was tremble in anticipation of his touch, flesh to flesh.

As exquisite as his touch to her breasts had been, this was better. Without hesitation, she opened her thighs to him, craving the heat of his hand, the experience of his caress.

If I had known it would be like this, Jillian thought, her mind awhirl, *I'd have bedded him that first night.*

Duncan's caress must surely have been magic because, of its own accord, her body began to move to the rhythm of his hand. Jillian stroked his broad back, his face, the corded muscles of his shoulders. Vaguely she wondered what it would be like to touch him, but she was lost to the moment. She couldn't speak. She couldn't reason.

When Jillian felt Duncan shift his body, she made no protest. He released the buckle on his breeches and lowered himself over her, pressing his hard frame against her softer one. It was then that she felt his manhood thick and hot on her bare thigh.

Jillian must have stiffened, because suddenly his face loomed above hers in the darkness. He was kissing her, brief fleeting kisses that soothed and calmed.

"Just a little pain," he whispered, "then never again. I swear it, Jilly. Then only pleasure."

She nodded, letting her eyes drift shut again. Her mother had instructed her on coupling. She had said it might hurt, but it was a woman's duty to bear the pain. Why had she never said anything of the pleasure?

Duncan kissed her long and hard, their breath mingling. With one hand, he guided his shaft.

In a movement born of some natural instinct, Jillian opened up to him. There was moment of uncomfortableness, not even pain that she could define, and then he was inside her, hot and pulsing.

He brushed back the lock of damp hair that clung to her forehead. "Are you all right?" he whispered.

Jillian wrapped her arms around his neck, reveling in the

feel of him inside her. "I'm fine," she whispered, smiling, touched by his thoughtfulness.

Then he began to move, and Jillian found herself in awe of the sensations he created. The pleasure came in waves, like those of the great ocean. Higher and higher the waves drew her, faster and faster.

Jillian found herself moving to meet Duncan's thrusts, panting, crying out with unabashed delight. Their bodies fit perfectly together, moving as one, moving toward some peak she knew not where.

Duncan's breath was now coming ragged in her ear. She clung to him, not knowing where he was taking her, only knowing that deep inside burned a desire only he could fulfill.

The end came with such force that it took Jillian's breath away. She rode the wave of pleasure on his stroke, and suddenly she felt as if she were thrust high into the sky. The pleasure burst into a thousand sparkling pieces, her body convulsing with its force.

A blink of an eyelash later, Jillian heard Duncan moan. He thrust one last time, hard and fast, and then lay still.

She found his weight over her comforting as she slowly drifted back to the reality of the dark attic and the dusty floor. Her body spent, Jillian now felt embarrassed. Was that really her own voice she had heard? Was that she, Jillian Elizabeth Hollingsworth Roderick, who had dug her fingernails into Duncan's back until she knew she must have left marks?

Jillian felt Duncan roll off her and onto his side, facing her. She kept her eyes screwed tightly shut, wishing she had something to hide her face with. She could still feel her heart pounding in her chest and her breath was still coming unevenly.

"You surprise me, wife," Duncan said after a moment.

"I'm sorry," she whispered, now mortally embarrassed. "I—I don't know what came over me."

He chuckled in the darkness, and she felt him lean over her and kiss her on the mouth. It was a husband's kiss. "You surprised me with your passion—pleasantly, I mean. Most women don't—" He searched for the right words. "—enjoy themselves so greatly their first time."

She opened her eyes, though she could see nothing of him but the shape of his face. "I—I was all right, then? Not too . . . loud or wanton?"

He laughed again, reaching out to draw her into his arms so that she could lay her head on his broad shoulder and curl up against him on the floor. Her gown and night rail were tangled around her waist, the front pulled open. Duncan wore his breeches somewhere down around his knees, but neither made a move to restore their clothing.

"You were definitely not too loud. You were perfect. A man likes to know if he's pleasing his woman."

His woman.

Jillian snuggled against Duncan, pleased with his remark. "I hadn't expected it to feel . . ." She sighed, giving up any modesty she might have once claimed to possess. "I hadn't realized it would feel so *good,* Duncan."

His laughter came again. Easy. Genuine. "I knew I would like you, Jilly. I knew the minute I spotted you chasing those goldfish in that pond—and you in nothing but your shift."

"That was a roguish thing you did. Spying on two ladies in their garden."

"And the best time I'd had all week." He pushed back a lock of her hair behind her ear and kissed her cheek. "I hate to say it, sweet, but perhaps we ought to rise and move to our bedchamber. Should a servant find the attic door open, I fear you'd be embarrassed."

Jillian sat up, pulling her gown and robe back over her shoulders. "Embarrassed? Why should I be embarrassed? I was but with my husband, seeing to a little autumn cleaning."

Chuckling at her comment, Duncan rose and buckled his breeches, then lowered his hand to lift her to her feet.

Jillian stared up at him, wishing desperately she could see his face, but not wanting to push the issue. Not tonight. So she stooped and picked up the puddle of silk at her feet she knew was his veil and handed it to him in silence. Then she turned her back on him and felt with her bare feet for her mules. When she had found them both and slipped them onto her feet, she turned back to her husband. Silhouctted in the darkness, she could see that he was wearing the veil.

Duncan put his arm out to her. "This way, my dear lady-wife."

She looped her arm through his. "Will you come to my chamber, Duncan? Will you sleep with me tonight in our room?" she asked softly.

There was no hesitation this time. "I will," he answered. Then he led her through the darkness.

Sometime in the middle of the night, Jillian woke to feel Duncan's hand on her breast, caressing her. Caught in that dreamy place between being asleep and awake, she gave herself to him, enjoying his lovemaking as much, if not more, than she had in the attic. And when both were spent from their passion, Duncan pulled her into his arms and she slept, her head pillowed on his hard, broad chest.

Jillian was disappointed in the morning when she awoke and found her husband gone. Yawning and stretching like a cat in the sunshine, she slid her bare feet over the side of the bed. She was shamelessly naked, her gown left near the door. Duncan had instructed her last night that wives didn't sleep in clothing. She had called him a liar, but allowed him to remove her gown just the same.

Jillian smiled at the memory, glancing at the case clock on the mantel.

Ten o'clock! God's eyeballs! She had never slept until ten in the morning in her life. No wonder Duncan was gone. He had to have left hours ago.

Jillian padded across the chilly floor to retrieve her gown and night rail. Duncan must have picked them up this morning and laid them over the chair. She dropped the gown over her head feeling terribly guilty. She should have risen with Duncan and broken the fast with him. She had wanted to get up with him this morning and start this first day as truly man and wife right. She had wanted to see his face in the light of the sun.

"Lazy chit," she murmured. *Ten o'clock. The dowager and Beatrice must be worried.*

A knock came at the door and Jillian slipped into her night rail to be more presentable. "Yes?"

"Your morning chocolate and biscuits, my lady. My lord ordered it be sent at ten," came the footman's voice through the closed door.

Jillian swept a handful of hair off her forehead, embarrassed to have a servant see her so disheveled. Surely he would know what she and Duncan had been up to.

But the thought of a cup of chocolate and a bit of bread was too tempting to turn away. She was near starved. "Come in," she called, walking away from the door.

She turned to look out the window as the servant entered and set the tray on the small table near the hearth. He added another log to the glowing coals. "Anything else, my lady?"

She parted the heavy drapes to look down into the garden below. "The dowager and Miss Beatrice, did they wait for me for breakfast?"

"No, my lady." The footman moved toward the door. "The dowager said not to set a place for you. She said you had had a late night and would sleep in."

Jillian knew her cheeks must have gone crimson. Was nothing a secret in this strange household? "That will be all, James."

"Yes, my lady." He bowed, and was gone, closing the door behind him.

Jillian walked to the table and poured herself a cup of

the frothy, thick chocolate. As she sipped it, she spotted a note with her name scrawled across it on the tray. She recognized Duncan's handwriting immediately.

Setting down her china cup, she picked up the note with a smile.

Hope you slept well, lady-wife.
Will return by dusk.
D

The note was simple—perhaps impersonal, at a glance, to a stranger—but Jillian was touched. She carefully refolded it, smoothing the seam, and clutched it to her bosom. A few short hours, and Duncan would come home to her. That was what he was saying. He was saying he couldn't wait to see her again. He was saying he cared for her. He was telling her everything was going to be all right.

Jillian reached for her cup of hot chocolate again. She had a noon meeting with the masons to discuss rebricking the southern wall. Then she'd see what Cook was preparing for the evening meal. Perhaps she'd have it brought upstairs so that she and Duncan could share an intimate supper. Perhaps they'd even eat it unclothed . . .

It was late afternoon, and the shadows were beginning to lengthen. Jillian was in Duncan's office, removing maps of the American Colonies from the walls, when she heard a horrendous crash. The sound was so loud, and so forceful, that the walls shook.

"My God," Jillian cried, leaping off the chair she stood on. She raced for the door, knowing instinctively what must have happened. For weeks she's been warning the workmen to take care with the scaffolding on the staircase. It had seemed unstable to her. God help them, the thing had come down!

Her skirts bunched in her hands, Jillian ran down the

seemingly endless hallway that led from the rear to the front of the house. She could hear men shouting sharp orders. A maid screamed.

Jillian came around the corner into the front hall so fast that she slid on the newly polished marble floor. She parted the canvas drop cloth that protected the fresh paint from the rest of the dusty house. “What is it? What’s happened?”

The hallway was crowded with ruddy-faced workers and assorted house servants. Even the gardener had beaten Jillian to the front hall. One of Daphne’s footmen stepped forward. “The scaffolding on the stairs, my lady. It’s all come down.”

“Who was there? Who’s hurt?” she demanded, running through the hall, forcing the footman to race after her. “Were there workmen? Has someone been injured?”

“Aye, there’s someone beneath it, they say.”

The tone in his voice made Jillian swing around, confused by the tone in his voice. “Who, for God’s sakc?”

“Thc carl, my lady . . .”

Eleven

Jillian reached the staircase in a split second. "Duncan! Duncan!" she screamed, terrified at the thought of becoming a widow, terrified at the thought of losing Duncan before she ever knew him.

She halted at the bottom of the staircase. What she saw turned her blood cold. The entire wooden scaffold, reaching two stories into the stairwell, had collapsed in a pile of timbers. Clouds of sawdust still rose in the air, choking the workmen.

Surely no one could survive beneath the weight of the timber, she thought in a brief instant of pain.

Several of the workman had already begun to drag pieces of the scaffold down the steps. Instinctively, Jillian reached out to move the nearest wooden girder. The raw, salt-treated timber was unbelievably heavy, but Jillian didn't care. All she could think was that Duncan lay somewhere beneath the weight of wood and nails, struggling to breathe.

"Help me!" Jillian ordered the nearest footman, her voice sounding strangely calm. "We've got to try and locate him. There's not time to remove all the pieces!"

The footman ran forward to help Jillian with the other end of the wood slab, some eight feet long. Just as she swung her end around, a hand closed over her shoulder.

"Jillian, there are others who can do this. Why not just go to your apartments, and wait?"

Jillian looked over her shoulder at Algernon. He pressed a lace handkerchief to his mouth to filter the dust.

"Get out of my way!" she demanded through clenched teeth. "This damned thing is heavy. Where's Atar? The one time I need him, and he's not anywhere to be seen."

"I haven't seen the man." He followed her as she backed into the hall and dropped her end of the beam. "Jillian, dearest, there's no need to hurry." His face was pasty white, his voice trembling. "I fear my cousin is already dead."

"He's not dead," she flung, clambering up the staircase heaped with rubble. She was trying not panic. Hysteria would do Duncan no good. "He's not dead," she repeated firmly. "I'd know if he were dead."

She crouched to looked beneath the nearest timber. "Duncan? Duncan, where are you? Duncan, answer me!" A tear slipped down her cheek as she climbed over a board onto the next step. "Damn you, don't do this to me!"

Men passed Jillian on the staircase, hauling pieces of the scaffold down. "Have you found him?" she called further up the stairs where she saw two men on their knees peering intently into a hole in the debris. "Have you found the earl?"

"Don't know," a red-bearded man answered. "See somethin'. Looks like cloth. His coat, maybe?"

Jillian ran up the stairs, lifting her skirts to her knees to climb over the splintered beams. "Where? Show me where!" She dropped to her knees beside the two men.

The one with the red beard pointed. "There."

Darkness was settling quickly over the house. The light inside was fading fast. Jillian squinted. "I can't see! I need a lamp." When no one responded immediately, she turned and shouted down the steps to Beatrice, who had appeared in the last minute. "Bea! Get me a lamp. Duncan's here somewhere! I have to see to find him!"

Beatrice raced from the hallway and returned with a lamp with surprising speed. She climbed over the rubble to reach her sister. "Here it is, Jilly." She thrust the lamp into her sister's hands, dropping to her knees behind her. "Where is he?" she sobbed. "Can you see him?"

Jillian pushed the lamp into a cubbyhole in the fallen timbers. At first she saw nothing; but then, she spotted a speck of color. It was not more than two inches of cloth, but it was bright blue. It had to be Duncan!

Jillian jerked the lamp out of the hole and pushed it into Beatrice's hands. "Hold the light. You!" She pointed to the bearded man. "Grab the beam; get it out of here. You!" She indicated the other man. "Grab that one. Easy," she bid him as he grasped the timber and the pile began to shift.

"I'm coming, Duncan!" she shouted into the hole. "It's Jillian, Duncan. Just hold on. I'm coming to get you!"

The men removed two more fallen timbers and Jillian turned to Beatrice, who was shaking all over. "Calm, down, Bea! Listen to me. I need you to hold the lamp, here." She pushed out her sister's trembling arm. "Over this section. I'm going to climb in there and see how badly he's injured.

"No!" Beatrice shrieked. "You'll be crushed if the wood moves."

Jillian glanced at the rubble around her. Beatrice was right. Already she could hear the agonizing groans as the wood shifted on the staircase.

But she didn't care. All that mattered was Duncan and reaching him.

"Do what I say," Jillian snapped. Then she dropped on all fours and crawled into the hole. She had to lie on her belly and pull herself along, but the light from the lamp shone through the spaces in the beams, illuminating her way.

She inched closer to the blue material. "Duncan," she called. "Duncan, can you hear me?"

She stretched out her hand, feeling the weight of the wood above her pressing down on her rib cage, preventing her from completely filling her lungs. The closeness of the tomb around her made her pulse race.

"Duncan?" She stretched again, groaning as she pulled

herself forward another few inches. Then her fingertips met the blue material.

It was he! It was his sleeve! His arm! She could feel him.

"Duncan," she called insistently, wiggling his arm. "Duncan, answer me."

But he didn't.

"I found him," Jillian called, rolling slowly onto her back so that she could reach up. "Here!" She thrust her hand through a hole above her head, hoping the workmen would see it. "He's here. We have to move enough rubble to get him out of here."

Slowly Jillian inched her way back out of the hole. Back on the staircase, she rested on her knees, panting. "Start pulling wood from off the top." She pointed to a place near where Duncan lay, a place where the boards weren't piled as high. "He's wedged in a space beneath a large beam. We'll dig and then pull him through—" She pointed. "—and pull him out this way."

The workmen looked skeptical, but they followed her bidding.

Coming to her feet, Jillian pointed down the staircase. "I need more light." Her gaze came to rest on Algernon's face as she scanned the crowd below. He had a strange look about him. He was very pale. What was it she saw in him? Fear? Terror? Was the coward afraid because it could have been him beneath the rubble? She pointed to two burly workmen below, not having the time or energy to be concerned with Algernon.

"And you two—get up here and haul the pieces we pull out down the steps. I want a walkway cleared."

One of the men she hollered to pushed his blue-felt cap back on his forehead, looking up at her. He shifted his weight from one foot to the other. "Um . . . we're masons. We don't haul timber, we do the brickwork, my lady."

"Well, you haul timber now!" She indicated with her hand, her tone icy. "So get your worthless hides up here!"

The two men took one look at Jillian poised on the staircase in the midst of the rubble . . . and leaped to do as she said.

For the next twenty minutes, Jillian stood among the workmen, overseeing the removal of the wooden beams of the scaffold. Twice she had to stop the men as they were forced to stand and listen to the giant beams groan ominously as they shifted.

Finally, Jillian thought they had cleared enough timber to pull Duncan out from beneath the rubble. She would have climbed in herself again, but she feared she wouldn't have the strength to pull Duncan out. She sent the burly red-bearded man in, promising him payment for his help.

"Try to be careful. He may have broken bones," she instructed as the workman climbed into the hole flat on his belly.

It seemed as if it took forever for the workman to reach Duncan and call out that he had the earl's feet. It took even longer for him to pull Duncan out of the hole. At last, the workman appeared, pulling Duncan by his booted feet.

"Is he conscious?" Jillian demanded, down on all fours again. She couldn't see anything of Duncan yet, but his feet.

"Ain't made a peep," the workman answered, looking doubtful.

She peered into the hole. Duncan was lying on his back, perfectly still. "Is he breathing?" she asked softly.

"Couldn't tell."

Jillian exhaled. "Hold the light over this mess," she told Beatrice, who had not left her side. "Good."

"What are you doing?" Bea asked. "Just pull him out."

Jillian shook her head as she crawled into the hole, flattening her body alongside his. He was still warm. That was a good sign. She inched her way forward, trying not to think about him naked beneath the sheets with her. When she laid her hand on his broad chest, she was relieved to feel it rise and fall.

Thank God, he was still alive.

Then, she reached his face. Just as she had suspected, his veil was pulled askew, down over his chin.

Even in the dim light from the lamp somewhere overhead, she could see his scarred cheek.

It was not scarred.

Jillian didn't have to time to think now. She didn't have time to try to understand her husband. All that mattered was getting him medical attention. Carefully, she pulled up the purple veil until once again it covered the tattoo on his left cheek.

Jillian quickly backed out of the hole. "All right," she ordered, thrusting her skirts down as she came to her feet. "Pull him the rest of the way out." She pointed. "You two. Pick him up and follow me." She had already started up the staircase, climbing over timber that blocked her way.

At the top of the stairs, she met Atar. "Sweet heaven, where have you been?" she snapped. "Your master's been hurt." She brushed past him, leading the workmen that carried Duncan's unconscious body. She didn't give the manservant time to respond. "Go find the physician I sent for. I want him in my bedchamber now!"

Half an hour later, Jillian sat beside Duncan, pressing a cold chamomile compress to his forehead. The chamber was empty but for her and her husband. Beatrice had gone to the dowager's apartments to comfort her. The physician had come and gone and been of little help. He had sewed and bandaged the wound on the back of Duncan's head and instructed Jillian to keep him warm. Either he would wake from the unconscious state or die, the physician had said. It was in God's hands now.

Jillian removed the compress and dropped it into the bowl at the bed stand, swishing it around. Duncan wasn't going to die. He wasn't. She looked down at his bare, handsome face. He was going to wake up, and then he was going to tell her what the tattoo on his cheek was. He was going to explain the meaning of the bear claw.

She pulled the linen sheet up, tucking it tightly around his chin. That wasn't all the explaining her husband had to do. Jillian had made everyone leave the room but Atar and then assisted the physician in undressing Duncan. It had been difficult for her not to react when she had seen his tattooed bare chest. But when the physician had responded in surprise, she'd said nothing. This matter was between her and her husband, and she'd not betray that union by admitting to anyone that she knew nothing more of the eerie tattoos than the stranger in the room.

Jillian wrung out the compress and placed it on Duncan's forehead again. Then with a finger, she hesitantly traced the bear claw on his cheek.

"Please God," she whispered in the warm, quiet bedchamber. "Please let him live to tell me. Please let him live long enough to make me understand."

Duncan woke slowly, the pain in his head excruciating. His entire body ached as if he'd been beaten by a Huron war club.

He made no effort to open his eyes as he attempted to recall where he was . . . what had happened.

Memories flashed through his head. He heard the beat of the Iroquois war drums. He smelled the blood of the enemy on his hands. He saw shadowy images of the Fire Dance.

But those were old memories. That was the past, long gone and buried.

Duncan forced himself to think of the present. He was in England. He had married.

Jillian was her name. Lithe, full-breasted Jilly . . .

The first thing Duncan remembered was making love to her. He remembered the feel of her in his arms. His virginal wife had taken him utterly by surprise. He remembered that clearly. He had expected her to be submissive, to tolerate his advances as a good English wife was instructed by her mother to do. But Jillian had reached out with innocent hands to caress him. She had accepted his offer of physical pleasure, giving herself to the moment. But more importantly, on an emotional level, she had given a part of herself to him when he'd touched her, something no other woman, whore or wife, had ever done before.

Then he remembered the ship. He'd overseen packing in the hold, but his mind hadn't really been on the precious cargo. All Duncan could remember thinking about all day was Jillian.

He'd returned to Breckenridge House early. He'd cut his workday early, cancelling an appointment, because he wanted to be with Jillian. He had brought her a gift, though what it was, he couldn't remember right now.

The last thing Duncan recalled was walking up the grand staircase humming to himself.

What had been that terrible sound?

"Duncan?"

The feminine voice Duncan heard from somewhere in the foggy distance startled him. Did it come from the past? Was it *Karonware* who called to him?

Karonware? Rone? Wife?

No. *Karonware* was dead, he reasoned, finding some comfort in logical thought. If she were calling him, it would be from the hereafter and he would be dead. Duncan didn't think he was dead, though his limbs felt weighted by mud, his thoughts drowned in rainwater. Besides, if it were his dead wife who called, she would use his Iroquois name. She would call him Tsitsho.

"Duncan. Are you awake? Can you hear me?"

It was the voice again, gentle, but urgent . . . the voice of someone who cared for him.

Duncan attempted to force his eyes open. His body reacted sluggishly.

"Duncan, you *are* awake!"

He felt her touch on his cheek.

Slowly her face came into view. "Jillian?" Duncan croaked, his voice sounding odd in his ears.

"Yes, it's me. I'm right here." She stroked his cheek, staring down intently.

He squinted, trying desperately to focus his eyes. "What—what the hell happened?"

"The scaffolding on the staircase, it collapsed. Don't you remember?"

He closed his eyes for a moment, the light of the candles piercing his mind like a dagger. He remembered the horrendous, crashing sound. Had that been the scaffold falling down around him he'd heard? "No. Not really."

She took his hand in hers. "You're lucky to be alive. I never thought we'd find you beneath the rubble."

"It collapsed on top of me?"

She was smiling. He liked her smile. "Yes."

Duncan attempted to sit up and winced as the pain in his head radiated to blinding proportions.

She pushed firmly on his shoulders, her strength surprising. "No. Don't try, not yet."

He relaxed on the pillow, giving in to the pain.

Jillian sat quietly on the edge of the bed beside him. After a moment, he opened his eyes again. Her face was clearer now. Too clear. Someone had removed his veil. She was looking at him . . . at it.

Slowly he lifted his hand to meet his cheek. "So, at last you see."

"I covered you up before they brought you out from under the timbers. No one else saw. No one but me, Atar, and the physician who attended you. I assumed Atar had seen it before."

He let his hand fall. It took too great an effort to hold it there. What was the sense anyway? She had seen the tattoo.

He could feel the soft, smooth cotton of the sheet that covered him. He knew she had seen them all.

He couldn't look her in the eye. It wasn't the tattoos as much as what they represented. "I suppose you'll want an explanation."

"Tonight isn't necessary." She stroked the back of his hand.

Duncan exhaled. He felt vulnerable lying before her, his head pounding so that he couldn't think. He didn't like feeling like this. It emasculated him.

"They . . ." His voice cracked as he spoke the first word. Something told him that if he didn't tell her now, he never would. Suddenly, it was important that she know. He realized she would never understand, but at least she would know the truth, or a small part of it.

"The . . . the Indians."

She didn't draw away. She held his hand tightly in hers. "That captured you?"

"Aye. It . . . the bear claw is the sign of the clan I was adopted into. Because I was a child when they took me from my family, they spared my life." He couldn't resist a sardonic smile. Spared, indeed. "You understand what I'm saying?" he asked, knowing she couldn't possibly. "I became one of them."

"It's really not *that* large a tattoo," she said after a moment. "Not *that* noticeable." She sounded so casual. "Not that shocking. I was expecting something far worse and not nearly so intriguing."

Again, his young wife surprised him. Slowly he lifted his arm to run his palm the length of his chest. "You saw the others?"

"Pictures," she said. There was almost a tone of amusement in her voice now. "I don't know why you didn't share them with me before. Some are very good."

"It was the way of the Mohawk. Many of the men wore them as proof of their virility, their family name, their successes in battle." He closed his eyes. It was too difficult to keep them open . . . too difficult to watch her watching him. "Ah, heaven help me, *I—I was one of them, Jilly."* His voice was barely a murmur. He felt a lump rise in his throat and for a moment feared he would come to tears. *"I did terrible things."*

"Shhh," Jillian soothed, bringing her face closer to his. She stroked his jawline. She pushed the hair back off his forehead in a tender gesture. "I don't want to talk about it anymore. Not tonight. Would you like a drink of water?"

He breathed deeply. Though he'd said barely a few words, it felt like a confession. And oddly, a weight seemed to have been lifted from his shoulders. No one knew the truth of what he'd done, what he'd been. Not even Will knew the full truth.

"Water would be good."

"Here." She cradled the back of his head with her hand, pressing a pewter cup to his lips. Duncan drank, letting his head rest against her hand. It still hurt so badly that he knew he wasn't thinking clearly. His words, hers, seemed to come from a fog somewhere beyond him.

She took the cup away, lowering his head to the pillow. "There're no broken bones as best we could find. Just the head wound." She chuckled. "You've a thick skull, husband. A lesser man would have died from the blow."

He smiled at her jest. "So you dug me out, did you, my fair lady-wife?"

"Just not ready to be a widow, I suppose." She paused for a moment, then went on. "Duncan, I know I said we wouldn't talk about it tonight, but who . . . who is Karen-wear? You spoke the name in your sleep."

Duncan smiled a bittersweet smile. He wouldn't lie to the chit. What would be the point? Besides, it would be wrong to betray her memory that way. *"Karonware."* It was not the way of The People to speak the name of the dead, but he wasn't one of them any longer. Was he? "My wife—dead wife."

She paused again. "An Indian?"

"We called ourselves *Kahnyen'kehaka.* The Mohawk Nation." *We . . . we. No matter how Duncan tried to bury the past, he couldn't. He still felt like one of them, somewhere deep in his bones.*

"You loved her?"

Duncan opened his eyes to look at Jillian. He could see her better now. She was a mess. She had been crying. Her rich, red hair was tumbled, her face streaked with dirt.

She was as lovely as he'd ever seen her. He closed his eyes again.

"Needle Woman was much older than I. Twenty years, probably. But she was good to me. She married me to save my life." He hadn't answered her question, and he wondered if she would call him on it. But he didn't know the answer.

Again Duncan felt Jillian's warm hand wrap around his. He had expected a bitter response. What woman would not be resentful to hear a man speak fondly of his previous wife? But when Jillian's voice came again, there was no ill-will in her tone.

"I'm sorry. I shouldn't have asked."

He would have shrugged, except he was too fatigued, too sore. "You have a right to know."

"Yes. But I shouldn't pry. You would have told me in due time. I shouldn't have looked at your face, either. I'm sorry. I apologize, Duncan. It was only that I wanted to understand."

Duncan was so tired now that he could barely open his eyes, but he had to see her. "I should have showed you sooner. You have a right to know." He patted the bed beside him, letting his eyes drift shut once again. "It's past bedtime; now come, wife. We can talk on the morrow."

Duncan heard her stand and heard the sound of her unclothing. She blew out the last lamp, and he lifted the edge of the counterpane for her. Jillian gingerly slid into the big bed beside him, and he wrapped his arm around her waist.

"Good night, wife," he whispered, already drifting into a dreamless sleep.

She snuggled against him. "Good night, husband . . ."

Twelve

"For me?" Jillian looked up from Duncan's desk where she was separating a pile of house repair bills. The office was freshly painted, his precious American Colony maps returned to the walls.

"Yes, for you . . . if you'd like it." Duncan stood in the doorway, a tiny yellow kitten curled in the crook of his muscular forearm.

The kitten mewed and attempted to climb up the sleeve of his doublet as Jillian came around the paneled desk. "You brought a kitten for me?" she repeated with disbelief. "Oh, Duncan, it looks just like my Sarah." She looked up at him as she took the cat into her hands. She was touched. "How did you know?"

He tucked his hands behind his back awkwardly. "I asked your sister. I wanted to get you a gift, but not another gown or jewels. I wanted to get you something special." He touched the back of his head lightly. The bandage was gone, but Jillian knew the wound was still tender. "It's not every day a wife risks her own life to save her husband."

Jillian lifted the kitten to her ear to listen to it purr. "I told you, you'd have done no less for me. I wasn't really in any danger."

He leaned against the doorjamb, apparently in no hurry to be anywhere. *"And I told you,* it's not the same thing." He crossed his arms over his chest. "You're a different kind of woman, Jilly. Different than I expected."

She lifted an eyebrow. "I'll take that as a compliment."

He watched her. "I meant it as one." Then he smiled and chuckled. "I'm only sorry I was resting beneath the scaffold there. I'd like to have seen you ordering those workmen about. Beatrice said you were rather impressive. She thinks you should go into the business of restoration."

"Business, indeed." Jillian cuddled the kitten to her breast. "Bea talks too much." She glanced up at him. "What shall I name—" She turned the kitten onto its back. "—her?"

"Whatever you like. Sarah would be all right, though I was always fond of the name for a child. I'm not certain I would want my daughter named after my wife's cat."

She turned her full attention to Duncan. The two weeks since the accident had not been perfect, but Jillian was satisfied with their progress. Though Duncan still had his moods, he and Jillian had begun the process of getting to know each other as a man and a wife should. Duncan did not volunteer information about himself often, but was revealing bits of his personality and of his past day by day. He had agreed not to wear the veil in the privacy of their bedchamber, and Jillian considered that a great step forward. She smiled a hesitant smile, her brow creasing. "You like the name for a girl?"

"A daughter. Our daughter."

This was the first Duncan had spoken of children since the degrading conversation he'd had with Jillian's mother the day he had come to sign Beatrice's betrothal agreement. "What about a boy?" Jillian prodded gently. "Have you a name picked out for a boy, too?"

"Forrest. My grandsire's name."

He acted as if he were going to say something else, but then hesitated. Jillian waited quietly.

Her patience was rewarded.

"I had a son once, a long time ago," he said after a moment.

Jillian tried not to appear surprised. Why would she be?

He had had a wife, why not children? "Does he live in the Colonies?" she asked carefully.

The kitten mewed.

Jillian watched as Duncan walked away from her toward the window. Whenever their conversations turned personal, he seemed unwilling, or perhaps unable, to look at her. "He died."

She felt a twinge in her chest. "I'm sorry."

"So was I." He continued to stare out the window at the autumn garden. "My wife died in childbirth and the babe . . . the babe was too small. He cried the first day . . . but after that, he didn't."

Jillian could have sworn she saw Duncan lift his arms as if holding an infant; but from where she stood behind him, she couldn't be certain. "How long did he live?" she asked.

"Three days. He died in my arms."

"Did he have a name?"

Duncan didn't answer immediately; but when he did, his voice seemed to come from a far-off place, a place Jillian knew she could never go. "The Mohawk say it is bad luck to speak the name of the dead." He chuckled, though there was no humor in his tone. "Of course everything was bad luck to them. His name was Winter's Spring, because he was born on a balmy day in December. I gave him the name. He didn't live long enough for the Women's Council to think he deserved a name, but I thought he deserved one." He balled his hand into a fist at his side. *"He deserved a name."*

Jillian's first impulse was to go to Duncan and put her arms around him. She could hear the pain in his voice. But she knew her advances wouldn't be welcome. She knew Duncan well enough now to know when to leave him alone.

After a moment of silence, Duncan turned away from the window. He was Jillian's again. "Will and I are going down to the dock. Would you care to meet us for supper tonight, at the Twin Cocks, perhaps?"

She stroked the kitten. "I'd love to."

"Good." He walked past her, toward the doorway. "I'll send a message from the shipyard as to the time. I can't tell you now when we'll be done."

"That will be fine."

Duncan waved a hand over his shoulder as he walked out of the office. "I'll see you then."

She waited until he had started down the hallway, then called after him. She ran to catch up. "Duncan!" She wanted to tell him she loved him. Watching him near the window, hearing him speak of his dead son, Jillian knew it was true. Somehow she had managed to fall in love with the Earl of Cleaves, the man they called the Colonial Devil.

"Yes? What is it?"

But when he turned to look at her, she knew this wasn't the time, it wasn't the place to speak of love. Duncan wasn't ready to hear such declarations; he would only pull away from her. She would lose the ground she'd gained. She looked down at the floor, cradling his gift in her arms. "Thank you for the kitten, husband," she said softly.

"You're welcome, wife."

Jillian leaned against the wall to watch him go.

Jillian laughed at Will's foolishness, picking up a discarded chestnut shell to toss at him.

Duncan broke into laughter as the shell reflected off Will's ear and fell into his lap.

"Can't you control your wife?" Will demanded, feigning gruffness. "I thought a wife was to be seen, but never heard, and never, ever, caught throwing objects at her husband's guests."

Duncan laughed harder, lifting a pewter cup of wine to his lips. "Not this wife. I fear I've chosen poorly, for I've no control over her whatsoever. I'm a failed man." He hung his head drolly. "A sorry excuse for an Englishman."

"I'll drink to that." Will wiped at his tears of laughter

and reached for his cup. His face was ruddy from drinking. "I make a toast to sorry Englishmen and to strong wives and the men who could make them happy *if they'd only try.*" He clinked his cup to Jillian's and then Duncan's, and all three drank the deep-red wine.

Jillian set her cup down on the table and pushed back in her chair, relaxing in the warmth of the cozy room and the friendliness of the atmosphere. Outside, thunder boomed and a cold rain pattered on the window glass. Inside, the blaze in the stone fireplace crackled and snapped, filling the room with the piquant smell of hickory smoke and the dancing light of a thousand candles.

Duncan had rented a private room above the Twin Cocks Tavern in Piccadilly, as was customary with gentlemen. The tavern's host had delivered a fine feast of oyster pie, roasted goose, potatoes and leeks, and sweet, hot bread. For dessert there was dried fruit and nuts. The two men and Jillian sat cracking nuts and tossing the shells to the floor, sharing the good wine and each other's company.

Will picked up the nutcracker and searched for a choice chestnut in the wooden bowl on the center of the table. "I've a meeting tomorrow with Dunbury concerning that land on the Chesapeake." He cracked the nut in half and began to pick the sweetmeat out with a knife and push it into his mouth with the sharp tip. "He says he'll sell. Could you possibly accompany me? I think I'd come up with a better price with your help. You're good at making prospective sellers squirm." He shrugged good-naturedly. "Good at making us all squirm at times."

Duncan ignored his remark, reaching for the iron nutcracker with the boar's head. "Can't tomorrow. I'm going to New Forest to my hunting lodge. My caretaker's grown too old and feeble to ride my property and keep his eye out for poachers. He's sent word his grandson could take the job, but I want to meet the boy before I lay down my coin, as well as my trust." He picked a bit of the nut's meat from a half shell and offered it to Jillian. "Why not take my wife? I wager she's a better negotiator than I. Only yesterday, a contractor accosted me in my own hallway claiming my wife had hired him to repair stone fencing for less than the cost of the materials."

Will laughed, slapping his palm on the trestle table still littered with dirty dishes and the goose carcass.

Jillian smiled, nibbling on the pungent, sweet nut her husband had given her. "No. Land purchases are beyond my understanding." She lifted her hand. "I can't fathom why a man would want to buy forest, then work himself to death to burn and dig up the stumps to plant tobacco, anyway. I can't understand wanting to live so far from London, in the wilderness, with nothing but bears and murdering red savages to keep you."

The moment the words were out of Jillian's mouth, she knew she'd made a mistake. Why had she not been more careful? Too much wine, she guessed. She'd let down her guard with Duncan when she knew better.

Duncan's chair scraped on the planked wood floor. "No. Perhaps a woman cannot understand a man's motive for hard work that leads to profit. Perhaps a woman can't understand a man's need to set his booted foot on land no man has walked before." Duncan scowled, squeezing the nutcracker in his hand so hard that the walnut burst with a snap and fell into dust in his hand. "And as for the red savages, *dear,* they are not all murderers. Some are good, some are evil. The same as Englishmen."

Will drew his chin down in an exaggerated frown, mimicking Duncan's sour face. Jillian knew he was only trying to lighten the mood, but she didn't smile. She folded her hands in her lap and stared at the floor.

So much for the enjoyable evening. It was like this with Duncan. One minute he was laughing and open with her; the next minute he was angry and glaring. His mood swings irritated her to no end.

After a moment of silence, Jillian rose. There was no point in staying any longer. "It's late, gentlemen. It's time I was abed. I've an early meeting with painters in the morning." She touched her quilted, amber petticoat, making a half dip of a curtsy. "Will."

"G'night, sweetheart."

She turned to Duncan. "Are you coming, sir, or do you stay longer?"

"You've the coach?" It was that cool, distant voice of his that she hated. Always efficient, always calm, always just a little cruel.

"Yes."

He didn't look at her. "I'll grab a hell cart later. I think Will and I will play a hand or two of knap and slur. I'm certain that whatever wench it is that waits for him can wait a little while longer."

"As you wish." She turned away, trying not to be angry or hurt. Even if nothing changed between her and Duncan, she knew she would have a better marriage than most Englishwomen. So why was she greedy? Why did she want more?

"I'll escort you downstairs if you wish," Duncan called after her, but he made no move to get up from his chair. Jillian could hear him already shuffling the cards he must have pulled from his doublet.

She snatched her blue wool cloak and lace vizard off the peg on the wall. "Don't bother, yourself, sir. I assure you, I can reach the coach on my own two feet. Atar will see that I get home."

When Jillian stepped out of the private room and closed the door, she stood on the landing, putting on her cloak. She half-hoped she would hear Duncan's footsteps behind her. She half-hoped he would come after her to apologize, to offer to come home to their bed with her now.

But he didn't. And Jillian rode home in the cold coach in the winter rain, alone.

* * *

Duncan picked up his horse's reins and led the animal toward the thatch cottage nestled at the edge of his property in New Forest. Smoke rose from the dwelling's clay chimney and curled heavenward.

In the distance, he could see the hunting lodge his grandfather had built of rough timber. Even at this distance, Duncan could make out the massive rack of stag antlers that ornamented the wide-cut plank door. The actual structure of the hunting lodge appeared to be in excellent condition, the windows battened down, the cedar shingles in good repair. Old Man Marshal had taken exceptional care of his property. Duncan made a mental note to remember to reward his loyalty to a master he'd not seen since he was a boy. All these years, the man had apparently cared for the property, even when he must have heard that the family had been murdered by savages.

A dog barked, and the cur came running from the cottage. Behind him came an ancient, shriveled man hunkered down over a twisted cane. "Who's there?" he demanded. "Who's there, I say?"

Duncan halted on the path, letting his horse's reins fall. It was Marshal, all right. Duncan could see that the old man's eyes were foggy and white, masked by cataracts. He had to be blind, or nearly so.

"It's the Earl of Cleaves, Marshal. It's Duncan."

The man broke into a spontaneous grin. "So it is. So it is! I can tell by your voice, though it's a mite deeper. It could be no other." He halted to wave his cane. "Come closer, let me see your face, boy."

Duncan chuckled. "A boy no longer, I fear. I'm sorry it took me so long to come." He offered his hand to the caretaker.

Marshal gripped it tightly. "Better than to have never made it at all, eh?"

The two men laughed easily. It had been almost twenty-five years since they had last met, but the time meant nothing to either of them. It was Old Man Marshal, who had seemed very old even then to Duncan, who had taught him to shoot and to hunt.

Marshal squinted, bringing his face only inches from Duncan's. "What the hell is that, boy? What you got on your face?" He shook his head. "I don't see like I used to. Couldn't bring down a deer now if it knocked me on my arse."

Duncan let go of the old man's hand. "A scarf. I wear it to cover my scars." It wasn't exactly a lie. Duncan just didn't want to have to discuss the matter with his old friend.

"Yeah, I heard some savages got ye in that faraway place. I'm just glad you got away from 'em." He looped his arm through Duncan's and led him toward the cottage. "Just glad ye made it home, boy."

Duncan let Marshal lead him. "I won't be here much longer. I'm going back to the Colonies."

Marshal made a clicking sound between his gums. His teeth appeared long gone. "Don't surprise me one bit. You was always hardheaded, and always determined." He slapped Duncan on the back, leaning against him for support. "So come share a nip of the jug with me. My grandson will be back after a bit and then you can talk to him. He's a good boy, my Eli."

Duncan had to duck to make it in the cottage door. He hadn't really intended to visit, but since he would have to wait for the boy, why not share a drink with an old friend?

A short time later, Marshal's grandson, Eli, came riding in with a hare flung over his back for the evening meal. Duncan's grandfather, then his father, and now he himself had given the caretaker and his family the right to hunt the Roderick land for food as they sold no pelts or abused the privilege in any way.

Duncan took an immediate liking to young Eli. The boy

was no more than sixteen or seventeen, but he'd been raised by his grandfather on the Roderick hunting grounds. He knew the boundaries by heart. He knew the herds that moved, and most importantly, he knew the poachers. When the King desired to hunt on Duncan's land, Duncan was certain there would be plenty of game.

Duncan hired the boy as the new caretaker of his lodge, said his goodbyes to Old Man Marshal, and then rode out, taking the same path he had come on. Suddenly, he was anxious to get home to Jillian.

He rode through the forest, enjoying the journey beneath the canopy of great oaks and maples, the last of leaves drifting through the air in a shower of autumn colors. Birds sang and squirrels chattered.

At a bridge, he slowed his mount to a walk, the horse's hooves clip-clopping on the old timber planks. Duncan was oblivious to his worldly cares until he heard the distinct sound of an arrow pierce the late afternoon air.

Duncan didn't know why he heard it, or how he had time to react. His Mohawk father must have taught him well.

One moment he was in his saddle, the next he was flying through the air, over the railing, taking his musket with him. He hit the cold, knee-deep water, then the gravel bottom, with a splash.

Duncan rolled hard, coming up on his feet at the stream's edge, spraying water. From where he crouched, he could see the feathered shaft of an arrow protruding from the bridge's rail. Had it been Duncan's chest the arrow had hit, he knew he'd have been breathing his last bloody, gurgling breath at this very moment.

With the instinct he had nurtured living among the savages, Duncan lifted his loaded musket to bead in on the enemy. He knew without seeing, without hearing, where his attacker lay in wait.

Duncan caught a flash of a brown coat in the crook of a tree and pulled the trigger, not needing to take time to aim.

The would-be assassin fell from the tree, dead before his grizzly face met the cold water of the riverbed. Duncan had shot him in the face, blowing away the top of his head.

Duncan crept along the shore, toward the would-be assassin, looking this way and that, fearing there might be another. With the single load in his musket discharged, he had nothing to rely on to defend himself but the sword he wore on his belt.

Duncan kicked the killer onto his back. He could barely recognize the face as human, but he didn't think he knew him. The man's wet, blond hair was cropped short, as if he'd recently come from sea; what was left of his head . . .

Duncan smiled grimly. He was comforted to know that he hadn't lost his ability to shoot true in these months he'd wasted as a gentleman in England. Once he returned to Maryland, he knew he would need to call on his capability to hunt and to protect himself, and others, once again.

Satisfied that the man was dead, Duncan reached down to pick up the bow that had fallen from the tree with him. It was not well made.

The sound of hurried hoofbeats sent Duncan hiding behind a massive oak. When the horse appeared, Duncan stepped out, recognizing the rider as young Eli.

"What happened?" He swung down off his mount. "I heard the musket-fire, my lord." He looked at the body at his feet. "Are you all right?"

Duncan gave the dead man's limp arm a kick. "Know him?"

Eli grimaced in shock.

Duncan guessed he'd never seen a man's face blown off before. *Never seen one skinned off either,* he speculated.

Duncan's saw the gamekeeper swallow hard. The boy was beginning to look a little green.

"Hard to tell," Eli said after a moment. "I don't think I know 'im. Look at his clothes. He ain't from these parts. Looks like he's out of London to me."

Duncan wiped his mouth with the back of his hand, staring out into the forest thoughtfully. "I'd guess the same."

Eli looked at Duncan. "Why—why would someone want to kill you, my lord?"

Duncan turned away to search for his horse, who had shied in the commotion. Already his mind was churning with theories. He didn't bother to answer the boy.

Was someone trying to kill him, or was this just a strange accident, a case of mistaken identity? He called to his mount, standing in the distance, and the horse trotted to him. Duncan picked up the leather reins. He'd have to go back to the cottage and borrow some clothing or dry his own. *And what about the scaffolding?* he wondered, shivering, from the cold. He was not a paranoid man, but neither was he a foolish one. *Had that been a freak accident as well . . . or not?*

Thirteen

Jillian stood near the fireplace, warming her hands. Duncan sat behind her at his desk, penning a letter. The hour was late; the tall case clock on the landing had just chimed eleven-thirty. Jillian was tired, but she had waited all day for Duncan. After going to bed without him last night, knowing he was annoyed with her, she wanted to make amends. Besides, she had something she wanted to discuss with him.

She heard him sprinkle sand on the paper to dry the ink.

"Duncan," she said softly.

"Yes?"

He had not given her his full attention, but she went on anyway. "Duncan, I've been thinking about Beatrice."

"Um hm."

"About a husband. Father has had no prospects, and now my sister Margaret wishes to wed."

"Um hm."

Jillian turned to him, putting her back to the warm fire. She was afraid if she didn't ask him now, she'd not get the nerve again, so she just blurted it out. "Duncan, could we take Beatrice with us when we go to the Colonies?" She went on a little faster, not giving him time to answer. "We could find her a husband there. I'm sure we could. Will says there's ten Englishmen for every woman in Maryland. He says everyone is looking for a wife with decent teeth." She twisted her hands in her white linen night rail with the Irish lace. "What do you think?"

He was staring at the letter on the desk, yet she knew he wasn't reading it. There was a long moment of silence before he spoke. He funneled the sand from the sheet of paper back into a small ceramic pot. "I'll consider it. I suppose finding her a husband would be the least I could do."

"Oh, Duncan." She came toward him. "I can't tell you what it would mean to me!" She stopped at his chair and dropped her hand to his shoulder. "Thank you."

He pushed back in his chair and stood. She remained beside him as he caught the hem of his linen shirt and pulled it over his head.

Jillian couldn't resist reaching out to touch the patterned tattoos that covered his chest. The colored figures fascinated her. Some were actual pictures that she could recognize, a bird, a dagger, but others were Mohawk symbols that Duncan had had to explain. "What's this one?" she asked.

Duncan's shirt fell from his fingertips to the floor. It was obvious to her that he enjoyed her touch, inexperienced or not. "It tells of a battle." He pointed to a blue cloud. "This is the smoke of the enemy's musket. This, the Mohawk victory." He indicated a flash of ochre lightening.

She nibbled on her lower lip, her hand still resting on his chest. She looked up at him.

His gaze met hers, and she knew that his anger over last night had passed. He leaned closer to kiss her, his movement deliciously slow and tantalizing.

Jillian sighed. If there were one thing that could be said for her marriage, it was that the sex between them was good. "Come to bed," she whispered.

He brushed his lips against hers, the sexual charge evident in the warm, still air of their bedchamber. "I'm coming."

Jillian stepped away from him and walked toward the bed, removing her night rail. She was still shy about allowing Duncan see her unclothed, but it was so obvious that he enjoyed it, that she found herself displaying herself, even when it wasn't necessary. She liked the way he watched her, as he watched her now.

She slipped out of the robe and laid it over a chair. She could hear Duncan undressing behind her. When she turned to sit on the edge of the bed, his gaze was on her. She smiled. She liked this power her sexual allure held over her husband. It was tangible proof that he cared for her on some level.

Jillian slipped between the sheets, but made no attempt to cover her bare breasts. Duncan had removed his boots and stockings and was now unlacing his breeches.

Jillian knew her cheeks colored as she stared shamelessly at her husband. His male organ fascinated her almost as much as the tattoos did. He slipped out of his breeches and his member sprang forth, already growing stiff with desire for her, from the confines of the broadcloth.

Duncan let his breeches lie on the floor where they fell and walked about the room extinguishing the candles. He left one burning on his side of the bed and then climbed beneath the sheets.

Jillian came to him immediately. She wasn't yet so bold that she would initiate their lovemaking, but she sought him out, at least for the comfort of his strong embrace, one thing he'd never denied her.

"Oh, Jilly, Jilly," he whispered in the near-darkness. "Aren't you a sight for tired eyes at the end of day?" His hand found her breast and stroked it. Already she could feel her nipple growing taut in anticipation.

She rested her head on his shoulder, running her hand over his chest. The sleek, hard muscles of his body fascinated her. Everything about his virile body was engaging; it was so different from her own, so full of strength and hardness.

Jillian could sense he was preoccupied—and certainly not with concern for finding Bea a husband. "You went to New Forest. Did you find a caretaker?"

"Aye." He caught her nipple between his thumb and fore-finger and rolled it.

Her breath caught in her throat.

"Nearly found an arrow in my chest, too."

"What?" Jillian sat up to look at him, peering into his face. "What do you mean? Someone shot at you?" He continued to caress her breast, but for the moment all Jillian could think of was his welfare. "Someone accidentally shot at you? I thought no one hunted your land except by permission."

"I'm not certain it was an accident."

Jillian searched his handsome face for understanding. Now that she had grown used to the bear claw tattoo on his cheek, she found she liked it. It made her husband different from any other man. "I don't understand. You think someone tried to kill you? Who?"

He brought his hand up beneath her chin. "Don't worry."

"Don't worry!" She stroked his cheek, now stubbled with a day's beard-growth. "Someone may be trying to kill you, and you say I shouldn't worry? What happened to the man who shot at you? What did he say?"

"Ouch."

She frowned. "Ouch?"

"I killed him."

Jillian stiffened. Just when she thought perhaps she was beginning to understand Duncan, she realized she knew nothing of him. Her husband had killed a man today and not thought to mention it until nearly midnight. Her voice wavered. "You killed someone today, Duncan?"

"Would you have rather he'd killed me?"

"No. No, of course not."

His hand was on her breast again, stroking her, comforting her. "The odd thing is that no one knew where I was going today," he said, kissing her forehead.

"No one? I knew. You must have told someone else."

"No, I didn't. I'm sure I didn't."

She traced the circle of flesh around his nipple with her forefinger. "You—you didn't tell Algernon, did you?"

"Algernon? I haven't spoke to my cousin since last week when he came to me for another advance on his allowance. He's been out about town—with one of his whores, no doubt." Duncan laid his hand over hers, ceasing her caress. "Why do you mention Algernon?"

Jillian hesitated. She wasn't a carrier of tales. She didn't want to see Algernon in trouble. The man was harmless; she actually felt sorry for him. But if Duncan were in danger, she knew it was her duty as his wife to tell him anything she knew. "Algernon . . . he's been speaking some nonsense about having the courts return the earldom to him."

Duncan tipped back his head and laughed genuinely. "Have the courts return the title? You jest."

She smiled. "He says they made a mistake. He's says it's all rightfully his."

"And what reason does he give?"

"No reason. He—he said I shouldn't have married you." She paused. "He said I should have waited for him."

Again, laughter. "So that's it. My cousin is jealous of my beautiful wife." He ran his hand down her bare arm. "And why shouldn't he be? Poor man. He thought we'd all been murdered and he'd inherited his uncle's fortune. He had for a few years. I can't blame him for being angry. After his parents died when he was a babe, he was passed about. He lived with us, with Grandmother, sometimes with his aunt. He truly got the short end of the stick being born the son of the younger Roderick brother."

"I knew he was harmless. That was why I didn't say anything before." She thought for a moment. "So you're certain you told no one you were going to New Forest today?"

He sighed. "Let's not talk about it anymore. Here in my bedchamber is the one place I want to get away from the world."

"All right." Jillian had more questions, but she wouldn't press him tonight. It was a wonder he'd said anything about the incident at all. She rested her head on his chest again. Her hand brushed his flat, hard belly, and went lower.

Duncan groaned. "Minx. I married a minx."

"You want me to stop?" Her voice grew sultry as her fingers met with the dark, curly hair of his groin. "I can stop if you want me to, husband."

"No." His voice came huskily in the darkness. "Don't stop . . ."

"He said what?" Beatrice giggled, reaching for the china coffeepot set on the table. She and Jillian were waiting for the dowager to join them for an afternoon refreshment.

Jillian turned from the hearth where she'd been stoking the fire. The chill of England's north winds had hit London hard last night, and suddenly winter was truly upon them. Jillian was actually relieved to see the month of December. Duncan hadn't mentioned when they would be sailing for the Colonies and she hadn't asked for fear of the answer, but she assumed that they would now wait until spring.

"Duncan said he would consider allowing you to go to the Colonies with us. He said he might help find a husband for you."

Beatrice clutched her woolen shawl tighter around her shoulders. "You're serious. Oh, I don't know, going so far across the ocean to that sinful land. Mary Maston said Indians walk right into your house whilst you dine. She says the conditions are dreadful. I don't know that I can do it. I don't know that I can go."

"Stuff and nonsense!" Jillian said, repeating the dowager's favorite saying. She came around the table set for tea. "You were perfectly willing to go when you were supposed to marry Duncan."

"That was different," Beatrice answered, wide-eyed, as she slipped into her seat. "That was when I was going with my husband. It was my duty. It's entirely different now."

Jillian leaned over the back of her chair. "Come, sister. Think of the adventure of it. I was looking at the maps on Duncan's wall. It looks like we'll take the southern route through the Caribbean Islands. We may even stop in Jamaica for supplies."

"I'm not the adventurous sort." Beatrice stared at her china plate, folding her hands neatly. "You are, but I'm just not."

"Such stuff and nonsense!" The dowager appeared in the doorway of the parlor. A footman trailing behind her lifted her cloak from her shoulders. It had grown cold enough in the house in the last few days that all three women had taken to wearing their cloaks when they moved from room to room in the drafty house.

"Daphne." Beatrice came out of her chair, smiling. "You look lovely today."

The dowager touched a red curl. "Madame Dupree just touched up my hair. It's not too bright, is it? I don't want to look like anyone's leman!"

Jillian linked her arm through the dowager's and led her to the table. "Not at all. It looks beautiful, especially for a woman your age."

Daphne allowed Jillian to help her into her seat. "That was what I told my husband, God rest his soul." She picked up her linen napkin and tucked it into the décolletage of her mint-green gown. "I said, Forrest, you'll carry me out in my coffin a redhead. No gray hair for me, not as long as the good lord is still making henna and French hairstylists!"

Jillian laughed, taking the chair beside her. "I may consider that thought myself someday." She ran a hand over her own red tresses.

"Indeed you should." The dowager turned to Beatrice. "Now what is this about your not being interested in a little adventure, Bea?" She reached for a cream-filled pastry.

"I . . ." Beatrice looked meekly to her sister for support.

Jillian poured the thick, hot coffee into tiny cups. "I've

asked Duncan if Beatrice can accompany us to Maryland. I want him to find her a husband there."

The old woman took a healthy bite of the sweet. "And you don't want to go?"

Beatrice wrung her hands. "I—I don't know."

"Ah, what a world you ladies have been born into. Me—I'm too feeble, too locked into my ways, but you have the chances of a lifetime. I'd have liked to have seen the American Colonies once. The Indians intrigue me." She waved her ring-encrusted hand. "I'm too old for that now, but not you." She pointed a bony finger at Beatrice. "You've just begun to live, woman. Use some good sense. Don't spend your life hiding behind a gilded chair. If my grandson will escort you to that wilderness of his, I say *go.* You'll meet the right man." She winked. "And then you'll be more than willing to share in an adventure or two with him."

Beatrice stared at her plate, chastised.

Jillian reached out to take her sister's hand and squeezed it. "Daphne's right. It will be an adventure, you and I going together to the colonies. And we *will* find you a husband."

"F—father would have to give his permission. I—I don't know that he will."

"Stuff and nonsense." The dowager reached for a chocolate-iced cake, still chewing on the cream puff. "He'll be more than willing to pass the responsibility of another daughter off to the earl." She glanced at Beatrice. "No offense meant, sweetling, but we all know that's the way men are."

"My sister forgets. Th—the earl didn't yet agree to take me."

Jillian gave a wave of confidence. "Leave both men to me. I'll see to it."

The dowager chuckled, wiping the corner of her mouth with her napkin. "No doubt you will, sweetling. I have utter faith in you and your feminine wiles."

Jillian was just reaching for the coffeepot to refill the dowager's cup when she heard an angry shout. All three women looked at each other. There was no mystery as to whom the voice belonged. The string of bellows that echoed through the east wing could come from no one but Duncan.

Jillian pushed out of her chair. "I'd best see what's about."

The dowager chuckled. "I suppose you had. Good luck." She returned her attention to her plate. "Now, Beatrice, dear, pass this old woman that plate of sweets, will you? I'm famished!"

Jillian picked her cloak off the chair near the parlor door and swung it over her shoulders as she went out. She could still hear Duncan shouting as she hurried down the passageway.

She found him in the front hallway, where the recently replaced swords hung in a grand circle over his head. She spotted a footman standing near the front door, trembling in his boots.

"And when I call for my horse," Duncan went on at the top of his lungs, "I mean for the horse to be saddled now. Not tomorrow, not come Candlemas Eve! Do I make myself unconditionally clear?"

The footman was bobbing his head in obvious terror, his Adam's apple rising and falling in his throat.

Jillian glided smoothly past her husband. "Go then, Maurice." She shooed him with her hand. "See to the earl's horse at once."

She waited until the footman had disappeared before she turned her attention to her husband. "Is it really necessary to shout at the servants like that, Duncan? You make them afraid of you."

His face was red with anger. "Is it too much for a man to ask to have his horse ready when he orders it?"

"Certainly not, but that's still no reason to lose your temper." She dropped her hand to her hip, hating that in public she had to speak to her husband through that ridiculous veil of his. She had tried to convince him that it was time to shed it, but he refused; worse, he refused to even discuss the matter with her.

He pointed his finger at her. "If the men and women we hire cannot do their jobs, then they need to seek employment elsewhere!"

She grabbed his accusing finger, trying to make light of the whole situation. "And where is it that you go in such a hurry? The king called for you, perhaps?"

He scowled, pulling his hand from her. "Banstead Downs."

"It's life and death that you make a bet at the horse races? I didn't even know they raced this time of year."

He didn't meet her gaze. "I seek Galloway. He's there purchasing some horses."

The tone in his voice set something off in Jillian's head. Something was wrong. Very wrong. "Will? *Why are you looking for Will?*"

He didn't answer.

"Duncan?" She rested her hand on his shoulder, making him face her.

"I've gone over and over in my head whom I might have told where I was going the other day." His words didn't come easily.

"And?"

"And the only ones who knew—" He balled his fist. "*—who knew,* were you and Galloway."

She watched his face. "Will would never harm you."

"No one else knew but the two of you, and you have nothing to gain, and much to lose, if I die. You'll inherit none of my acquisitions, nor privileges, unless you provide an heir."

"What if I were pregnant?" She didn't know what made her ask. Obviously he didn't suspect her.

"Then you will be well provided for." He smiled grimly, gripping her shoulder. "I have to go, Jillian."

"I'll go with you," she offered anxiously. She hated to

see him go alone, so angry. She feared for Will's well-being. "I know Will had nothing to do with this. *I know it.*"

He started for the front door. "No. You stay here where it's warm. This is between Will and me if he's betrayed me. You're not involved."

Jillian followed him out the door onto the front stoop. It had been repaired only last week by the masons. The wind whipped at her hair and she lifted her hood, shivering. As Duncan caught his horse's reins from the stable boy and swung into his saddle, she saw his pistol tucked into the waistband of his breeches. She was truly frightened. "Duncan!" she shouted above the howl of the wind. "You can't go off half cocked like this! Please let me go with you!"

He sank his heels into the horse's flanks, and his mount reared and bolted.

Jillian whipped around, furious with Duncan, furious with herself for not being able to stop him. Her hand had just touched the doorknob when she turned back. "Maurice!" she called to the retreating stable hand.

He turned back. "My lady?"

"Saddle a horse for me."

"My lady?"

"You've been chastised once today for not getting a horse quickly enough. Don't repeat your mistakes," she snapped. "Saddle a horse for me. I'm going up to my apartments to get a heavier cloak. I want my horse here when I come down. Is that clear?"

He gave a jerky bow. "Yes, my lady."

Jillian raced back up the steps. If she couldn't stop Duncan from confronting Will in his anger, at least she could be there when he did.

Fourteen

Jillian calculated that, escorted by a groom, she had reached Banstead Downs not five minutes later than Duncan. So where was he? She tugged her mount's reins, and the horse shied, prancing sideways.

It had begun to sleet. Snow mixed with freezing rain fell, the white haze reducing her visibility. She yanked at the hood of her ermine-lined cloak, pulling it off her head to get a better view of the deserted field. She ignored the wet sleet that stung her face. Some of her hair had come unpinned and whipped in the wind; she smoothed it irritably. "Where the blast are you, Duncan?" she murmured, keeping a steady hand on the reins.

Then she heard a voice carrying on the wind—an angry voice. It was the same voice she had heard in the hallway at Breckenridge House only a short time ago.

"Duncan?" She turned her horse around in a tight circle.

There in the distance she saw a group of men and horses. But even at this range, Jillian could make out her husband's form as he narrowed the gap between himself and the men standing with the horses.

Jillian urged her mount into a trot, headed directly for Duncan, who'd left his horse standing near a thicket of leafless trees.

"Duncan!" she called into the howl of the wind. She watched as a man broke from the group and started toward him with a wave of greeting. It had to be Will.

"Duncan!" she shouted again. She rode her horse right between the two friends, her groom close at her heels.

Duncan turned his angry gaze on her. "Jillian, what the hell are you doing here?"

She put out her hand to Will, and he helped her down from her sidesaddle. The groom caught the reins of her mount and discreetly led it away.

"Answer me, wife. Why have you come?" Duncan shouted at her. "I told you this was between Galloway and me."

Out of the corner of her eye, Jillian could see the other men in the group turn their heads, hoping to pick up part of the private conversation among the Earl of Cleaves, his wife, and Will Galloway.

Jillian took Will's hand in her gloved one and led him farther from the prying eyes and ears of the horse traders.

Duncan was left with no choice but to stomp after them. "Answer me, damn you! I told you to stay home! I told you this was not your concern!"

Will looked utterly perplexed. "What's he talking about, Jilly?" He looked at Duncan. "What the hell are you talking about?"

"New Forest." Duncan shoved his black wool cloak off his shoulders so that it rippled and snapped in the wind behind him. He seemed unaffected by the frigid wind and falling sleet.

Will's brow creased. *"New Forest?"* He looked to Jillian for understanding. "What the sweet hell's gotten into him?"

Jillian took Duncan's arm, trying another tack. "Let's go somewhere and have a drink. Somewhere in private where we can discuss this calmly."

Duncan pushed her off his arm. "Go home, wife. Where you belong."

She dropped her hands to her hips. "The hell I will!"

Both men looked at her, surprised by her reaction.

"I won't go home and let the two of you get into some

damned duel!" she shouted into her husband's face. "I won't do it."

"Duel? What are you talking about?" Will looked at Jillian, then his longtime friend. "Duncan, I'm lost here." He plucked at his chin, still apparently not understanding the seriousness of Duncan's anger. "Why are we going to duel?"

"New Forest, what do you know of it?" Duncan's tone was as cold and biting at the sleet that now fell in daggered sheets from the darkening sky.

"Good hunting. You've a lodge there." Will turned his palms heavenward. He was wearing a fine pair of black, calfskin gloves. "What else should I know?"

"You knew I was going to my lodge yesterday."

"Yes. So?"

"Please," Jillian begged. "Not here. Let's go home; it's freezing out here. A little brandywine would do us all some good."

"Go home, Jillian." Duncan spoke through clenched teeth, never taking his eyes from Will's. "You were the only one who knew," he told his friend. "You and my wife, and she would have no reason to make an attempt on my life."

"Attempt on your life?" Will seemed genuinely baffled, then greatly concerned. "Someone tried to kill you, *again?"*

"Again?" Duncan's eye, unobscured by the purple veil, glinted. "What do you mean *again?"*

"Well, you said yourself that whole scaffolding incident was odd. We talked about the possibility that someone might have it in for you."

"Odd? Odd how?" Jillian attempted to interrupt.

Duncan was either ignoring her or didn't hear her to begin with. "And what do you know of that, Will? Did the scaffold collapse by accident, *conveniently,* just as I went up the stairs?"

Will looked at Jillian as if to ask if Duncan were in earnest.

Jillian placed a hand on Will's shoulder. "An archer tried to shoot Duncan on his own land in New Forest yesterday."

"I can speak for myself!" Duncan bellowed.

Will was attempting to follow the conversation. "A freak accident?"

She shook her head. "He doesn't think so. He had to kill the man."

"Jillian, stay out of this," Duncan ordered. "I don't need you here protecting me. I don't want you here, *damn it!*"

"Why would I want to kill you?" Galloway asked, now seeming hurt. "You're the best friend I've got in the world, Duncan. My only true friend. I'd die for you or yours." He offered his hand. "You know that."

With his fist, Duncan hit the hand Will extended with a viciousness that frightened Jillian. "You were the only one who knew! You betrayed me, you son of a bitching whore!"

"Listen to yourself!" Now Will was shouting. "You're being irrational. Why in sweet Charles' name would I try to kill *you?*"

Duncan grabbed Will by his cloak with both hands, knocking him backward a step. "How the hell should I know?"

"Duncan!" Jillian intoned, refusing to become an hysterical wife. She thrust her arm between the two men. "Take your hands off him!"

"I wouldn't betray you. I wouldn't," Will said gently, but firmly, his gaze locked on Duncan's. "I'm not her. I wouldn't do that."

Who was Will talking about? Jillian sensed that there was something more here than met the eye, something she didn't understand. Will was right; Duncan wasn't behaving rationally.

Jillian's mind ticked. Wasn't it the thought of betrayal that had set Duncan off when she had met with Jacob? That and his thought that she was abandoning him?

"Duncan, listen to me," Will reasoned. "Think. There would be no reason for me to kill you. I could gain nothing. You had to have told someone else. Someone on the ship, at court, in a tavern."

Duncan shook his head adamantly. "No . . . no. Only you and Jillian knew."

Suddenly, Will paled visibly. His gaze shifted to the slick, icy grass at their feet. "Sweet Jesus."

"What?" Duncan demanded. "Galloway?"

Slowly, painfully, Will lifted his gaze to meet his friend's. "I may have told someone where you were going." He raised a hand weakly. "Just in passing, just in conversation."

"Who?"

Jillian sensed the answer before he spoke the name.

"Who?" Duncan repeated, still gripping Will by his cloak. "Tell me, damn you!"

Jillian could have sworn she saw tears in Will's eyes. "Algernon."

"Algernon?" Duncan let Will go so abruptly that he stumbled backward, barely catching himself before he would have fallen. "Where the hell did you see Algernon? What are you doing conversing with him? You hate the sniveling son of a bitch, you said so yourself."

Will looked past Duncan, past Jillian, to somewhere in the distance, his eyes losing focus. "Let's go somewhere and talk. I've something to tell you." His voice cracked. "Something to confess."

Duncan hesitated. Jillian could tell by the look on his face that he wanted it out now. He wanted to hear what Will had to say here, here in the driving sleet.

She touched his arm gently. "Will's right. This conversation shouldn't be shared with these gentlemen." She motioned to the men standing in the distance with their horses. They were far enough away that Jillian knew they couldn't have heard the conversation, but certainly close enough to realize there'd been a confrontation between the earl and his friend. As it was, every anteroom in London would be buzzing with defamation and speculation by nightfall. The gossips needed no more fuel to feed their fires.

When Duncan didn't answer at once, she squeezed his

arm, praying she'd somehow gotten through. "Please, Duncan. For me."

He loosened his stance. "Now, Galloway. Today. I'll not put this off."

"I'll come to your house. Just let me get my horse."

Jillian had never seen a man look so beaten.

"Not my house," her husband denounced. "You'll not step foot in my house."

"Sweet, Jesus, Duncan," Will swore. "All right then, my apartments."

Duncan shook his head stubbornly.

Jillian fought the urge to roll her eyes. Duncan was just being childish now. "The Three Cocks in half an hour," she said, settling the matter as she signaled to her groom to bring both her horse and his master's. "We could all use a libation, wouldn't you say?"

Will rode off immediately. Jillian and Duncan mounted their horses and headed in the direction of the designated tavern.

The moment Jillian rode up beside her husband, he turned to her angrily. "I want you to go home now."

She raised the hood of her cloak. It was bitter on horseback, and the sleet was still falling. Jillian wasn't accustomed to riding in bad weather; already the road was beginning to turn to icy mud. She had to concentrate to keep her seat as her mount slipped and slid in the frozen muck.

"I'm not going home."

"You're my wife. The law says you must obey me."

She set her jaw. "So what are you going to do?" She was angry now. "Are you going to wrestle me off this horse, tie me to yours, and take me home?" She tightened up on the reins, riding around a deep puddle covered by skim ice. "You could slap me around. Perhaps that would work."

"I would never hit you," he grunted, staring straight ahead into the wind, "though I'm sorely tempted now."

"Will's the best friend you've got." She urged her horse

forward so that they rode side by side again. "By my calculation, he's the only friend you've got."

"He told Algernon where I'd gone. I suspected my dear cousin. I didn't want to believe he'd be so stupid, but I suspected. Now I find out my friend is in league with him."

"You don't know that."

"That slimy bastard, Algernon." Duncan put out a gloved hand and slowly closed it as if choking a man. "I'll kill him. I swear by all that's holy I will! And Galloway may well go to his reward in the same breath."

"Just hear Will out and stop jumping to conclusions. He's always been honest with you, you told me so yourself."

"Honest with me?" He gave a snort of derision. "He and Algernon have been in on this little game since I arrived, I'd suspect. With me out of the way, Algernon gets the title, monies, and holdings in England and Galloway gets my land in Maryland." He clenched his fist, swinging it in the air. "I knew I should never have trusted him. Either of them. Damn it! Why did I try to be reasonable with Algernon? Why did I try to be fair?"

Recognizing that she could do nothing at this point but try to keep anyone from being injured, Jillian listened to Duncan's ranting the remainder of the ride to the Twin Cocks.

When Jillian and Duncan arrived at the tavern, they went straight upstairs to the private room they had shared with Will only a few nights ago. He was already waiting for them, seated at the table, a drink in his hand.

Jillian removed her gloves, then her wet cloak, and moved to the fireplace to warm her chilled bones. Duncan stayed near the door, as if he didn't intend on remaining long.

"Well, Galloway?" Duncan's voice rang off the plastered walls.

Will peered into his brandy glass. "I didn't do it on purpose, Duncan. I've been careful not to speak of you or your doings to him."

"The two of you conspired against me!"

"No." Will shook his head. "I can only speak for myself, but I swear by my father's grave that I had nothing to do with the attempt or attempts on your life."

"What were you doing, if not conspiring with him, then? Answer me that, Galloway."

Jillian watched the men closely. Her heart ached for them both.

"I . . ." Will hesitated. "My only sin, friend, was that of fornication." He glanced at Jillian, tears in his eyes. "My apologies, my lady."

Jillian smiled. She would have gone to Will, but she feared Duncan would see that action, too, as a betrayal.

"Fornication?" Duncan boomed. "What are you talking about? Speak plainly, man. I'll not stand here all day."

Will exhaled. Then he turned his head to meet Duncan's hostile gaze. "I did not conspire with your cousin, I only slept with him."

Jillian knew her jaw must have dropped. Will? Have sex with another man? Certainly she had heard of such debauchery, whispered by servants in the shadows, but she had assumed such men were monsters. Will couldn't possibly be one of them.

Jillian covered her mouth with her hand, feeling tears well in her eyes.

Duncan remained frozen beside the doorjamb, stunned. "No, Will," Jillian heard him whisper. "I—I've seen you with women. Whores."

"Women yes, but men, too." Will came out of his chair, taking a step toward his friend. "I never meant to harm you, even inadvertently. That was why I kept my, um, *appetite* from you."

Duncan was shaking his head. "But not Algernon. Not my cousin."

"I can make no excuses for myself, but you must believe me when I tell you I had nothing to do with what transpired at New Forest. I know nothing of any attempts on your life, though I wonder now why I'd never considered it. Algernon's been babbling for months about what was rightfully his."

"You said you disliked him." Duncan spoke flatly. "You barely spoke to him when he entered the room."

"I can't explain it to you." Will lifted his hand toward Duncan, then let it fall with futility. "I do dislike him. It was a physical relationship, like many others. Nothing more. You have to believe me."

Duncan wiped his mouth with the back of his hand, as if trying to get rid of a bad taste in his mouth. "How can I? How can I believe anything you say?"

Will turned away. "I don't understand. What of that tolerance you said the savages taught you?"

"It's not that and you know it!" Duncan pointed, his voice barely restrained. "It's not the sex, damn you! You could have confided in me. I'd not have loved you any less for that. I'd not have approved, but I'd not have condemned you!"

"Then what is it?" Will was openly crying now, tears spilling down his ruddy face.

Jillian had never seen a man cry before. She wanted so badly to go and comfort him. She knew his heart was breaking.

"Jillian, let's go." Duncan yanked her cloak off the wall peg.

Jillian came to him without hesitation. Instinctively, she knew when to resist and when he needed her.

"Answer me, damn you! You and I are practically brothers!" Will wiped his running nose with the velvet sleeve of his doublet. "You owe me an answer!"

Duncan dropped the cloak over Jillian's shoulders and pushed her in front of him, out the door. "You betrayed me, Galloway. You abandoned my friendship for his."

"It wasn't like that. Surely you know—"

"You and I—" Duncan swept a hand through the air. "—we are no longer brothers. Let's go, Jillian."

"You can't do this, Duncan." Tears ran down her cheeks.

She reached for his arm. "I believe Will when he says he knows nothing of the shooting. Don't part like this. You have to forgive him."

Duncan glanced over his shoulder. "Do not set foot on my step again, do you hear me, Galloway? Do it, and I'll kill you."

Then Duncan grasped Jillian's arm and led her down the narrow staircase, leaving Will to stand alone.

Duncan entered the front hall of Breckenridge House, slamming the door behind him. The stable boy had informed the earl that his cousin had arrived only a few minutes before.

"Algernon?" Duncan boomed, headed down the hall toward his cousin's apartments.

"Is something amiss, my lord?" Atar called after them.

Duncan glanced over his shoulder at his faithful servant. "Not a thing, Atar. You're dismissed. I'll not need you again until tomorrow."

The black man hesitated in the dark hallway, then he was gone.

Jillian hurried behind Duncan. "You've got to get control of your temper," she warned. "You have no proof it was Algernon. The archer died with the evidence. You kill Algernon, and you'll be the one hanging from the gallows by your neck."

"His life is forfeit. The little bastard knows it. Why do you think he skulks about? I have the legal right to take his life." Duncan's muddy boots pounded on the freshly polished floor. " 'Twould be in self defense."

"You don't have to kill him. We're going to the Colonies. He can't harm you there," she reasoned, grasping for straws. She didn't want Algernon's death on Duncan's conscience, a conscience she feared was already burdened by the past.

Duncan halted in the hallway at the door that led to his cousin's two-room apartment. Jillian had never been inside.

"Go to our bedchamber and wait for me there."

She reached out to him. "Think before you act. Promise me. Have him arrested. Let the courts be the condemners."

He brushed her hand aside. "Wait for me upstairs, damn it, woman!"

Before Jillian could answer, he had burst through the door and slammed it behind him, shutting her out.

"Algernon!"

She heard Duncan's voice clearly through the paneled door. She didn't care that he had ordered her to return to their apartments. She couldn't tear herself from the spot. She wanted no blood shed in her house, certainly not family blood.

"And where do you think you're going?" she heard Duncan say.

Algernon's voice was lower, a meek whine. She couldn't make out his reply.

Suddenly there was a loud crash and the sound of splintering wood. Jillian winced.

"No you don't, you cowardly swine," came her husband's voice.

Jillian pressed her ear to the door. She could hear Algernon whimpering. She couldn't make out what he was saying, only that he was protesting.

They must have moved farther from the door, because now she could only hear snatches of the conversation.

"New Forest . . ." Duncan intoned.

She heard swearing and the mention of an arrow in his gut.

Algernon was denying the entire incident.

"And what of the scaffolding . . ." came Duncan's voice. ". . . unfortunate accident, too . . ."

Jillian leaned against the door, her hands clasped in prayer. "Don't kill him," she whispered. "He's not worth it."

Suddenly the room behind the door burst into a cacophony of shouting.

"Took what was rightfully mine . . ." Algernon babbled. "Stole my inheritance . . ."

"Kill you right now . . ." Duncan threatened. ". . . be done with your lousy pelt before supper . . ."

There was another scuffle. Jillian heard what sounded like a table turning over. Glass shattered.

She wondered if she should go in. Not yet, she decided. She had begged Duncan to control his temper; and actually, for him, she assessed, he was doing quite well so far. He'd not shot Algernon with his pistol yet, nor run him through with his sword.

Duncan was right about what he said, of course. With even the slightest proof that Algernon had attempted to kill him, the courts would deem the Earl of Cleaves had possessed the right to kill his cousin in self-defense. But Jillian didn't want it to end that way. For Duncan's sake.

There was more shouting, Duncan's voice booming over Algernon's weak whining.

At some point Algernon must have attempted to escape Duncan's grip, because Jillian heard running footsteps and the sound of Duncan's heavy boots pounding on the wood floor. They moved even farther away, into Algernon's sleeping chamber she guessed, and now she could hear nothing but the rumble of Duncan's voice.

"Please," Jillian prayed, squeezing her eyes tightly shut. "Don't let him kill him, God. Save Algernon's skin, and I swear I'll work harder for our marriage; I swear it, dear Lord. I'll rescue Duncan from his inner torment."

One minute stretched into two, then three, then five, and still Jillian couldn't tell what was going on behind the door. Just when she'd made up her mind to go in, she heard hurried footsteps in the apartment.

Jillian jumped out of the way of the door just as it swung open with a bang. Algernon ran out, dragging a leather traveling bag behind him. He was half dressed, wearing only one shoe. His neat periwig was cocked to one side, his nose bloodied.

Algernon never saw Jillian as he raced down the hall, sobbing, dragging his belongings behind him. "Not right, not fair," he repeated over and over again.

Jillian met Duncan in the doorway, and they turned to watch his cousin retreat.

She looped her arm through Duncan's, hugging him around the waist. "Thank you," she whispered. "Thank you for not killing him."

Duncan, who held his purple veil in his hand, reached up to replace it and cover the bear claw tattoo. "I should have killed him, but I decided it wasn't worth the time the inquiry would take."

Jillian could feel Duncan's entire body trembling with rage.

"Where's he going?" she asked gently.

"France. Switzerland. Denmark? I don't give a fat rat's ass, just as long as he never sets foot in Mother England again," he shouted down the hallway after him.

She looked up at her husband, proud of his restraint. She did love him. "You're not going to have him prosecuted?"

He dropped his hand to her shoulder, actually seeking her comfort. Algernon was gone. "No. I told him I wouldn't bother. My goldsmith will send his allowance to him. If my dear, loyal cousin sets foot here on English soil again, I'll have him killed—and not without pain. He's running scared now. He knows I'll do it. He won't be back."

Jillian stared down the empty hallway, a strange sinking feeling in her chest. Duncan was so sure of himself and of Algernon's fear of him that she knew she should trust her husband. Why would Algernon come back at the risk of his life for such false claims? He wouldn't.

Why then, was she suddenly afraid this was not the last they would hear of Algernon Roderick?

Fifteen

"Are you certain?"

Jillian set down the paperwork and looked up at Duncan, who sat across from her, reading a book. Her kitten curled into a tighter ball on her lap and purred harmoniously.

It was a cold night in mid-December. Outside, the wind moaned, the shutters rattled, and branches of a tree scraped window glass somewhere in the house. After supper with Beatrice, Jillian and Duncan had retreated to the warmth and intimacy of their own chambers. Beatrice had gone to sit with the dowager, who was ill with a touch of the quartan ague.

It had been quiet the last two weeks, too quiet to suit Jillian. Algernon was gone to France by now, and there had been no word from Will Galloway. He had made no attempt to seek out Duncan; and no matter what Jillian said, Duncan refused to reconsider his judgment of his friend.

She looked at her husband, her amusement plain on her face. "Of course I'm certain." She laughed, pleased that he was pleased. "Why is it that men always ask that question? Every man since Adam has asked his wife if she were certain she was with child when she said she was."

He was smiling, too. "Well, it's such a mystery to men, I suppose. The idea of one human being growing inside another. We can't fathom it." He had let his book fall shut on his lap. "And honestly, women sometimes lie about such matters."

"Lie?" She laughed. "Why would I lie?"

"I didn't say *you* would lie, Jillian. I said some women. Women lie to get husbands, sometimes to keep them."

She grew serious. She studied Duncan's face, realizing she barely noticed the bear claw tattoo anymore. It was a part of him, a part of her now. "Was it necessary that I get pregnant with your heir in order to keep you?"

He came out of his chair to kneel before hers. He pushed the cat out of her lap. Sarah mewed in protest as she skittered across the cold floor.

"When I spoke my vows before God almighty, they were forever, Jillian." He took her hand in his, turning it, studying it. "With or without an heir, I'll be your husband unto death. I'll always provide for you and always keep you within the protection of my name."

Jillian leaned forward to kiss him.

"Of course, a son will be nice," he murmured playfully against her lips.

She looked directly at him, lifting a feather brow. "And what about a daughter?"

"A son to inherit, a daughter to spoil with my riches."

Their laughter mingled.

"Oh, Duncan, we're going to be all right, aren't we, you and I?" She wrapped her arms around his neck and hugged him tightly. "I feared this marriage wasn't going to work. I feared it would make us both unhappy. But it hasn't, and it won't, will it?"

He made no response but to return her embrace. After a moment, he broke away. He got up and crossed the room to his linen press. "I have something for you. I've been saving it for just this occasion."

Jillian remained in her seat, watching him dig through his clothing. He was handsome, this husband of hers, and frighteningly masculine. Just watching him made her tingle with desire for him. But it wasn't only his male body that attracted her. It was the sensitivity beneath his rough exterior that drew her, that made her love him.

God knew the man was frustrating. He behaved irrationally at times, such as how he'd dealt with Will. He could be abrupt and harsh with servants. Yet there were other times when she was in awe of his caring, his understanding. His giving her the kitten had been a small gesture, yet it had touched her heart. He treated Beatrice, the woman who should have been his wife, with the utmost respect. They had grown familiar enough with each other that he even dared to tease her. He was making inquiries into finding her the husband her father couldn't find.

Then there was the case of their French servant's daughters. In passing, Duncan had heard one of the maids speak of her daughters living in poverty in the slums of Paris. Not only had he fished enough coins from his breeches to pay for the girls' passage to England, but he had offered to find them both employment, if not in his household, then nearby.

Duncan growled and grumbled, yet he was a good man. He brought Jillian gifts; he read to her; he played her favorite card games by the hour. When they made love, he seemed more concerned with her pleasure than his own. He made her laugh. He made her think as no man had ever required. How could Jillian not love him? Now if only he would love her back, Jillian's world would be perfect.

Duncan returned, a small wooden box in his hand. "It was my Grandmother Daphne's, but she gave it to me to give to my wife." He offered her the box, acting awkward—as he often did when he gave her things. "The story is that it belonged to an Irish princess a long time ago. She had red hair and eyes of midnight. Supposedly, her husband gave it to her on the eve of some great battle, saying that as long as she wore it, he would be safe on the battlefield. The Irish woman's husband was gone three years, and for three years she wore it."

Jillian sat perched on the edge of her chair, staring at

Duncan, awed by the strange tale. "And did he? Did he come home to her safely?"

"He did. And they lived to grow very old together."

Jillian took the box from his hand and opened it. "Oh, Duncan," she breathed. Carefully, she lifted his gift from its black velvet-lined box. It was a necklace, shaped like a collar, made of hundreds of emeralds and diamonds. Hanging from the center was a rectangular-cut-emerald larger than her thumb nail. She looked up at him, hoping she wasn't going to tear up. Duncan hated tears, even of happiness. "It's beautiful."

He put out his hands. "Want to try it on? I knew it would look beautiful with your hair."

"In my night clothes?" She laughed at the prospect.

He shrugged. "Why not?"

So she rose from her chair, dressed in a silky blue sleeping gown, covered by a white flannel-and-lace night rail. On her feet she wore warm flannel mules. She spun around. This was one of the reasons that she could bear Duncan's tirades. He made her feel special in a way that no one had ever made her feel before.

He held up the hair that fell loose down her back and kissed the nape of her neck. Then, gingerly, he placed the necklace on her, fastened it, and let her hair fall down over her back again.

She spun around to face him. "So, what do you think?" Her fingers spanned the green jewels that sparkled in the firelight.

"Beautiful," he murmured. "You're beautiful. I thought so the day I found you in your father's garden."

She frowned. "The necklace, I mean. Does it suit me?"

He took her hand, leading her in a circle around him. "It becomes you. I think the next time we're invited to Whitehall to sup with the king, you should wear it . . . with the sleeping gown of course."

He sounded so serious that it was a moment before Jillian

laughed. Then he swept her into his arms and her heart swelled. She was going to have Duncan's baby. He was going to take her to the American Colonies; they were going to have many healthy children. And he was going to love her. She was certain of it.

He brought her close to him and nibbled at her earlobe. "Shall we go to bed, wife?"

She rested her hands on his chest, looking up at him. "Actually, I thought I'd call for a bit of bread and honey. I'm terribly hungry."

"After what you ate for supper?" he teased.

She gave him a push. "Well, I'm not just eating for myself now, my lord. I have to think of your son."

"Or daughter," he corrected.

She nodded. "Or daughter."

He waved. "Don't call for Atar or a servant." He took her hand. "I'll make you something to eat."

She let him lead her to their bedchamber door. *"You will?* I've never seen you set foot in the kitchen since I came here. I wasn't aware you knew where it was."

He grabbed a lit candle as they went through the door and into the darkness of the cold hallway. "No need for me to cook here. But in Maryland—"

"Ah, yes. The land of milk and honey. The land of glory and riches," she teased. "The promised land . . ."

He swatted her backside as they went down the steps. "In Maryland," he went on, "I cook my own meals often."

"You've no servants besides your man?"

"In the house?" He led her down the dark staircase, holding her hand tightly. "Only one. Most everyone else works in the tobacco fields. Labor is shorthanded there. That's why I'll be taking bondsmen back with me."

"It's a woman?" she asked, wondering if some things were better left unsaid. Will had once inferred that Duncan had a leman back in the Colonies.

"Yes. Her name is Morning Glory."

"An Indian?"

"Mm-hm."

"And she cleans your house and cooks?"

They turned at the bottom of the steps, headed for the kitchen wing. "Out with it, Jillian. Ask what you wish."

"Does she only cook and clean or does she . . ." Jillian searched for a lady-like word, then exhaled. "Hells bells, Duncan! Do you sleep with her?"

He tightened his hand around hers. "Yes."

They walked down the hallway in silence for moment. She was trying not to feel jealous. Duncan was older than she was; he'd been alone a long time. Of course, he had sought the release of a woman. "Well," she said finally. "At least you're honest, which is more than I can say for most men. My cousin Elizabeth hadn't been married three months when her husband had two of her maids pregnant." When Duncan didn't say anything, she looked at him. "Children?"

"No. I have no living children, illegitimate or otherwise."

Jillian wanted to ask him what would become of Morning Glory when he arrived in the Colonies with a pregnant wife. But she didn't. She would bide her time; and once she arrived in Maryland, Morning Glory would simply have to seek employment elsewhere. That would take care of that!

They entered the kitchen and Duncan lit the candles on the great candelabra that hung over the center of the room. The kitchen was warm from the fireplace with its banked coals. The entire room smelled of cinnamon and flour.

"So, what's your pleasure, wife?" He set her down on a stool at the worktable and went to the food cupboard, peeking inside. "Boar's tripe and herring?"

She pretended to gag.

He looked into the cupboard again, feigning seriousness. "Blood sausage with thyme gravy?"

She stuck her finger in her mouth, grimacing. "Bread and honey. Just bread and honey."

"I know, I know. I have it!" He pulled out half a pie. "A slice of eel pie with mint jelly?"

She threw herself onto the table that was sprinkled with a fine layer of flour and pretended to be in the throes of death.

A minute later, Duncan appeared at her side with a loaf of the day's bread and a jar of honey. He put a pot of water on to boil, and the two shared bread and honey and tea and laughed and talked for another hour.

Finally, Duncan extinguished the candles and, together, hand and hand, they retired to their bedchamber to make love.

Daphne studied the ivory chessboard. "You'll break her heart, you big fool."

Duncan crossed his arms over his chest, defensively. He had dreaded having this conversation with his grandmother, and rightfully so. Still, he felt he owed her an explanation. "It's best for her and the child."

"Stuff and nonsense!" Daphne picked up her rook, then replaced it in contemplation. She glared across the game table at him. "Better for them or you, grandson?"

"The Colonies are not a place for delicate women."

"Jillian? Delicate? The same delicate woman who crawled beneath a collapsed scaffold to save your sorry arse?" She gave a snort of derision. "Besides that, a woman's place is with her husband. She can keep him out of trouble that way."

Duncan shook his head. "You don't understand, Grandmother. The supplies are short. The winters are harsh. She would have little female companionship."

"So take Bea. Marry her off there. Or I could go. I've been contemplating it. I think I'd like to see this blessed Maryland of yours." She picked up the rook again, this time setting it down precisely in a new position.

"With all due respect, madame, the thought is absurd.

You don't understand the hardships. I'd ask that you would trust me in my saying my wife would be better left here in London caring for you."

"Horse shit." Daphne slapped the gaming table. "You're a coward, Duncan Roderick. I hate to say it, but it's the truth of the matter!" She pointed a ringed finger. "You're running."

He laughed without humor, glancing away. "I never intended to take my English wife back to the Colonies. It was never my intention."

"You thought you were going to marry some bit of fluff, get her with child, and forget her. You thought you were marrying Beatrice. I understand. Many an Englishman has done the same. They've been doing it since time began. Some run off on their adventures across the oceans. Others just ship their wives to the country, only visiting them for an annual breeding."

"Grandmother—"

"Don't you *grandmother* me! Hear me out. You may well have intended to leave your wife. It would have been wrong then, but acceptable. But I'm telling you, boy, you leave *this* wife, you leave this redhead, and you will never ever put your life back together. You will never forgive that bitch of a mother of yours, and you will never heal."

Duncan rose out of his seat angrily. "You'll not change my mind."

"Then you're a bigger fool than I thought." She frowned, shaking her head of red ringlets. "I don't know why you're so afraid. Jillian loves you."

He exhaled. "She doesn't love me. She's infatuated, perhaps. But she doesn't know me. She doesn't know the things I've done."

"Martyrdom can be a lonely life, child." Shaking her head, she pulled a handkerchief from her sleeve and patted her rouged lips. "She loves you as no woman will ever love you. And if you weren't walking around with your head tucked under your wing, you'd realize you love her, too."

He started for the door. "This is a pointless conversation. I came to inform you of my departure out of respect for you, madame. I am the head of this family, and you all will do as I see fit."

"Fool! Fool!" the dowager called after him, fluttering the handkerchief. "You think you have regrets now? Just wait. Your only chance at forgiving yourself, forgiving Constance, is with Jillian and the life you could have with her."

"Good day, Grandmother. It will still be a fortnight before I sail." He stopped, his hand on the doorknob. "I'd like to tell my wife myself, so I'd ask that you not discuss the matter with her or her sister until I have."

Then Duncan went out the door and closed it softly behind him. But rather than immediately starting down the hallway, he leaned against the wall. His hands were shaking, though why, he couldn't fathom. The dowager meant well, he knew, but her words echoed in his ears like a Tyburn Hill death sentence.

Of course he didn't love the chit. He was fond of Jillian. She was amusing; she was entertaining. But he didn't love her, damn it. He would never love her, or any woman again.

Images of the day he was captured flashed through his head. He smelled his sister's warm blood on his hands. He heard a small boy call for his mother. He saw the Iroquois brave running straight for him.

Duncan squeezed his eyes shut violently, balling his fists at his sides, forcing the memories back into the recesses of his mind.

Love Jillian? Certainly not. He'd made that mistake once. He'd neither love nor trust another female again.

Jillian rested on her side beneath the warm coverlet, reading a book, waiting for Duncan to come to bed. He seemed preoccupied tonight, not himself. The emotional bond she had sensed for the last week felt strained. He was distantly polite, inquiring about her health, concerned for her well-being, but cool and detached.

Jillian reread the same paragraph from Chaucer's *Book Of The Duchess* for the third time and finally gave up. She marked the book with a blue ribbon and set it on the side table beside the bed. She needed to be able to concentrate to read Chaucer. "Duncan."

"Yes?" He didn't look up from the charts spread across his small desk.

"Could I ask you a question . . . a personal question?"

She heard him exhale. "I suppose."

"Will—"

"I said I wasn't interested in discussing Galloway."

"No. It's something he said. He referred to a *her*. He said he wouldn't betray you. He said he wasn't *her*."

Duncan looked up at the wall ahead of him, apparently lost in thought.

"Whom was he speaking of, Duncan?"

After another moment of silence, he replied. "My mother."

"She died in the Indian attack with the rest of your family, right?" she probed gently.

Duncan blew out his candle and came out of the chair, wood scraping wood. "No."

Jillian blinked. She could have sworn Duncan said they were dead, they were all dead. "She's alive?"

He began to disrobe. Still, he made no eye contact with her. "Aye. She lives in Maryland with her husband and other children."

"You have half-brothers and sisters? You never told me."

"I'd rather not speak of this, Jillian."

Jillian couldn't resist. "Duncan, what did Will mean when he said he wasn't your mother? What did she do?"

He blew out the candles on the mantel and came to the

bed, leaving a trail of clothing behind him. "Put out the candle. I said I don't want to talk about this."

Jillian opened her mouth to speak again, then closed it. Again, she sensed when she had penetrated far enough into his past. Bit by bit, shred by shred, she was piecing Duncan's life together. She sat up, blew out the last candle, and then snuggled beneath the warm blankets beside her husband.

She lifted his arm and ducked beneath it, drawing close against his chest. She refused tonight to let him withdraw as he often did when his past was discussed. She kissed his shoulder blade. "I missed you today," she whispered in the darkness. "I thought you'd never come home from the shipyards."

He said nothing.

Jillian sighed, stroking his bare chest, thinking of the multi-colored tattoos beneath her fingertips. She had finally come to the conclusion that it was not the tattoos that he hated as much as what they represented. What that was, she didn't know, but she could feel she was drawing closer to the truth.

"Duncan?"

"Please, Jilly. No more talk tonight." He smoothed her hair.

Jillian could feel him reaching out for intimacy, not just sex, but real intimacy. He needed her. Even if he didn't know it, she knew it.

So there was hope.

She lifted up on her elbow to look at him in the darkness. Slowly, she lowered her mouth to his. He didn't respond immediately; but when he did, it was with fierce abandon.

Duncan threaded his fingers through her hair, pulling her closer, thrusting his tongue between her lips. Jillian sensed he was angry, but not with her. He ran his hand over her bare back, her buttocks.

When they parted to breathe, she dropped her head to his chest, pressing hot, fervored kisses to the muscular plane.

"Jilly . . . Jilly . . ." She heard him murmur.

She slid her leg over his and boldly climbed on top. So many times Duncan had comforted her with his body, why couldn't she do the same for him with her own?

She kissed his mouth; she kissed the tattoo on his cheek. She nibbled his earlobe. She pressed warm kisses to the pulse of his throat, all the while moving her body against his.

Kissing him solidly on the mouth, she straddled his hips, already feeling him growing hard beneath her. The feel of his hot flesh against hers ignited the familiar flame of desire in her. She leaned forward and he raised his head, his mouth meeting her nipple.

Jillian moaned softly. She liked this being astride.

He sucked one nipple into a stiff nub, then the other. Despite the chill in the air, Jillian flung back the blanket, feeling nothing but the heat of their passion.

She was stroking him now, her thighs against his. She could feel him throbbing, hard and hot against the softness of her woman's place. And she could feel her own body growing hot and slick with want of him.

He kneaded her buttocks with his callused hands. She lowered her mouth to his male nipple and suckled as he had suckled her.

She heard him moan and call her name.

She kissed him again and again, moving her body against his. "I won't leave you," she whispered. "I would never betray you, do you hear me, husband?"

The she lifted up, and guiding his shaft with her hand, she took him inside her.

As Duncan moaned with satisfaction and Jillian struggled to catch her breath, her veins pulsed with desire, desire that demanded release.

Duncan rested his hands on her hips, and she began to move to a rhythm that was only theirs. She could hear their labored breathing, mixing as one, as they drove closer to that pinion of pleasure they both knew was somewhere in the distance.

Jillian flattened her body against his, molding her soft contours to the male hardness of his frame. She stroked him, stroking herself, calling his name. Faster they moved, closer to sweet ecstasy.

Jillian suddenly attempted to slow the rhythm. She was losing her concentration on pleasing Duncan. Her own throbbing need was overpowering.

Duncan caught her hips, refusing to let her slow down. Another stroke and Jillian's world burst into a thousand shards of glorious light. A heartbeat behind her, she heard Duncan groan and felt him thrust one last time in release.

Jillian's muscles contracted and relaxed again and again in ultimate pleasure. A moment later, she found herself on the bed beside Duncan, cradled in his arms. He was brushing the damp hair off her forehead, holding her close, kissing her face.

"I love you," she whispered, her eyes still closed.

He pressed his finger to her lips, still breathing heavily. "Don't say it," he answered softly, his voice choked with emotion. "*Please* don't say it, Jilly."

She opened her eyes, looking up at him, sensing his withdrawal even as she spoke. "But I do, Duncan. I love you."

He sat back on his pillow to stare up at the ceiling, no longer touching her.

She rolled over, refusing to let him separate them so quickly. "I know you don't love me, not yet. But that's all right. Right now I have enough love for the both of us. But someday . . . someday—"

"Jillian, you're not going." His voice was cool and distant.

"What did you say?" She stared at him in the darkness, knowing she must have misunderstood.

"I said, you're not going to Maryland with me. You never were."

Jillian grabbed a bolster from beneath her and hit him as hard as she could across the face. "You son of a bitch!"

Sixteen

Giving him a shove, Jillian leaped out of bed. "You lied to me."

He threw the bolster and it soared through the air, hitting the floor and sliding under his desk. "I didn't lie." He sat up. "I never said you were going! *Never.*"

She padded, naked, to the fireplace and thrust a candle into the flame. She wanted to see his face. *The bastard! He was going to leave her.* The wick of the candle flared, and feeble yellow light shadowed the room. "Every time I mentioned our going to the Colonies, you never said any differently. You let me believe I was going! You even said Bea could go with us!"

"I didn't want to argue with you." He ran his fingers through his hair. "I wanted you to be happy with the time we had together."

"What?" She dropped a hand to her still-slender waist. "You didn't think I would notice when you went off and abandoned me?"

"I am not abandoning you! Don't say that." He gritted his teeth. "My tobacco plantation is in the Colonies. That's where I belong. You belong here with the fine house, money, and servants that I'm providing for you. Why the hell did you think I let you spend that bloody fortune to repair the house? So you would be comfortable. So you would be happy."

She refused to be diverted. "You never told my father you

intended to leave me here in England. He'd not have permitted the union if he'd known you would be leaving me."

Duncan sat up and swung his bare feet over the side of the bed. "Your father had no choice. He could never have repaid his debt to my family."

She stared at the floor. "Son of a bitch," she whispered. Then she looked up at him. "I won't stay here. I don't care about the hardships, or the Indians. I don't care if I have to live in a dirt-floor cottage, milk my own cow, and make my own butter. I want to go with you," she shouted fiercely. "I want this child to be born on the land you love."

"It's out of the question, Jillian." He walked around the bed and picked up her night rail. "It's cold. Put this on."

"Don't touch me." She snatched the flannel robe from his hand and slipped into it, covering her nakedness. "Why won't you even discuss the matter with me?" She knotted the tie on the robe securely. "Why do I have no say?"

He removed a man's silk banyan from his clothes press and tugged it on. "You have no say because you are my legal wife. A man's wife must follow her husband's bidding; it's her duty."

"And what, pray tell, is the husband's duty?" she fumed.

"To protect and care for his wife and their children."

"Saints in hell, Duncan! And you think you're going to be able to do that from thousands of miles away?"

"I'm protecting you by leaving you here in London with my grandmother. You couldn't possibly cross the ocean in your condition."

"So, we'll go after the baby is born."

"No. You're not going." He shook his head. "You were never going."

She thrust the candle into the candlestand and threw up her arms. "This is absurd. It's an absurd conversation."

"Jillian, there's no need for a conversation. The decision was made before I arrived in London. Don't you hear what

I'm saying? *I never intended for my wife to accompany me to Maryland.*"

Jillian was afraid she might cry, but she was too angry for tears. "I cannot believe you'd do this to me." She shook her head. "I thought you cared for me. I thought maybe . . ." She wiped at her eyes. "I thought that maybe in time you would come to love me."

He stood at the door, his face a mask. He shook his finger. "I never promised that, Jillian. Never."

She turned her back to him, a sob rising in her throat. "I was never anything more to you than a brood mare."

"That's not true. I care for you. That's why I'm leaving you here where you'll be safe. I'll be back in two or three years. You'll have the child to keep you company."

She whipped around. "And what of the child? You don't want to be here to see him or her grow up?"

"I'd make a poor father. I think we both know that." He put his hand on the doorknob. "I'd make as poor a father as I have a husband."

He was running from her and her love again. But this time he would cross the ocean to escape.

He turned the doorknob and the paneled door swung open.

"Duncan," she whispered. she was at a loss. She didn't know what to say or what to do. She didn't know how to stop him. She only knew she must.

Jillian started after him. "You're abandoning me."

He stiffened visibly. "I said, don't say that!"

"You are. You're leaving me. You've got some fear of people abandoning you, so you just drive us all off. Your grandmother, Will, me . . . you're abandoning us before we have the chance to abandon you."

"Don't say that!" he shouted, his voice reverberating off the plastered walls. "You don't know what you're talking about! You don't know what she did."

Jillian took another step toward him. He was losing control. She knew she should back off, but damn him to hell and back, she was tired of always tiptoeing around this mysterious past of his. "You're right, I don't know what happened. So, tell me! It was your mother, wasn't it?"

He was shaking his head back and forth. He no longer seemed to be entirely with Jillian. His thoughts were at another place, in another time.

"When the Mohawk came," he said in a voice that sent a chill down her spine, "my sister and I were playing a hide-and-find-me game." He looked at Jillian, but she knew he didn't see her. "She must have gone outside. She cheated."

Jillian wanted to reach out to Duncan to comfort him. Her heart ached for the boy he had been, yet she feared she would break the spell if she touched him. She stood her ground. She had to know the truth. She had to know so that she could help him.

He shrugged, his movements not quite his own. "I couldn't find her. Then I heard the musket-shots. I heard the war whoops, the women screaming. My father ran through the kitchen with his weapon. He never made it out the door." Duncan pointed mechanically to the center of his forehead. "A war club, here." He paused, as if seeing his dead father for the very first time. Then, haltingly, he went on.

"I hid under the kitchen table, coward that I was."

"You were just a little boy," she whispered.

"I could hear the screaming. Musket-fire. The hogs squealed. They were slaughtering the animals, too. For the sport of it." He wrapped his arms around his waist. "When I didn't hear any more sounds, I went out of the house the other way. I walked up into the field. That's when I saw my little sister . . . raped . . . scalped." His lower lip trembled. "They peeled off part of her face. I don't know why."

Jillian caught her breath.

"That was when I saw him. The Mohawk. He was coming toward me, his bloody war hatchet in his hand. There were dried human fingers hanging from the handle. I was so scared, Jilly, that I couldn't move. I knew I should run—" He shook his head slowly. "—but I couldn't. I just couldn't.

"Then, out of the corner of my eye, I saw my mother." He smiled as a boy would smile. "She was on a horse. She was coming to get me. She was going to save me from the red savages. She saw me. She saw the Mohawk." His face hardened suddenly. "She . . ."

Tears ran freely down Jillian's cheeks. "What?" she whispered.

"She looked me in the eye; she looked at the Mohawk, then she wheeled the horse around and rode away." He lifted his hand weakly. "Mama . . ."

Jillian didn't know what to say . . . how to comfort him. She couldn't imagine his terror. "But he didn't kill you."

"No. I wish he had. I've wished it a thousand times." He looked at her. "Instead, he took me home and adopted me. I became his son as if I were of his blood. I became one of them." His last words came out with such a hatred that it frightened her.

Jillian started toward Duncan, but he shrank back. "Go to bed," he said. Then he turned away and, before she could reach him, he had disappeared into the darkness of the hallway.

Jillian thought about following him, but decided it would be better to leave him to himself tonight. It had to have been hard for him to tell her that story, that hideous story. Tomorrow, she would go to him. Tomorrow, she would convince him that he had to let her go to Maryland. Tomorrow, she would fix everything.

So, wearily, Jillian returned to her bed and slept, all too aware of the empty place beside her.

It was early morning. She still wore her sleeping gown and robe. The moment she'd woken, she'd come downstairs in search of Duncan. She'd assumed he'd slept in his office, but the room had been empty. Mysteriously, his maps and charts were missing.

Jillian paled. "Gone? What do you mean? Gone where?" She stood at the door of the orangery, watching the dowager water a lime tree.

"Gone to the docks, coward that he is. Woke me at dawn to say goodbye."

Jillian froze as the dowager's words slowly sank in. "Goodbye? You mean he left already? He left without telling me?"

The dowager moved on to the next tree. "He wasn't supposed to go for another fortnight. He didn't even take that Atar with him. The manservant came down ill this morning, so he's leaving him behind to follow on one of Duncan's own merchant ships."

"But why didn't you wake me?"

"He made me promise I wouldn't. Said I would be interfering in his life." She chuckled. "You've got my grandson running scared."

"Me? It was his idea to go to Maryland without me. I thought I was going." She gripped the door frame, feeling faint in the knees. *He'd gone without her. He didn't care. He hadn't even said goodbye.* "I *wanted* to go to the Colonies with him."

The dowager peered through a leafy branch in the tree. "I thought as much." She shrugged. "But what are we poor, helpless women to do?"

"Do?" Jillian stepped into the orangery, the warm, humid air hitting her full in the face. The glass-walled room smelled of oranges, limes, and lemons. "I'm going to Maryland, that's what I'm doing."

"Are you?" Daphne moved to the next tree and plucked a dead leaf, playing the devil's advocate. "But how? He says he's leaving on the evening tide. He won't wait for the passenger ship to sail. It's some merchant vessel. He didn't say which one."

Jillian tightened the tie on her robe. "I'll find him."

"He won't let you on board."

"I'll stow away."

"That's my girl." She winked. "It's the red hair. I've had confidence in you since the first day you set foot in this house and set Algernon on his ear."

"I won't let Duncan leave me behind," Jillian said, as much to herself as to Daphne. She looked up at her. "He told me about his mother. Last night. He told me what she did." Jillian followed her around the tree. "Why didn't you tell me?"

"Wasn't my place, child. Besides, it wouldn't have been the same, coming from my mouth as his. He hasn't told but a handful of people, not in twenty-five years, he hasn't. My grandson must care for you deeply, else he wouldn't have told you."

"Oh, certainly." Jillian was awash with doubt. "He cares for me so deeply that he's run off to the Colonies without so much as a goodbye."

The dowager came around the tree. "You have to understand something about Duncan, Jillian. The man hurts inside."

"I know that. And I want to help."

"That's the trouble. He can't let go. He can't forgive himself."

"Forgive himself for what?" Jillian opened her arms in confusion. "He was a child. His mother left him, and he was forced to live among savages."

"He says he became one of them."

"To survive."

Daphne shook her head. "He says he did terrible things in the name of survival. He thinks he should have died in the field with his sweet sister."

"That's ridiculous." Jillian rested her hand on her hip. "What terrible things did he do?"

"I don't know, and I don't know that I'd tell you if I did.

All I know is that the Earl of Cleaves is going to have to forgive himself before his past kills him."

Jillian sighed, staring off into the lush greenery of the orangery. "I'm with child, Daphne."

"He told me this morning."

"Would I be risking the baby's life if I made the journey."

The dowager's eyes narrowed speculatively. "How far gone are you?"

"About two months."

She threw up a hand. "I rode a camel across a desert eight months gone with Duncan's uncle. Did him no harm."

"How long will the journey take if I make it on board this merchant vessel?"

"Three to four months by the southern route you'll be taking. 'Course you might find another vessel willing to take you by the northern route in less time." She slapped her thigh. "Wouldn't that be something, to beat the smug bastard there?"

"No." Jillian was emphatic. "I have to be with him. I have to make him understand that I'll never leave him." She looked at the old woman whom she admired so greatly. "I love him."

The dowager smiled. "Then go. Go and have a good life."

"I hate to leave you."

The old woman kissed her wrinkled palm and blew Jillian a kiss. "I'll be fine, sweetling. Go, go, and take that sister of yours." She chuckled, reaching for her watering can again. "Marry her to one of those redmen if you have to, but see her wed. Do that for me."

"I don't know if she'll dare go."

"She'll go. For you, she'll do it."

Jillian smiled. "Thank you."

Daphne ducked beneath the branch of a lemon tree with the agility of a woman half her age. "What for?"

"For your advice. For your support."

"Stuff and nonsense. What else are the old and weary here for but to show the young the path?" Then she turned away, moving on to the next plant, and Jillian ran out of the orangery. She had a million things to do, and the first involved an audience with Will Galloway.

"This is wrong," Beatrice whispered, hurrying down the dock behind Jillian, who walked behind Will. "Father will be terribly angry that I've gone. That you've gone."

"Think, Bea," Jillian whispered harshly. The salt air and the heady scent of stagnant water assaulted her nostrils. "When was the last time we heard from Father or Mother? I don't mean to be cruel, but they consider their work done. We won't be terribly missed, you or I." Jillian didn't mention her parents' relief at no longer having to try to find their eldest daughter a suitable match. There was no need to hurt Bea's feelings any more than necessary. Jillian could speak the truth without speaking the whole truth.

"But what of Daphne? I—I should stay and care for her."

Jillian stopped and spun around, both hands occupied by large, heavy carpetbags. *Only what they could carry,* that was what Will said they could bring. The merchant vessel would have very little room for passengers. The quarters would be cramped. The only reason there would be room at all for them was that the captain of this particular ship had altered the vessel so that he could carry a few passengers with each trip as a means to earn extra money.

"You can stay if you want, Bea." Jillian set down one of the bags to ease the ache in her shoulder. "That's up to you. But you heard what the dowager said. Your best chance at finding a husband is in the Colonies. Besides, I need you."

"Hurry," Will called under his breath "The dockworker I bribed won't wait. Seven on the hour is when he said he would load the last crate. The ship sails on the tide at eight."

Jillian scooped up her bag and ran down the uneven

planks of the dock to catch up. In the shadows, she saw a rat scuttle by. She prayed Beatrice hadn't spotted it.

"Wait for me," Bea murmured. "I'm coming! I'm coming."

"That's the sport," Jillian whispered over her shoulder. "This is an adventure you'll never forget, sister."

"An adventure I'll regret is more likely." Beatrice stopped to stare up at the hull of a merchant vessel that loomed over their heads. "Is this what we're going to sail on?"

By the light of the shipboard lanterns and the torches that illuminated the dock, Jillian could make out the gold letters that bore the ship's name. *Kelsey Marie.* It was a three masted Dutch-built flute, Will had informed her. The length was fifty feet on the keel, with a beam of sixteen feet. He had assured her the *Kelsey Marie* had crossed the Atlantic many times and was as seaworthy as any vessel.

"This is it," Jillian reassured her sister. "Duncan is on board. Will confirmed it."

"Hurry, ladies." Will stopped near a stack of barrels and waved them on. "I see the boy now. They've already got the pulleys in place to load the crate. Are you coming?"

"We're coming, we're coming." Jillian followed in his footsteps to the stern of the *Kelsey Marie.*

Will told Beatrice and Jillian to wait while he went to speak with the dockworker who had agreed to help them. The two sisters watched nervously, from a distance, as money exchanged hands. Then Will waved them on again.

Before Jillian knew what was happening, she, her sister, and Will were seated inside a five-by-ten-foot wooden crate and the side was being nailed on. Suddenly, they were immersed in darkness.

Beatrice gave a start as the dockworker sank the first nail home.

"It's all right," Will assured them. "He's just putting enough nails in to keep the crate shut. When we're ready to show ourselves, there'll be no problem getting out."

Jillian heard the squeak of rope against rope. The box shifted and creaked ominously.

Beatrice grabbed Jillian's hand and hung onto it.

"It'll be all right," Jillian whispered as the crate was lifted and swung precariously in the air. "We're going to be fine. I'm going to be with Duncan, and you're going to find yourself a handsome tobacco planter."

As the crate went higher and began to swing toward the deck of the ship, Jillian looked through the darkness to where she knew Will sat. Nervous energy coursed through her veins. She was so intent on reaching Duncan that she wasn't even afraid. "Everything's happened so quickly," she said. "I haven't had a chance to thank you, Will."

"No need." His voice came out of the darkness. "I'd had enough of London. Enough to last me years."

"But your things—"

"Not a problem. What little I own of value will be shipped. I told you, the arrangements have all been made. It's time I returned to the Tidewater, too. It's my home now, just as it's Duncan's and will be yours."

In their preparation to stow away, neither Jillian nor Will had mentioned what had taken place between him and Duncan. "But your friends . . ."

"There was no one to say goodbye to. All I have is Duncan, and you. What have I got to lose? I just hope that once I get the Colonial Devil trapped on the bowsprit, I'll be able to talk some sense into him."

The crate was beginning to lower. They could hear the shouts of sailors as the last of the cargo was loaded on board ship.

"He'll have to listen to you then, won't he?" she asked, hoping he read the support in her voice.

"If he doesn't, I guess I'll just have to push him overboard into the ocean, won't I?" His laughter came easily. Then after a moment, he whispered. "Shhhh. We'll touch down on the deck in a moment. The sailors will have to strap us down. We wouldn't want them to hear us." He tossed a blanket to the two women. "Cover up, my ladies. It's going to be a cold, damp night."

Seventeen

That night in the crate, on the deck of the *Kelsey Marie,* was the longest Jillian had ever spent. She slipped in and out of sleep due to sheer exhaustion, but was plagued with nightmares. She dreamed Duncan wouldn't take her back. She dreamed he set her afloat on a raft in the ocean. She dreamed her baby was born, a boy, with his father's bear claw tattoo on his cheek.

Dawn's light was just beginning to seep through the cracks in the crate when the gentle roll of the ship began to change. Within minutes, all three occupants were fully awake and clinging to the sides of the crate to keep from sliding to and fro with the movement of the ship.

Will said they were hitting rougher water, that it wasn't unusual. Jillian hung onto Beatrice, huddling under the wool blanket for warmth, and prayed she had not made a mistake in coming after Duncan.

By the dull morning light, Jillian could make out her sister's face. She was as green as one of Daphne's houseplants.

Jillian reached under the blanket to take Beatrice's hand. "Bea?"

"Oh, sweet heaven, Jilly, I feel so sick," she muttered.

"Are you going to be ill?"

"I—I don't know." She panted, pressing her hand to her stomach. "I haven't eaten since yesterday noon."

Jillian dug through the closest carpetbag and pulled out

a bundle of bread wrapped in a linen napkin. "I've sweet muffins and water. Would that make you feel better?"

At that moment, Beatrice turned her head and delicately wretched into the corner of the crate.

Will groaned.

"Hush," Jillian hissed, stuffing the muffins back into her bag. "It's rough. She can't help it if she's sick!" She got up on her knees, trying to comfort poor Bea.

"I told you this would be no picnic at Banstead Downs, Jillian," Will said from his corner. "I told you to think twice about bringing her."

Jillian hugged her sister, smoothing her damp hair. Beatrice was sweating profusely. "It's all right, sweetheart. I'll take care of you."

Beatrice moaned and pressed her face into Jillian's shoulder.

"We've got to get her into a bed," Jillian whispered to Will.

"No. It's too soon. If they find us now, Duncan will just order the ship back to the dock. I told you when we agreed to try this, a full twenty-four hours in the box is required. And even then, I can't guarantee the captain won't turn back. It depends on how hefty a bag of coins the good Earl of Cleaves offers him, I suppose."

Beatrice lifted her hand weakly. "I'm fine. Really. Just let me sleep. I don't want to ruin this for you. I won't."

Holding Beatrice with one arm, Jillian retrieved a bottle of fresh water from her bag. "Will, have you a knife?"

"Yes, why?"

"Give it to me. I want to make a compress."

Will crossed the short distance between them at a crawl. "Want me to help?"

"No." She took the knife, speaking coolly. She was annoyed that Will didn't have more compassion. "I can do it myself."

Will retreated to his corner. "Sure stinks in here, now."

"Hush!" Jillian chastised. "Count your luck it's not you." She tore a square from the bottom of her shift with the aid of Will's knife and saturated the cloth with water. "There. How's that?" she asked Bea, as she pressed the cloth to her perspiring forehead. "Better, dear?"

Beatrice could manage nothing more than a limp nod.

After a few minutes of silence, Will spoke. "This wasn't a good idea." He cradled his head. "I should never have agreed to this crazed notion of yours. Your sister's not up to it."

"She's only seasick. We'll be fine."

"How about you?" he asked. "Feeling ill?"

"I'm fine." The truth was, Jillian was a little queasy, but she refused to give in. She'd not get sick. She just wouldn't. She had to stay well so she could care for Beatrice.

"Duncan will have my head if you get sick or injured. For that, I vow, he'd never forgive me."

"I said I'm fine," Jillian repeated, wedging herself into a corner of the crate so she wouldn't sway with the roll of the ship.

She could hear the howl of the wind and the splash of the water that now surrounded them. Dampness seeped from the walls of the box. From somewhere in the distance she could hear the faint call of one of the ship's crew as they trimmed the sails.

"Promise me that if you feel poorly, you'll tell me."

"I promise."

He chuckled in the semi-darkness. "You lie."

After a moment she laughed with him, any anger she felt toward him dissipating.

"It's not fair," Will chided.

"What?"

"That Duncan found you first. I'd have married you in a heartbeat, Jillian."

She laughed at the prospect. "You and I wed, indeed!"

"Well, it's not *that* funny! I could have provided for you

as well as he can. Well, not as well, but certainly comfortably."

Jillian only laughed harder. "Oh, I'm sorry, Will." She dabbed at a tear in the corner of her eye. He was right. It wasn't that funny. It was just nerves that were making her behave so foolishly. "I didn't mean it as an insult, only—"

"Only you love him. You love the Colonial Devil, the lucky bastard."

She looked at him through the gloom. It had never occurred to her before that Will might find her attractive. She was flattered. "I do, Will, I do love him," she said gently. "More than I realized, until he was gone."

He picked at the sleeve of his doublet. "And I as well." Then he looked up quickly. *"I didn't mean it that way."*

"I knew exactly what you meant," she answered evenly. "I'll not judge you, Will Galloway. It's not my right, and it's not Duncan's either. You've been a good friend to him and to me. He shouldn't have treated you as he has."

"I forgive the devil." He drew up his knees to lean on them. "It's not his fault. It's all this crap with his past. The Mohawk. His mother."

Jillian's arm was beginning to ache with pinpricks from the weight of her sister's limp body. She shifted Beatrice carefully. Her sister slept on. "He told me what she did."

"Damn shame, isn't it? What's really a shame is that Duncan can't get over it. He can't accept the fact that Constance was a piss-poor mother. Somehow in that twisted mind of his, he blames everything on himself. His capture, his Indian wife's death, the baby's death, even his brother's."

"What brother? I thought he only had the one sister who died in the attack."

"He had an Iroquois brother."

"Oh," Jillian said softly, looking away. The ship was beginning to rock more violently. The carpetbags slid across the floor of the crate. "There's so much I don't know about Duncan. So much I don't understand."

"You can't expect to understand what he doesn't. All you can do is love him, Jillian."

She nodded. "That's all either of us can do, isn't it?"

Jillian's words were barely out of her mouth when Beatrice sat up and was violently ill again. Comforting her sister as best she could, Jillian looked at Will, but said nothing.

Hours passed. The sea grew rougher; the ship pitched harder, and Beatrice seemed to grow sicker. Either water was beginning to splash onto the deck or it was raining, because the blanket Jillian and Beatrice covered themselves with was growing wet. Even in her cloak and heavy woolen skirts, Jillian was cold.

It had to have been sometime in midafternoon when Will finally crawled from his corner toward the two women.

He touched Beatrice's forehead. "We need to get some water in her."

"I've tried. She can't keep it down."

He crouched, steadying himself with a hand pressed against the wall behind Jillian's head. "Men die of dehydration."

"Die of seasickness?" Jillian laughed without mirth. "Surely you're not serious?"

Will pulled his timepiece from inside the waistband of his breeches. "It's not yet three."

Jillian looked at her sister. She was pasty white, her skin cool and clammy, and she was shivering uncontrollably. Jillian knew what Will was thinking. If they made their presence known now, the ship might turn back.

Jillian looked at her sister, then back at Will. "We've got to get her out of here."

"Agreed." He crawled back to his corner and pulled a claw hammer from his single bag. He immediately began to work on the edge of the crate.

Beatrice barely stirred at the sound of the banging.

True to his word, Will had the wall of the crate loose in minutes. He gave the crate one hard kick, and the wall fell.

The first thing Jillian saw was a crewman in a black wool coat, staring at them with a mixture of surprise and fear.

Will jumped out of the box and reached in for Beatrice. "I need some help, here, man," he said, taking over completely. "Can't you see I've a sick woman, here?"

"Stowaways," the sailor murmured, adjusting his wool stocking cap so he could get a better look at the two women. "I—I'll have to tell me captain."

"All in good time. Now help me get her out of here."

The sailor hedged, but when Will caught his sleeve, he jumped into action.

As Will took Beatrice from her arms, Jillian stared out onto the open deck. She could tell that they were on the stern because the boat deck loomed before them. It was just beginning to rain. She could barely see the difference between the gray sky overhead and the gray sea that stretched out on every side of them.

The ship rocked violently as Jillian crawled from her hiding place, dragging Beatrice and her bags behind her. She could hear the waves splashing against the hull and onto the deck. Suddenly the *Kelsey Marie* didn't seem as large as she had at the dock.

Quite a crowd was beginning to gather. Sailors circled the packing crate, staring in awe. One brave soul with two tarred pigtails reached in to help Jillian with her carpetbags.

Will slung Beatrice over his shoulder, trying to steady himself on the rolling deck. She lay slumped and motionless like a worn rag doll. Waves crashed against the ships hull, nearly drowning out Will's voice. "The lady's in need of a bunk, boy. Show me the way."

Jillian hurried behind them, shivering beneath her cloak. Overhead, the canvas sail cracked and snapped ominously in the bitter wind. Not halfway across the deck, a man of obvious authority appeared. The response of the sailors indicated he was the captain.

"Where did you come from, might I ask?"

Will halted before the captain. "My apologies, sir. We were in a bit of a hurry to reach the Colonies. We've coin to pay our passage, I assure you."

The captain was a tall, thin man with a head of curly blond hair and a close-cropped blond beard and mustache. He was dressed all in black wool with a military cap on his head. "This is highly irregular," he shouted into the wind. "Stowaways can be criminally prosecuted. I could feed you to the sharks if I wished."

"We can pay well," Will insisted. Then he named a price.

Jillian blanched. She had had no idea the cost of such an expedition. She had no money to give Will. She had no money but Duncan's and a small dowry she had sewn into the hem of her petticoat.

The captain immediately appeared less hostile. "Well, it just so happens that we have a lady traveling with us. There're only two racks, so the three will have to share."

Jillian stepped forward, lowering her head against the blinding rain. "Sir, I must ask you. Have you a passenger by the name of—"

"Jillian?" A voice that could belong to no other cut through the wind.

Jillian looked up to see Duncan stomping toward them. "Galloway, what the hell is going on here?"

Duncan had shed his veil, leaving his tattoo plain for all who cared to stare. He had discarded his gentleman's clothing and now wore plain broadcloth breeches, an unbleached muslin shirt without the stock, and a black wool cloak. It appeared that when he left the dock at London, he left behind whatever shred of Englishman he had been. Gone was his periwig; his dark hair rippled down his back. Jillian had not realized how long it had grown since she'd first met him.

She brushed past the captain, Will, and her sister. "Duncan, you can't blame him. This was my idea."

He took her arm none-too-gently. "You shouldn't have

come," he hissed. Then, "Captain, we'll have to turn the ship around. My lady-wife will not be accompanying us."

"Turn her around?" The captain squinted in the driving rain. "Are you as mad as they say? Do you see which way the wind blows, Roderick? 'Twould be suicide to turn back now." He shook his head emphatically. "Lady or none, we head for open sea and hope we can outrun the storm."

Jillian had to suppress the urge to smile smugly. She had won! She had found Duncan, and the ship would not turn back.

"I'll pay you," Duncan shouted, not to be bested. "Whatever you ask. Christ, I'll buy the ship, Adam."

The captain shook his head, already turning around, and headed for cover below deck. "The *Kelsey Marie* is not for sale. Not for any price. And she'll not be turning back." He threw his hand up. "Do what you will with your wife, Roderick. Throw her overboard if it suits you."

The captain signaled to Will. "Bring that one this way. There's no cabin for you, sir. You'll have to sleep with the crew, but the price will not change," he warned.

Will followed the captain, leaving Jillian to stand on the rolling deck, her carpetbag in her hand. From the look on Duncan's face, she feared he might do just what the captain had suggested. He might well throw her overboard.

"What the hell are you looking at?" he bellowed at the sailors who had gathered around. "Have you no tasks to keep this tub afloat?"

The men immediately skulked away, much like the rats Jillian had seen on the dock.

Jillian stared at Duncan. She no longer felt the chill of the wailing wind or the dismal rain. She refused to be the one to break eye contact. She refused to admit she'd made a mistake.

Duncan opened his mouth to speak, then clamped it shut. He snatched the carpetbag from her hand and took her arm, leading her across the slippery, wet deck.

Jillian followed Duncan down a narrow ladder below the deck, then down a passageway barely wide enough to accommodate her husband's broad shoulders.

"You shouldn't have come, Jillian," he repeated like a chant under his breath. "You shouldn't have done it."

Jillian said nothing until he pushed open a door and stepped over a small ledge into a cabin. She followed behind him. The room was tiny, eight by eight feet, perhaps, and spartan. On one side was a narrow bed that hung by ropes from the wall. On the opposite side was a desk and stool. Duncan's maps and charts littered the desk and floor around it. The room smelled of polished wood and wet wool.

He slammed the door behind her so loudly that she jumped.

"Well?" he demanded.

She spun around. "Well, what? You left me and I wasn't ready to be left. I wasn't ready to give up on you, Duncan. You're my husband. The vows were until death do us part, not the bloody ocean!"

"This was Galloway's filthy scheme, wasn't it?"

She frowned. "You don't honestly believe that, do you?" She scrutinized his face, reading a mixture of anger and incredulity. "I said I wouldn't be left behind."

"Yes, but women say things," he scoffed. "I never thought—"

"You never thought I'd follow through with my word?" She removed her damp cloak. "Well, you've a lot to learn about me, haven't you husband?"

For a moment, Duncan actually seemed speechless. He picked up her carpetbag and tossed it onto the bed. "I cannot believe you did this. If someone had told me this would happen, I'd have laid every coin I owned against it and thought it an excellent wager."

"I suppose you'd have been a poor beggar then, wouldn't you?" She didn't mean to be smug. But it annoyed her that after the months they had been together, he still didn't realize the strength of her convictions. He didn't understand that she truly loved him.

When he turned to face her, he let his hands fall at his sides. "So now what do I do with you?" he asked, much of the power and anger gone from his voice.

She studied him from where she stood, three feet from him. She lifted her arms lamely. "Accept the fact that I'm here and make the best of it? Accept the fact that I'm not going to be as easy to discard as you'd anticipated?"

To her surprise, he laughed. Then he put his arms out to her and pulled her close. She melted into his embrace, savoring his warmth.

"Oh, Jilly . . ." He smoothed her tangled, damp hair. "You shouldn't have come. You should have just let me go. It was for your own good."

"But I love you," she cried passionately. "I want to be with you."

He sighed. "But don't you see, I can't love you like you want me to? And it's not you, sweetheart." He kissed the top of her head, almost pleading with her. "Understand that it's me. I just don't have it in me."

She clung to him, holding him tightly. "It's not true," she whispered, fighting tears. Her heart ached for the pain she knew he felt. "Give yourself time," she whispered, reaching up to stroke his cheek, where the tattoo would forever be emblazoned. "Give us a chance, that's all I'm asking."

Eighteen

The *Kelsey Marie* caught the north winds off Portugal and headed for the American Colonies by the southern course. As the captain had stated, there was no turning back. Like it or not, Duncan was bound for home with his red-haired English wife at his side.

Despite Duncan's anger that Jillian had followed him, they fell easily into a shipboard routine. With Beatrice almost constantly ill and wanting no company, Jillian spent most of her time with Duncan, alone, in the tiny cabin they shared. The only time he allowed her to set foot above deck was when he accompanied her, which, due to the weather, was rare.

The truth was, after Duncan had gotten over his initial fury, he found himself almost pleased to have Jillian along. She sure as hell made a better cabin-companion than Atar. To his surprise, she was fairing well in the confinement of the cabin. She never complained of boredom or claustrophobia. She occupied herself with the chest full of books Duncan had brought with him. Oddly, he found himself comforted by Jillian's presence. With her beside him, he no longer had to fight the nagging suspicion that Algernon might make another sorry attempt to regain the Roderick fortune. Algernon and his whining voice was nothing but a bad taste in Duncan's memory now, along with many others.

Sometimes, to break up the boredom of the hours aboard ship, Duncan escorted Jillian to the captain's cabin for the evening meal. But he preferred not to share his wife's laughter with the captain, his first officer, Mrs. Amstead (the other female passenger), and Beatrice, if she could manage to get out of bed.

By remaining alone with his wife, Duncan could also avoid Will, whom he still refused to converse with other than when absolutely necessary. As far as he was concerned, Will had betrayed him. Perhaps he had not been in on Algernon's little stunt in New Forest, but Galloway had betrayed him by association just the same. Duncan refused to discuss that matter with either him or Jillian. He didn't think he needed to justify his sentiments. When the ship docked in Maryland, Galloway would go one way and Duncan another. The friendship was over.

So, most days, Duncan and Jillian remained in their own cabin, trying to keep warm around the small brass box the cabin boy filled with hot coals. Here the turmoil of the past months in England and the future that lay ahead in Maryland seemed far removed. Here, alone in the cabin with Jillian, Duncan felt he could lower his guard. It was a well-needed rest.

Duncan watched absently as Jillian, seated at the table, gave a tug on her second layer of wool stockings and reached for another slice of bread. In the crew's berthing area he had found a table only as wide as a man's shoulders, and installed it in the center of their cabin. There he and Jillian took their meals and played cards. The only trouble with the table was that, because it was not fastened down as the desk and bed were, it slid back and forth with the rolling rhythm of the ship. When the seas grew rough, Duncan had to tie it to the desk with a length of rope.

Jillian bit off a piece of bread and, licking the honey from her fingertips, turned the page of her book. Duncan imagined the taste of her mouth and his thoughts strayed. The best way he and Jillian had found to pass the hours was making love on the narrow bunk they shared. To his never-ending surprise, Jillian's appetite for bed sport matched his own.

Duncan pushed aside the Chesapeake Bay map he was copying. How could he concentrate on correct measurements with Jillian sitting there, honey sweetening her sensuous lips? "Are you eating, again, wife?" he teased.

It was a running joke between the two of them. While her sister Beatrice spent most of her time lying in her rack with Mrs. Amstead nursing her, Jillian continued to be in perfect health. Even when the sea grew so rough that Duncan felt queasy, Jillian's stomach remained unaffected. She claimed it was the freshly baked bread and sweet honey she consumed along with cups of strong tea sugared with the same honey that kept her well. He was beginning to think the woman just couldn't be defeated. Not by distance, not by the sea, nor by his own foul moods.

"I'm hungry," she retorted. "The baby's hungry."

"The baby?" He rose from his chair and walked behind her to rub her shoulders. "Your waist is no thicker than it was the day I married you. I've a mind to have you treated by the ship's surgeon for worms."

She laughed, tucking a strip of bread crust into her mouth. "Now, you complain I'm thin. In a few months, you'll be complaining that I'm too fat." She set down her book and leaned back against him with a sigh. "Mmmm. You're just never happy, are you?"

"Well, I wouldn't be so quick to say that. I'm always relatively content when you . . ." He whispered into her ear, and her hair tickled his mouth.

Jillian chuckled sensually. "Oh, is that what you've a mind for, now? And I was going to ask if you wanted me to beat you at a hand of cards."

"I didn't say that was what I had in mind, but since you offered." He slipped his hand beneath the wool cloak she was forced to wear almost constantly into the low-cut neckline of her woolen gown. It was true, her abdomen had not yet expanded, but he couldn't help but notice the recent swell in her breasts. She had the most beautiful breasts he'd ever seen, and they fit perfectly in his cupped hand.

Jillian leaned her head against his chest, baring the creamy skin of her neck. Duncan kissed the pulse of her throat. How it was that this woman could smell like spring flowers in the dead of winter on a ship crossing the ocean, Duncan couldn't fathom. When he closed his eyes, her scent reminded him of the patches of flowers that grew around his house in Maryland. She reminded him of the home he longed for.

Jillian turned her head and kissed his cheek. Like the other men aboard ship, he had given up his razor upon setting sail. His beard, which grew in red, was beginning to thicken and now covered his bear claw tattoo. Jillian said she liked it. She said it tickled when he kissed her in certain places.

It was just those places he was thinking of now.

She turned in her chair to face him and raised her hands to rest on his shoulders. Their mouths met and Duncan thrust his tongue between her lips, anxious to taste the honey she'd consumed.

He was not disappointed. She tasted of rich fireweed honey and desire for him.

"Let me escort you to a place where you might be more comfortable," Duncan whispered in her ear. Then he took his lady-wife by her hand and led her to their ship's rack.

Standing beside the hanging bunk that swung gently with the roll of the ship, Duncan lifted Jillian's cloak from her shoulders and laid it over the wool blanket. At night, they added their cloaks to the covers for extra warmth.

Jillian turned to him, smiling, her face already flushed in anticipation of their lovemaking.

How she could look at him with such devotion, Duncan couldn't comprehend. She claimed she loved him. Perhaps it was true. But if she knew the truth, if she knew the horrors he'd witnessed, hell, he'd committed, she would despise him.

But even knowing that, Duncan couldn't keep himself

from her. He was finding it more difficult each day, not just to resist her physically, but emotionally. She constantly hammered at his soul with her innocent questions, her laughter. He knew what she was doing. She was trying to discover what was inside his black heart. She was trying to make him fall in love with her. And he feared, deep inside his soul, that she was succeeding.

"Duncan," Jillian whispered as she lifted her chin to meet his mouth.

Her hands, which grew more experienced in pleasing him each day, grazed over his cloak, making their way to his shirt.

Her warm fingers found the bare patch of skin between the neckline and his Adam's apple. She unlaced the ties and slipped her warm hand inside.

Duncan sucked in his breath as she brushed against the already-hardening nubs of his nipples.

He nipped at her earlobe as his fingers found the hooks that ran the length of her sturdy wool gown. He had to give his wife credit where credit was due. She'd certainly packed appropriately for the cold journey across the Atlantic. She had nothing but heavy wool gowns and underthings. It seemed to Duncan that it took hours to unclothe her. But then, that had become part of the delicious ritual, hadn't it?

Again their mouths met greedily. Duncan fumbled to push her gown off her shoulders. She yanked his shirt over his head, tossing it carelessly to the floor. Next came her stays and an armful of woolen petticoats.

Finally, he was reaching her warm skin.

Duncan kicked off his boots, then gently pushed her back onto the bunk so that she sat on the edge. She was wearing nothing now but a sheer shift, her thick wool stockings, and a pair of riding boots.

"Hurry, Duncan," she murmured in his ear as he tugged on her boot. She ran her hands over arms covered with goosebumps.

"Hurry because you're anxious to have me?" He brushed his lips against hers. "Or hurry because you're cold?" The second boot removed, he tackled her ribbon garters and stockings.

She giggled, her voice husky with passion. "Both."

He removed one pair of stockings and started on the next. "Hell's bells, Jilly. How many pairs are you wearing? We'll reach Port Royal before I get you undressed."

"I'm just trying to keep warm. Of course, we could do it as we did yesterday, me fully clothed and you with your breeches around your ankles."

When he looked up at her, she was laughing, and it occurred to Duncan that if only he had her strength of spirit, perhaps he could laugh as she did, again. "I'll keep you warm," he assured her.

"All right," she whispered, taking her stockings from his hand and adding them to the growing pile of discarded clothing on the floor. "Stand up."

So, he stood, exhaling as her hands moved from his hips to the tie of his black woolen breeches.

He leaned forward to kiss her soft, tumbling hair. He loved it down as she wore it now, pouring over her shoulders like some magical red waterfall of the tropics. She didn't know it, but at night when she slept, he stroked the red locks, reveling in the silkiness between his fingers. The Mohawk had claimed redheads to be touched by the spirits, and honored them as such. Perhaps, somewhere deep in his mind, Duncan still believed such superstitious nonsense, for surely he was enchanted.

Jillian tugged his breeches down over his hips and he felt his member spring forth, released from the confines of the fabric.

She leaned to help him pull his feet from the breeches, and he felt her cheek brush his throbbing, tumescent shaft. Christ, if he didn't get a hold on his thoughts, he'd ejaculate before he ever took her. Duncan didn't know how she did it, but the moment he got Jillian naked in his arms, he felt like a fourteen-year-old boy again, lying with his first woman. At times he felt he was bumbling, yet he couldn't get enough of her.

Duncan stepped out of his breeches, and the cold air of the cabin hit his backside. "Brrr, it *is* cold. Move over," he told her, his mouth against hers.

She ducked her head to press a kiss to the warm place between his thigh and groin. "But I was just getting comfortable here." Her laughter came easily as she wrapped her warm fingers around his manhood.

Duncan groaned, giving her a gentle push. "Get in before we both freeze." That was something else about Jillian. She actually seemed to take pleasure in giving him pleasure. He'd never experienced that with another woman. Oh, certainly they were willing to do what he told them, but it was for the coin or favors expected, never out of love. . . . *Love* . . . Christ, there was that word again! Duncan knew he'd been locked up too long when he was becoming as notional as his wife.

Jillian slipped under the covers and Duncan followed. She wiggled out of her shift and pulled it from beneath the blankets. She laughed as she threw it over his head and it floated to the cabin floor.

"Now, what is it you have in mind?" she purred. Her hand brushed his stomach and drifted lower.

"What have I in mind? Hmmm . . ." He ducked his head beneath the wool blankets to bury his face in the valley between her breasts.

As he took her nipple between his lips, he heard her make soft sounds of pleasure. When they made love, her voice excited him almost as much as the sight of her.

Jillian ran her fingers through his hair. She stroked his back, cradling him between her breasts. He sucked greedily.

Duncan could feel Jillian's body tense with anticipation

as he stroked her hip with his hand, moving lower to her shapely thigh.

"Touch me," she whispered.

"Here?" He brushed her kneecap.

She giggled huskily. "Not there. You know . . ."

"Ah . . . so sorry I misunderstood. I'm here but to be of service, my lady." His fingers brushed the bed of red curls at the apex of her thighs. More magic . . .

Jillian lifted her hips, parting her thighs. She was breathing faster already.

He stroked her woman's mound until he felt her grow moist. She was moaning softly now, moving her hips to the rhythm of his hand.

She lifted the blanket, allowing the light to enter his warm, musky cave. He could see her face now, her eyes closed, her cheeks flushed with pleasure. "Duncan . . ."

It wasn't a request, just a sigh of delight. Duncan loved to give her pleasure. It was one way he knew he could make her happy.

"Jilly . . . Jilly," he whispered. "*Yoruhhote,* Jillian. *Teyottsikhetare,* Jilly." Then he scooted up on the narrow bed so that he could kiss her. As their lips met in sudden urgency, he delved deeper with his fingers.

She moaned, her tongue meeting his in a dance that was theirs alone. She still tasted of honey.

She lifted her hips to the rhythm of his touch, twisting against him. She was warm and wet on his fingers.

Duncan could feel his own desire mounting. . . . Everywhere she touched him, his flesh was aflame.

They were both damp with perspiration beneath the heavy wool blankets. Her face was flushed, her breathing short and shallow. Jillian kept her eyes shut much of the time, but Duncan refused to close his. He wouldn't miss a moment of the pleasure so plain on her face.

She threaded her fingers through his hair, kissing him hard on the mouth. "Now, Duncan. I need you, *now.*"

Slipping his hand from that warm, sweet place between her thighs, he rolled over, holding himself up with his elbows above her. He touched a fingertip to his tongue.

That taste. That musky scent. Thirty years from now, when he was old and gray and most likely alone, he would remember the taste and smell of her nectar. It was forever emblazoned in his mind.

She smiled up at him, her eyes open and searching his.

"Now?" he teased.

She lifted hips so that they met his in perfect alignment. "Now," she whispered urgently.

As if it had a mind of its own, he felt his organ press against her soft cleft, throbbing.

She moved erotically against him, her dark eyes dancing with mischief. "Well, perhaps not yet, my lord." She started to slide out from under him, but he pinned her against the cotton tick beneath them.

"Oh no you don't." He brushed a thick lock of her magical hair off her forehead. "You said the word," he whispered. "It's now, sweet, or not until much later." He guided his thick staff with his hand. He could feel her part her thighs in anticipation of the union. "I've only so much restraint, you know."

She was still looking up at him when, with one thrust, he slipped inside her.

A moan escaped from Jillian's love-bruised lips.

Duncan showered her face with kisses, hesitant to begin the motion that would hurl them both into final bliss. Then it would be over, and he didn't want it to be over. Not so soon. These days he craved the intimacy as much as the act. More foolishness . . .

Duncan lifted his hips and lowered them, meeting Jillian halfway. Faster and faster they moved, he whispering to her with words of encouragement, she filling his head with her moans of pleasure.

All too soon the act was done, both were spent, and,

reluctantly, Duncan disengaged himself from her and pulled her into his arms so that she could cuddle as he knew she liked. They must have drifted off to sleep, because the next thing Duncan knew, there was a sound at the cabin door.

"Yes?" he called out gruffly, embarrassed to be caught asleep in mid-afternoon.

To Duncan's surprise, the door swung open. The cabin boy's towhead poked through the door.

Duncan heard Jillian give a squeak as she pulled the blankets over her head.

"I didn't mean, *yes, come in,* you oaf! I meant, *yes, what do you want!*" Duncan scooped up one of Jillian's boots and hurled it at the door, striking the wall beside the boy.

The cabin boy ducked and jumped back through the door, slamming it shut.

Duncan dropped his head onto the pillow, snaking his arm around Jillian's warm shoulders. She still had her head beneath the blankets, but now she was giggling.

"That's better," Duncan bellowed to the boy on the other side of the door. "Now, what the hell do you want?"

"Um—uh sir, the captain he uh . . . he wanted you to know we've spotted a whale."

"Oh, goody," he snapped sarcastically.

Jillian punched him in the ribs. She was laughing harder now.

"So?" Duncan called. "Was that it? Was that why you disturbed me?"

"The captain . . . he thought you might want to bring the ladies above deck. Thought they might like to see the beast . . . relieve your boredom, he said."

Duncan brushed his hand against one of Jillian's full breasts. "Can't say that I'm bored; what of you, wife?" he said only loud enough for Jillian to hear.

She snickered under the blanket.

"Thank you," Duncan hollered to the cabin boy. "That

will be all." Then as an afterthought, he yelled. "Hey, boy . . ."

"Chuck . . . his name is Chuck," Jillian chided.

"Chuck?"

"Sir?"

"Next time you set foot in my cabin, you make certain you have permission, else you'll be shark bait."

"Yes, my lord."

Duncan heard the sound of the boy's footsteps as he ran, not walked, down the passageway.

The minute the boy was gone, Jillian threw back the covers. "You're terrible! You shouldn't have hollered at the poor boy like that! He was only following his captain's orders."

"He came into my cabin!" Duncan rolled onto his side to face her on the narrow bunk. "He nearly saw my wife naked."

"He caught you unaware. You didn't even have your tomahawk ready. You were asleep."

"I was not! And that's not a tomahawk in my trunk, woman. It's a war club."

She shook her head, smiling. He just couldn't intimidate her these days. Now, Duncan was beginning to wonder if he ever had been able to.

"What?" she questioned. "My great Lord Roderick, the Earl of Cleaves, is such a virile man that he need not even sleep?" She spoke in a pseudo-masculine voice. "The Earl of Cleaves, he does not sleep, he does not eat, he does not spit. He is not human like the rest of us. He is invincible . . ."

Duncan tickled her belly.

She burst into laughter. "He is beyond reproach . . ."

He tickled her harder.

He . . . he . . . he is—" She broke into peals of laughter. "Stop! Stop!" She gave him a shove, pushing him onto his back, and then climbed on top.

Duncan caught her waist with his hands. Already he could feel his desire quickening again. Just the feel of her velvety skin against his made him hard. "This is nice," he whispered in her ear.

She was still laughing as she ground her hips against his. "And this, too?"

He let his eyes drift shut for a moment. "That, too . . ."

"Then how about . . ." She suddenly ducked beneath the covers and slid down. As she moved, she dragged her warm, wet tongue along his belly, burning a path lower.

"Better," he whispered with a groan. "Even better . . ." Then he lifted the wool blanket and ducked underneath with her.

They never made it to the deck that day, nor did they even bother to redress. Instead, the cabin boy brought them their evening meal of stew and biscuits and Duncan and Jillian ate naked beneath the covers, secluded in their own private world.

Jillian stood on the stern of the deck, leaning over the rail, sucking in great breaths of the warm, tropical air. Ever since they had reached the Canary Islands, where they had gone to shore for fresh water, the weather had been warm, too warm to suit her. Weeks ago she had shed her woolen gown for a lighter cotton one and done away with most of her undergarments. They had sailed through the Horse Latitudes and were now bound for the Caribbean, Duncan had explained, showing her one of his maps a few mornings ago. They were making excellent time and, if their luck continued, they'd be in Maryland in another six weeks.

Jillian turned away from the sparkling sea to lean against the rail. High above the deck she spotted Duncan, fiddling with some lines. She smiled at the sight of him. A stranger wouldn't have been able to distinguish him from the other sailors with his wild red beard, unbound hair, and bare chest. He wasn't even the only man on board with tattooed skin. She had noticed that one of the sailors had red dragons that snaked around his chest to his back. Duncan said he'd gotten them in the Orient. He said that tattoos were not uncommon on the open sea.

"There you are!"

Jillian squinted in the bright sunlight and tipped the straw hat Mrs. Amstead had loaned her to see Will approaching. Unlike Duncan, he'd not taken to the casual dress of the sailors. He wore cotton breeches and an immaculate white-linen shirt with a broad-brimmed cocked hat on his head to protect his face from the sun. He truly looked the part of the Colonial planter in contrast to Jillian's *Colonial Devil* of a husband.

"I thought I'd find you here."

She smiled up at Will, annoyed that her husband still insisted upon holding his grudge against his friend. Duncan was definitely beginning to weaken, though. Last night, Jillian had invited Will to come to their cabin for supper and cards. Duncan had nearly been civil.

"I know I'm going to be as freckled as a goose girl, but I just can't resist the sunshine!"

He came to lean against the wooden rail beside her. "How's Bea?"

Jillian rolled her eyes. "About the same. I really think she'd enjoy the sunshine, but she rarely comes above deck with me. She says she can only keep her stomach stable by lying flat on her back. Thank heaven, Mrs. Amstead wants to care for her. I fear I'd be an impatient nurse."

Will laughed. "So where's the earl? I know he can't be far. He barely lets you out of his sight."

She pointed to the foremast.

Will squinted, his tone droll. "Rot his soul, what's he doing up there? Trying to hang himself?"

She shrugged. "Something about tangled lines and an inexperienced crew. I don't think they need him; he just likes playing sailor. After all these weeks of being cooped up with me, I think he's bored."

"Cooped up with you?" Will brushed his hand against her arm. "The man looks happier than I've ever seen him. Do you know that last night when I left, he said he wanted to talk to me about Algernon. Not then, of course, but later."

She crossed her arms over her chest sternly. "It's time he forgave you, and he knows it."

"The man just needs time. I think it would take something more than this to separate us permanently. I know what's in his heart, even if he doesn't. That's all that matters."

Jillian turned to look at him. "You're a good man, Will Galloway." She looked back up at her husband casually. "Perhaps you were right. Perhaps I should have married you instead of him."

He laughed easily. "No. You two were meant for each other. I just want to see Duncan happy. I want to see him at peace with himself. If I could have one wish in this world, that would be it. And I think you're the answer, Jilly."

Jillian took his hand and squeezed it. "I—" She stopped short. Duncan was coming fast down a rope toward the deck.

A bosun's mate had called an alarm. Instantly, the deck was alive with the movement of sailors as they raced to their stations.

Duncan was shouting something to her as he came down the line, but she couldn't make out what he was saying.

Jillian looked to Will in confusion. "What's wrong? What did he see?"

"Ah, hell, sweetheart." Will took her arm. "He's saying you've got to get below deck." He started for the nearest ladder. "It's pirates."

Nineteen

Duncan hit the deck of the *Kelsey Marie* running. All day he'd had a nagging premonition that something was wrong, but it had never occurred to him that the ship might be overtaken. Pirates, God rot their black souls, what were they doing in these waters? They were still a good two days out of the Caribbean. It wasn't like the lazy bastards to sail so far from their lairs.

"Jillian! Go below deck!" Duncan ordered.

Will was leading her by the hand.

"I don't want to go down there, not without you," she protested over her shoulder.

"Will!" Duncan caught up to the two of them. "See what munitions this vessel's carrying. Get your pistol and sword and meet me here. I'll see to Jillian." He took his wife by the arm and pushed her toward the ladder. "Hurry, Jilly, this isn't the time to be stubborn."

She raced down the ladder ahead of him. "Pirates? Will said pirates."

"Aye."

"But this is an English vessel. I thought it was the Spanish they attacked."

"Only if they're English themselves, and not even that precludes an attack on an English merchant vessel." He halted at Beatrice's cabin door and pushed it open without knocking.

Bea gave a squeak of surprise. "Beatrice." Duncan

stepped inside the room. Mrs. Amstead was seated beside the bunk where Beatrice lay prostrate. He waved. "You and Mrs. Amstead follow me. *Now,* damn it."

Mrs. Amstead, a tall, thin woman with a sour face, jumped up from her chair. "What is it? What's wrong, my lord?"

"Jillian?" Beatrice cried. "What's going on? What's happening? Why are all the sailors shouting?"

"Just do as he says, Bea," Jillian insisted. "I'll explain."

Duncan came back out of the cabin with Mrs. Amstead and Beatrice directly behind him. Jillian led the way.

Inside his and Jillian's cabin, Duncan scrambled to locate the two ivory-handled blunderbuss pistols he carried with him. He found them at the bottom of a small leather trunk he kept beneath the bed. He checked to be certain both were loaded. Then he pushed one into Jillian's trembling hands. "Someone comes through this door other than me or Will and you send him to his maker, you understand me?"

She was trying to be brave, and yet Duncan could tell she was petrified. "You keep both women inside here and keep them quiet." He left extra shot and powder on the crumpled bedcovers where he and Jillian had made love only this morning. "Can you reload?"

"I—I'm not certain. If I have to, I suppose I can do it." She held the pistol against her chest, pointed at Duncan.

He reached out with one finger and moved the barrel so that it wasn't aimed directly into his gut. "Good answer, because I haven't the time to show you. When I go, you push the table in front of the door after you've locked it, and then my sea trunk."

She nodded, following him to the door, the pistol still clutched in her hands.

Mrs. Amstead was demanding over and over again in her high-pitched voice to know what was going on. Beatrice, huddled on the edge of the bed, was crying softly, trying not to disturb anyone. Duncan ignored them both.

"It's going to be all right, isn't it?" Jillian pleaded. "You can outrun them?"

"No. They're sailing in a shallow draft brigantine. We can't outrun them, not with the weight we're carrying."

"What of firepower? What about the cannons on the decks? You said just the other day that they could be used if someone tried to attack us. You said the captain kept her well-armed."

"Perhaps." He strapped his sword belt on his hips and slid his cutlass into its sheath. The weight of the weapon added to his confidence. He crammed the other pistol into the waistband of his breeches. From his sea trunk near the door, he retrieved a thin-bladed knife with Mohawk markings across the hilt. He tucked it into the waistband of his breeches, against his back. Lastly, he added to the sword belt his war club, with the blood of past enemies stained in the wood.

"Oh, Duncan. We're not going to die, are we?" She looked up at him with her cinnamon eyes, her red hair pulled back off her face, curling at her temples.

"I sure as hell hope not." Then he kissed her hard against the mouth. "Do as I say, Jilly, and you'll be all right."

He wanted to kiss her one last time, but he didn't. He had become the warrior he despised once again. He could feel it in his bones, coursing hot in his veins. All these years he had not fought, and yet, suddenly, his hackles went up; he tasted the blood of his enemy again as if it were only yesterday he'd fought the Shawnee and Delaware. Warriors did not weaken themselves with emotions or thoughts of women and children. All that mattered was the success of the battle.

Duncan walked out the cabin door and slammed it behind him. "The chest and table, Jillian," he ordered, barely recognizing his own voice. Then he ran down the narrow passageway and climbed the ladder into the sunlight and the smell of battle.

The deck of the *Kelsey Marie* was already swarming with

sailors as they made for their battle stations. Although she was not a fighting ship, like all merchant vessels that traveled through the Caribbean waters, she carried a few light guns.

Duncan had just set foot on the deck when he heard the first sounds of cannon blast from the pirate vessel approaching from the rear. Chain shot hurled through the air, ripping at the *Kelsey Marie*'s rigging. Men shouted, and the bosun's mate's shrill whistle could be heard above the melee.

Duncan ducked as canvas and line fell from the clear sky overhead.

The *Kelsey Marie* responded with the boom of a four-pound cannon volley.

"Sweet heaven, what are they carrying?" Will shouted, running toward him.

Duncan squinted in the bright sunlight. The brigantine was approaching fast, keeping its keel at an efficient angle to the wind, its boarding nets already erected. Her intention was clear. From where Duncan stood, he could see at least a dozen six-pound cannon and a host of deadly swivel guns. The miniature cannons were mounted on the elevated poop deck, giving a commanding sweep of the *Kelsey Marie*'s topside. One was even mounted on the crow's nest high about the pirate vessel, giving it an even better vantage point.

The *Kesley Marie*'s cannons returned fire again and again, belching black smoke, and the air was filled with the stench of burnt black powder.

The first cry of a dying man sent a shiver down Duncan's spine. No matter what language they spoke, all men sounded the same as they died.

"What can we do?" Will questioned.

"Not much, until they board, then slit their gullets." Duncan stepped over a pile of tangled rigging. "See if any of the gunners could use some help."

"Aye, captain," Will answered, forever keeping his sense of humor.

Out of impulse and completely unlike himself, Duncan reached out and squeezed Will's arm. "Take care, friend. Don't let them roast your liver."

Laughing, Will ran off across the deck toward the nearest cannon, shouting he would fetch more lead.

The pirate vessel was now so close that Duncan could make out her name on the hull. *Royal Fortune,* she read, in metallic gold lettering.

Fortune, indeed. If Duncan had his way, the pirate brigantine would sink this day into the depths of the hellish sea.

A sailor crossed Duncan's path with a bucket of four-pound shot for the cannon. "Let me take that and you go back for more," Duncan hollered above the sound of the cannon-fire.

The pigtailed mate nodded, pushing the bucket into Duncan's hand and disappearing aft in the smoke.

Duncan carried the bucket of lead to the nearest cannoneer. "More shot," he told the man who was ramming a powder cartridge down the bore of his cannon.

"Going to need more cartridges, too." The cannoneer never even looked up at Duncan. In battle, every man knew a wasted moment could mean death.

"Christ, almighty," Duncan murmured, watching the pirate ship as she passed the *Kelsey Marie* on her windward side. "She's armed to the teeth. She could take three vessels with that cannon." He and the cannoneer ducked as the deck was sprayed with walnut-size shot from one of the pirate ship's six-pounders.

"Aye," the cannoneer agreed, returning to his task. "It don't seem like happenstance, does it? The way she's attacking, it don't seem like she wants the *Kelsey Marie* or her cargo, else she wouldn't be fillin' the hull so full a' lead."

The cannoneer was right. Something was wrong here, very wrong, but he couldn't put his finger on it. *So what do they want?* Duncan deliberated, the hair bristling on the back of his neck.

The *Royal Fortune* passed the *Kelsey Marie* by two lengths and shivered her sails.

Cries went out about the merchant vessel's deck. The pirate vessel intended to collide with her. The captain shouted to turn the *Kelsey Marie*'s helm hard about to avoid the collision, but it was too late.

The clever captain of the *Royal Fortune* put her helm hard alee and locked her bow into the merchant vessel's rigging. The ship was so close that Duncan could make out the pirate captain in an azure-blue coat as he called, "Prepare to board!"

The collision rocked the *Kelsey Marie* so hard that Duncan had to struggle to stay on his feet. One sailor was hurled from the mainmast to his death on the deck far below. Another went overboard with an agonizing scream as he was crushed between the hulls of the two ships.

Duncan drew his cutlass as the pirates poured over the boarding rigging onto the deck of the merchant vessel like rats fleeing a shipboard fire. There must have been thirty or forty of them, trained fighters, to the two-dozen sailors. As Duncan swung his cutlass over his shoulder and brought it around, neatly detaching the first pirate's head from his shoulders, he realized this would be a slaughter.

Only Duncan's Iroquois training kept him from being paralyzed by the thought of Jillian below deck. If Duncan fell, he knew what her fate would be. He only prayed she had the sense to kill herself before the pirates took her captive.

Duncan stepped over the decapitated body with a sense of detachment and took on his next attacker. The pirate who faced him wore a short white coat over his red-and-white-striped shirt. The white lines of the shirt turned crimson as the tip of Duncan's cutlass sank into the man's heart. As Duncan pulled back his sword from the man's chest, arterial blood gushed forth. Duncan had only to step out of the way to let the pirate fall.

Even in the confusion of the shouting, the musket-fire, and the men's screams, Duncan could tell the crew of the *Kelsey Marie* was no match for the blood-thirsty pirates. The pirate captain was shouting for surrender or no quarter. If he called for no quarter, every man and woman would die.

Behind Duncan, along the port rail, a fire spread, its flames licking the deck. The *Kelsey Marie* was floundering in the waves, taking water on fast.

How odd it was, Duncan thought calmly, *that the sun could shine down so brilliantly, the water sparkle like jewels of a royal crown while men died, screaming in pain.*

Duncan had just turned to search for another opponent when he heard Will's strangled cry. A pirate had him pinned against the starboard rail, his sword knocked uselessly to the deck. Duncan let his own cutlass fall from his hands and, without thinking, he drew his blunderbuss. The shot was true and clean. The pirate pitched forward under the impact of the lead ball to his head, and Will heaved him out of the way. With a gentlemanly touch to the brim of the cocked hat he still wore, Will retrieved his own sword, plus the pirate's, and dove into the center of the fight again, swinging both weapons over his head.

As Duncan turned to search out his next victim, he caught the eye of the merchant vessel's captain. Adam Percy, standing overhead on the poop deck, was bleeding heavily from a shoulder wound, his arm dangling uselessly at his side. Duncan read surrender in his eyes. Of course, a Mohawk never surrendered. He died fighting, but the matter wasn't up to Duncan, was it?

Sure enough, Captain Percy threw up his arms, shouting to the blue-coated pirate captain who sat on his own bowsprit, sipping from a silver flask. "We surrender!" He looked down from the poop deck at the crewmen still standing. "Lay down your arms!" he cried in defeat.

Duncan pressed his back to the side of the poop deck and slipped around the corner. He wasn't ready to surrender, not yet. He wanted to see what these pirates were about, first. He had to come up with some plan to save Jillian, that or he'd kill her himself. He'd not let these monsters take her.

From the other side of the elevated poop deck, Duncan could hear everything that was taking place, though he could see very little.

"You know my orders," the pirate captain called in well-spoken English as he boarded the *Kelsey Marie.* The fire was spreading, but no one made any attempt to put it out. "Find him and be done with it. Salvage what cargo can be salvaged before she sinks and take what prisoners are willing to join us. Throw the others to the sharks."

Him, him who? Who were they looking for? Before Duncan could think, he heard a voice shout, "I've got him. I've found the gentleman! I've found the earl, I did!"

"Kill him."

Duncan's breath caught in his throat. They were looking for him. This was all his fault. And if they didn't have him, who did they have? The answer, horrifying, came to him too late.

"Nooo!" Duncan roared, stepping around the corner of the poop deck just in time to hear the musket-shot and see Will Galloway crumple to the deck.

Jillian stood beside the cabin door, her pistol poised. The sound of the cannon's roar had been terrifying. When the pirate ship had collided with the *Kelsey Marie,* Jillian had been nearly paralyzed by her stark fear. But now, the silence was even more frightening. There was no cannon fire, no shouting. Only the creaking of the boat and the rushing of water somewhere along the hull.

Jillian knew that the ship was taking on water; she could feel by the way it listed to one side. Still, the water had not reached her cabin, so she decided to stay put just a little longer. Duncan would come for her, she knew he would . . . if he survived.

"We've got to do something," Mrs. Amstead whined, wringing her hands.

Beatrice sat on the edge of Jillian's bunk, her knees drawn up. She was no longer crying, only rocking back and forth, hugging herself.

"Hush, Mrs. Amstead. My husband said *stay put,* and stay put we will!"

Just then she heard the sounds of footsteps in the passageway. Men were running and flinging open doors. Wood splintered, and Jillian heard the distinctive sound of water rushing through the passageway.

"Oh, sweet Mary, Mother of God, we're going to die!" Mrs. Amstead went down on her spindly knees. "I'll never live to see my Rupert again."

Jillian rolled her eyes. "Nonsense. I'm not ready to give up yet. You shouldn't be either."

Mrs. Amstead clasped her fingers and began to recite the twenty-third psalm. " 'The Lord is my shepherd, I shall not want . . .' "

Jillian listened, her ear pressed to the wall as the men approached the end of the passageway where her and Duncan's cabin was located.

" 'He leadeth me in the paths of righteousness for his name's sake . . .' "

First, the doorknob turned. Jillian took a step back.

"Someone there?" called a deep voice. "Let me in, else I'll come in after you!"

" 'I fear no evil, for thou art with me,' " Mrs. Amstead moaned.

"Let me in!" A fist pounded on the door.

Jillian took a step back at the sound of the splintering wood. The lock had not held more than a few seconds.

" 'Thou preparest a table before me, in the presence of thine enemies . . .' "

"Bea, get something to use as a weapon!" Jillian ordered, her voice amazingly calm. The door opened a crack, and through it, she could see a giant of a man with a red kerchief tied around his head. "Bea!"

Beatrice leaped up with a stool and stepped around Mrs. Amstead, who was still on her knees in the center of the room.

Jillian watched as the desk and sea trunk slowly slid across the floor from the weight against the door.

"Shoot him," Beatrice insisted in her sister's ear. "Shoot the pirate, Jilly!"

Salt water was rushing in though the crack in the door.

Jillian shook her head. Not yet. Not until he was closer, not until she had him in full view. She only had one shot; she'd make it a good one.

When the pirate finally broke through the door and the barricades, Jillian gave an involuntary cry. He was wielding a sword covered with blood. In the back of her mind, she heard Mrs. Amstead still reciting.

" 'Surely goodness and mercy shall follow me all the . . .' "

Jillian outstretched her arms, aiming the pistol. "Back up or I'll shoot!" she ordered.

Beatrice screamed as the giant sailor swung his cutlass.

The pistol sounded, and the recoil sent Jillian stumbling backward into her sister.

Hit in the shoulder, the giant pitched backward, and Beatrice stepped around Jillian to bring the stool crashing onto his head.

"Petey!" a voice came. Another pirate, a small man with a dark complexion, appeared in the doorway. "Petey!" He looked at Jillian. "You shot my amigo."

Now what was Jillian to do?

The small pirate pulled a derringer from the waistband of his canvas breeches. "Get topside and we will see what the capi'tan will do with you. *Ahora!*" He waved the derringer, going down on one knee to examine his unconscious friend.

"Get Mrs. Amstead," Jillian told Beatrice. "We're going to drown if we don't get up on the deck."

"Drown?" Mrs. Amstead blubbered as Beatrice pulled her to her feet. "What difference does it make? Better to drown than to be raped by pirates!"

Beatrice looked at Jillian, stricken.

"We're going to be all right," Jillian insisted. "I'll find a way to get us out of this, I swear I will, Bea."

A strange calmness came over Beatrice's face. "I know you will, sister."

The small pirate dragged Petey through the rising water to the door and passed him off to another man in the passageway. Then the little man stepped back into the cabin and grabbed Jillian by a hank of hair. He started to drag her toward the doorway. She struggled to keep up in the water that was now knee-deep. Tears came to her eyes as the pirate yanked her hair again.

"I'm going, you little troll," she shouted. "I'm going!"

Duncan went down on his knees to cradle Will in his arms. His friend was still breathing, but barely. "Will, Will," Duncan cried. "Hang on!"

Will shook his head, his eyes closed.

Blood was gushing from his chest wound. Duncan had seen this type of wound often enough to know that he would bleed to death in a matter of minutes, and that nothing could be done.

"Will." Duncan shook his shoulders, not wanting to let him go.

"Too late, friend." Will managed to smile. "They thought I was you," he whispered. Duncan's massive shoulders blocked the view of the other sailors and pirates. "Shhhh." Will lifted a finger to touch his lips, his movement sluggish.

"Let them think they got their man. Play the game and save that pretty wife of yours."

He closed his eyes and Duncan shook him. "Will, Will . . ."

Slowly, with great effort, his friend opened his eyes once more. "Don't be hard on yourself over this . . ." His breath came ragged and wheezing. "Always friends, you and I. Always . . ."

"Oh, hell, Will, I'm—" Duncan halted in mid-sentence. He was gone. Will Galloway was dead.

Duncan leaped up, yanking his war club from his sword belt.

Someone came up behind him and brought the flat blade of his sword down over his head. Duncan went down on his knees at the impact, seeing stars in his head, but he didn't lose consciousness. He couldn't.

Two pirates wrestled his weapons from his belt and tied his wrists together before he had enough wits about him to fight them.

The other sailors from the *Kelsey Marie* were being tied up as well. Will was right. They had mistaken him for the Earl of Cleaves. Who would have thought such a man would be bared to the chest? It was a logical mistake, one that had cost Will his life and saved Duncan, at least for the time being.

Fate . . . the Mohawk said all was fate.

Duncan struggled to remain cognizant. Blood trickled down over both ears. The pirates were gathering the crew members. Jillian. Where was she?

A sudden scuffle broke out in front of Duncan. A musket-blast sounded and the sailor with the dragon tattoos pitched backward to stare up at the sky, unseeing.

Duncan squeezed his eyes shut, trying to get control of his senses.

"Lookie, lookie, there be another one!" one of the pirates declared.

Duncan opened his eyes to stare down the long barrel of a blunderbuss musket. His gaze met the pirate's. A Mohawk died looking into the face of the enemy.

"What are you doing?" asked one of the pirates to the one holding the musket. He wore a filthy blue handkerchief tied around his throat. "The cap'ain said only kill the earlie. He wants the others fer crew."

"Yea, but didn't he say somethin' about a tattoo?"

Duncan knew he should pray to his God above, but all he could think of was Jillian and their child and what would become of them. Why the Christ hadn't he stayed in England with her? Why had he been so stubborn about returning to Maryland? It suddenly occurred to him in crystal-clear irony that Jillian had been right. He had been running from her.

"I know that's what 'e said, and that's why I'm killin' 'im."

The one in the blue scarf rolled his eyes, placing his hand on the barrel. "We already kilt the gentleman and then the one with the dragon tattoos for good measure."

"Yeah, but I want to be sure. The cap'ain said there was an extra shilling for the man who brought the cur down."

The man in the blue scarf raised his hand and turned away. "So fine, Freckles, kill 'im. Kill 'im all if ye like."

Twenty

The picaroon shoved Jillian so hard on to the deck that she tripped and fell. When she lifted her head, she saw Duncan on his knees, a pistol aimed at his face. Her first instinct was to scream, but something kept her from making a sound.

"What the hell are you doing?" a commanding voice boomed.

Stumbling to her feet, Jillian spotted an imposing man with an attractive, chiseled face, in a gentleman's blue coat. His tall, polished boots hit the deck rhythmically as he strode across the deck toward Duncan.

Duncan's gaze darted in her direction, though he didn't move his head. Jillian understood his thoughts as effortlessly as if he had spoken aloud. *Keep your mouth shut,* he told her with his green eyes. *And I may yet live.*

"Freckles. Respond. I asked what you were doing." The tall man spoke the King's English of a London-born-and-educated gentleman.

The pirate holding the blunderbuss pistol on Duncan lowered it quickly. He snatched his knit cap off his head. "K—killin' the prisoner, I was, sir. Killin' the earl."

"I thought *that* was the Earl of Cleaves." The authority figure gestured with a manicured hand.

Jillian followed his gaze. Bile rose suddenly in her throat, and for a moment she feared she would be ill. Will . . . Sweet heaven, it was Will, and he was dead. Dead, like so many men lying on the ship's deck, where blood dissipated in the rising water. Jillian reached behind to take her sister's hand, hoping she understood to keep silent. She didn't dare look directly at Duncan.

"We—I thought 'e might be 'im," the one called Freckles answered hesitantly. " 'E bein' the only one in fancy clothes like yourself, cap'ain."

"And what of that one?" The captain pointed to the sailor with the dragon tattoos, who was also lying dead on the deck, his throat cut.

"Why, he—he 'ad tattoos, cap'ain. Chuma said something 'bout tattoos back in port. I jest wanted to be sure I was gettin' our man."

The gentleman-pirate swore beneath his breath and lifted his hands heavenward. "Why am I cursed with such stupidity around me? Why?" He turned his gaze to Freckles, much as a father addresses a foolish child. "Freckles, if I had a wart on my ass, would you kill me, too?" He flipped his hand. "Just to be certain you got your man?"

Some of the pirates cackled, but one look from their captain silenced them all.

Freckles twisted his knit cap in his hand. "N—no, sir, I would never kill you. Sure not."

"So is that man you're holding at bay the earl or not? Because if he's not, and you kill him, you'll be responsible for replacing him." The pirate spoke slowly, enunciating each word. "I told you, Freckles, as I told you all, that I require more able-bodied men. There will be no needless killing today."

Freckles looked at Duncan, then back at his captain. He shifted his weight uneasily from one bare foot to the other.

"Well, Freckles?" The captain removed a silk lace handkerchief from the sleeve of his doublet and pressed it to his forehead. "How shall we determine if this is the man you seek or not?"

Freckles glanced at one of his companions, obviously at a loss.

The captain sighed with boredom. "Freckles, does this man look like an English earl?"

Everyone aboard the ship, including Jillian, stared at Duncan with his wild red beard and tattooed bare chest. His breeches were torn and soiled; his arms, chest, and face splattered with blood. He looked more like a murdering Saracen than an Englishman.

"Ah, no . . ." Freckles answered after a hard look at Duncan. " 'E don't look like you, sir—you bein' the only gentleman I ever knowed."

"No. He doesn't, does he? So, now what?"

Freckles grimaced. Then, after a second, his face lit up. "I cou'd ask 'im, sir."

The captain pirate swung his fist enthusiastically. "There you have it. Ask him."

Freckles looked at Duncan, narrowing his beady eyes. "You the earl?"

That moment stretched into an eternity as Jillian watched Duncan's face. *No,* she prayed, *say no. Will is already dead. Let him help you. Don't let his death be an absolute waste.*

Duncan drew back his head casually and spat on the deck at the pirate's bare feet. "I looks like a bloody earl to ye?" His tone of voice had changed; his pattern of speech, even his eyes, looked different. There was something savage about them, something feral and untamed. Something that frightened even Jillian.

Freckles looked at his captain. " 'E says 'e ain't the earl."

The captain chuckled. "So ask him if he's willing to join us. If not, feed him to the sharks."

"Aye, I'm with ye," Jillian heard Duncan say.

The crewmen of the *Kelsey Marie* left still alive made no attempt to rectify the error, and Jillian exhaled for what seemed the first time in minutes.

The captain started to turn away, but then on second thought looked back. "Oh, and Freckles?"

"Cap'ain?"

"You can go ahead and join them."

"S—sir?"

"The sharks. You're too stupid to remain on my crew." The captain snapped his fingers crisply, his voice sharp and cold. "Three Eyes! See to it. Toss Freckles overboard and get these prisoners onto the *Royal Fortune.*" He lifted one boot, shaking the water from it. "I fear this fair ship is about to sink."

Freckles screamed as two scoundrels lifted him over their heads and carried him across the deck.

Jillian closed her eyes tightly in anticipation of the splash as the pirates went to heave him overboard into the shark-infested waters.

"Nooo, nooo!" Freckles wailed.

Jillian didn't know what made her react. She should have known better than to interfere. Her life and Bea's were at stake. But she couldn't help herself. "Hasn't there been enough killing for one day?" She took a few steps forward toward the captain, her skirts dragging in the rising water.

"Well, my stars, what was that you said?"

The pirates hesitated at the ship's side, Freckles' body hanging precariously over the rail.

Jillian blinked in the glare. She heard the pirate captain's voice suddenly very near her, but the sun was so bright that she couldn't see anything but his silhouette as he approached. She shaded her eyes with her hand, knowing he spoke to her. "I—I said we've had enough killing for one day. I have, at least. Haven't you?"

The captain held his hand to his heart, dramatically. "A lady? A lady aboard ship?" He lifted his plumed hat from his head and bowed gracefully, presenting a fetching leg. "Heavens, but I do believe I'm in love."

Jillian stared at the pirate, her eyes filled with hatred.

"You think my punishment too harsh for my man."

"Yes," she challenged.

He thought for a moment, then gave a wave of his hand

in the direction of the man about to be thrown overboard. "The lady is right. There's been enough death today. Let him go. I imagine he's learned his lesson."

The men lowered Freckles to the deck. "Thank ye, sir. Thank ye." Freckles groveled.

But the captain paid no attention. His eyes were on Jillian. "I am called Captain Indigo Muldune, but you, my beloved, may call me Indigo." He returned his hat to his head. "That or *my wretched love* would be acceptable."

Jillian made no response. All she could do was stare straight ahead to where Will Galloway lay slumped in death.

"Oh, heavens." The pirate captain touched his cheek. "Don't tell me the earl was your husband. Oh, I am so sorry. Truly I am. I hope you won't take it as a personal affront. It was business, madame, merely business."

Jillian stared at the pirate. "You can't do this. You can't take us against our will."

He sighed. "I agree. The trouble is, that this ship is sinking, my lady." He offered his arm. "So, please allow me to escort you onto my fair ship. She's called the *Royal Fortune*. I assure you, you will be made comfortable."

Jillian looked out on the deck. Indigo was right. Water was rising fast on the deck, and the *Kelsey Marie* was listing hard. The merchant ship wouldn't remain afloat much longer, thanks to the pirates' cannonballs.

Jillian scanned the deck, trying not to be obvious. She couldn't see Duncan now. He'd been led away with the other crewmen, bound hand and foot. She hesitated in indecision. What did she do now?

Play along, of course, just as Duncan had. Really, she had no other choice.

Jillian refused the captain's arm, lifting her chin arrogantly.—"My name is Jillian, Jillian Roderick. You may show me the way to your ship, sir, but I shall require whatever belongings are left of mine below deck, as shall my traveling companions, my sister and Mrs. Amstead."

For the first time, Indigo glanced at the two women behind Jillian. "Ladies." He dismissed them immediately with a wayward glance, snapping his fingers. "Portence," he called to the small man who had dragged Jillian from below deck. "Go back down and see what you can salvage of the ladies' belongings."

"But, cap'ain! She nearly killed Petey, the redhead did."

Indigo broke into a handsome smile, his clear blue eyes sparkling with sincerity. "Oh, dear, and a spine, too." He touched his chest. "Ods fish, but I fear I'm madly in love with you already, madame." He glanced at the pirate, sharply. "Portence?"

"But, cap'ain. She's already floodin' below deck."

He sighed. "Then I suggest you hurry and fetch the ladies' possessions." Then he turned to escort the women across the deck to his ship. "Because this charming lady is going to be my wife."

For two days, Jillian, Beatrice, and Mrs. Amstead remained locked in the captain's quarters aboard the pirate ship the *Royal Fortune.* Several times each day, food and water was brought; a half-grown boy even cleaned the cabin and removed the chamber pot. The three women were made comfortable, just as promised, yet remained completely isolated from whatever was taking place beyond the tiny room.

Jillian saw no sign of the pirate captain, Indigo, or any of his crew. She had no idea what had happened to Duncan and the others. She assumed they remained on board; the only other possibility was beyond consideration.

When Jillian attempted to bribe the cabin boy for information with coins from inside the hem of her petticoat, he refused her and the payment. All he would say was that no amount of gold was worth kissing the bottom of the sea.

Mid-morning on the third day, Jillian heard sounds above deck. There was a great deal of activity: pounding feet, the shrill call of the bosun's pipe, a voice shouting orders. Jillian was trying to ascertain what was happening, but Mrs. Amstead's droning voice made it difficult.

"Hush, Mrs. Amstead, please," she snapped crossly. For more than two days she had listened to the woman's fervored prayers and lengthy Biblical recitations, and she was sorely on edge. It wasn't that Jillian didn't believe in the power of prayer, only that she also believed in doing something for one's self besides wailing about the predicament. "Listen. Something's happening. Do you hear them racing about? The boat seems to be altering its course."

Beatrice rose from the bunk where she had remained curled on her side for most of the journey. "What is it, Jilly?" she asked excitedly. "Have we made a port, do you think?"

Jillian was greatly relieved by how calm her sister had managed to remain throughout their ordeal. Accepting her plight and trying to make the best of it, she had been far easier to deal with than Mrs. Amstead. She had even remarked several times that Indigo couldn't be all bad. She rationalized that he had let them live, hadn't he? It was odd how Beatrice was that way. Despite her weak nature on some points, when a crisis arose, she was able to meet it head-on with surprising strength.

"Perhaps someone will help us! Perhaps, we can escape," Bea offered with enthusiasm.

Jillian walked to the cabin door, locked from the outside. She heard sailors go by in the passageway and could have sworn she heard the pirate captain's voice. She wiped her perspiring forehead with the back of her hand.

It had grown hotter and more humid in the last two days as they'd approached the Caribbean Islands. It was so warm that both she and her sister had shed their petticoats and stockings. Now they walked barefoot about the cabin unencumbered by as little clothing as possible. From their belongings saved from the *Kelsey Marie* they had changed into their lightest cotton gowns and put their hair up on their heads.

Mrs. Amstead, on the other hand, refused to remove any of her proper attire. She said it was inappropriate; so consequently, she spent most of her days seated on a stool, sweltering as she prayed.

"I think you're right, Bea." Jillian listened to the movement beyond the locked door. "I think we've hit port. All she could think of was Duncan. Was he all right? She had missed him so much these last few days, sleeping alone without his arms to comfort her, that she refused to even consider the possibility of life without him.

Jillian heard footsteps approach their cabin, then the sound of the door being unlocked. She took a step back just as it swung open and Indigo appeared, dressed in pale-blue breeches, a loose white coat, and a wide-brimmed straw hat. He was dressed as crisply as if her were about to go bowling on a London Town lawn.

"Good morning, ladies." He bowed. "I hope you've been made quite comfortable." His gaze was fixed on Jillian. "I apologize for not seeing to your needs myself; but honestly, I thought you could use a little time to adjust. I understand that this could be difficult for you." He smiled a handsome smile, opening his arms wide. "So, there you have it."

Jillian refused to acknowledge his charm. "Where are we? Where have you taken us?"

"Why, dearest, we've arrived home. Port Royal, Jamaica, home of the sweetest rum and the most magnificent scenery you have ever laid eyes upon. I just know you're going to like it here."

He spoke as if she were to remain here forever. Had he been serious when he'd told the picaroon that he intended to make her his wife? *God's teeth,* she thought, *I can only handle one problem at a time.* She turned her sharp gaze on Indigo. "What's happened to the crew members?" She went on without hesitation, not wanting him to become suspicious. "As the earl's widow, I'm responsible for their plight. I'm simply interested to know if they've survived with the same care the ladies and I have."

"I commend you for concern for the underlings. If we don't watch after them, who will?" He smiled, flicking a bit of lint from his pressed coat. "For your information, madame, the prisoners will be off-loaded shortly and dispersed where needed. I have a dozen ships, you know."

Jillian arched an eyebrow. "A dozen pirate ships? Heaven's sir, you have become quite profitable at the sake of others."

He chuckled. "Ah, Jillian—I may call you Jillian, may I not, Mrs. Roderick?—considering the circumstances, of course."

She made an exaggerated smile. "Of course."

"Jillian, dear, I do appreciate your sense of humor, though I must correct your term, *pirate.*"

"Picaroon? Picaro?"

"I am not a pirate. I am a privateer, ofttimes called a buccaneer."

She smoothed a lock of damp hair that had escaped her loose coiffure. "So the crewmen of the sunken merchant ship will be forced to join one of your privateering crews."

"Oh, it's not as bad as all that, my dear. I pay my men well for their loyalty." He glanced at the other two women. "Which is your sister, might I ask?"

Beatrice surprised Jillian by taking a half step forward from where she stood near the bunk. "I am, sir." She dipped a slight curtsy. "Beatrice Hollingsworth, your servant."

He lifted his hat, presenting his leg. "Mademoiselle, charming . . . charming." He returned his hat to his head. "And the other lady?" he addressed Jillian.

"A fellow passenger, Mrs. Amstead, bound to meet her husband in the Virginia Colony."

Indigo nodded in Mrs. Amstead's direction. "Well, my darling . . ." He returned his attention to Jillian. "I thought you'd enjoy a breath of fresh air. I'd like to escort you above deck. I want all of Jamaica to see you as we arrive in port."

The thought of going topside into the sunshine, perhaps even seeing Duncan, excited her. "Oh, yes, I'd like that, sir. Just let my sister and me get our hats." She started across the cabin to retrieve the straw hat that had survived the *Kelsey Marie*'s demise.

"No, no, you don't understand. *You'll* be going topside, my love. The other ladies will remain here in my cabin."

Jillian turned, her hat already on her head. She wanted desperately to see if Duncan were all right, but she'd not be separated from her sister. It would be too easy for the pirate to have her carried off that way. "Oh, sir, I'm sorry, then." She removed the hat. "I fear I'll not be able to accompany you without my sister and Mrs. Amstead."

"I'll not go," Mrs. Amstead burst. "I'll go nowhere with a murdering pirate!"

Indigo studied Jillian's face. She didn't blink. After a moment of indecision, he sighed. "How could I possibly resist a beautiful face *and* willfulness? Very well, my darling." He swept his hand. "They may accompany us as well."

Beatrice scrambled to find her hat. "Hurry, Mrs. Amstead," she whispered into the older woman's ear. "We're going topside."

The women stepped back. "I'm not going."

Jillian was just slipping her bare feet into her shoes. "Mrs. Amstead," she snapped, "it's come along or perhaps be carried off by one of them!" She indicated upward with her chin in the direction of the pounding feet.

Mrs. Amstead's eyes grew round with fright. "Heavens! I'll need my parasol. I freckle so easily."

Jillian snatched the woman's parasol from the top of a sea trunk where they'd been drying out their belongings. "Hurry, ladies," she whispered, then walked to the door where Indigo waited patiently.

He nodded, offering his arm. "Madame?"

Jillian considered, then accepted it. She'd do what she had to, within reason, to save herself, her sister, and her husband. She'd come too far to turn back now. "Sir . . ."

Topside, Indigo led Jillian and the other two women to the stern of the boat where they could watch as the ship sailed into the harbor. From where they stood, Jillian couldn't see the prisoners or Duncan.

Her first impression of Jamaica was how crystal-clear blue the water was. It was like perfectly blown glass. From the poop deck she could see below the surface of the water. She spotted brilliantly colored fish and even painted coral, things she had only read about, or heard about from Duncan. What immediately struck her was the heady scent of tropical vegetation. Even from offshore, the hot wind carried the smell of the lush, green foliage and bright flowers, filling her nostrils with the intoxicating scent of the tropics.

The sails filled with the warm winds of the northeast trades, the *Royal Fortune* sailed into the harbor and set anchor in the clear, glassy water of the town of Port Royal. At Indigo's orders, the three women immediately disembarked into a small rowboat and were taken to shore. Jillian didn't want to leave the pirate ship without seeing Duncan, but Beatrice gripped her arm and whispered into her ear. "Play the game, sister, like you said. It's what he would want you to do."

So Jillian rode to shore with Beatrice and Mrs. Amstead. *Duncan could not escape surrounded by water and pirates,* she reasoned. He would wait until they reached solid ground; it only made sense.

On the docks, three pirates and Indigo escorted the women to an awaiting carriage. The dock was alive with the activity of a busy afternoon at a country market. Dark-skinned men and women dressed in colorful robes with baskets of fruit and vegetables balanced on their heads were everywhere. The air was abuzz with soft, liquid voices and foreign words.

"Aha, my carriage." Indigo stepped ahead of Jillian and opened the door to the French-made vehicle with a fringed, linen top. Four white horses danced in their traces. "I'll have you escorted to my plantation, where you can get settled in. I'll be along, shortly, my love."

She gritted her teeth. "Please, do not say that," she said under her breath.

"What? My endearment was not meant as an affront to you. It's only that I'm so taken with you that I'm quite beside myself." He lifted a hand, indicating the carriage. "Please board."

Jillian stepped into the carriage. What else was she going to do, surrounded by Indigo and his three armed pirates? If she managed to escape on her own with Bea in tow, where would she go on this island of foreigners?

Next, Indigo offered Beatrice his hand. When she took it to be aided into the open carriage, he leaned over and kissed the back of her hand. "Another time, another place, mademoiselle," he said softly, "and I would make you mine, my hibiscus flower."

Beatrice blushed like a simpleton, and Jillian rolled her eyes. "Bea! Get into the carriage!" she snapped.

Almost reluctantly, her sister let go of the pirate captain's hand and sat down on the bench across from Jillian. Mrs. Amstead put up her hand to be helped into the carriage, but the captain made no attempt to offer his assistance.

"Oh, heavens—Mrs. Amstead, is it?"

She looked at him from beneath her parasol, still dressed in her woolens, stockings and all. Her face was so bright red and she was breathing with such labor that Jillian feared she would succumb to heat stroke. "Yes," she answered. "It is."

"I fear there's been a bit of a misunderstanding." He tipped his hat, smiling that charming smile of his. "You see, you'll be going along with Chuma here, my second in command.

Jillian didn't know where the black-haired man with skin the color of chocolate and watery brown eyes came from, he just appeared.

"Chuma will see that your belongings go with you."

"No! No," Jillian said firmly, sticking her head out the carriage. "She goes with us, too, Indigo." It was the first time she had addressed him by name.

Indigo glanced at Jillian. "I'm sorry, love; but again, it's merely a matter of business. Now, if you insist Mrs. Amstead must stay, I fear your sister will have to go."

Jillian's gaze met Indigo's. Despite his pleasant tone and polite words, she knew he meant it. She looked at Mrs. Amstead. "I'm sorry," she whispered.

"So, there you have it." Again, Indigo was smiling. "Now, as I was saying—" He turned back to the dark-skinned man, a man Jillian took an immediate disliking to. "—Chuma, you're to take Mrs. Amstead out to Pierre Luz's place. He's paid handsomely for a new wife."

"A wife!" Mrs. Amstead shrieked. "But I'm already married."

The pirate captain never as much as blinked. He went on with his instructions. "I've already received payment, so all you need to do is deliver."

Chuma looked suspiciously at Mrs. Amstead. "She's old, cap'ain. Old and gristly." The man had a slight French accent to his liquid-smooth voice.

Indigo shrugged, answering matter-of-factly. "He'll take her or lose his twenty pounds. God's bowels, Chuma. The man is seventy-eight. How much do you think he intends to use her?"

Chuma frowned, staring at Mrs. Amstead, who was beginning to hyperventilate. "And if he won't take her?"

"Then Mr. Buckler will. He's paid for a wife as well." Indigo brushed Chuma away with his hand. "Go, go, and then see to the merchandise we brought in on the *Royal Fortune*. I'll see you at *Lily's Fortune* tonight."

Chuma grasped Mrs. Amstead's thin arm and dragged her down the dock.

It tore at Jillian's heart to see her go; she had to turn away and cover her ears to block out the poor woman's screams. But Jillian was no fool. She knew when to push the pirate captain and when not to. And she had come too close to losing Beatrice not to be more careful in the future.

With Mrs. Amstead gone, Indigo closed the coach door. "So, there we have it," he declared, dismissing the entire incident. "Now, you'll be escorted to my sugarcane plantation, that's *Lily's Fortune,* named after my dearly departed mother. You'll be cared for there. I do hope I won't be late for supper, darling, but I can make no promises."

Jillian gripped the edge of the open window. "You . . . you're sending us away?"

He patted her hand affectionately. "Don't worry, love; we won't be separated for long." He glanced behind him. "Ah, here come the prisoners now. I must see to them."

The pirate captain swaggered away, and Jillian scanned the bustling crowd in search of Duncan's face. The driver of the carriage was attempting to turn the vehicle around, but the dock was so congested that he was having a difficult time of it.

Through the sea of faces, Jillian spotted a line of white men in chains marching down the center of the dock toward them. She held her breath in search of that familiar face. When she saw Duncan—wild-bearded and dirty, but otherwise healthy—she had to cover her mouth with her hand to keep from crying out in relief. *Thank you, God,* she repeated over and over in her head. *Thank you for saving him.*

Jillian's gaze was fixed on Duncan as the line of prisoners walked straight toward the carriage. He was going to walk right by her! Perhaps even close enough to speak! He would tell her what to do. Surely he had a plan.

The first prisoner marched by Jillian's window and she

turned in the carriage, thinking perhaps she might even touch Duncan. The second man passed. Duncan was next . . .

But when he walked by the carriage, he never turned his head. He could not possibly have not seen her, and yet he never acknowledged her presence.

"Duncan . . ." she whispered.

She knew he must have heard her. But his wild green eyes stared straight ahead, and he passed her without a glance.

Jillian dropped back onto the seat, tears filling her eyes. Her heart was pounding. Her hand went to her abdomen where she knew her baby grew.

What was Duncan doing? Didn't he care about what was happening to her? Wasn't he going to save her from the pirate captain?

Then a thought crept into her head. Duncan had intended to leave her behind in England. He hadn't wanted to bring her to Maryland. He had never wanted her at his side to begin with. So, what was he doing now?

Just saving himself?

Twenty-one

Jillian stood on the verandah on the upper floor, staring out over the tangled jungle that surrounded the manor house of Indigo's sugarcane plantation. She paced back and forth restlessly, the folds of the pale-green organza gown she'd been given fluttering in the hot breeze.

Suddenly nothing seemed real to her. The decaying smell of the jungle was overwhelming, as was its closeness. Though the large, leafy plants that surrounded the house were obviously trimmed back often, it seemed to Jillian that she could actually see the jungle closing in on the outer walls, and on her.

There were huge insects everywhere, flying, crawling. Flat, black beetles the size of her finger crept up the sides of the stucco walls of the great, white house. Small green lizards ran along the tiled floor beneath Jillian's feet, and snakes slithered in the grass on the lawn below. Now, as darkness fell, the air was filled with a cacophony of insect song so loud that it disturbed her thoughts. From somewhere in the distance came the steady, mournful beat of a hollow drum.

"I think it's beautiful here," Jillian heard her sister remark. "Paradise."

Beatrice was dressed in a gown almost identical to Jillian's, her blonde hair swept up gracefully on her head. She was seated on a bamboo chair, sipping an icy tropical fruit drink.

"Beautiful? Are you addlepated?" Jillian paced past her sister, dabbing the perspiration from her throat with a large white handkerchief. "Aren't you hot? I can't breathe here. I can't think."

"No, I'm not hot. I find the warmth invigorating, in fact." She sighed. "Duncan will come for you, Jilly. He'll come for you because he loves you."

She shook her head. "You don't understand. You didn't see his face when he passed the carriage. You know he didn't want me to go to the Colonies in the first place. He wanted to leave me behind, to rid himself of me—of the child, too, I suspect."

Beatrice rose and went to her sister, wrapping her arms around her shoulders and hugging her tightly. Jillian returned the embrace, fighting tears.

"It's going to be all right," Beatrice soothed. "You just have to wait until Duncan finds a way to escape. He'll come for you then, but you have to remain calm, as you've told me to a hundred times before." She smoothed Jillian's damp hair. "No harm will come to you here. You just have to wait."

"No harm?" Jillian sniffed, lifting her head from Beatrice's shoulder. "Did you hear that crazy pirate? He wants to marry me!"

Beatrice lowered her hands to her hips. The white gown had transformed her from a dull sparrow to a dove. "He's taken with you."

Jillian walked away with a groan. "Well, if you think he's so wonderful, have him for yourself! The man is a pirate, Bea. He steals and murders for profit."

"He said he was a privateer."

"Is there a difference in these waters?" Jillian walked to the edge of the balcony to lean on the white iron rail.

Below, a pirate, one of many who guarded the perimeter of the manor house, was sitting on a fallen log, skinning a snake some six feet long. He tipped his hat when he spotted her, then went back to his snake.

"Oh, Bea . . ." Jillian whispered, staring out at the strange jungle that surrounded them. "Why didn't my husband look at me when he went by the carriage today? Just a glance and I could have waited a lifetime for him." She twisted her hands, unable to stop going over and over in her mind what had happened. "If he had cared just a little, if he'd had just a little compassion, he'd have at least looked at me."

"No, he wouldn't. He's not your husband, the Earl of Cleaves, any longer, remember? That man is dead. He's just another crewman from the *Kelsey Marie,* trying to stay alive. If he'd acknowledged you, someone might have become suspicious."

Jillian sighed. "Perhaps you're right."

"I am. Think logically, Jilly. If Indigo suspected that crewman with the red beard was your husband, he'd have had him killed. Duncan knew that. He was playing it safe."

"What you're saying makes sense. I know that." Jillian pressed her handkerchief to her forehead. "It's just that I'm having a difficult time trying to think with my head and not my emotions."

Beatrice went back to her drink. "You're overwrought. Now, hush about this nonsense. You'll make yourself and the baby sick."

Jillian spun around, pressing a finger to her lips. She knew the housekeeper, Maria, wasn't far away; and below the balcony, a picaroon in a red cap stood watch. "We mustn't let anyone know I'm with child," she whispered. "Right now, it's Indigo's infatuation with me that's saving our hides. If he finds out I'm going to have Duncan's baby, he's liable to sell us both as he did poor Mrs. Amstead. I wouldn't—"

"Ladies, ladies . . ."

The distinct sound of Indigo's voice silenced Jillian.

Indigo swept onto the balcony. He was wearing a pair of ankle-length white, wide-legged breeches and a turquoise shirt that fell loosely to his hips. With his suntanned skin and dark hair pulled neatly into a queue, he looked much like one of the natives. "I hope this evening finds you well." He nodded cordially to Beatrice, but then turned his attention to Jillian. "Dearest?"

"I don't want to be here," Jillian stated flatly.

"Well, where do you want to go?"

Jillian's voice caught in her throat. All she could think of was Duncan. Back on the boat, in those days they had shared alone in their cabin, she had thought she and her husband had grown much closer. She had thought Duncan had begun to fall in love with her, even if he couldn't yet admit it. Now, she was riddled with doubt. Perhaps she should have remained in London with the dowager. At least there, the baby wouldn't have been at risk.

"I don't know where I want to be," she whispered, as much to herself as to the pirate, as she stared into the jungle that was now growing dark. "Just not here."

Indigo sighed. "I understand, my darling, that the notion of remaining here with me will take some adjustment. I'm certain you were quite fond of your husband. But in time, your memory of him will fade. *I* will become your protector, your companion, your lover."

Jillian stared dismally into the darkness. The pirate was mad, stark raving mad. He honestly thought she could come to care for him, after all he'd done. The intentions weren't even worth addressing. "Tell me something," she said softly. "You said that the attack on our ship was a business arrangement."

"Yes, purely business."

"Then someone hired you to kill . . . my husband."

Indigo sighed. "I'm ashamed of myself, my darling, but yes."

"Who?"

Indigo leaned against the balcony, facing her. A small green lizard ran along the railing past his hand. "I wish that I could tell you, but I was merely hired to do the job. No names passed hands, only cold coin."

"It was Algernon, of course," Jillian whispered softly. "Duncan's cousin Algernon sent you to kill us."

"No, no, not all of you." Indigo raised his index finger. "There was some discussion of that, but I said I was not a killer of women or children. I have my standards."

She was still staring out off the verandah, but not really seeing the jungle. Behind her, she heard a servant lighting torches, and suddenly they were bathed in soft light. "So what was supposed to be done with my sister and me?"

Indigo clasped his hands, staring down at the tile floor. "It was left up to me, as long as you were never heard from again."

"So, officially, I went down with the ship with my husband."

"Officially, yes."

Jillian didn't say anything else. What was to be said? She and Duncan had both misjudged Algernon. The depth of his hatred ran deeper than either had ever suspected, as did his tenacity.

Indigo glanced at Beatrice. "Mademoiselle, let my housekeeper take you to your room beside your sister's. She has a charming meal prepared for you." Indigo nodded to Jillian. "I do hope you'll excuse my ill manners, but we have private matters to discuss."

Beatrice rose. "Jillian?"

"I'll be all right," she answered without much conviction. "I'll come in to say good night soon."

Indigo clapped his hands softly, and Maria appeared out of nowhere. A thin woman in her mid-forties, she was dressed in a colorful sarong that fell just below her knees.

"Oui, Master?" The older woman nodded her head with respect, but looked Indigo directly in the eye.

"See to Miss Beatrice, Maria. Fetch for her whatever she desires; but remember, her room is to be locked from the hallway."

Maria dipped a brief curtsy. *"Oui."*

Indigo waited until Beatrice had departed and then produced a tiny lacquered black box. "I have something for you, Jillian."

She shot him a cold glare. "I don't want it."

He opened the box as if he could entice her. "Of course you do; every woman from babe to wrinkles likes jewels. Look, here. It's just come in from the Orient."

The light from the torches caught the amber stone of the ring he displayed, and it sparkled like a thousand twinkling stars. It was, indeed, very beautiful. The pirate had excellent taste.

"I want you to wear it."

"I don't want it."

Indigo took her limp hand. "Now, dearest, I will try to be patient; but I must warn you, my patience is not endless. Sulking is not becoming to a woman." He slipped the ring over her finger. "Now, I will allow you a certain time of mourning; but in the meantime, I want you to be civil—pleasant is preferable."

"You expect me to be pleasant when you attack my ship and sink it, kill my—" Her voice caught in her throat as she thought of Will lying dead on the deck of the sinking ship. "You murder my husband, sell off a companion, and now keep my sister and me prisoner, and you suggest I be pleasant!"

"I expect you to adjust as women must. It's all quite simple, really. You were married off to this Earl of Cleaves, and he's dead. I'm sorry. It wasn't meant to be personal. But I'll make it up to you. I want to make you my wife."

"And if I refuse?"

"As much as it hurts me to say this, you'll be sold to another man, dear. I know it sounds cold, but it's simply—"

"Business," she finished for him, sarcastically.

He smiled. "Exactly. I knew we would see eye to eye, you and I, Jillian. You're a bright woman and you're resilient. I knew that the first time I laid eyes upon your lovely face." He took her arm and led her to a table that was being set by two Jamaican girls. "Now, let's be finished with this nasty business of the rules. As long as you please me, you and your sister may stay together here at *Lily's Fortune.* Please me, and whatever you wish for, within reason, will be yours. Displease me, and I'll be forced to send you and your sister on your merry ways. I already know a man on the far side of the island who would greatly appreciate your sister's lovely face. Do you understand my terms?"

Jillian looked up at him, studying his clear blue eyes. His words were not in jest. "I understand," she said softly.

"Excellent. So there we have it. Now, shall we dine?" He pulled out a chair for her and she sat down.

She didn't know what she was going to do. All she knew was that she wouldn't allow Beatrice and herself to be separated. She took her napkin, unfolded it in her lap, and reached for the cold drink one of the little Jamaican girls offered.

Perhaps tomorrow this would all make more sense. Perhaps tomorrow she'd awaken to find this was all a horrendous dream.

"Melon, darling?" Indigo offered her a plate of fresh fruit.

Jillian forced a cordial smile. "Thank you, sir. Now, tell me about your plantation. You say it's sugarcane you grow?"

The hot breeze wafted through the floor-to-ceiling windows of Jillian's bedchamber, and the mosquito netting that covered her carved rice bed swayed. The steady, unending rhythm of the mournful native drums filled the bedchamber . . . filled her head. Haunting voices that chanted rose out of the darkness to mingle with the night sounds of the jungle until they beat as one.

Jillian rolled restlessly on the smooth, cool, linen sheets.

Duncan? Duncan where are you?

She found herself racing through the jungle, barefoot, her long white gown tangled in her legs. Sweat trickled down her face, stinging her eyes.

The Jamaican drums beat faster.

Someone was chasing her . . . something . . .

The overgrown vegetation of the jungle floor suddenly came alive, closing in around her. Vines slithered along the ground, catching her ankles as she ran.

It . . . he was gaining on her.

Duncan! Her mind screamed, but no sound came from her throat.

Jillian flailed her arms, tearing at the thick leaves and branches that blocked her way. Thorns tore at her hair and filmy gown. She beat at the broad, green leaves, refusing to give up, refusing to surrender.

The vines rose out of the ground to grasp her wrists like iron chains.

No, no . . . she screamed silently, fighting the ghostly apparitions. A moment before, the trees that stretched overhead had been harmless coconut palms, pine, and gum; but now they were long-limbed creatures of the dark, humid night closing in on her.

Insects swarmed over her head, buzzing angrily. They flew into her eyes, blinding her; down her throat, choking her. Again and again she broke free of the tentacle-like vines that snatched at her hands and feet, only to be caught again.

And still the unknown force behind her grew closer. She couldn't hear it, or see it, not even when she dared a look over her shoulder. But she knew it was there and she knew it was gaining on her.

A giant snake abruptly shot up out of the tangled path ahead of her. A scream froze in Jillian's throat. Not a snake, but a snake skin, thick and transparent, floating above the jungle floor, its eyes glowing red.

For the first time, a strangled sound escaped her lips. "Duncan!"

A hand came out of nowhere to cover her mouth, to stifle the cry for help.

Jillian fought frantically, trying to tear away the giant hand.

"Jillian . . . Jillian, hush, it's me . . ."

The voice was trying to trick her. It sounded like Duncan.

Jillian struggled toward consciousness, the weight of her dream heavy on her mind. "D—Duncan?" she muttered beneath the hand.

"Who else?"

Jillian's eyes flew open as she sat straight up in the pirate's bed, gasping for breath. "Duncan!"

It *was* he! Sweet Jesus, it was Duncan, half-naked, his face painted with mud and green pulp from leaves.

He knelt among the white sheets, pulling her against his chest. A huge, half-moon hung in the sky outside the window, casting white light across the floor, through the mosquito netting, and onto the bed. He was covered with mud and smelled of the rotting jungle. His leggings had been cut off so that they were not much more than a savage's loincloth, and he carried a curved saber. But Jillian didn't care what he looked or smelled like as she flung her arms around him.

"You came for me! You came for me," she repeated over and over again.

"Of course I came for you," he whispered into her ear. "I would never abandon you. I came for you because . . . because I love you, Jillian."

She lifted her head from his shoulder to stare into his green eyes. She wondered if she were still dreaming. She was almost afraid to speak for fear of breaking the spell. *"What did you say?"*

He smoothed her cheek with his muddy hand. "You're not going to make this easy for me, are you? I said, *I love you,* Jilly." He exhaled. "It took Will's death, it took having you torn from my arms to know it, but I love ye. I've loved you since I first set eyes on you in your father's garden. I was just too stubborn, too stupid, to know it." He was breathing heavily, as if his words had taken great effort. But the tone of his voice was witness to his sincerity. "Will was right, you were right, even Grandmother was right. It's time I stopped being so bullheaded about the past and got on with my life. I can't change what I did, but I can control what I do now."

Jillian grasped a handful of his full red beard and pressed her mouth to his. "I love you, too, Duncan: I love you; I love you." Then she smiled at him mischievously, looking into his eyes. "Though I must admit those were not my feelings that first day."

He laughed softly. "I knew you'd be all right until I got here. I just knew it." Tentatively, he reached to brush his fingertip against her belly. "And the babe?"

She smiled. "Fine."

"Good, now let's see what we can do about finding Bea and getting out of this bloody place."

He scooted back out of the mosquito netting of the bed and Jillian followed him, not yet willing to let go of his hand. "How did you find me?" She went on with nervous excitement. "I have so much to tell you. I know who did this to us."

"Shhhh," he hushed. "We'll talk later, when we're far from this rotting hellhole. Now tell me where your sister is. She's all right, isn't she?"

"Bea's fine. We'll have to go down the hallway. She's in the next room, but it's at the end of the corridor."

"We haven't much time. The entire perimeter of this place is patrolled by pirates with sabers. You would think it was the Tower of London Indigo was protecting, instead of just a futtering, bug-infested house."

Jillian released Duncan's hand to grab up a few of her belongings. "They took all of my clothes to launder," she whispered.

Duncan had walked to her bedchamber balcony to look

out the window through the filmy curtains. He glanced at her. "Wear that for now, then. We'll get decent clothing as soon as we can."

She grabbed a pillow off the bed, removed its case, and began to fill the makeshift bag with the few belongings she didn't want to leave behind—the petticoat with her coin and jewelry sewn into the hem, the mirror and brush Duncan had given her, a tiny book from her childhood, now water stained but still intact.

Duncan came to her side, glancing at the large stone ring that rested at the bedside. Even in the moonlight, she saw him lift his eyebrow. "A gift from an admirer?"

She frowned, glancing away from his camouflage-painted face. "Indigo. He fancies himself in love with me. He's actually been a gentleman." She rolled her eyes. "He wants to marry me."

Duncan chuckled, but without mirth. "Thank goodness I came when I did, eh? Otherwise I'd have had to wait in line."

She took his hand. "Let's go. I'm ready. I've no shoes, but—"

"You'll be better off without them anyway, sweet." He took her pillowcase sack from her hands and tossed it over his shoulder. "We'll have to cut through the jungle into the town. We can't risk being seen on the road." He took her hand. "When we reach Maryland, I'll buy you a pair of shoes for every day of the year if you like." He clasped her hand. "Now, let's get the hell out of here."

Cautiously, he opened the door to the hallway, and stood stock still, staring into the blackness.

"Indigo sleeps downstairs," she whispered. "Everyone's asleep, let's go."

"Shhhh," he hushed.

"What is it? Do you hear—" The instant Jillian's bare feet hit the cool tile, a huge dog leapt from the darkness to sink its teeth into Duncan's arm. A cry of alarm rang out in the house as Duncan fought the snarling cur.

Jillian screamed as the black hallway filled with torch light and charging pirates.

Twenty-two

In a matter of seconds, the corridor was in utter confusion. Duncan kicked the vicious black dog so hard with his bare foot that the cur hit the far wall with a yelp and slumped, dazed, to the tiled floor, its tongue lolling.

The pirates shouted in a mixture of French, English, and Jamaican as they filled the hallway from the stairwell, trapping Jillian and Duncan.

Behind her, Jillian could hear Bea shouting and pounding desperately on her locked bedchamber door.

Duncan drew his saber as the first two brigands approached, their own swords ready-handed.

"Behind me," Duncan ordered Jillian tersely. Then under his breath, "If we can get to Bea's room and out her window . . ."

Jillian nodded in understanding as she retreated down the hallway, protected from the attackers by Duncan's massive form. Though her sister's bedchamber was their only chance of escape, she knew it was not likely they would make it. She didn't understand how Duncan thought they could escape with so many pirates in the corridor, so many surrounding Indigo's house. But she didn't take the time to question the feasibility. She only wanted desperately to escape with him with her and sister still alive.

"Surrender!" the piccaroon Jillian recognized as Chuma shouted, swinging a saber.

Duncan backed up slowly, fighting inch by inch, moving

Jillian closer to her sister's door. But it was still so far, at least fifteen feet.

The corridor stank of burning pitch torches and unwashed bodies. The pirates jabbered in half-a-dozen languages, shouting in the excitement of the moment.

Chuma lunged at Duncan, and Duncan stepped back smoothly, blocking the parry. With the ease of one of the king's own swordsmen, he returned the offensive move with one of his own. The tip of his saber cut smoothly into the Jamaican's arm, and the pirate howled with anger. Duncan barely drew back his saber before another scoundrel lunged, and yet another. Like wild curs, the pack was closing in on him. Metal clanked against metal as Duncan ducked and dove, trying to always keep one step away from the pirates' swords.

Jillian wished desperately that she had a weapon, anything, to help defend herself, her sister, and her husband. Behind her, she could still hear Bea pounding on the door, crying her sister's name, begging to be released.

"We're coming," Jillian shouted. "Hold on, Bea!"

Everything was happening so quickly.

Duncan struck down the pirate she had seen skinning the snake, but others charged over him, crushing him beneath their feet.

Beyond the eight or ten men, Jillian caught sight of Indigo as he appeared in the torch light, dressed in a linen banyon. "Sweet Christ, get him!" the pirate captain ordered, running his fingers through his rumpled black hair. "And don't hurt the woman. God's ass! Can't you do anything right, Chuma? How did he get into my house?" he ranted. "How did he get past the guards? I'll have you all strung up by your gonads, by Christ, I will!"

Jillian rested her hand on Duncan's back. They had almost reached Beatrice's door now. Duncan was sweating profusely, gasping from the exertion. Blood trickled down his chest where he'd been nicked by the tip of a sword, the blood mingling with the ochre paint of his tattoos.

Duncan swung his saber over his head and struck a pirate in a red-knit cap at the neck. Jillian grimaced, squeezing her eyes shut, as blood spurted from the wound, splattering the white stucco wall, Duncan, and the other pirates with the gore. The man fell like a brick; but once again, the pirates paid no attention to their fallen comrade. It almost seemed as if the grisly blood added to their frenzied excitement. It made no difference that it was the blood of one of their own, only that it was a kill.

Jillian was shocked by how savagely Duncan fought. She couldn't fathom how this man who could be so gentle, so tender, could fight with such unabashed ferocity. He swung the saber again and again with swift, calculated movements, moving gracefully, more like a macabre dancer than a swordsman.

"Jillian!" The door rattled over Jillian's left shoulder as she heard her sister shouting frantically. "Let me out!"

"We're coming," Jillian cried, too frightened for tears. "He's come for us! Duncan's here!"

Jillian felt the door with her hand, and she turned to fumble with the knob.

Finally, the lock clicked, and Beatrice flung the door open. Jillian backed in, with Duncan directly in front of her. He made a quick repartee, stepping forward, driving the two closest pirates back.

"He's getting away! Damn you, stupid asses!" Jillian heard Indigo shouting. "Give me one of those frigging sabers and let me cut him down!"

Once the pirates backed up to avoid the deadly blade of Duncan's saber, he retreated rapidly through the bedchamber door and slammed it shut. "Run," he shouted, his voice booming. "Run, Jilly! Take your sister and run! Through the window, into the jungle!"

"Aren't you coming?" She was already racing for the

window, her sister's trembling hand in hers. "I won't go without you!"

"I'll catch up!"

She heard the lock click from the inside.

"This will only hold them a minute. They'll break down the door!"

Uncontrollable tears streamed down Jillian's face. She had lost Duncan once; the thought of being separated again, even for a short time, was almost unbearable. But she ran anyway. She ran for the sake of Duncan's child whom she carried in her womb; she ran for her sister.

Out on the bedchamber balcony, Jillian peered over the iron rail. A stream of moonlight shone a path through the jungle, across the grassy lawn. "We'll have to jump," she told her sister.

"Jump? I can't jump!"

Hiking the filmy skirt of her sleeping gown to her thighs, Jillian threw her bare leg over the painted railing. "Yes, you can, and you will!" She flung the other leg over, holding onto the rail so that she was balanced on a ledge only three or four inches wide. "Come on, Bea! Else I'll leave you here, by God!" She put out her hand to her sister.

After an instant's hesitation, Beatrice climbed over the rail. "I should have stayed in London," she moaned, gripping the iron. "I wasn't cut out for adventure: I told you I wasn't!"

The bedchamber was filled with the sound of splintering wood and crumbling plaster as the door came crashing in.

"Quit your bellow-weathering and come on before the guards see us!" Jillian cried. Then, taking a deep breath, she grasped the bottom of the rail, then the ledge, and let herself down. "Come on! It's not that far when you lower yourself."

Then Jillian let go. A moment later, she felt herself hit the soft grass of the lawn below. She scrambled to her feet. Overhead, Beatrice was dangling from the ledge, the skirting of her semi-transparent sleeping gown swaying in the breeze.

"Jump!"

"I can't," Bea moaned. "It's so far."

Jillian could hear the sound of metal meeting metal as swords clashed again. The pirates had managed to get into the bedchamber.

"Jump!"

Beatrice let go of the ledge and came tumbling down. The moment she hit the soft earth, Jillian was at her side, pulling her to her feet. "We have to run," she insisted, dragging her sister. "Into the jungle. Duncan will find us there!"

A hand clasped a handful of Jillian's tangled hair and she whipped around, knowing even before she looked who it was. He had come from nowhere, out of the darkness.

Beatrice screamed.

"You're hurting me." Jillian breathed, tears of pain stinging her eyes as she turned to see a man's leering face.

"Let her go," came Indigo's voice. "I'll not have women treated roughly!"

The pirate released Jillian's hair and stepped back out of his captain's way.

Indigo made a clicking sound between his teeth. "Jillian, you surprise me." He took her arm firmly. "After our little talk, I would have thought you would have more sense."

She tried to twist away, but he was surprisingly strong. Another pirate came out of the shadows of the house to grab Beatrice.

"Let her go!" Jillian cried fiercely. "This wasn't her fault. It was mine!"

"Get her out of here," Indigo barked.

"No, no," Jillian cried, turning to Indigo, ignoring the pain of his hold on her. She clasped her hands, trying not to become hysterical. "Please, don't hurt her; please, don't sell her! I'll do what you ask. *Anything!*" And she meant it.

"Take her to her room and stand guard at her door and balcony. But lay a hand on her and you die."

"And what do you want us to do with him?" called Chuma from the balcony.

Jillian looked up, trapped by Indigo's grasp, to see Chuma leaning over a rail. Two burly pirates held Duncan, who was now without his weapon, a chain wrapped around his neck.

Indigo sighed impatiently, looking to Jillian. "Don't tell me this is your husband. Don't tell me those idiots bungled the job."

Jillian gritted her teeth.

"Is this your husband, the Earl of Cleaves?"

She couldn't help but look up at Duncan. He was covered with blood, struggling for breath as the chain around his neck cut off his airway. Her eyes met his.

"No," she whispered. She tore her gaze from Duncan's to look back at Indigo. "No, that is not my husband. My husband is dead, lying on the bottom of the sea. You murdered him, remember?"

"Yes," Duncan shouted from the balcony, his voice reverberating in the hot, humid night-wind. "Yes, I'm her husband. Yes, she's my wife; and by God, you harm her and I will come back to haunt every generation of yours from here to eternity. Harm a hair on her precious head and you and yours will weep for a thousand years, ten thousand!"

Indigo blinked, his sun bronzed skin paling in the moonlight.

Jillian was confused. Surely he didn't believe in such nonsense as being cursed.

"What do we do with 'im, Capi'tan?" Chuma repeated.

Indigo glanced at Jillian, as if contemplating his decision. A full minute passed before he spoke, a minute that seemed to Jillian to stretch into an eternity.

"Kill him," Jillian finally heard Indigo say. His next sentence echoed in her head. "Bury him up to his neck on the beach and let the tide come in and take his black soul."

"No!" Jillian screamed, covering her head with her hands, trying to block out the pirate's voice. "Noooo!"

"I love you, Jilly," Duncan shouted from the balcony. "Remember, Jilly, I love you . . . I always loved you!"

She looked up just in time to get a glimpse of his face; then he was gone, dragged away by Chuma and the others.

"How touching," Indigo murmured, thoughtfully. "I only hope that you will come to be so devoted to me. Now, come along, darling. You'll have to spend the remainder of the night with me in my chambers."

Jillian sank to her knees in the grass, oblivious to Indigo's words, left numb by what had happened.

"Oh, Jillian," Indigo sighed. "I am sorry, sweetheart." Then he lifted her in his arms and carried her into the house.

Duncan winced as the chain was pulled tighter around his neck. The pirates half-carried, half-dragged him down the steps. If he didn't catch a breath, he knew he was going to lose consciousness.

Jilly, Jilly, his mind raged. *I'm sorry, sweet. I'm sorry I failed you . . .*

The pirates dragged him out of the stucco house and across the lawn. When he tripped and went down on one knee, he was rewarded with a hard kick to his abdomen. Duncan grunted with pain.

These pirates had no honor.

He began to think not as Duncan Roderick, the Earl of Cleaves, but as Tsitsho of the Mohawk.

He spat blood into the grass, his mind whirling with activity. Anything to remain conscious.

Now a Mohawk, he knew how to kill the enemy with honor. There were many ways. A man could toss his enemy into a pit of wolves and let him battle his way to death. A man could place his enemy in a canoe and let him paddle over a waterfall hundreds of feet high. Yes, there were many honorable deaths for a warrior, but burying him in the sand to let the tide and the crabs eat away at him was not one of them.

Duncan blinked. Blood from his head wound was trickling into his eyes, stinging them and blurring his vision. As the pirates dragged him through the jungle, down a narrow path, he heard the sound of the natives' hollow drums and their mournful chants.

What would become of Jillian? he wondered. He had failed her.

Then he smiled. Somehow, in his heart, he knew she would be all right. She would save herself and her sister because she was a survivor, she was a fighter. The thought of her bedding Indigo made him physically sick, and yet he hoped she would have the sense to give herself to him. The pirate captain was her only chance. He only wished he'd had the opportunity to tell her . . .

Duncan stumbled over a twisted vine and went down on his knees again. This time the pirate called Chuma yanked so hard on the chain around Duncan's neck that everything went black.

When Duncan opened his eyes again, they were on the beach. He could feel the sand beneath his bare feet. He could smell the salty ocean and hear the breakers offshore. Moonlight streamed from the sky, giving the beach an almost ethereal look.

Not a bad place to die . . .

Chuma shoved him into the wet sand, placing a bare foot on the center of his spine to shove him face-down. The chain was pulled taut around his neck and attached to a stake pounded into the sand. Again, he struggled to keep his head as his air was cut off.

He heard the sound of shovels sinking into the sand. The hole they would bury him in was being dug.

But of course he didn't want to die. Not yet. A year ago, it wouldn't have mattered. In the past, he had been a man that tempted the grim reaper often. But now he had something to live for. Someone . . .

After a few minutes passed, Duncan dared to raise his head an inch or two to survey his surroundings. Two pirates held muskets to his head. Behind him was the beach, and beyond that, the path that led to the house. In front of him, beyond the sloping sand, was the warm ocean.

Someone must have seen him move his head, because suddenly he saw one of the pirates swing the butt of his musket. Duncan felt the wood meet the crown of his skull as his head filled with pain and bright starlight.

Then, nothing.

When Duncan woke again, he couldn't move. He was paralyzed from the tips of his toes to his Adam's apple by the crushing weight of the wet sand. He could only breathe in shallow, short breaths. As he blinked away the sand in his eyes, he heard the pirates cackle.

"Don't guess he'll be goin' anywhere, will 'e?" someone said from behind him.

"Nowhere but to his maker!"

The two broke into gruesome laughter.

Then Duncan heard them retreat across the sand and he was alone, except for the tide that faced him.

So, what did a Mohawk warrior do when he was buried up to his neck in sand and the tide was coming in?

Duncan closed his eyes. He thanked sweet heaven he'd been baptized, and then he prayed to God Almighty.

Twenty-three

Daphne Roderick stood on the poop deck of the three-masted sailing ship watching the ocean spray cascade over the bowsprit. She pushed the hood of her wool cloak off her head and took a deep breath, finding the cold, crisp air invigorating. She smiled to herself, giving her silver-tipped cane a tap. Old woman or not, she still had a little spunk left in her! She was headed for Duncan's blessed American Colonies. Be damned if she wasn't going to see a red savage before she died, after all.

Daphne glanced at her grandson's manservant, who stood at an appropriate distance from her, huddled beneath his cloak. The man had quickly recovered from whatever had ailed him the day Duncan sailed and was now returning on the ship to meet with his master in the Maryland Colony. Atar was obviously not pleased at her decision to go to the Colonies; but, of course, what a servant thought was of no consequence to anyone. How could this slave understand her desire to see the outcome of the relationship between Duncan and Jillian? To see her first great-grandchild? How could a man with no family understand her need to see her grandson Duncan happy before she died?

A man's voice carried on the wind that beat at the canvas sails, and the dowager frowned as she looked over her shoulder. Now *that grandson,* that was the one who truly worried her. She looked down onto the deck to see Alger-non, huddled against a wooden crate of chickens, speaking to one of the crewmen. She turned her back on him to gaze out over the white-capped sea again.

When Daphne had sent word to Algernon in France that she was going to the Colonies, her grandson had appeared in London immediately, almost as if he'd anticipated her departure. He insisted upon escorting her across the ocean, saying a woman shouldn't travel alone with only a Negro slave to guard her. Daphne suggested Algernon might be better served to remain at Breckenridge House. What made him think he would be safe in Duncan's presence in the Colonies? Hadn't Duncan threatened to kill Algernon if he ever laid eyes on him again?

Daphne had tried not to involve herself in that whole matter. She didn't really believe Algernon capable of attempting to murder Duncan. The boy didn't have the spine, or the stomach, for it. Perhaps the scaffolding incident and the hunter in New Forest had been coincidence. Fact always was stranger than fiction. But Daphne had agreed that Duncan's suspicions were well founded enough to send Algernon off until Duncan left England. All along, Daphne had intended to allow Algernon to return to Breckenridge as soon as Duncan was a safe distance away. After all, where did Algernon have to go, whom did he have but his family? Considering the tragic circumstances of his birth, circumstances that Duncan wasn't aware of, the boy was at least owed a roof over his head.

Algernon had told Daphne that he wanted to go to the Colonies to make amends with his cousin. He didn't admit to the alleged attempted murders of Duncan, but he said he had a confession to make. He proclaimed that even if Duncan did run him through with a sword, at least he would die with his soul cleansed. So, what was Daphne to do? She couldn't physically keep the boy from setting sail at her side.

Daphne ran her fingers through a handful of her freshly dyed red curls. It was bitter here in the wind. She knew she should return to her tiny cabin before she caught a chill, but it felt good to be out in the elements. The cold air and the wind made her feel alive; it made her feel twenty years younger.

"Madame, it's cold," Atar said, coming to her side. "Let me escort you below deck and make you a cup of your favorite tea. Your grandson wouldn't want you to catch your death crossing the sea to be with him."

Daphne smiled. Atar was a good man. Despite his disapproval of her journey, he'd been attentive since they'd set sail.

She glanced at him. "In a minute. But I have a matter to discuss with you first."

"My lady . . ." He bowed his head, listening.

"I want you to do something for me."

"What is your wish, my lady?"

"I want you to keep an eye on that grandson of mine."

The slave in his red coat and worn shoes never blinked. "Master Algernon?"

"Yes. The boy's behaving entirely too agreeably. It's simply not in his disposition. He's too old to have suddenly gotten a conscience. I'm concerned that he may have ulterior motives behind his desire to go to Maryland." She glanced at the manservant. "I fear your master may have been correct in his suspicions concerning those so-called accidents at our home and at New Forest. When we get to Maryland, to Duncan's home, I want you to keep an eye on that one." She gestured toward Algernon with a ringed finger. "I want no more accidents."

"I would give my life for Master Duncan."

"I know you would, so just keep sharp, will you?"

Atar nodded, glancing at Algernon on the deck below. The two men's gazes met for an instant, then Atar turned away.

* * *

By the first light of the dawning red sun, Chuma walked onto the beach. He liked the early morning. It was a time when a man could think, unencumbered by his daily duties.

The smooth, white sand was scattered with shells brought in on the incoming tide. In the distance, he spotted the prisoner, or what was visible of him. Chuma chuckled . . . just a head. Gulls flew above it, scavengers that they were, diving in search of a morning meal. Crabs scurried in the fresh surf around the head, pincer claws snapping.

Chuma walked across the wet sand, a shovel over his shoulder, feeling the warmth of the Caribbean sun on his face. Indigo, or Master, as he liked to be called, had instructed that when the prisoner was dead, he was to be dug up and tossed into the jungle. Indigo hated to have the beauty of his private beach disturbed by the stench of rotting, crab-eaten body parts washing ashore.

Chuma do this. Chuma do that.

It had always been that way between them, even when they were boys. Indigo was the elder brother, and only half Jamaican. His mother had been a beautiful French woman from Paris, part of their father's booty one night on the open sea. Lily had been her name.

Chuma, on the other hand, didn't know who his mother was. One of the slaves, no doubt, Jamaican most likely, African perhaps. Their father had always preferred Indigo with his lighter skin and fine French features. It was Indigo that had been sent to London and Paris to be schooled like a gentleman, while Chuma remained home to run the plantation. It was Indigo that had been given the ships, the money, even the land, when their father died. And it was Indigo that had not one, but two Englishwomen now.

Chuma spat into the sand. His brother was infatuated with the redhead. He fancied himself in love with the haughty bitch. He laughed, but without humor, and the gulls overhead scattered, frightened by the human sounds. Chuma preferred the blonde, who was softer, gentler. Bea was her name. She knew when to keep her pert mouth shut. Chuma had asked Indigo for her. He said he might pass her on later, but Chuma wasn't going to hold his breath waiting. Indigo always made promises. Some he didn't keep.

No, Chuma, he had to look out for himself and for his own interests. He knew it. He'd known it since the day he was four and Indigo was six and their father had brought home a stick of unrefined sugar from the mill for his eldest son. There'd been no sugar for Chuma. It didn't matter that later, in the darkness of their bedchamber, Indigo had shared the sticky sweet with Chuma. Their father's betrayal had been no less real; it had hurt no less.

So Chuma accepted his fate. He stole what he could, took advantage when he saw the opportunity. He looked at the head in the sand.

And there was an opportunity.

Chuma stared at the head for moment, cocking his head. The crewman, or whatever the hell he was, had been a worthy opponent. Chuma couldn't recall having ever fought a man who parried a saber so well.

Chuma sank his shovel into the warm sand. Water pooled where he made the hole, baring the head's attached shoulder. A crab scuttled over the shoulder, and Chuma flicked it with a dirty finger. "Off with ye," he muttered. "This 'ne's mine."

Chuma dug for a while, resting when he tired. Sweat trickled down his temples. It was barely dawn and already hotter than an afternoon in hell. But the water was coming in fast, so he knew he had to hurry or he'd lose the head to the tide.

After a few minutes of digging, the body began to slump. The face fell into the water, and Chuma had to grab it by a hank of hair and yank it back.

He had dug to the knees now, but the hole was filled with churning water. Chuma leaned over and tried to lift the dead weight, cursing beneath his breath. It wasn't fair that he had to work so much harder for everything than Indigo did. It just wasn't fair.

Reaching the ankles, Chuma set the shovel in the sand; and when he gave the grotesquely tattooed chest a hard push, the body popped up, out of the hole, and into the water with a splash.

Chuma grabbed the two bare feet and began to haul the body up the beach. "Good thing I caught ye before the tide did, eh?" he cackled.

He heard the man begin to retch, coughing up the salty water that had nearly taken his life.

Chuma grinned to himself as the sun appeared in its full burning glory above the horizon of the jungle.

He knew Indigo had ordered the tattooed man to be buried until dead, but what good was a dead man?

Now, a live one, and one as healthy as this, *that* was worth something. The slave market on Jamaica was brisk. The foreman of the sugarcane plantation on the lee side of the island would be pleased to have him. Slaves died so quickly in sugarcane fields that he was always in need of fresh blood. And the foreman never asked questions.

Chuma smiled to himself, dragging the body along. He could almost taste the gold coin now. Damn if he wouldn't have himself a decent bottle of rum, and a warm wench, tonight!

"You have to eat."

Jillian rested her head on the crisp pillowcase, her skin as bleached as the linen. "I can't."

"You have to; if not for your sake, then for that of the baby's." Beatrice sat on the edge of the bed, the bowl of warm tortoise soup in her hand. "Duncan would want you to eat."

"Duncan's dead." Jillian stared at the mosquito netting, blowing in the hot breeze.

Beatrice set the bowl on the bedside table and dipped the soft rag into a clean bowl of water brought by one of the servants. She pressed the cool cloth to her sister's sweaty forehead. "All the more reason why you have to eat. The baby only has you now, Jilly. You have to think of the baby."

Jillian turned her head to look up at her sister. She'd cried so many tears that there were none left. Now, she was numb, just numb. She couldn't think; she couldn't even pray. Duncan had said he loved her, and now he was gone, drowned by the sea. "What am I going to do?" she whispered.

Beatrice dropped the rag into the bowl of water and vinegar and picked up the hearty soup again. "First, you're going to eat. Then, you're going to dress and sit out on the verandah and get some sun. You're piqued."

"It's hot out there." She pushed away the spoon Beatrice offered. "It's hot in here. I can't get my breath."

Beatrice set the bowl down with a thump and left Jillian's bedside. She walked to the open windows to stare out at the verdant jungle.

Jillian rolled onto her back, throwing one hand over her forehead. *"What?"*

Beatrice kept her back to her sister. "Nothing. I didn't say a word."

"But you're thinking it! You're thinking that I'm just feeling sorry for myself. But you don't understand. I loved him. He loved me, and now he's gone."

"Can you change that?"

Jillian opened her eyes to look at her sister. This didn't sound like meek Bea. Why, she almost sounded angry. "No, I can't do anything about that," Jillian flung back.

"So, now what? Do you lie down and die, taking his child with you?"

"Indigo would never let me keep the baby. It would be sold off, just like Mrs. Amstead."

"So you give in now, four months gone? You don't give yourself a chance? You don't give the baby a chance?"

"We don't have a chance."

Beatrice shook her head. "I'm surprised by you, Jilly. I

can't believe you're actually going to let someone get the best of you."

"He's dead!" Jillian shouted, picking up a pillow and throwing it at her sister. "Don't you understand? The only man I will ever love is dead and gone!"

Beatrice turned around, crossing her arms over her silky pink day gown. "Don't get angry at me. Why don't you use that anger to make the best of the situation?"

Jillian flung herself back on the bed. "You don't know what you're saying. That man, that futtering pirate who killed my husband, wants to marry me. He wants me to have his children."

"At least, you'd be alive. Duncan's child would have a chance."

"You're being ridiculous now, Bea. I can't marry a pirate. I won't." She picked up a pillow and covered her face.

Beatrice strode toward the bed, jerking the pillow away from Jillian. "I'm being sensible. It's what Duncan would want you to do."

"He'd want me to sleep with another man?"

"He'd want you to survive." Bea was almost shouting now. "He'd want his child to survive."

Tears ran down Jillian's cheeks. All these years she had been the strong one, and now suddenly the roles were reversed. "Oh, Bea," she whispered. "I'm scared. I'm so scared."

Beatrice sat down on the edge of the bed and took her sister's hand in hers. "I know you are. So am I. But I'm not ready to give up. And neither are you." She kissed Jillian's hand. "Now, why not get up and have a little soup on the verandah? It's already cooler outside. Can't you feel the breeze?"

Jillian allowed Beatrice to help her up out of bed and, arm in arm, they walked out onto the verandah. Jillian's heart ached to the very bottom of her soul, but she knew Bea was right. She wasn't ready to give up. For the sake of Duncan's child, the child she carried in her womb, she just couldn't.

Twenty-four

Days passed; weeks slipped through her fingers like the powder-fine sand from the white beach as Jillian struggled to pull herself out of depression. Her life seemed so unfair. There were mornings that she didn't want to get out of bed. She wasn't certain she wanted to live without Duncan. But for the sake of the baby, she knew she had to.

"Let's go for a walk," Beatrice said, patting Jillian's arm.

Jillian had been sitting on the porch for more than an hour, a book lying open on her lap, unread. "I don't feel like a walk." Idly, she watched a small green lizard skitter along the bottom step.

"Well, I do, and you're coming." Beatrice took her sister's hand and pulled her out of the chair. "It's a beautiful day. The sun's not even too bright." She adjusted the brim of Jillian's beribboned straw hat, a gift from Indigo. One of many.

Reluctantly, Jillian followed Beatrice through the open, airy house and into the hot sunshine. She had to give Indigo credit for one thing: The man was persistent. He brought her gifts daily, even exotic foods to sample. To amuse her, he brought guests to the house. Last week he'd given her a small lap dog to keep her company. Jillian hadn't wanted to accept the gifts, not even the puppy, but Beatrice had insisted. She'd said it was rude not to accept; and considering their precarious circumstances, Jillian couldn't afford to anger the pirate captain. It was only his *hospitality* that was keeping the two sisters alive, together, and in good health.

Hand in hand, Jillian and Beatrice walked through the garden Indigo was attempting to establish. The air was filled with the sweet, humid fragrance of his success. Not halfway through the tangle of transplanted hibiscus flowers and exotic vines, they encountered him, on his hands and knees, tending a withered white rosebush.

"Ladies." The moment Indigo spotted them, he jumped to his feet, wiping his soiled hands on a towel he wore tucked into his pristine breeches.

"Sir." Beatrice dipped a curtsy.

Jillian nodded. "Indigo." It grated on her nerves to call her husband's murderer by his Christian name, but Jillian knew it was a fine-line she walked these days.

Indigo was anxious to be wed to Jillian. He was now pressing her daily. She knew that not only her life and the baby's, but Beatrice's as well, hung on how she responded to the pirate. If she made him too angry, if she turned him away too many times, he might well sell her and Beatrice, something she suspected was not an idle threat. Still, she hadn't yet been able to bring herself to agree to wed Indigo. For the time being, she tried to remain cool, but polite, telling him she was still in mourning for her husband and needed more time to recover.

Indigo wiped his perspiration-dotted forehead with a handkerchief. "And how are you two ladies today? I apologize for not making the morning meal, but Chuma had trouble with the slaves again. I was forced to go down and settle it myself."

When Jillian made no response, Beatrice jumped into the conversation. "I hope there were no injuries."

"No, no, no. It was all settled. The little monkeys are always demanding this and that. More food. A better freshwater supply. It's something different every fortnight." He tucked his handkerchief into the sleeve of his loose, woven white shirt. "So, there you have it." He was smiling at Jillian.

Jillian looked down at her feet, knowing she was expected to say something. "We—we were just going for a walk. Bea thought I needed to get out."

Indigo took her hand and leaned to kiss her mouth. Jillian moved her head so that his lips only brushed her cheek. Every time that he attempted to kiss her, all she could think of was the taste of Duncan's mouth on hers . . . all she could think of was his heady masculine scent, the feel of his touch. It was nearly enough to make her go mad.

"And wise she is, this sister of yours," Indigo continued, smiling at Bea. "She's absolutely right. You spend entirely too much time doing nothing but sitting and staring." He turned her hand in his as if to search for a tidbit of information that would please her. "Oh!" He looked up. "I'd almost forgotten, darling. We've been invited to sup tonight with the Carletons. They've just returned from Paris with oodles of gossip."

Jillian looked away. "I'm not sure that I'm up to it."

"Now, dear, you know we've talked about this. I want you at my side. I want everyone on the island to meet my intended. I want them all to love you as I do."

Jillian could feel Beatrice glaring at her. "Oh, all right." She finally gave in under her sister's scrutiny. "What time shall I be ready?"

He squeezed her hand before letting it go. "Seven on the clock. So there you have it."

She nodded, walking away.

"And dearest . . ."

Jillian halted on the path. She didn't look back at him. "Indigo?"

"Do wear that darling de' shabille' I just brought you. I'm anxious to see how the fabric plays against the color of your hair."

"All right."

"Have a good walk," he called after the two women.

Jillian waited until she was out of earshot before she spoke. "I hate it when he touches me," she whispered.

"He's really not a bad man, Jillian. He honestly seems to care for you."

"He killed Duncan."

"Forgiveness is the key to a Christian woman's life. You can't go on hating him forever. It'll eat you up inside." Bea squeezed her hand. "Indigo simply needs some guidance. He had no one to look up to as a child. For heaven's sake, his father marched whores in and out of the house for decades."

"Guidance?" Jillian couldn't suppress her laughter, and she had to admit that it felt good inside. "I swear, Beatrice, you sound as if you're attracted to the monster."

Beatrice's eyes grew wide, her rosy cheeks coloring. "Don't be ridiculous. What would I do with a man like Indigo?" They took the fork in the garden path that led into the jungle. "He's entirely too . . . too virile for me!"

Jillian threw back her head and laughed harder. She couldn't imagine her sister using such a word. Though she had to admit, Beatrice was right in thinking the man had an attractive nature about him. He seemed to have a way of charming females from young to old. It was unfortunate that Jillian couldn't see him in that light. It would have made her inevitable plight easier to swallow.

"Where are you taking me?" Jillian asked as they walked deeper into the jungle. "If it's to see another snake that's eaten a goat, I'm going to be ill."

"It's not a snake. I just wanted you to see the slave housing."

"So, you do have ulterior motives to getting me out in the blasted heat."

"Now you're beginning to sound like your old self again." Beatrice tugged on her hand. "Come on. It's not much farther."

The two sisters followed the path that wound through the jungle for another quarter of a mile before they reached an open place crowded with native huts. The dome-shaped structures were built from a few supporting beams of wood with woven mats making up the walls and roofs.

"So, this is where the slaves live and you wanted me to see it?" Jillian took her handkerchief from her short sleeve and dabbed her neck. "Why?"

"Jillian, I think it's time we took some responsibility here."

A naked toddler appeared from one of the round huts. The minute the little girl saw Beatrice, she came racing toward her. To Jillian's surprise, her sister lifted the baby into her arms.

"You've been here before," Jillian remarked in disbelief. "That child knows you."

Beatrice tickled the toddler's chin. "This is Maria. She stays here with her grandmother while her parents work in the fields. Isn't that right?" She addressed the little girl. "Isn't that right, sweetie?"

Jillian rested a hand on her hip, glancing at the camp. The huts were in ruin. Thin, mangy dogs wandered about, scavenging for food. In the distance, Jillian saw an ancient, stoop-shouldered Jamaican woman appear out of the jungle carrying a basket balanced on her head. As she walked, droplets of water splashed from the pitch-covered container.

"I want you to talk to Indigo about making some improvements here."

Jillian looked at her sister, wondering if she were suffering from a touch of heat stroke. "You want me to do what?"

"I want you to talk to Indigo." She pressed a kiss to the baby's forehead and put her on the ground. The child ran off in the direction of the old woman. "I couldn't ask. I have no influence over him, but you do."

Jillian ran a hand over her swollen abdomen. By her calculations, she was at least five months pregnant. Only the voluminous skirts of her gowns, and the fact that the baby was small, kept her secret. "I'm not exactly in a position to be asking favors. At some point the man is going to realize this isn't a basket of fruit I'm carrying under my skirt."

"Exactly why you should ask now."

Before Jillian could respond, Beatrice went on. "Why not do something good for someone? Why not let someone profit from this horrible thing that's happened to you?"

Jillian shook her head. Beatrice was serious. She was absolutely serious. "Indigo isn't going to do anything for these people because I ask. They're slaves, Bea. Cheap labor. Their lives mean nothing to men like Indigo."

"He treats his slaves like this because he knows no better. It's the same all over the island." Bea took Jillian's hand. "He will do it for you. He wants so badly to please you, to see you smile." She looked her in the eyes. "Please, Jilly, will you just try? This is important to me."

Jillian sighed with exasperation. The entire idea was absurd. "What do they need?"

"Decent wood to repair the huts." Beatrice began to rattle off a list, counting on her fingers. "More food or, better yet, permission to grow their own. Cloth to cover their nakedness. Medicine when they need it. And a well. They have to have a well, Jilly. The old women carry the fresh water here from nearly a mile away."

Jillian stood in the middle of the jungle clearing, shaking her head. The toddler had picked up a stick and was now pounding on one of the kettledrums near the central fire pit in the middle of the Jamaican slave village. It was the hollow sound that Jillian heard each night when she lay in her bed unable to sleep. It was the same sound that haunted her dreams. It was the sound that brought Duncan's image to her when she slept.

"All right," she conceded after a moment. She threw up her hands. "I can try. What can he do but say no?"

With a shout of delight, Beatrice threw her arms around

her sister's shoulders and hugged her. "I knew you would do it! I knew it. Thank you. Thank you."

"Don't be so quick to thank me," Jillian answered drolly. "You and I may yet see Mrs. Amstead's fate."

The iron bars of the door slammed shut and Duncan fell to his knees in the filthy straw that lined the jail cell. He rubbed his aching shoulders, wincing at the touch of the raw spot where the oxen yoke cut into his flesh. Day in and day out, seven days a week, twelve to fifteen hours a day, he served as a beast of burden, pulling carts of loaded sugarcane through the rutted fields beneath the scorching sun.

"Easy day, eh?" Duncan heard a man's voice call out of the darkness of the tiny, crowded cell.

Duncan chuckled, reaching for the ladle in the water bucket he knew was near the door. It was too dark to actually see anything. That bastard foreman always worked the men until well past sunset.

Duncan sipped the stale water greedily, spitting out a bit of straw he took with it. "Relaxing day, Jake, and you?"

"A stroll in the gardens . . ." The black man who had befriended Duncan laughed easily.

The first week Duncan had arrived at the sugarcane plantation, he'd heard Jake's voice in the communal cell beside his. He had recognized his accent immediately as coming from the Chesapeake Bay area. Jake was a freeman, a ship's first officer by trade. He and his crew had been captured when their ship had sunk in the Caribbean waters, taking their captain with it. Most of Jake's crew was here, those who were still living, working the sugarcane fields.

Duncan dropped the ladle into the water bucket and crawled across the fetid straw to his spot against the back wall. The cell reeked of sweat, human excrement, and suffering. Men parted the way to make room for him. It was a territorial thing, Duncan had learned his first night in the cell. He'd been forced to fight a man to have a bit of warped wall-board to rest his weary head against. When a worker died and was pulled out of the stall, bare feet first, all of the men lunged for his sleeping spot. Duncan didn't blame them. It was a matter of survival.

Duncan backed into his corner, in the space beside Jake, and let his head fall back, closing his eyes.

"Saved ye a bit of bread," Jake murmured, pressing it into Duncan's hand. "I had to clobber Clyde to get it, but get it, I did. Only got a few bugs in it."

Duncan accepted the weevil-infested heel of bread and gobbled it ravenously. It made no logical sense to him to expect a man to work as hard as the foreman expected his men to work and then not to feed them. It was poor business. But Jake said it was cheaper for the master to buy new men than to feed the ones he had.

His supper over, Duncan closed his eyes again. This was his favorite part of the day, if a slave could have a favorite part working a sugarcane field. Now was the time he could close his eyes and think of Jillian. Now was when he could remember the taste of her lips; the smell of her clean, bright hair; the feel of her hand touching his. He remembered the oddest things about her: The sound of her laughter when together they'd discovered the rocking horse from his childhood . . . the contented, drowsy smile on her lips when they'd just made love . . .

Duncan sighed. At nighttime he allowed himself to remember such precious moments. Now was the time that he could plan how he would torture Indigo before he killed him. Now was when he made his plans to rescue Jilly.

"How many wagonloads you haul today?" Jake asked, making conversation.

"Hell, I don't know. Lost count after awhile. Twenty, thirty maybe."

Jake chuckled. "I watch those men cut down that cane as I roll my wheels by and I drool."

"You want to cut?" Duncan opened one eye. A thin strip of moonlight came through a crack in one of the ceiling boards overhead, the same board that leaked water when it rained.

Jake grinned, his black eyes twinkling. "Christ no, I don't want to cut! But I want to rid myself of that wagon I'm haulin'. Hard for a man to escape through the jungle, pullin' a wagon he's chained to."

"You really think you could do it?" Duncan had both eyes open now. ". . . *we* could do it?"

" 'Course we could, with the right circumstances." Jake winked. "That and a prayer."

Duncan lowered his voice. The man beside him was snoring, but he would take no chances. A man could be rewarded with food for telling tales; and if the foreman learned he and Jake were even discussing escape, he'd have them both beheaded without as much as a blink of his eye. "And then what?"

Jake shrugged. "We set my crewmen free and anyone else willin' to go with us, and we head for the Port Royal harbor, of course."

"And what, might I ask, friend, is in the harbor?"

"That filthy pirate Indigo's ships, of course. You sure are stupid for an earl, man."

Duncan chuckled. It was Jake's sense of humor and thoughts of his Jilly that had gotten him through those first few days of work in the sugarcane fields. It was Jake who had convinced him he would see his Jillian again if he wanted it badly enough. "We take the ship?"

"Why not? I got me a decent crew, those still left livin.' "

"And then what?"

Jake grinned ear to ear. "We pick up that pretty red-haired wife of yours and we sail for paradise, home to the Chesapeake, which, I swear by God a'mighty, I'll never leave if He'll get me there safely once more!"

Duncan smiled. It was far-fetched, wishful thinking, nothing more. He knew no one escaped the cane fields, except by death. "And just how are we going to lead this mutiny of ours, friend?" Duncan closed his eyes, too weary to keep them open any longer. His shoulders ached and his hands, with their open wounds, smarted. He didn't know how long he could stay in decent health without food or rest. Soon he would begin to lose his strength, and then he would no longer be able to fight. He'd not be fit enough to escape.

But then he thought of Jillian and her laughter. He thought of the baby, his baby, nestled in her womb. He thought of the son who had died in his arms, and Duncan knew he wasn't ready to die yet. He wasn't ready to give up, not as long as he thought his lady-wife Jillian lived. "I said, how do you intend to lead this mutiny?" Duncan repeated.

Jake grinned, his even white teeth shining in the darkness. "Machetes."

"Machetes?"

Jake raised a meaty hand, slicing an invisible weapon through the air. "You and I get called to the cane fields, and we're as good as free." He winked at Duncan. "As good as home."

Jillian sat on the edge of her bed, dressed for her supper with Indigo. But her head was aching, her stomach churning. The baby was growing larger by the day now, the girth of her abdomen increasing. Jillian couldn't imagine how Indigo had not yet noticed, and she had begun to live in fear.

Beatrice came across the room, a sparkling topaz necklace in her hands. "Wear this. It'll look lovely with your gown."

Jillian groaned as she allowed her sister to climb onto the bed and fasten the necklace. It was a gift from Indigo, of course.

"I don't want to go."

"You have to. He's expecting you. Besides, he gave the

order to start digging that well for the slaves today. You have to be nice to him."

"I don't want to be nice to him." She fiddled with one of the folds of her gown. "Bea, he talks about touching me."

Beatrice peered over her sister's shoulder, blushing. "He *talks* about it?"

Jillian sighed. "He talks about little else these days, but the wedding and the consummation." She shivered. "It's disgusting. I just can't imagine letting another man touch me where only Duncan has."

Beatrice climbed down off the bed, moistening her lower lip with the tip of her tongue. The little lap dog Indigo had given Jillian followed her, playing at her heels. "What—what does he say?"

"He says he's going to bathe me with rose water from the petals of that futtering rosebush of his. Then he'll lay me out on his bed and dry me with soft cloths."

Beatrice listened wide-eyed.

"Then he says he's going to rub scented oil on his hands and touch me."

"Men do that?"

"Well, I suppose they do, with their wives," Jillian snapped, not meaning to.

But Beatrice took no offense. "Did—did Duncan ever do those things to you?"

Jillian smiled, remembering. Without realizing it, she brushed her breast with her fingertips. "Not oil, but he once dripped honey all over my breasts and licked it off. Then he dribbled it—" She caught her breath, suddenly embarrassed.

Beatrice's eyes were wide, her mouth forming a perfect "o." "I didn't realize it . . . it could be like that. Mother just called it a *duty,* like mending. Something a wife had to endure because it was what was expected of her."

Jillian chuckled, getting off the bed to retrieve her hairbrush. Her silky blue gown, sewn for the tropics, made a swishing sound as she walked. "Oh, Bea, it's nothing like what Mother told us—not when you care about each other, at least. Duncan called it making love. It was . . . it was, oh, I can't explain it to you." She turned to her sister, running the brush through her thick, auburn hair. "But one day you'll understand, if you're so lucky as to find someone you love."

Beatrice scooped the puppy off the floor and walked to the open window, stroking the pet that had become her own. "I'm beginning to lose hope in that dream."

"Well, don't. Your life isn't over, and neither is mine. Something will happen to change all this. We'll make something happen, you and I."

Beatrice turned to look at her sister. "I'm so glad to hear you say that. You're beginning to sound like the Jillian I've always known and loved."

A knock came at the door, interrupting the women's conversation. "Yes?" Jillian called, knowing who it was.

"Might I come in, darling?"

Jillian gave a sigh. "Certainly."

Indigo appeared in the doorway, dressed as handsomely as ever in a grass-green doublet and matching wide-legged breeches. At his waist, he wore a jewel-encrusted saber. "Ready, darling? I thought we'd have a little liquid refreshment on the balcony and then retire to my chambers for a more . . . intimate supper."

Jillian pressed her hand to her forehead. She truly wasn't feeling well. She just hadn't been able to adjust to the climate as her sister had. "Indigo, I'm not feeling well."

He crossed his arms over his chest. "I'm losing my patience with this, my love."

"I'm sorry; I am. I think I spent too much time in the sun today. Bea and I were overseeing the rebuilding of the slave quarters."

He sighed irritably. "I told you not to stay too long. And I had such a lovely supper prepared. Blackened swordfish.

I was dearly looking forward to a little feminine company after a long day of toil."

To Jillian's surprise, Beatrice suddenly stepped forward. "If . . . if it would please you, sir, I'd be willing to sup with you."

Indigo turned to look at Beatrice, lifting an eyebrow. He stared for a long moment, as if seeing her for the very first time. "You wouldn't find my company boring?"

She smiled graciously. "Not at all, sir."

Indigo extended his hand, and Beatrice came forward to take it. Why, her sister was behaving as if the pirate were her consort!

"Then, please, do join me." Indigo pressed a kiss to the back of Beatrice's hand.

Jillian rolled her eyes.

"You wouldn't mind, darling?" Indigo asked Jillian.

She smiled. "Not at all. If you could just send Maria up with a little fruit and cheese and to help me remove my gown, I'll need nothing else."

He bowed graciously. "I'll send her up immediately." Then he stepped aside to make way for Beatrice. "Mademoiselle . . ."

Beatrice and Indigo had just stepped into the hallway when Jillian called after her sister. "Bea, wait!"

Hurrying across the room, Jillian removed her necklace. She caught up to her sister in the doorway. "You wear it," she whispered. "It matches your beautiful eyes."

Before Beatrice could protest, Jillian fastened the jeweled necklace around her sister's throat. "See you in the morning," she whispered in her sister's ear. "Call me if you need me." Then she slipped back into her room and closed the door, looking forward to an evening alone.

Twenty-five

"He wants to see you."

A long shadow cast across her feet, and Jillian looked up from where she sat on the top step of the porch. Beatrice stood in the grass in front of her, her lap dog curled in her arm. Jillian had given her the puppy because she'd felt she couldn't care for it properly. Besides, she liked cats better and still missed the orange tabby kitten Duncan had given her after the scaffolding incident.

"Is he angry?"

"He's impatient." Beatrice dropped down beside Jillian on the step. "Jilly, I need to talk to you. It's time to make a decision. We need a plan, you and I."

Jillian held her head, trying to keep herself together. She knew where this conversation was going. "It's too soon."

"It's been nearly two months since Duncan . . . died. We're not going to escape, at least not anytime soon. You heard what the man told us in the market: No one crosses Indigo Muldune. No one's going to help us at the risk of their own lives."

Jillian ran her hand over her abdomen; and as if in response, her baby kicked heartily. Her sister was right. She knew it. She just hated the thought of admitting defeat. "I'm six months along. I won't be able to hide the baby much longer, will I?"

Bea shook her head, scratching her little brown dog behind the ears. "I'm afraid not.

With a sigh, Jillian stared out into the tangled jungle. It had just stopped raining, and the air was hot and humid and filled with the scent of blooming flowers. Enormous droplets of rainwater fell from a broad, leafy plant beside the stone step, and she put out her hand to catch one. "What would you do if you were in my situation, Bea?"

"I'm not you, Jilly. I could never be like you. I'm just not as strong. I despise confrontation, I—"

"What would you do?"

Beatrice put her hands together, threading her fingers. "You're six months gone. You'll not be able to hide the baby much longer beneath your gown. I'd marry Indigo with the agreement I would keep my child and my sister. I would marry him and change his ways."

Jillian lifted her wide-brimmed straw hat off her head and wiped her perspiration-dotted forehead with her handkerchief. "I'd be betraying Duncan's memory."

"In England you'd have had to remarry."

"Not my husband's murderer."

Beatrice stared out at the jungle. "Perhaps not, but odder things happen. Remember when Mrs. Olsen died in childbed and Jane had to marry her stepfather?"

A lump rose in Jillian's throat. "It's not the same thing."

Bea looked at her sister. "I'm sorry. I don't know what to say, except choose the lesser of the evils. You're not going to get what you want. You heard Chuma's report to Indigo. They buried your husband's body in the jungle."

"Without as much as a Christian burial." Jillian laughed morosely. "Or even a pagan one."

"Duncan isn't Lazarus. He can't rise from the dead," Beatrice went on gently. "But perhaps you can keep your baby . . . his baby."

Jillian rose, dropping her hat back on her head. "Where is he?"

Beatrice pointed toward the back lawn. "Bowling with Chuma."

"I'll go talk to him."

Beatrice looked up from where she sat on the step, her pretty peach-colored gown in billows of sheer linen around her. "Want me to come with you?"

Jillian shook her head with resignation. "No. I have to do this myself."

"Jillian?" Beatrice called after her.

Jillian turned around. "Yes?"

Bea was smiling bittersweetly. "I love you, sister, and I'm glad I came. I'm glad I can be here with you through this."

Jillian smiled back, then went to find Indigo.

She located him on the back verandah, sipping a glass of frozen lemonade. It never ceased to amaze Jillian that no matter how hot it got, Indigo still had ice in his ice house, shipped from the north.

"Darling!" Indigo called to her when he spotted Jillian coming across the lawn.

She kicked a stray wooden bowling ball as she walked. "So who won, you or Chuma?"

Chuma stood on the end of the verandah, a glass of ale in his hand. He didn't seem to care much for Jillian or her presence, but the feeling was mutual. The bastard had been the one who had actually murdered her Duncan.

"Oh, blast him, Chuma won." Indigo came down off the verandah to take her hand and lead her up the steps. "But he cheated, of course."

Jillian smiled. Bea was right; Indigo could be rather charming when he wanted to. "So demand a rematch." She sat down on the two-seated swing made from woven palm leaves.

"Lemonade, love?"

"Thank you." Jillian accepted the glass from Indigo's hand. He was dressed impeccably this afternoon, as always, with his dark hair smoothed back over his head and tied neatly with a blue ribbon from one of her own smocks.

Indigo picked up his glass and sat in the swing beside her. "Chuma, thank you for the game. You may go."

Chuma looked at Indigo with his watery brown eyes, and Jillian wondered why Indigo didn't see the hatred in his stare. She wondered why he trusted Chuma as he did. The man was always skulking about.

Indigo patted Jillian's hand, taking her from her idle thoughts. "Such a pleasant surprise to see you smiling, darling."

She sipped her lemonade, unable to bring herself to look at him. "You wanted to see me?"

He crossed his legs, giving the hammock-like swing a push. They drifted back. "Yes, I did. It's time we had one of our little talks."

She stared straight ahead as they swung forward. Chuma was out on the lawn retrieving the bowling balls, just out of earshot. "Yes?"

"I'd like to set a wedding date."

She gave a push with the toe of her slipper, and the swing drifted back with the two of them again. "I see."

She heard him sip from his glass.

"Does that mean you agree?"

She thought long and hard before she spoke. Images of Duncan flashed through her head. There was so much she had never learned about him . . . so many pieces of the puzzle she had never had a chance to put together. Duncan had lost his first child and she knew that it had hurt him. At least she could save this one. "Indigo . . ."

"Jillian?"

She made herself look into his sharp blue eyes. "Indigo, before I agree to the wedding, a deal will have to be struck between you and me."

Indigo sighed good-naturedly. "No matter what you give a female, she always wants more." He fluttered his hand. "Well, come, come, tell me your terms."

"I have something to confess, first . . ." A lump rose in

her throat; tears stung her eyes. Suddenly she couldn't speak . . .

"The baby?" Indigo prompted after a moment.

She looked up at him in surprise "You know?"

He shrugged his shoulders and reached for his handkerchief from his sleeve, taking her glass from her. "I'm an observant man. Here, darling, wipe your eyes."

She accepted his handkerchief and dabbed her face. "How long have you known?"

"Oh, weeks. More than a month."

She sniffed. "Why didn't you say anything?"

"I wanted you to come to me. I wanted you to feel that you could trust me."

"Trust the man that had my husband murdered?"

"I've explained all that to you numerous times. I'm a businessman."

"And it was just business," she intoned.

"Perhaps poor business. But I cannot change the past, only alter the future."

Jillian took a deep breath. "I won't give up my baby."

"Your husband's child, I assume."

"Yes." She crumpled the handkerchief in her hand, feeling stronger already. She would come out the winner in this deal. The pirate wouldn't get the best of her. She wouldn't let him. "And my sister will not be taken from me, not ever. She will not be forced to marry a man she doesn't want. She will be no one's concubine. Chuma will not have her."

He raised an eyebrow. "Chuma?"

"I see how he looks at her. I also know you can be generous to a fault. I wouldn't put it past you to give my sister to a man as a gift."

He chuckled at her observation. "Considering your plight, your request is lengthy."

Jillian got out of the swing, suddenly impatient to have this matter settled between them. "So why ask my terms?

Why not rape me? Forget this farce of marriage. Force me against my will. I don't know why you haven't already."

He put her glass on a table beside the swing, slapping it down so hard that sweet lemonade splashed over the side. "I told you!" he insisted. "I want something good in my life. Something decent. My father filled this house with whores. My mother was nothing more than a slave. I want better for my children."

She opened her hands, beseeching. "So you kidnap me?"

Indigo rose from the swing to pace the verandah. "What decent woman would have me? Look at what I am. What I've become." He grabbed one of the supporting posts and stared into the jungle. "My father," he muttered. "I've become what I swore I would never become. The bastard . . ."

Jillian, in turn, stared at Indigo. For the first time, she actually felt sorry for him, and she hated herself for it. This was the man who had killed her beloved, her Duncan. "If I agree, do we have a bargain?"

"You have to give yourself to me honestly. You have to try."

"I can make no promises. I loved my husband deeply; but for the sake of my child, I would try to come to care for you as a wife should her husband."

Indigo turned to face her. "Does that mean you'll marry me, Jillian?"

It was on the tip of tongue. She almost said yes, but she couldn't. Logic told her to say it and get it over with. But her heart told her she couldn't give in. Not yet. "It means you will have my decision shortly."

"More stalling." He came toward her. "You don't have a choice."

"Two more days, Indigo. I ask two more days."

He caught her hand, turning it in his own. "I shouldn't give in to you. Chuma says I'm too easily manipulated by you and your sister."

"Two days," Jillian repeated, looking the pirate directly in the eyes.

"Two days," he whispered. Then he leaned forward and brushed his mouth against hers.

The moment their lips met, Jillian knew she couldn't marry him.

Duncan woke to the disturbing clang of metal against metal.

"Get your lazy arses up and out," shouted the one-eyed foreman as he went down the row of slave cells, rattling the bars with the metal staff he always carried. "Ye've slept half the day away already!"

Duncan blinked in the feeble light that filtered through the crack in the roof overhead. It was barely dawn, and he was certain he hadn't come in from the fields last night until almost midnight. He didn't know how long he could physically hold up under this stress. It had been two months of working past exhaustion only to be fed a crust of bread, given a few hours rest, and returned to the fields again. Two months since he had last seen his Jillian. Duncan wiped his filthy, sweaty brow.

And what had become of her? He tried not to think about it. She was safe, of course. She had done what she had to to save herself. He tried not to think about that either. All that mattered was that she was still alive, that she would stay alive until he could come for her. That was what he lived for now. Jillian's memory was what kept him strong.

The foreman passed Duncan's cell again, beating on the bars. "Up, up, you lazy bastards. We got work to do. The master wants the south field cut afore it rains."

Duncan jabbed his friend in the stomach, playfully. "Jake, wake up. Mother calls."

Jake came awake slowly. He looked terrible. In the last few weeks, Duncan had seen his friend's face begin to sag gauntly, dark circles appearing under his eyes. His skin hung on his bones. He was starving to death. Duncan could only guess the toll taken on his own body by watching the changes in Jake's. Most men survived six months to a year. Jake had already been here nine months. Duncan couldn't help but wonder how much longer Jake had.

The iron door on Duncan's cell swung open, and the slaves began to file out. One man started to crawl toward the door, and another helped him to his feet. Duncan guessed that there would be one fewer man to feed in the cell tonight, one extra heel of moldy, bug-infested bread to fight over.

"Let's go," Duncan told Jake, giving him his hand as he got to his feet. "Time to get a little fresh air, lover."

Jake chuckled, accepting Duncan's assistance.

"You're a good man, Duncan Roderick, even if you are a scurvy earl."

The two men had just reached the door, the last out of the cell, when the foreman came back down the filthy corridor between the cells. "Need a couple extra cane-cutters today."

Duncan's gaze immediately met Jake's, a smile twitching on his lips.

"It'll mean an extra piece a' bread and a hunk a' cheese," the foreman called as he slunk by.

"We'll go," Duncan offered, hooking a thumb in Jake's direction. "We'll cut cane."

The foreman turned around, wrinkling his brow. "No. You two ain't to be trusted. Ye got too much life left in yer eyes." He started to move on to the next cell.

"So we ain't starved yet," Duncan said, knowing intuitively that this might be his only chance at escape. "That means we can cut more cane, my friend and I."

The foreman turned around and spat a stream of tobacco into the straw at Duncan's bare feet. "And why ye so anxious to cut cane, Tattoo Man? You and your niggard friend lookin' for trouble?"

Duncan touched the scabbed wounds across one shoulder. "No. We ain't stupid. We're just lookin' for a change."

The foreman studied Duncan, following him with his beady rat eyes.

"But it'll take two extra pieces of bread," Duncan put in for good measure. "Me and my friend, we don't work for free."

One of the slaves passing the cell cackled. The foreman struck him on the back of the calf with his metal staff as he went by. "Shut up, afore I shut you up for good!"

The foreman looked back at Duncan.

Duncan prayed as hard as he had ever prayed in his life.

The foreman spun his staff. "What the bloody hell. Follow me, boys; but I warn ye, ye so much as look cross-eyed, and I'll order the guards to shoot your balls off."

Duncan fell into step behind the foreman, glancing over his shoulder at Jake.

The black man winked, his dark eyes twinkling. *Home,* he mouthed.

Twenty-six

"You can't."

"You coming or not?"

"Jillian, think about what you're saying. What you're doing," Beatrice pleaded. She stood near the open window in her night robe, the darkness of the jungle oppressive. "You can't think just of yourself. You have to think about the baby."

"I am thinking about the baby." Jillian fastened the emerald-and-diamond necklace Duncan had given her around her neck. "And for the baby I have to try."

Beatrice followed Jillian as she moved about the room, gathering the few belongings she had come to Jamaica with. "This is insane. Even if you could make it into town, even if you could find someone to help you, you'd never make it out of the Port Royal harbor alive. Indigo owns half the ships in these waters, and half the men. He won't let you go."

"I have to try. I should have tried weeks ago. Now, are you coming with me, or not?"

Beatrice set her jaw. "If something happened to you or the baby, it would be partly my fault."

Jillian shrugged. "So, stay here if you're frightened. I'll send back help as soon as I can."

Beatrice grabbed her sister's hand as she went by. "Please, don't do this," she begged, near tears. "Just marry him. He'll provide for you. He'll let no harm come to you or the child."

"I can't do that."

"You were willing to do it in England." Beatrice crossed her arms over her breasts. "When Father signed that betrothal agreement, you were going to marry a suitor you didn't know as well as you know Indigo. The Earl of Cleaves could have been a cruel man, a brutal one."

"But he wasn't." Jillian held up one finger, keeping her voice low so as not to disturb anyone else in the household. "He wasn't cruel or brutal. I came to love him and he me."

"So now you expect that in another marriage?" She laughed at the ridiculous thought. "You expect what no woman has ever expected?"

Jillian looked at her sister, lifting her chin a notch. It was the memory of Duncan that made her strong. "I suppose I do."

Beatrice walked away, her bare feet padding on the cool tile floor. "You're making a mistake."

Jillian stuffed her few coins into a small cotton bag she dropped over her neck. "I'm not going to argue with you anymore. I'm leaving. I'm going to escape."

"You're going to get past the guards?"

"I have to. Now, you make your decision and make it quickly. I won't blame you if you stay."

Beatrice frowned. "This is madness."

"You'll go?"

"I'll have to change. I refuse to traipse about the jungle in my sleeping gown."

Jillian smiled, watching her sister head for the door. "Hurry. In another hour, everyone will begin to rise; in two, they'll realize we're missing. I want to get a good head start on them."

Beatrice closed the door behind her quietly.

Jillian had just walked to her bedstand to retrieve the silver hairbrush Duncan had given her when she heard a noise on her balcony. She froze, listening. For a long moment, there was silence. She heard the sound of the wind blowing in the treetops, the swish of the curtain in the open windows.

Then she heard the sound again. A single footstep . . . barefoot.

Had Indigo sent someone to spy on her? Had he suspected she would flee rather than agree to marry him? Her two-day pardon was up. Today, Indigo expected an answer, and he expected a *yes*.

Jillian glanced at the fruit bowl on a table near the door. A shiny paring knife used to peel the sweet fruit lay beside it. Noiselessly, she walked to the table and picked up the knife. The blade was short, but razor-sharp. The weight of it in her palm gave her confidence.

Slowly she crept toward the swaying, transparent curtains that hung in the open windows and doorway. Before she reached the door that led to the balcony, she spotted a silhouette through the drapes. A man . . .

Jillian gripped the knife tightly in her hand, gritting her teeth. This man wasn't going to stop her. No one was going to keep her from getting away. For too many months she'd sat paralyzed by her grief and done nothing. But this morning was her time for action. She'd not allow others to control her fate another moment longer.

"Who's there?" Jillian demanded.

The movement came so quickly that she barely had time to react. He came at her through the thin drapes, his identity masked by the filmy white material.

Jillian lashed out with the knife, stifling her urge to scream.

The man grunted with pain as her knife sunk into his arm. He struggled to grab her, tangled in the curtains.

Jillian drew back the knife, stained by her attacker's blood, to strike again.

"Jillian . . . Christ . . . stop. . . . It's me . . ."

She froze. *Holy God . . . he had come back from the dead.*

Or was this someone playing a cruel trick on her? Had her ears deceived her?

"D—Duncan?" She couldn't move.

"Hell, yes, it's me." He struggled in the curtains, ripping a sheet down, trying to untangle himself. He looked like an apparition.

"You're dead. Buried in the sand." Her voice trembled. "Drowned by the tide. I heard them say they'd buried you."

"Apparently not well enough. Sweet Christ, will you help get me out of this mess?"

Jillian nearly laughed out loud. It had to be Duncan. No one else had the sense of humor he possessed. She grabbed at the thin drapes, frantically tearing them away. *"Duncan, Duncan,"* she sobbed, nearly hysterical.

"Jilly . . ." He put his arms around her, a portion of the curtain falling over her shoulder.

She yanked a bit of material from his face. It was him! Sweet heaven above, it was her husband!

Jillian threw her arms around his neck, heaving her body against his. "Duncan . . . Duncan . . ." She ran her hands over his bare shoulders, his tattooed chest, trying to convince herself he was no ghost.

"Jilly, I knew you were safe. I knew it," he murmured in her ear. He covered her face with kisses, catching her tears on the tip of his tongue.

She rested her head against his broad chest, running her fingertips over the multi-colored tattoos. "I . . . thought you were dead."

"I thought I was too, for a while."

"How . . . why . . ." She couldn't catch her breath. "I don't understand. Chuma *said* you were dead."

He grinned. "Lucky for you and me, our friend Chuma had his own agenda. He didn't leave me to drown, buried on the beach."

Jillian peered up at Duncan. He was freshly shaven, the

bear claw tattoo evident on his gaunt cheek. "What happened?"

"He sold me to a sugarcane plantation on the far side of the island." He kissed her lips once, then a second time. "Slave labor."

She kissed him back. "So, how did you get—"

"Enough talk, woman. Once we're safe, far from here, I'll tell you the story, start to finish; but right now, I just want to get the hell out of here. Where's Beatrice? Is she all right?"

Jillian smiled, her heart still pounding in her chest as if it would burst. "She's fine."

Duncan let his hand slide from where it rested on her full breast to her swelling abdomen. "The baby?"

She covered his hand with her own. "He's very strong." She laughed with a joy she hadn't felt in months. "He keeps me awake at night."

Duncan lifted an eyebrow. His dark hair was pulled back in a neat queue, but Jillian could see signs of gray he hadn't had before they'd left England. "He?"

" 'Twould be my bet if I were a betting woman."

Duncan's green eyes twinkled. "Let's get your sister and get the hell out of here, Jilly, so we can get on with our lives."

She dropped her hand on her hip, still holding on to him with her other hand. She was trying to think with her head instead of her emotions. "Bea's in her room, but she should be back any minute."

"You were expecting her at midnight?"

She touched the emerald necklace and the cotton bag she wore on her neck. "We were just on our way out."

He stared at her with a look of bemusement. "Oh, you were, were you?"

"It was that or become a bride again."

Duncan's face darkened suddenly. "I'll have that bastard Indigo on the tip of my sword before we sail."

"No." Jillian touched his thick, muscled forearm near the place where she had stabbed him with the paring knife. "I don't want him harmed if we can help it."

"Jillian, the man tried to kill me. He kidnapped you." Duncan looked away.

"That's all true, but he could have killed Beatrice and me. He could have sold us into slavery, too. But he didn't." She looked into his eyes. "Let's just go home," she said softly.

Just then the door swung open. Beatrice gave an involuntary squeak at the sight of Duncan.

"Look what the lizards dragged in," Jillian said, grinning ear to ear.

Beatrice stared wide-eyed. "A miracle," she whispered.

"Indeed that," Duncan retorted. "Now, let's hope the good Lord isn't out of them today, because it's going to take another one to get us out of here."

Jillian turned to him, suddenly filled with fear. She remembered all too well what had happened the last time they had tried to escape from this room. She also knew that, if they were caught, Indigo would make certain Duncan was dead this time. "Which way?" Jillian whispered.

"We're going to try the window. The corridor didn't work for us last time."

Jillian couldn't help but smile. How Duncan could keep his sense of humor at a time like this, she didn't know. It was odd, but she didn't remember his having a humorous side when they'd first met. It was something that seemed to have developed along with their relationship.

Duncan walked toward the balcony to stare out between the twisted drapes. Jillian stood beside him. "Where are the guards?" she whispered.

"Two are asleep. One's dead."

Jillian looked at him.

Duncan shrugged. "Natural causes."

She frowned. "I understand defending ourselves, but I just want to get out of here, Duncan. I want no blood path."

"I agree, sweet. I've seen enough suffering and death to last two lifetimes. Now here's the plan . . ."

A few minutes later, Jillian, Beatrice, and Duncan slipped out onto the balcony. In the darkness, she prayed they would be able to escape. She and Duncan were going home, home to Maryland, home to their newfound love. In her heart she knew everything was going to be all right.

The two women followed Duncan to the edge of the balcony. Duncan went over the side first, followed by Beatrice. When Bea was safely on the ground, Duncan waved to Jillian. "Hang over the side, and I'll catch you before you touch the ground." He held out his arms. "It won't be far then."

Gingerly, Jillian climbed over the railing. She'd done this two months ago, but without the encumbrance of an extended abdomen. Now, suddenly, she was afraid.

"Come on, sweet. We haven't much time."

The words had barely left his mouth when a voice came from the path in the distance. "Ship off the beach!" the voice cried.

A bell clanged, sounding the alarm. A guard appeared around the corner of the house.

"Jillian!" Duncan urged. "Now!" Then he spun around to meet the pirate guard, saber to saber.

A musket shot rang out in the still, humid air, and Jillian heard the sound of the lead ball as it whirred by her head. Giving an involuntary cry, she let go of the railing and fell.

She hit the ground hard, a sharp pain streaking up her shin. For a second she lay still in the grass, cradling her abdomen, waiting for the pain to pass.

"Jilly?" Beatrice went down on her knees beside her sister. "Jilly, are you all right?"

"Yes," she panted. "Just . . . just help me up."

But when Jillian took her sister's arm and tried to stand, she found she couldn't put any pressure on her leg.

Jillian paled, her heart fluttering. The fear was worse than the pain. She fought back her tears. "I—I don't know if I can walk."

"Go! Go!" Duncan was shouting as he sidestepped the pirate's parry. "Run for the jungle. There are men there who will help you to the ship."

"I'm not going without you!" Jillian cried fiercely. Hanging onto her sister, she twisted around to see Duncan slice the pirate's sword arm.

The pirate yelped in pain, blood gushing from the wound as the sword fell to the grass.

Duncan gave the bleeding pirate a hard kick in the stomach, and the pirate went down on all fours.

Half a dozen dangerous-looking men brandishing machetes appeared out of the darkness. "Let's go!" Duncan cried. "This is our escort."

A volley of musket-shots sounded. Someone fired off Jillian's balcony into the men pouring out of the jungle.

"She's hurt!" Bea hollered. "Jilly can't walk."

Duncan came running.

"The shots, they scared me," Jillian apologized, fighting her tears. "I fell."

"Sweet Mary!" came a familiar voice.

Jillian looked to see Indigo coming around the corner of the house from the front, a pistol in his hand. He was only half-dressed, in riding breeches and slippers. His black hair fell loose to his shoulders in disarray. Bare-chested as he was, it was evident that, though slender, Indigo was a strong man.

"Does this man not die?" Indigo demanded incredulously. "You kill him and he doesn't die? Chuma! Chuma, where the hell are you?" He swung his pistol in fury. "I'll have your ass in a sling for this one."

More shots rang out. Duncan's men that had come from the jungle met Indigo's pirates head on. The clash of sabers rang through the jungle.

Duncan swung Jillian into his arms.

"Put her down and back away!" Indigo shouted.

Jillian hung onto Duncan's neck. "Let me go, Indigo," she pleaded. "You know this won't work. It will never work."

"No!" he shouted stubbornly. "You're mine. I'll have you or no one will."

Jillian's gaze met the pirate's. "So, kill me," she said softly. "Kill me or let me go."

With a growl of anger, Indigo lunged forward. Duncan dropped Jillian to the ground on her good leg, and Beatrice came up behind her to support her.

Duncan's fist connected with Indigo's jaw, making a sickening crack. "Let us go!" Duncan called.

"Never! She's mine!" Indigo slurred through his broken jaw. He attempted to aim the blunderbuss pistol, but Duncan lifted his leg high and kicked Indigo in the forearm. The pistol flew out of the pirate's hand and slid across the damp grass.

Indigo hurled himself at Duncan in fury, hitting him soundly in the stomach with his fist.

"Stand on your own," Beatrice whispered.

Before Jillian could answer, Beatrice let go of Jillian and slipped away behind her.

Trying to keep her balance on her good leg, Jillian cringed as Duncan slammed his fists into Indigo's face again and again. But for a small man, in comparison to Duncan, Indigo was an excellent fighter. Both men were covered in blood.

"All right, Indigo, that will be enough," came Beatrice's voice from behind Jillian.

Jillian turned to see her sister aiming the pistol at Indigo.

Panting, Duncan backed up, coming around toward Jillian.

"Put that down, Bea," Indigo ordered. "That's very naughty. You'll be punished."

"You have to let my sister and her husband go now."

Indigo wiped at his bloody nose with the back of his hand. "You wouldn't shoot me."

Bea smiled. "That's where you're wrong. I would." She glanced at Jillian and Duncan, but still kept her aim. "Get her to the ship, Duncan. I'll hold him. If any of his men go after you, I'll shoot him." She looked at Indigo. "Now, call off your men."

When he didn't immediately respond, she shook the pistol. "Call off your men, Indigo, else I swear by all that's holy I'll kill you."

"Lay down your arms!" Indigo ordered. "Let them go."

Slowly, the clang of sabers ceased and the jungle was nearly silent except for the rustle of the trees and the insect song.

Duncan swung Jillian into his arms, starting toward the jungle. "To the ship!" he ordered his men.

Jillian clutched Duncan's neck, calling desperately. "No, you can't do this, Bea." She looked at Duncan. "I won't do this. I won't leave Bea behind."

Duncan halted.

"Go!" Beatrice shouted. "I'll be all right. He won't hurt me. I know he won't."

"Put down that blessed pistol," Indigo intoned through clenched teeth. "You're making me very angry, Beatrice dear."

"Run!" Beatrice shouted. "Take her, Duncan, take her home to Maryland. This is where I want to be. Here." She looked at Indigo. "With him," she added softly.

Jillian's frightened gaze met Duncan's. "Don't make me do this."

"It's our only chance."

"She's my sister. I can't leave her."

"Would you do it for her?"

Jillian hung her head.

"Answer me," Duncan demanded harshly.

"Yes," Jillian sobbed. "Yes, I'd do it for her."

Duncan took off at a dead run.

"I love you," Beatrice called as they entered the edge of the jungle.

"We'll come back for you," Jillian sobbed.

Beatrice waved goodbye, and then Jillian lost sight of her in the darkness.

Twenty-seven

Nervously, Algernon shifted his weight from one foot to the other. He fingered the lace of his sleeve as he watched Constance Abbott move from one knot of guests to the next. The Colonials had come from miles around to attend the funeral; some traveled days.

She was a lovely lady, Constance, dressed in her heavy silk-and-taffeta mourning gown. Her honey curls, piled high on her head in a tor, were as thick and shiny as market taffy. Her hands were smooth, her nails well manicured. Her pursed lips were darkened with red paste. She had plucked and powdered her face, but her cheeks were properly lacking rouge. She was, indeed, a lovely woman. Algernon surmised that few of the mourners guessed she was fifty-five.

"Algernon? Algernon, come here."

Algernon heard his grandmother call and knew that he should go to her; but then, to his delight, he caught Constance's eye. He hurried across the room in the opposite direction from the dowager, toward the fair-haired hostess. He left his brandywine glass on a cherry sideboard as he went by. "M—"

"Don't say it!" Constance hissed. She smiled sadly at the guest who passed, then turned to Algernon with a frown, whispering, "I told you never to call me that, didn't I?" Her breath was scented with a heavy mixture of French brandy and toilet water.

"Y—yes. I—I apologize. It's only that I'm overwrought,

as are you, madame. This is a difficult time for us both." He looked up at her, hoping for a pat on the shoulder, perhaps a hug, some small demonstration of her affection.

One of the mourners, a tall man with a bobbing Adam's apple, took Constance's hand. "I'm so sorry for your loss, Constance. I cannot imagine what you must be going through, having lost your son once to the savages, only to have had him returned again, and now to have had him meet his death so tragically. And to think, his wife and unborn child perished, too."

"I know, I know." She rolled her head dramatically, then leaned on the man for support, pressing her breasts against him.

"Duncan was a fine man."

Constance produced a scented handkerchief and dabbed her nose, giving a convincing sniff. "Thank you so much, dear Myron. It's only due to my dear friends and family that I'm able to keep my wits about me."

Algernon bowed stiffly, introducing himself to the mourner whose hand Constance was holding so tightly. "Algernon Roderick, sir."

"My nephew," Constance interjected quickly.

"Myron Welsh." The man bowed. "Your servant, sir." Then he turned his attention back to Constance. "Please, do let us know if there's anything you need, dear." He smiled grimly. "And I am sorry for your loss."

She pursed her lips as he walked away. "Thank you so much, Myron, and do send dear Jane my love." Then, under her breath, as he walked away, she whispered, "It's just too bad your whore-wife is in childbed with a another man's son, again."

Algernon stared at Constance.

"Well, she is," she whispered. "Everyone knows Jane Welsh sleeps with anything with three legs. Now, go get me a drink—brandy. I'm parched. Grief does that, you know." She touched the sleeve of his new pink-and-bayberry doublet. "No, two. And don't you dare sip from either glass. Get your own."

"Yes, madame."

"Meet me in Peter's office. You and I have a matter to discuss, and I'm sick of these horse's asses. Peter must have invited everyone in the colony. They'll not go home until they've drunk every bottle of English liqueur, eaten every crumb of meat and pastry, and slept on every sheet in my house."

Algernon watched Constance flounce away and then ran to fetch her drinks. A few minutes later, he found her in her husband's private office, seated at a desk.

"Come in, come in." She gestured. "And shut the blasted door. Do you want someone to see us?" She snatched one of the glasses from his hand, and a portion of the amber liquid spilled onto the cherry desktop. "Sit, sit. You make me nervous hovering the way you do."

Algernon did as he was told.

Constance drained half the glass of brandywine before she came up for air. "Now, I've had my solicitor draw up the papers." She pushed a pile of legal documents and a quill and inkwell across the desk. "Just sign, and the matter will be settled."

Algernon glanced at the papers, then at Constance, not quite certain of himself. He wanted so badly for her to like him. "Sh—should I read it first?"

"Ods fish, no. I told you, my solicitor drew it up. Don't you trust me?" She let her words sink in and then went on faster than before. "It's all quite in order. I will manage your estates and monies. You will carry the title, *my lord.*" She batted her eyelashes. "We'll discuss your payment later, of course."

"Just so that I understand, madame," Algernon hedged. "*Why* am I giving you control of my inheritance?"

Constance slapped her hand so hard on the desk that Algernon jumped. "Because of your nervous disposition, of course." She gestured to him, as if his reaction were proof enough. "I'm better able to look after your interests—" Her voice softened *"—darling."*

Algernon smiled. She was so lovely. She could be so sweet. "Of course," he murmured and reached for the quill, anxious to sign.

Constance relaxed in the leather chair and retrieved her brandy.

The office door swung open, and Algernon looked up, startled. It was just Alfred, Constance and Peter's whiny son.

"Mama! Father says I mustn't have another sweet." He came around the desk to his mother, pouting. His pock-marked face was covered with sticky sugar and jelly. "He says I'll pop like an overinflated pig's bladder if I eat another bite. But if I don't taste Martha's crumpet, I fear I shall perish!"

Constance reached out to adjust one of the pale-blue ribbons tied in her son's hair. "Just sneak into the kitchen, love, and tell Martha you must have one," she crooned. "Father need never know."

The ten-year-old boy crossed his fleshy arms over his chest "And what if they're gone, Mother? What shall I do, then?"

"Well, Martha shall have to make you some more crumpets, of course." She smiled. "Now, run along, dearest, and do try to stay out of your father's way."

As the boy exited the office, Peter entered. The child ducked under his father's arm and ran down the hall.

"Alfred, come back here! Alfred!"

"Peter, hush." Constance reached for her second glass, the first one now empty. "Our guests will hear you, and what will they think? Shame on you, behaving so harshly on the children and it being the day of my eldest son's funeral."

Algernon glanced up at Constance, suddenly wishing he weren't in the middle of this conversation.

Peter closed the door behind him. "You're drunk, again," he accused distastefully.

"I'm in a state of grief." She lifted her chin so that the wrinkles of her neck were barely visible. Seated so closely to her, Algernon could see where the thick make-up on her face was beginning to crack. "I have a right to a glass of refreshment."

"Refreshment, my ass. I saw the maid bring you a bottle at breakfast." He scowled. "You disgust me, Connie. You've turned our son into a worthless, whining milksop. Our daughter can barely speak by her own wits, she's so downtrodden, and you spend your days getting soused and plucking your futtering eyebrows!"

A single, well-rehearsed tear ran down Constance's rice-powdered face. "My son is dead, and you speak to me this way?"

"*Your son,* to whom you barely gave the time of day after he returned from the savages? *Your son,* to whom you said 'good riddance' the day we received the message of his death at sea?" Peter spat. "Oh please, spare me, Constance. Save your histrionics for someone who doesn't know you as well as I do." He glanced at Algernon. "Save them for that little turd."

Algernon's mouth dropped open, shocked a husband would address his wife in such a manner.

Peter slammed the door behind him.

"Oh, what are you staring at? Eavesdropper!" Constance picked up a small leather-bound receipt book and threw it at Algernon. It glanced off his ear.

He jumped up out of the leather armchair.

"Did you sign it?" she demanded.

"Y—yes."

"Then get the blast out of here."

Algernon backed toward the door. Constance was overwrought, that was all. Today was the day of Duncan's funeral. She wasn't really herself. "I—I'll speak with you later, madame." He clasped the doorknob. "When you're feeling better."

She snatched up the documents, still damp with his signature. He'd signed them *Algernon Roderick, Earl of Cleaves.*

"Get out!" Constance shouted. "Get out, all of you! This gray hair, it's your fault; the wrinkles, your fault," she ranted. "You did this to me, all of you! You made me old . . ."

Algernon reached the paneled door just before the second book struck.

Jillian tucked her hands behind her head, sitting up, but resting against a pillow. She was seated on the bunk in the captain's quarters of the *Royal Fortune.* Duncan and Jake had stolen the pirate ship out of the Port Royal harbor. "But it's been weeks," she protested, watching Duncan carry her dirty plate to a bucket near the door. "I'm going stir-crazy."

He came back across the small, but comfortable cabin, a glass of wine in his hand. "I want the leg to heal properly."

"I thought you said it was going to be fine. No limp."

He sat on the edge of the bunk. "It is." He brushed his lips against hers, tasting of wine. "It's going to be fine because I made an excellent splint and because you're going to do as I say and continue your bed rest for another month."

Jillian laughed, running her hand over her rounded belly. "By then I won't be able to walk. You'll have to roll me."

He covered her hand with his. "I told you, Jilly, I find your change in shape rather attractive." He ran his hand back and forth over her abdomen. "A trim waist has nothing over this."

She was seven and a half months pregnant now. Duncan thought they'd be in Maryland within the next ten days, depending on the winds offshore. By the time they were settled in their house on the Chesapeake, the baby would be arriving.

Jillian smiled sadly. If only Bea were going to be with her when it came time for her lying-in. But, of course, that was impossible. Bea was still in Jamaica, safe she hoped . . . she prayed.

Duncan brushed her chin with his fingertip. "What is it, sweet?"

She made a face. "I was just thinking about my sister."

"She'll be fine. You said yourself, Indigo wouldn't harm her. I'll be back to get her before she knows it."

Jillian gripped his muscular forearm. After only a month of decent food, Duncan already looked robust and healthy again. He seemed none the worse for wear for the two months he had spent on the sugarcane plantation, the only lasting evidence being a few gray hairs. "As soon as we reach Maryland, you'll go back for her? You promise?"

He held up his right hand. "Promise." Then he kissed her again.

Jillian licked her upper lip. "Good wine. Where did you get it?"

Duncan climbed into the bunk, and she wiggled over, making room for him, her leg still propped on a rolled blanket. "There are definite advantages to acquiring a pirate ship."

She lifted a feathery eyebrow. *"Acquire?* Now, you sound like Indigo. I thought it was called stealing."

He stared at her incredulously. "Not if the ship was never his to begin with."

She laughed. "But of course."

For a moment they lay side by side on the bunk, just happy to be together, pleased to have resolved their differences to the point where they knew they would live out their lives in content. Of course, there were still matters to iron out. So much of Duncan's past was still a mystery to her; but brick by brick, she was pulling down the wall that had once threatened to separate them forever.

"Duncan?"

"Yes?"

She rolled gingerly onto her side so that she faced him. "I know you said you don't want to talk about it, but what are you going to do about Algernon? I have a right to know."

He groaned. "I suppose word was sent immediately to the Colonies that the *Kelsey Marie* sank with all hands. Once word reaches London, if it hasn't already, the conniving bastard will have my inheritance again."

"So, what's to be done?"

"My solicitor will have to deal with the matter. I've got tobacco to plant."

"No." She traced the bear claw tattoo on his cheek. "I mean, what are you going to *do* about him? He has to be stopped."

"I'll have to kill him or have him killed, I suppose," Duncan answered flatly. "I've no choice. I'll not be safe—you and the babe'll not be safe—until the matter is settled."

"Couldn't you leave it to the courts?"

"And what proof do I have that my cousin attempted to have me murdered? The *Kelsey Marie* was not the first ship to go down under a pirate attack, nor will it be the last. You think Indigo is going to go under oath and say who hired him?"

"I suppose not."

"It's Algernon or us, Jilly. And shortly, we'll have the child to think of."

"You're right." Jillian closed her eyes. *Death.* She didn't like to think about it, but it was the only logical answer.

"So, what would you like to do this evening?" Duncan questioned, changing the subject. He caught a stray lock of her hair and wrapped it around his finger.

She looked at him. "Go for a walk on the deck?"

"Nope. But I can carry you up, if you'd like."

She frowned. "It's not the same thing. Besides, Jake's sailors gawk at me."

"They can't help it. Some haven't seen a white woman

in years, and certainly not one with such beautiful hair and charming freckles." He ran his finger along the bridge of her nose.

Jillian sighed with boredom. "We could play cards."

"Dice," Duncan offered.

"Or, we could . . ." She whispered in his ear.

Duncan grinned. "Precisely what I was thinking, but I didn't want to be accused of being insensitive to my wife's delicate condition."

She laughed huskily, curling against him. "It's the only physical activity you'll let me participate in these days."

He set his glass of wine on a stool beside the bunk and took her in his arms, cupping one full breast with his hand. "Love-making is actually known to encourage broken bones to knit faster." He pressed his mouth to the valley between her breasts.

"I'd never heard that." She laughed, lifting her head to feel his lips at the pulse of her throat.

"So, tell me what you had in mind, lady-wife. Your wish is my wish."

She ran her fingers through his unbound hair, reveling in the scent of his masculinity. "I want you to kiss me."

He raised up on one elbow to brush his lips against hers. "Here?"

"Yes," she whispered.

He scooted down in the narrow bunk. "And what of here?"

Jillian ran her hands over his broad shoulders as he nuzzled her breasts, making a wet spot on the thin linen of her gown with his tongue.

"Yes," she whispered. She could already feel a warmth spreading over her, a warmth that kindled in the pit of her belly and radiated outward to her limbs.

Duncan pushed aside the thin material of the dressing gown he'd found for her in a trunk in the hold and caught her nipple between his teeth. He drew it into his mouth and sucked gently at first, then with greater demand.

Jillian sighed . . . then she moaned. Duncan knew her better than she knew herself. He knew what she liked . . . what she craved.

"Jilly, my sweet Jilly," he crooned. His tongue teased her nipple to an aching torment. He found one breast and then the other, tugging, teasing her into a frenzy.

He unbuttoned her gown and flung it open. The cool cabin air made her skin prickle with goosebumps, adding to her sensitivity. His hot, callused hands roamed over her, sending shivers of desire down her spine.

She ran her hands freely over his rippling, muscular form, reveling in the feel of his skin against hers. "Take your clothing off," she murmured in his ear, nipping at his lobe. "Take it off, love."

Duncan complied with her wishes; and in an instant, he was stretched out beside her again, naked, his rigid member proof of his desire for her.

Jillian explored the colorful tattoos on his chest, the bulging biceps and triceps of his arms. She could never get enough of this man's body. She fantasized about it during the day; she dreamed of it at night. Since they had been reunited, she couldn't get enough of him. No matter how many times they made love in a day, it wasn't enough.

Their mouths met hungrily, and she tasted the wine he'd drunk, their tongues twisting in a dance of passion.

"Where else shall I kiss you?" Duncan murmured.

Her breath was ragged. "You know . . ."

He laughed, his voice husky with excitement. "I know, but tell me. Show me . . ."

Slowly, Jillian ran her hand over her belly to the source of her pleasure. She brushed the bed of red curls with her fingertips. "Here, touch me here, husband. Kiss me here."

"Of course . . ." Then he slid further down in the bunk, taking care not to disturb her injured leg. When he had lowered his head between her legs, she closed her eyes, arching her back against the hot, sweet heat of his probing tongue.

Jillian entangled her fingers in his long, dark hair. "Duncan," she moaned. "Duncan . . ."

He fanned the flames of her desire, teasing her into a frenzy of aching want. Then, finally sensing how near she was to the brink of release, he slid up in the bed again and lay beside her so that they were facing each other. She was panting heavily.

Duncan reached for his glass of wine.

Jillian open her eyes. "What are you doing?" she asked, her voice strained and breathy.

"Resting." He sipped the wine. "I'm in no hurry, are you, love?"

"Resting!" Jillian flung her arm over her face, trying to catch her breath. Her heart was pounding, her blood racing. "You're a tease," she accused.

"Just the way you like me." He winked.

Jillian grabbed him by the shoulders and pressed her lips hard against his, sharing the wine still in his mouth.

A little liquid spilled from the glass onto his chest. When he went to wipe it up with the corner of the sheet, she pushed aside his hand. Two could play this game of exquisite torture . . .

"What are you doing?"

She flattened her tongue against his chest and licked up the wine.

"Jilly, I was just teasing." He tried to roll on top of her, but she pushed him back onto his side. She dipped her finger into his wine glass.

"Now what?"

She laughed deep in her throat, touching her fingertip to his nipple. He shrank back in reaction to the cool liquid.

Jillian brushed his nipple with the tip of her tongue, then pressed her lips against it to suck.

Duncan groaned, lifting his head. "Where did you learn that?"

"From you." She dipped her finger into the glass again, this time painting a red trail of wine down the middle of his tattooed chest and lower . . .

Duncan lay back as she began to lick up the dark wine, following the path she'd drawn. Lifting her head, she took a drink of the wine and, holding it in her mouth, she let it dribble onto his tumescent member.

"And that?" He lifted her thick curtain of hair so that he could watch. "Where did you learn that, sweet?"

She looked up, licking the wine from her lips. "I thought of that on my own," she whispered. Then she lowered her head over him, touching her tongue to the tip of his throbbing, engorged shaft, tasting the wine and his saltiness

"Jilly," he moaned as she explored his length, taking her time as he had taken his.

"Jillian, you don't have to . . . your leg . . . the baby . . ." His words were coming in short bursts.

"Shhhh," she hushed, lifting her head to stare into his green eyes. "I want to. Lie back and let me give you the pleasure you've given me so often."

So, Duncan lay back, watching her, his eyes full of passion.

Again and again, Jillian took him to the edge. . . . He moaned, he called her name; she delighted in his pleasure.

Finally, when Jillian sensed her husband couldn't stand her sweet torture much longer, she slid up, throwing her good leg over him so that she could mount him.

"Jillian, your leg."

"Just a fracture," she answered. "Remember?" Then, before he could protest further, she raised up, guiding him with her hand until he penetrated her.

Jillian dug her knees into the feather tick, unaffected by the splint on her calf. Suddenly, her own desire was urgent once again.

Duncan caught her around the waist, his broad hands spanning her hips, his eyes drifting shut as she moved to the rhythm that was only theirs. Again and again, she raised and lowered her body over him, taking him deeply, her moans of pleasure mingling with his. Fire spread from her loins outward as she moved closer to that precipice she knew only Duncan could take her to.

Then, against her will, it was all over too quickly. She reached the edge and fell, dissolving into pulsing, molten ecstasy she could never experience often enough.

"Duncan," she cried as he lifted his hips beneath her.

"Jillian . . ." He pulled her hard against him, and then he, too, was satiated.

Jillian rolled onto her side, curling up against him, her back to his chest. She wiggled until her buttocks were settled against his groin. He wrapped his arm around her waist, kissing the damp curls at the back of her neck.

"I love you, Jillian," he murmured.

She smiled in the semi-darkness. "And I, you."

She wanted to just lie beside Duncan and bathe in her happiness, but there was one thing that she still felt separated them, something even more important than his past. It was a matter that Duncan refused to discuss.

"Duncan," she said after a few minutes. "It's important that you believe me."

He didn't look at her. "I told you it didn't matter to me. I wanted you to live at any cost. Whatever you did for the sake of our unborn child was honorable."

"But I didn't do anything with Indigo."

Duncan got out of bed and picked up his clothing. He dressed, his back to her. "You don't really expect me to believe that, do you?"

She pulled the sheet up over her bare breasts, suddenly chilled. "Yes, I do."

"I told you, it's not important to me. After all, if a man sips from the well, it's not drunk up."

"I don't want to hear any of that Mohawk nonsense!" she flung, hurt . . . angry. "I want you to tell me you believe me when I say Indigo never touched me."

He tucked his shirt into his breeches and sat down to pull on his boots, more booty from the hold of the pirate ship. "I can't do that." He stood, turning to look at her with those green eyes she had come to love and, at times like this, to hate. "All I can say is that I forgive you. I will never bring up the subject again, and you'd be wise to do the same." He started for the door.

"Come back here!" she cried, throwing her legs over the side of the bunk. He was running from her, the son of a bitch. "Come back here and finish this! I won't be your wife with you thinking I betrayed you! I swear to God, I won't! I'll leave you, Duncan! I'll go home to London."

He stopped at the cabin door, glancing first at her broken leg, then at her protruding abdomen.

"I don't think you'll be going anywhere anytime soon."

Gone was her beloved Duncan. In his place stood the cold, arrogant man that she had met that warm day in her father's garden. Suddenly, Jillian realized she was fool if she ever thought she could change him.

He opened the door. "I'm going up on deck for some air." Then he was gone.

Jillian flung herself back on the bunk, too furious for tears. He thought she had spoken her words in anger, but she was utterly serious. She'd leave Duncan if he thought she betrayed their love. Even if it broke her heart.

Constance rested against a silk pillow, an herbal poultice covering her eyes. It was late at night; the house was quiet. "How dare you come here?" she whispered harshly. "How dare you come to my private chambers uninvited?"

"I did everything you asked and, now, I want my payment," came the male voice.

Constance chuckled. "Considering the circumstances, considering who did what, I wouldn't think you'd be in a position to demand anything."

"But it was your idea. I only followed your instructions."

She adjusted the soothing eye-poultice. A mixture of chamomile, rose water, and cow dung, it was supposed to eliminate crow's feet. "You have no proof of that. You have no proof of anything, twit."

He exhaled. "Just give me the entire payment, and I'll go. I'm afraid the dowager is suspicious. She keeps asking questions."

"Old, nosy fool. I never liked her and her brassy hair." Constance sighed. "Well, I don't keep those sums about. You'll have to give me a few days."

"You've been saying that for weeks."

"Well, I'm saying it again, damn it!" She ripped off the eye-poultice and flung it at him.

He retreated into the shadows of the doorway so that she couldn't see his face.

"Come back in a few days." She reached for the glass beside her bed.

"Just give me my due, and I'll never trouble you again."

"Get out," she hissed, "or I'll call Peter. Get out!"

He closed the door quietly behind him.

Twenty-eight

"It is beautiful," Jillian conceded. She stood on the deck of the *Royal Fortune* beside Duncan, leaning against him for support. It was early June, and the bright sunshine was warm on her face. Last night, they had sailed into the Chesapeake Bay and were now approaching the cove used by Duncan's tobacco ships.

"There's the house." He pointed. "Do you see it?"

In the distance, she spotted a three-story, white-brick house far off the bank. It was surrounded by trees and a grassy lawn that led down to the water's edge. Were circumstances different, she would have thought the view nearly perfect.

"It's nothing like the homes in England, but for here, it's quite nice. Once we have furniture—"

"I'm certain it will be fine," she said, cutting him off. They had not settled the matter of Indigo. Duncan refused to discuss it and so, once again, their relationship was strained. He obviously thought she would get over her anger and resentment. He obviously didn't know her as well as he thought he did.

Jake called to set anchor and the ship slowed, came about, and drifted to a halt. A dingy was lowered over the side and, within half an hour's time, Jillian found herself in the small boat, being rowed to shore. Duncan was at her side.

"My land runs to the north and south along the bay and then to the west." He stood on the bow of the boat as they neared the grassy shore. "Once you're up to riding again, I'll show you the tobacco fields. Last summer, we were cutting one to the northwest. I sure as hell hope the men finished in my absence."

Someone appeared on the shore, waving. Duncan waved back. "It's good to be home," he said softly, dropping his hand to Jillian's shoulder. "Good to be home."

Home? Jillian thought dismally. *Where was her home, now?* She could not, she would not, remain in Maryland if Duncan wouldn't believe she'd not had relations with Indigo. Where would she go? To England, she supposed. Back to Breckenridge, for surely her father wouldn't take her in.

Jake's men rowed the boat onto the sandy shore beside a wooden dock. An old black man in a red shirt jumped up and down excitedly. When Duncan stepped onto the beach, in the shallow water, the old man went down on his knees clasping his hands.

"That's Atar's father, William," Duncan explained.

"A ghostie!" the man wailed. "Ghosts have set upon us."

"No ghosts, Billy," Duncan called, good-naturedly. "It's me in the flesh."

The man got to his feet, squinting in the sunlight. "You certain that's you, masta', and not a spirit?" He still appeared suspicious, even upon closer inspection.

Duncan laughed, hitting his broad chest. "It's me, all right."

"But . . . but yer dead. We got the word weeks ago, masta'. We done had your funeral. Yer dead and sunk to the bottom of the sea wit' yer new wife."

"I'm telling you, I'm not dead." He leaned over the side of the boat and swept Jillian into his arms. "And here's my new wife, come to set this household straight. Just as I promised."

"Put me down, please, Duncan," Jillian said in his ear. "I can walk. I've been walking on the ship for weeks whenever you weren't about." She hung onto his shoulders. "This is not how I want to meet your staff."

"Hush, Jillian. There'll be no argument. It's too far for you to walk to the house." He started up the gently sloping bank. "And when we get there, you're going straight to bed."

Jillian gritted her teeth. She didn't want to make a scene out of Duncan's homecoming, but neither did she want to be treated like a child, too foolish to know what was good for her. In the last week, she'd had just about enough of Duncan Roderick and his cool control.

Halfway up the lawn, a familiar figure appeared on the steps of the great white house, surprising them both.

Jillian looked at Duncan. "Daphne? It can't be . . ."

The old woman with her bright red hair came down the steps and trotted across the lawn. A young manservant chased after her. "Your cane, madame," he called, waving it. "You've forgotten your cane."

"Grandmother!" Duncan hollered.

When the dowager reached them, she threw her arms around Duncan, embracing Jillian as well. Tears ran down her wrinkled cheeks. "I thought you were dead," she said over and over again. "Drowned at sea. That's what the message was. Constance said the ship went down with all hands."

Duncan seemed genuinely delighted to see her. "You don't think a few pirates would get the best of me, do you, Grandmother?"

She laughed, patting his arm. "Oh, and heavens, child, what's happened to you?" she asked, noticing at once Jillian's splinted leg.

"It was broken, but I'm much better now, as good as new." She glared at Duncan. "I could walk if he would let me."

"It's wise to keep her off her feet," the dowager said, falling into step beside Duncan. "How much longer before the baby comes?"

"Six weeks, I would guess." Jillian answered before Duncan could. "Now, what in sweet heaven's name are you doing here, Daphne? We left you in London."

She threw up a hand. "I decided to come and see Duncan's Maryland for myself. That and my great-grandchild."

They reached the simple, three-story, white-washed brick house and Duncan carried Jillian up the front steps with the dowager directly behind him.

"Take her to the master chamber," Daphne ordered. "I've been staying there, but of course you and Jillian must have it." She clapped her hands to get her manservant's attention. "Joshua, run to the kitchen and tell Mary we'll need clean linens and tea. Decent English tea for the new mistress!"

"Yes, madame."

Duncan carried Jillian up the grand staircase as she turned in his arms to catch a glimpse of the sparse, yet elegantly furnished house.

"Stop wiggling," Duncan chastised. "There'll be plenty of time for exploring the house later."

The dowager hurried up the staircase behind Duncan, holding onto the polished oak banister for support. "So tell me how it is that you managed to survive, grandson. I still can't believe it's you!"

Duncan took Jillian down the hall and, with his foot, pushed open a door. The bedchamber was large and airy with a masculine tone.

Carefully, he set her on the bed. He reached behind her to arrange a pillow. "Comfortable?"

"I'd be more comfortable in the chair. I'm not sick, Duncan, just pregnant."

"With a broken leg." He crossed the room to adjust the thick, burgundy drapes so that the sun didn't shine directly in her eyes.

"A mended fractured leg," Jillian corrected, turning her attention to the dowager. "Our ship was captured by pirates and it was sunk, but we managed to get away."

"It's a very long story, Grandmother." Duncan came to

the bedside. "Perhaps we should let Jillian rest and talk later."

"I'm not tired," Jillian snapped, glancing at Duncan. "Tell her what happened. He's her grandson, too. She has a right to know."

Duncan frowned. "Jillian."

The dowager grabbed Duncan's hand. "What is she talking about? I have a right to know what? Tell me, boy. I'm not so old that you must shield me from truths."

Duncan crossed his arms, looking over the bedchamber he'd not set foot in in nearly a year. "We *were* attacked by pirates in Caribbean waters, Grandmother. Pirates sent by my dear cousin, Algernon. I've proof this time or, at least, proof enough for me. The pirate captain said he was hired by an Englishman to murder me and my family. It was only by luck and through Will's death that we survived."

The dowager covered her mouth with her hand. "No," she whispered.

"Listen, Grandmother, I understand that you love Algernon. I understand that you—"

"No, no," she insisted. Her rosy complexion went pale. "You don't understand. He's here."

Duncan's hands fell to his sides. "Here? Here, where?"

"Here in the Colonies. In Maryland." The dowager rose, her ringed hands trembling. "Why . . . I brought him with me on the ship. He said he hadn't tried to harm you in London. He said he had to make amends."

Duncan swore foully under his breath. "Where is he?" His hand came to rest on the hilt of his dagger.

"At your mother's."

Duncan stared at the dowager in angry astonishment. "At Constance's? What's he doing there?"

She clasped her hands. "He—he's been staying with her. Since we got word of your death."

"I don't understand," Jillian said, sliding across the bed to sit up.

"Why is he staying there? If he thinks I'm dead, *this* is his home."

The dowager swayed slightly, and Duncan reached out to steady her. "Tell me."

Jillian didn't know what was going on. Only that the dowager obviously knew something Duncan didn't.

"Grandmother?"

"A seat," she said softly. "Get me a seat, boy."

He left her side for only a moment, bringing her a straight-backed chair. He helped her into it. "Tell me."

The old woman hung her head. "I'm ashamed."

"Grandmother, tell me!"

The old woman sighed, looking up. "I swore I wouldn't. I swore to your father before God that I would never speak of her."

Duncan knelt before his grandmother, taking her trembling hand in his. "You swore to my father you would never tell about *whom?*"

She bit down on her ruby-pasted lower lip. "Your mother."

Jillian slid further onto the edge of the bed so that her feet touched the floor. She was confused, too. "You swore to Constance?"

The dowager shook her head no. "His real mother," she whispered. "I swore I wouldn't tell. I swore I would take the truth to my grave."

Duncan let go of his grandmother's hand. "Just tell me. Constance isn't my real mother?"

"No," Daphne answered, defeated. "Constance is not your mother. It's a strange tale. They say nothing's stranger than fact."

"I'm waiting . . ."

Jillian wanted to reach out to Duncan because, despite their troubles, she still loved him. But she sat where she was. "Just tell us what this is about, Daphne."

The dowager took a deep breath. "*Your father,* Duncan, was a good man, but he . . . he enjoyed the company of the ladies. Your Uncle Hamlet was wed to a young woman who came to his marriage bed already with child." She paused. "Your father was the father of the child."

"Who was the woman?" Duncan demanded. "Who was the child?"

"The woman was Constance. The child, Algernon."

"Algernon is my elder brother?"

"Half-brother. It was a terrible family scandal."

"Go on, Grandmother."

"Your father married a short time later. His wife gave birth to a son."

"Me?"

"Yes, my dearest." The dowager patted his hand. "She gave birth to you whilst your father was attending his brother's deathbed. Hamlet fell from his horse, hunting, and broke his neck. He only lived a day."

"The day I was born?"

Daphne nodded, patting her lips with her scented handkerchief. She seemed so much older than she had only a few moments before. "The birth was a hard one. We sent word to your father." She stared off, as if lost in her memories. "She wouldn't stop bleeding. The poor child was Catholic. I thought what harm would it do, bringing a priest to the house?" Her eyes filling with tears, she looked up at Duncan. "Jane was dying, barely seventeen years old and dying in childbed . . ." She shook her head. "I didn't realize how angry your father would be. I didn't understand how deeply his hatred for her Catholic religion ran."

"You're not making sense, Grandmother—"

Daphne lifted her tear-filled gaze. "I called the priest to give Jane her last rites. Your father arrived. I went to greet him. When we returned to Jane's room, the priest was baptizing you!"

Duncan chuckled, but without a glimmer of humor in his voice. "My mother had me baptized Catholic?"

"She said it was the only way to save your soul. Those

were her last words. Then she died." Daphne sighed, gaining control of her emotions. "Oh, how your father ranted and raved. He sent the priest away. He made me swear I would never tell."

"About the baptism?"

"Any of it. No one was ever permitted to speak Jane's name again in the household. That's how furious he was."

"And then he married Constance?"

Daphne nodded. "And she became your mother. Of course he couldn't claim Algernon as his eldest."

"Because he was a bastard," Duncan murmured, walking to the window. "It all makes so much more sense now . . . my entire childhood." He spoke as much to himself as to Jillian and Daphne.

"That's why Algernon always resented you."

"Because I was the heir, though he was the oldest of our father's children. I had the money, the title . . ."

"And his mother," the dowager offered.

"That son of a bitch!" He strode toward the door.

"Duncan!" Jillian rose out of the bed, walking stiffly toward him. "Where are you going?"

"You know where I'm going. Get back in bed!"

"Duncan!" she pleaded, following him. "Look at this from Algernon's point of view."

"He knew we were brothers, and yet he still tried to kill me! That makes his offense even more dishonorable!"

Jillian grabbed Duncan's arm. "So, now that you know the truth, you're going to kill him? You're going to murder your own brother?"

"Get back in the bed." He pushed her gently aside and went out the door.

"Duncan!" she called down the hall. "Duncan, please don't!" But he was already gone. She hurried across the room to look out the window at the ground below. A moment later, he burst through the front door onto the open porch.

"Get me that horse, David." She heard his shout through the paned glass windows.

A man appeared leading a horse already saddled.

"Good to see you, sir," the man said, obviously flustered. "I—I thought you were dead, sir."

Duncan slung himself into the saddle. "Do I look dead to you, David?"

"N—no, sir."

"Out of my way!" Then Duncan sank his heels into the horse's flanks and the mount leaped forward.

Jillian spun around. Daphne was headed for the door. "Where are you going?"

"To stop him," she answered. "If Algernon was responsible for the attempts on Duncan's life, then the courts need to tend to the matter. I know Duncan. If he kills Algernon in anger, knowing he's his half-brother, he'll never forgive himself."

"I'm going, too." Jillian hobbled toward the door, lifting her petticoats high.

"Stuff and nonsense! You shouldn't be about!"

Jillian passed the dowager in the doorway. "If he were your husband, would you go?"

The two women's gazes met.

"I'll, get the dogcart," Daphne conceded finally. "It's only a few miles to Constance's."

Walking stiffly with her splinted leg, Jillian followed the dowager down the servants' back staircase, through the kitchen, and out of Duncan's house. Before they were across the back lawn, a stable boy came bursting out of the barn. "Help him! He's gonna do it! He's gonna do it!" the frightened boy cried.

Daphne reached for his flailing arms. "James, calm down and tell me what's wrong. Is it your master?"

James shook his head. "Master Duncan rode off."

"Then what is it?"

The boy could only point in terror toward the barn.

Daphne lifted her black skirts and dashed off, moving faster than Jillian imagined possible for a woman her age. Jillian ran after her, limping.

Daphne threw open the barn door and halted in shock.

Jillian came up directly behind her, staring into the dimmer light of the stable.

What she saw made her blood run cold. It was a man . . . a man standing on a barrel, a noose thrown over the rafters and fastened securely around his neck.

A man she knew . . .

Twenty-nine

"Atar," Jillian said softly for fear she would startle him. "Atar, why are you doing this?"

Duncan's manservant stood stiffly on the barrel, dressed in his impeccable red coat, his hands on the noose at his neck. "My master . . ." he mumbled.

"He's alive, Atar." She moved slowly toward him. "He didn't perish on the sea. The claims were false. It was Algernon, he was the one trying to kill your master.

Atar trembled. "No . . ." He put up his hand. "Don't come closer!"

Jillian halted. "It's true. It was Algernon. Duncan went to find him now. To kill him, I fear."

"You don't understand." Atar's upper lip curled in a sneer. "I did it."

Jillian blanched. "What?"

The dowager moved up behind Jillian slowly. "What are you talking about, Atar?" she snapped. "Get off that barrel. I don't know what you want, but you'll not get it threatening suicide."

His brow creased. "You don't understand; none of you understand. I did it. I tried to kill him. I failed."

"You tried to kill Duncan?" Jillian whispered.

"Yes."

She believed him. It was the look on his face, the tone of his defeated voice. "Why? Why would you try to kill a man who was so good to you? He freed your father. He was going to free you, Atar."

"And who is he to give me my freedom?" Atar mocked venomously. "Who is he to have all when I, when my people, have nothing?"

He moved on the barrel, and Jillian's breath caught in her throat. "But he didn't die, Atar. You don't have to do this. If what you say is true, you only attempted to kill him. It's not the same thing."

"Same thing to a slave. They'll hang me the same." His mind seemed to wander as he steadied his footing on the barrel. "It was her fault, you know."

"It was whose fault?"

"The white bitch. She promised to pay me handsomely. 'What good is freedom without coin?' she asked. She said she understood the oppressed. She said she wanted to help me." He adjusted the thick rope around his neck. "Of course, she didn't. She only wanted me to do what her cowardly son couldn't."

"Atar, you don't have to do this. Duncan is a reasonable man. You were his faithful servant for years. He won't forget that."

"Only one way out for a slave—"

Jillian anticipated his move, but a second too late. She screamed and reached into the air as he leaped off the barrel.

Atar's neck made a sickening crack as it broke.

"No," Jillian whispered, squeezing her eyes shut.

The dowager grabbed her by the shoulders. "It's all right, child," she whispered. "You couldn't stop him. He was crazy."

The stable boy came running in through the door, leading the old black man, William. "No, no," the man moaned, going down on his knees in the clean straw. He clasped his hands in prayer, swaying. "Not my son. Not my boy."

Jillian rubbed her abdomen where she felt a sudden tightening. She made herself open her eyes, knowing she had to get hold of herself. Someone had to take control; someone had to be in charge.

Atar hung from the rope, swaying.

"Cut him down," Jillian ordered, turning away. "You!" She pointed to a young man who appeared in the barn. "Get someone to help you." She turned to the half-grown stable boy. "I want the dogcart hitched," she ordered.

The boy stared at her with frightened dark eyes.

"Now, I said." She took a deep breath, fighting what she assumed must be another contraction. But it was too soon for the baby. It would pass.

Jillian turned to Daphne. "We have to stop Duncan before he kills Algernon. Atar's story rang true."

The dowager nodded gravely. "It did, indeed."

A few minutes later, the stable boy led the dogcart, hitched to a dappled mare, to the barn's entrance. Jillian climbed in with his assistance.

"Are you all right, child?" Daphne questioned, sitting beside her.

She took another deep breath, not wanting the dowager to be suspicious. "Fine."

"I can do this alone. They're my grandsons, my responsibility. You should be in bed."

Jillian pushed the reins into the dowager's hands and handed her the buggy whip. "Let's go. We have to get there before Duncan kills him. He won't listen to Algernon, and it would never occur to him that Constance and Atar were responsible for the plot to kill him."

The dowager loosened the reins, and the dogcart rolled off, headed south.

"Not there, here, twit." Constance reached out and slapped the serving girl across the cheek.

The servant jumped, still clutching the cut-crystal brandy decanter.

"Here," Constance insisted. "How many times must I tell you simpletons where I want my refreshment?"

Fighting tears, the girl pushed the glass across the small table and set the decanter beside it. "Anything else, mistress?" she whispered, remaining an arm's length from Constance.

"No, you're dismissed. Get out!"

Algernon stepped aside to let the girl pass. He had come to see his mother because he'd been told she'd taken ill. He smoothed his thin mustache with his thumb and forefinger nervously. "Is . . . is there something I can do for you, madame? You seem vexed."

She leaned back in her chair and propped one heel on her footstool. "And why shouldn't I be?" She took a sip of brandy. "Peter came to me last night. He hasn't in weeks." Her lower lip trembled.

His mother didn't look herself to Algernon today. She was dressed in a floral silk banyon, her yellow hair covered by a matching turban. Her rouged cheeks were smudged, the kohl eye pencil smeared black beneath her lower eyelids. In the strong sunlight that poured through the windows, she looked older, less vibrant.

"I see," Algernon commented, not knowing what else to say.

"He came to my bed, wanting me . . ." She took another drink from the glass, then sneered, "He came to my bed smelling of another woman's perfume! Bastard!" She reached for the decanter, and glass clinked against glass as she removed the stopper. "It takes a lot for a woman my age to hold a man like my Peter, you know."

"Of course," Algernon answered, drifting toward the door.

"He gambles. It takes a great deal of money to keep him happy. To keep him here. That's why I need some of your inheritance, son, just a few hundred pounds a year. Just to keep him happy. To keep him from straying too far."

Algernon reached behind him to touch the doorknob. He didn't want to hear this. He didn't care about money. All he cared about was Mother. "I'll just leave you to yourself now, madame. Perhaps we can sup together tonight if you're feeling better." He tried to turn the knob, but it was yanked from his hand. The door swung open, and Algernon turned in surprise. "Duncan?" he croaked.

Duncan charged into Constance's bedchamber. He had hoped the ride would clear his head, alleviate some of his anger. He didn't want to kill in anger; he wanted to kill in revenge, in defense of his family. One glimpse of Algernon's face, however, and the rage returned.

"Surprised to see me?" Duncan feigned a smile. Algernon paled to the hue of milk glass. "And, dear mother—" He swung around "—what of you?"

Constance fluttered a painted fan, her face as ashen as her son's. "You . . . you're alive. The report," she gasped. "They said you were dead." Then she threw out her arms with all the drama Duncan knew she was capable of. "My beloved son, come home to me!"

Algernon had begun to inch toward the door. Duncan intercepted him, putting out his arm. "Not so fast, cousin. You and I have a matter or two to discuss . . . brother."

Algernon gasped.

"What do you know of the attack on my ship?"

Algernon's eyes widened. "N—nothing. O only what was said in the message. What . . . what madame told me."

"You had no prior knowledge of the attack in the Caribbean? Will died in that attack. The pirates killed him, thinking he was me."

"How horrid," Algernon breathed, seeming genuinely upset. "I—I liked Will."

"I don't want to hear about that!" Duncan snapped in disgust. "Just tell me how you did it so smoothly. I left a week early on a different ship than intended. Did you have someone watching for me in the Canary Islands? Was word sent on to the pirates when we put in those two days for water?"

Algernon was trembling from head to ribboned foot now. "I—I didn't do it; I swear I didn't!"

Duncan lunged forward, grabbing Algernon by the throat. "You little, cowering bastard. Just admit it! At least die with honor!

"Tell him!" Algernon screamed to Constance. "Tell him what happened, Mother. Please . . ."

Duncan's gaze met Constance's. She had the same blue eyes that Algernon possessed, something he had never noticed until this moment. "Tell me what?" Was Constance in on this as well? Nothing would surprise him at this point. He had been naive, entirely too naive. He tightened his grip on Algernon's throat, and Algernon began to gasp.

"Tell him," Algernon begged.

"Tell him what?" Constance arranged the folds of her silk banyon, as cool as Duncan had ever seen her. As cool as she had been that day in the field when she had turned around and ridden away, leaving him to the Mohawks. Of course she had left him behind. He wasn't her child.

Constance sighed. "I wanted to protect you, Algernon. You know I wanted to save you if I could." She looked at him sadly. "Because of the past, of course. But the game is up." She lifted her manicured hands in a helpless motion. "I can do no more."

"Mama, please . . ." Algernon pleaded.

"He did it, of course." Constance looked at Duncan. "I was wrong not to have tried to stop him, but what is a woman to do? I was here; he was so far across the ocean."

"Mother . . ."

"He wanted what he could never have." She went on faster with her confession. "He wanted your title, Duncan; he wanted your money, your respect."

Algernon was crying openly now.

Constance glanced away. "I suppose you shall have to kill him. How else will you be safe, Duncan?"

"No!" Algernon moaned, tears running freely down his cheeks. He struggled against Duncan's grip, clawing at the hands at his neck, begging for mercy. "She's a liar. It was her idea!" he bawled. "She wanted me to do it. I didn't want to kill you. I just wanted to make her love me."

Duncan stared into Algernon's frightened eyes. Something about the tone of his pitiful voice made him believe him. He wouldn't put it past Constance to play a part in his attempted murder. She had left him for dead once before, hadn't she? "So you did it for her?" he questioned.

"Yes," Algernon sobbed. "No . . . I . . . I didn't do it. I knew about it, but I didn't do it."

Constance rose to her feet. "Just kill him, Duncan. You'll not be safe until he's dead. He's a madman. None of you will be safe."

Struggling for each breath, Algernon pointed. "She had Atar help her. It was he, not I, that cut the boards on the scaffolding. He hired the man in New Forest. He found the pirates willing to murder you. I was just supposed to keep my mouth shut."

Duncan loosened his grasp on Algernon's neck, but only enough to allow him to catch a breath.

Where was the truth here? Could his faithful man Atar have done such a thing? The logistics were farfetched, but not impossible.

Duncan grabbed Algernon by his shoulders and shoved him into a chair. "Is it true, Constance? Did Atar do it? Did you ask him to?"

There were sounds of footsteps in the hallway and shouting. The door to Constance's bedchamber banged open, and Jillian appeared in the doorway. "Don't kill him!" she cried, stumbling in. "He didn't do it!" She was breathing heavily, her clothing rumpled. Sweat beaded above her upper lip. "It was Atar, Duncan," Jillian panted. "I'm sorry."

"But not alone," the dowager announced, following Jillian into the bedchamber. She swung a buggy whip. "He didn't do it alone, did he, Connie?"

"I don't know what you're talking about." Constance backed up toward her four-poster bed. She hugged herself tightly, shaking her head, her voice suddenly odd. *"I don't know what any of you're talking about. Care for tea? What of a sweet? My cook makes an excellent raspberry tart."*

"Don't know what we're talking about, indeed!" Daphne shouted, crossing the room. She cracked the buggy whip in the air. "Let's see what a few welts will do for your memory, shall we?"

Duncan reached out to take the whip. "Grandmother, no." He looked to Jillian. She was very pale. "Where's Atar?"

With great effort, she walked toward him. "D—dead. He hanged himself before we could stop him. He must have seen you leave on horseback headed this way. He must have known the ruse was over."

"Jillian, you shouldn't be up. You shouldn't have come." He frowned. "Are you all right?"

Duncan put his arms out to catch her as she crumpled.

"Oh," she moaned, gripping her distended abdomen.

When he caught her in his arms, he realized her gown was wet. "The baby?" he whispered in her ear, praying it wasn't true.

She nodded, grimacing as another contraction gripped her.

"But it's too soon." Gently, he helped her to her feet.

"Sorry." Somehow she managed a guilty smile. "Too much excitement. I guess he's decided to make his entrance into the world a little early."

Duncan swung Jillian into his arms. "Out of here, all of you but Grandmother!" He glared at Algernon as he slipped by. "I'm not done with you, cousin. Don't you disappear on me!" He gestured toward Constance, who was now doing some sort of dance in the corner of her room. It was as if she had suddenly gone as mad as May butter. "And get her out of here before I kill her, too."

Algernon went around Duncan and Jillian and caught his mother's hand. "This way, Mother. Let's go."

Constance looked at Algernon. "You'll dance with me, young man, won't you?"

Duncan carried Jillian to Constance's bed and laid her down. "I'll send for help," he told Daphne. "But it will have to be someone from your place. I wouldn't trust anyone here. You stay with her. I'll be back as quickly as I can." Then he brushed his lips against Jillian's feverish forehead and hurried from the room.

The following morning, Jillian lay in Constance's bed drifting in and out of sleep, her newborn son cradled in her arm.

She heard the door open and sleepily lifted her eyelids. Someone had drawn the heavy crimson drapes so that only a few rays of sunlight illuminated the room.

"Jilly?"

She smiled weakly, exhausted. It had been a long night. "Duncan?"

"How's our son?"

She pulled back the counterpane. "Look for yourself. He's tiny, but Daphne says he's in good health." She brushed her finger against his cheek; and in his sleep, he turned his head to suckle.

Duncan sat carefully on the edge of the bed. "I've never seen anything so beautiful," he whispered, looking down at the precious bundle.

Her gaze met his. "Does he look like your other son?" she asked gently. "The one who died."

He shook his no. "But he touches me in the same place." He brushed his chest at his heart. "Here."

"Want to hold him?"

"No. Let him sleep." But then he put out his arms. "Yes."

Jillian couldn't help but smile as she tucked the infant into his father's arm. Who would have thought the Colonial Devil would have been so sentimental over a child's being born, even his own? Most men barely gave a thought to the birth of offspring. It was simply something expected of a wife . . . a duty.

Duncan ran his forefinger over the crown of the baby's head. "Do you think he'll have red hair?"

Jillian tucked her hand behind her head. She was tired, but actually felt good, considering the number of hours she'd been in labor. She was hungry, too. "I don't know. He hasn't much hair at all right now. Bald as an apple, Daphne said." She studied her husband with amusement. "She said he looks just like you did as a babe."

He grinned. "She would. She's the only one who would dare."

Then Jillian brushed his arm. "So, how do you feel about this turn of events?"

He took a moment to answer. "I think I'm mostly relieved about Constance. Hurt Atar would betray me. Saddened by Algernon and his pathetic ways."

Jillian tucked the corner of the flannel blanket over the baby. In those three short sentences, Duncan had revealed more about his feelings than he had in the last six months. She was pleased. "So, what do you want to name him? Your son?"

The infant squirmed, and Duncan lifted him onto his shoulder and patted his padded bottom as if it were the most natural thing to him. "I was thinking William. Will."

Jillian nodded. "Good choice." She watched Duncan as he brushed his cheek against their son's downy head. "You know he forgave you for what happened back in London."

"I know."

"Do you forgive yourself, Duncan?"

He sighed. "I think so. I reacted in anger. I was hurt. I

think Will knew that. He was always the one who understood me better than I understood myself."

The baby began to make mewing sounds, rooting against Duncan's shoulder. "Is he hungry?"

She put out her arms to take him. "Yes."

Duncan handed little Will to Jillian and then got up from the bed. He watched as she opened her sleeping gown and put the baby to her breast. "We're going to have a good life, Jilly. You and I and the boy." He took a deep breath. "I can feel it in my bones."

Jillian toyed with the edge of the infant blanket. She really didn't want to discuss this matter right now, but he was the one who had brought it. As far as she was concerned, nothing had changed between them. "Duncan, I'm not staying."

"That's ridiculous."

"It's not. I told you I won't live my life with you, knowing you think I slept with another man."

"But I forgive you."

"You can't forgive me for something I didn't do!" She paused. This hurt so badly. All she wanted was Duncan and his love, but she'd not sacrifice herself for the sake of that love. Besides, she didn't care what he said. How could it not matter to him that he thought his wife had slept with another man? How could he help but wonder if it would happen again? "The point is," she went on with a sigh, "that you think I betrayed you and I didn't."

"I won't let you go."

"You can't hold me here forever."

"I love you." His green-eyed gaze met hers. "Isn't that enough?"

She shook her head, turning her attention back to the baby. "I'm sorry, Duncan, but it's not." It took great effort for her not to cry. They'd been through so much together. It seemed so unfair that it should end this way. "I need you to go back to Jamaica and bring my sister here, if she's still alive. Then she and I will return to London. I'll live at

Breckenridge House as you originally intended. There'll be no scandal. Your name will remain unscathed."

"But I want you here, Jilly, here with me." He balled his hands into fists, his voice filled with emotion. "Please . . ."

She closed her eyes, knowing she was right in her conviction, fearing it would break her heart. "I'm tired now, Duncan. Could you leave us?"

"I'll fight for you, Jilly. I won't let you go."

When she opened her eyes again, he was gone.

Thirty

Jillian sat on the front porch with Will tucked into his cradle at her feet. She was busy shelling fresh peas from Daphne's garden, enjoying the late August breeze that came in off the bay. Though it was warm on the Chesapeake in the late summer, thankfully, the heat was nothing like what she'd experienced in Jamaica.

"You don't have to do that," Duncan said, surprising her with his sudden appearance. She'd thought he was in the tobacco fields overseeing the cutting. She hadn't been expecting him until after sunset.

"I know. But since you sent Morning Glory on to the Robertsons and I've hired the new woman, things just haven't run smoothly in the kitchen." She dropped a handful of peas into her wooden bowl and tossed the shells into a basket. "Besides, it gives me something to do while Will naps.

Duncan peered into the cradle and touched one small bare foot. The infant slept on. "He's getting so big, so quickly.

The tension between them was like an electrical charge in the air. It had been almost three months since Will's birth, three months of stilted conversation, three months of sleeping alone. But Jillian had held to her decision. Either Duncan had to believe she'd not slept with Indigo Muldune or she would leave him.

Unfortunately, he held the last card. So far, he had refused to go to Jamaica to look for Beatrice, saying he knew Jillian would go as soon as he set sail. Jillian promised she would remain on the Tidewater until he returned with her sister or word of her death, but he refused to trust her. They had reached a stalemate, each as determined as the other.

Jillian's only hope was the cryptic note she had received when Will was about six-weeks-old. It came by way of a merchant ship. Jillian still read it daily, trying to make sense of her sister's words.

> *J,*
> *You once told me I would find*
> *a man to love. Don't come*
> *to me. I'll come to you.*
> *B.*

Jillian gave Will's cradle a push with her foot and reached for another handful of peas. All she could do for now was try to be patient. With or without Beatrice, she would have to wait until spring before she could return to London with her son. He was still too young to endure such a journey, and she wouldn't risk a winter crossing.

She looked up at Duncan, who seemed to be in no hurry. "Daphne said you went to see Constance this morning," she said, making conversation. "Is she any better?"

Duncan crouched on the top step, looking out over the wide lawn that led down to the water. One of the bond servants was cutting tall grass with a scythe near the shore. "No. Well, it's hard to say. Algernon swears she's lost her bread crumbs, but . . ."

"But Algernon would say or do anything for her; we already know that."

"Exactly."

Jillian continued to shell the peas. "I know it happens. Men and women do lose their senses, but this seems rather convenient to me. You discover she was trying to have you murdered to get your money, and suddenly she's no longer sane."

Duncan stroked his chin. He was a picture of health once again, his months in the sugarcane fields seeming to have had no lasting effects. He was as robust and handsome as Jillian had ever seen him. "Aye. It seems convenient to me as well. What kind of man would I be to call the High Sheriff on a deranged woman?"

"So, what are you going to do with her? Daphne says her husband wants her out of his house. The children will remain with him, but the marriage is over and he'll no longer be responsible for keeping her. He claims she drank herself into insanity."

"Peter is a more sensible man than I realized." Duncan plucked a blade of grass from beside the step and poked it between his teeth. "I was considering sending Algernon and Constance back to England. They could stay at one of my properties. Hell, Algernon can have a house if he wishes. I can afford an allowance to keep them both, though perhaps not to the lifestyle they'd prefer."

"That's very generous when they tried to kill you."

He shrugged, rising to look at something on the water. "I've found I don't have time for thoughts of revenge or justice. I don't want either of them dead or imprisoned. I just want them out of my life."

Jillian couldn't resist a smile. "You're a good man, Duncan Roderick."

"Good enough to—" He halted in mid-sentence.

"What is it?" She rose from her seat to stare at the bay. "Duncan?" Fear trickled down her spine. It was a ship, and her first thought was of pirates. Each summer, Duncan had admitted, there was trouble with marauders on the Chesapeake. Most of the pirates only came for booty, but a few came for blood.

"We're not expecting any vessels, are we?"

Duncan started down the steps. "Take Will inside."

"Duncan!"

"Jillian, do as I say." He broke into a run across the yard

toward the bell that would warn all the nearby workers of the potential danger. It was a call to arms. "Get the women and children and take them into the root cellar."

"But—"

"No argument for once, Jilly, just do it . . ."

The bell clanged, breaking the serenity of the summer morning.

Jillian took one last look at the ship sailing fast into their cove and ran. She scooped Will up out his cradle, shouting for Daphne. She would see to the safety of the women and children, but she'd not hide in the hole with them.

Not five minutes later, Jillian had the female serving staff and their offspring settled in the root cellar. With a kiss, she pressed Will into his great-grandmother's arms and started back up the cellar steps. In the kitchen, she retrieved a loaded blunderbuss kept for this very purpose.

By the time Jillian reached the front lawn, Duncan and a dozen men, some armed with muskets, others with scythes and farm implements, were standing on the shore, waiting, watching. Jillian ran down the hill to the water, her petticoats bunched in her free hand.

"Is that a white flag they're hoisting?" she asked, squinting in the bright sunlight.

Duncan glanced at her, surprised by her appearance. "I thought I told you to put the women and children in the root cellar."

"I did."

"I meant you, too, Jillian, and you know it. Now, I want you to go back to the house and down into the cellar until I figure out what's going on here."

She watched the ship as it grew closer, ignoring him. "Is that a flag of surrender?"

"It is."

"I don't understand. Why would a ship sail into your cove and surrender to you?"

He shook his head. "I've never seen such a thing in all my days."

"Is it a pirate ship?"

"Could be. It's the right size; it has a shallow draft, the right rigging."

"And you have no idea who it is?"

Duncan glanced at the weapon she carried in her hand. "I've my suspicions."

They watched, standing side by side as the unknown ship set anchor beside the *Royal Fortune.* "Could it be Indigo?" she breathed.

"That would be an educated guess." He looked at her. "Jilly, I'd really rather you went up to the house."

"He's my son, too. I have the same right to protect him that you do." She looked out onto the water. "I have the same right to know who that is as you do."

"Jillian, I . . . Look, they're putting a small boat over." Duncan pulled a spyglass from his breeches and peered through it. "I'll be damned."

Jillian could feel her heart pounding. Did this have something to do with Beatrice? Could the pirate have possibly sent her to the Colonies? "Who is it? Is it Indigo?" Then she spotted a woman in a bonnet with billowing white petticoats. "Duncan?" She could barely get her breath. "Is it Bea? Has he brought her home to us?"

"See for yourself." Duncan passed her the spyglass. "Back off, men," he ordered. "The two come alone. Just watch for fire from the ship."

Jillian raised the glass to her eye, almost afraid to look, for fear of what she would see. What if it weren't Bea? "Oh, I can't believe it!" she whispered, breaking into a smile. "It *is* Bea! It's she. Duncan, it's Bea!" She grabbed his bare, suntanned arm. "He's brought her home to me!"

Duncan was grinning, perhaps because she was so happy. "I suppose I won't need to make the trip to Jamaica now, will I?" He took the gun from her hand and passed it to one of his men who was retreating up the hill. "Shall we greet your sister, Jilly?" He offered his hand.

Jillian couldn't resist a smile, realizing that no matter how far from Duncan she ever went, she would always love him. There would never be another man for her. "Let's go."

So, hand in hand, they walked up the beach to where the small boat was landing. A salty breeze blew in off the bay, ruffling her hair. The blue-green water lapped at her shoes.

Jillian ran the last few feet, leaving Duncan behind. "Bea! Bea!" she cried.

The boat slid up onto the beach.

"Jilly!" Beatrice smiled from beneath her parasol. She was wearing a French-cut white gown and a broad-brimmed straw hat. Diamond earbobs glimmered from beneath her silky blond hair, which was pulled back in a sleek coiffure.

Indigo offered his hand to help her from the boat; and the minute Beatrice's slippers touched the sand, Jillian was in her arms. "Bea, Bea . . ." Jillian was laughing, but Duncan could see she was near to tears with relief. "You came home to me!"

"But just for a visit." Beatrice brushed her lips against her sister's cheek. "Then I'll be sailing back to Jamaica."

"Back to Jamaica?"

Beatrice turned to Duncan. "It's good to see you."

He nodded, then awkwardly took a step forward and brushed her cheek with a kiss. "Good to see you safe, sister."

"I take it from Jillian's appearance that you're now a father," she said, adjusting her bonnet.

Duncan grinned, unable to conceal his pride. "Of a fine, healthy son."

"I'm so happy for you." Bea reached behind her to take Indigo's hand. He was dressed all in white as well, with a hat nearly identical to Beatrice's. "Jillian, Duncan, I want you to meet my husband." She smiled shyly at Indigo, who seemed to have eyes only for her. "Indigo Muldune."

Duncan watched Jillian's jaw drop.

"Your . . . your husband?" Jillian was barely able to speak. "Is this why you're not staying with me? You . . . you married a pirate? You married the man who tried to kill us?"

"He is no longer a pirate, and he is deeply ashamed of his past transgressions. From now on, my Indigo will be using his talents to improve his sugarcane operation. It will be entirely legitimate, I can guarantee."

Jillian couldn't stop staring at the two of them.

"We're on our way to the Carolina Colonies. My husband will be receiving a full pardon from the Royal Governor there."

Duncan chuckled. This was not the first time he'd heard of such pardons. The cost came high, but it was all perfectly legal. A Royal Governor had free rein to do as he saw fit, including making money where he saw the opportunity. "For a price, he'll receive a pardon," he offered.

Beatrice looked at him. "Of course. But then his debt to society will be paid, won't it?"

Indigo removed his hat, sweeping a full bow, speaking for the first time. "It is good to see you again, my lord, this time under better circumstances. I'm glad to have this opportunity to ask your forgiveness for my past errors . . . in judgment, shall we say? It took Beatrice to make me understand that."

Duncan nearly laughed out loud. It all sounded so ridiculous, but the truly funny thing was that he believed them both. They looked in love. And he guessed they were a hell of a lot happier with each other than he and Jillian were right now.

"I understand that you cannot forget what I did; I only ask that, as a Christian, you find it in your heart to forgive me," Indigo continued.

Duncan took a step toward him, his eyes narrowing. "Are you sincere in your intentions to my wife's sister? Or is this a farce to clear your name so that you can return to pirating?"

He opened his arms. "I'm a changed man, sir. I love her." He took Bea's hand, raising it to his lips to kiss her palm. "Thank goodness I realized it in time. Thank goodness I didn't betray that budding love by consorting with her sister." He leaned to kiss Beatrice's painted mouth.

Duncan blanched. "What did you say?"

"I said, I am thankful I didn't have relations with dear Jillian here, though I was sorely tempted. No offense intended, but you were supposed to be dead." His gaze was on Beatrice again. "I'm thankful I saved myself for my wife."

Jillian glanced at Duncan, as if to say *didn't I tell you so?*

All he could do was stare at her lovely face, seeing the hurt in her cinnamon eyes. Suddenly, he realized he'd made a grave error, perhaps the gravest in his lifetime—and he'd certainly made many. He'd not believed Jillian; and now, he knew for a fact that she'd spoken the truth. He knew it as well as he knew his own name. It wasn't the pirate's words. A man could say anything. It was the look on his face.

"Excuse me," Duncan said, not sounding quite like himself. "I need to speak to Jillian privately. Would you care to come onto the porch for a cool drink?"

Beatrice looped her arm through Indigo's. "You two go ahead. We'll take a walk on the beach first. We've been cooped up too long on the ship."

Duncan took Jillian's hand and led her toward the house.

"What is it?" she asked, annoyed.

"I need to talk to you."

"Now? When my sister's just returned?"

"Now, Jilly."

"Where are you taking me?"

He led her up the lawn, onto the front porch. "Somewhere where we speak in private." He clasped her hand tightly. "I've made a terrible mistake, Jilly."

He pushed through the front door. Daphne was standing in the airy hallway, little Will perched on her hip. "Grandmother," he said. "Beatrice has arrived with her new husband. Could you see to getting something to drink for them? I have to talk to Jillian alone."

His grandmother looked surprised, but she said nothing. She had certainly known of the rift between him and Jillian since their arrival, but she had not questioned him on the matter. Perhaps she sensed this had something to do with it. "Go." She waved. "I'll see to your guests."

Duncan opened the parlor door and gestured for her to go in.

Jillian walked past him, entering the parlor that still lacked furniture, and moved to the window. She knew what he was going to say. She just wasn't sure what her reaction would be. She was wrung out with emotion. She didn't know how much more she could stand in one day. "What is it, Duncan?" Her tone was cool.

"Jillian, I've made a mistake. You didn't sleep with Indigo."

"I told you that months ago. Why should you believe Indigo if you didn't believe me?"

He exhaled. "I deserved that."

"You deserve worse."

"Jilly, I'm sorry." He went to her, reaching for her, then drawing back. His voice was filled with remorse.

Jillian kept her back to him, petting her orange tabby cat. Daphne had brought Sarah from London, and she was sitting on the windowsill. The cat purred.

Jillian didn't know what was wrong with her. This was what she had wanted, wasn't it? Why did it matter how he came to believe her, as long as he did? "Duncan, I think it's too late for this."

"I said I'm sorry," he repeated. He was silent for a moment before he spoke again. "Jillian, maybe I didn't believe you because I didn't want to."

She turned to look at him, thinking he merited at least that. "I don't understand what you're saying."

"Don't you see? I've felt betrayed my whole life."

"But I didn't betray you!"

"But if you did, I could always use that as an insulatio between us," he explained haltingly. "So that when thing did go wrong . . . it wouldn't hurt so much."

Jillian studied his face—his pensive green eyes, the bea claw tattoo on his suntanned cheek. She loved him so much and yet . . . yet she was afraid. They were so different. Thei love for each other had not changed Duncan's past, nothin could. The ghosts would always be there. Perhaps she woul be better off in England. Perhaps he had been right all alon when he had intended to leave his wife behind.

"Duncan—"

There was a sharp rap on the door.

"Go away," Duncan hollered. "We're busy."

To Jillian's surprise, the door swung open. It was Daphne No one else would have dared disobey Duncan.

"Grandmother, please. This is a private conversation."

She closed the door behind her. "So it is. But now I'r a part of it." She pointed at him. "Now, listen to me. I hav tried to keep to my own affairs. I have not interfered i your relationship with your wife, but I'll be damned if it' not time I did." She turned on Jillian. "All this stuff an nonsense. Be realistic, girl. He said he was sorry. He sai he was wrong. He knows now you didn't bed the pirate, s stop being so stubborn and forgive him!"

Jillian was shocked. "You eavesdropped?"

"A person can't help what they hear through these walls What's important is that the two of you love each othe You don't belong in London, Jillian. You belong here wit my grandson."

"But I'm afraid this will never end, Daphne." She fough tears of frustration. "It's one thing after another. I feel lik I'm fighting his past day in and day out."

She swung her fist. "So fight it! He's come so far. Yo can't give up now."

Daphne looked at Duncan. "Go to her, boy. Tell her you love her. Beg her to stay." She shook her finger. "Let her go, and you'll regret it the rest of your days."

Duncan looked at Jillian. She looked at him.

"Do you really want to leave me?" he asked her.

Jillian could feel a lump rising in her throat. She shook her head no, not sure she trusted her own voice.

Duncan came to her, wrapping his arms around her and pulling her into his embrace she'd missed so much. "Ah, Jilly," he whispered, kissing her temple.

The door closed quietly, and Daphne was gone.

"I love you," he whispered. "I'll try harder. Just don't leave me. Don't let me chase you away. I need you. I need our son."

"Duncan . . ." A tear slipped from the corner of her eye as she brushed her fingertips across his tattoo. "I do love you."

"Does that mean you'll stay? Does it mean you'll come back to my bed, Jilly?" Now his eyes were filled with tears. "Because I need you there. I need you to hold me."

She wrapped her arms around his neck and looked up into his eyes. "I'll stay," she whispered. "I'll stay and I'll love you forever, Duncan. I'll love you for your past. I'll love you in spite of it. You were destined to be mine."

And then Duncan kissed her as only he could . . .

Epilogue

Ten Years Later

"No. The molding is still not right." Jillian stood in th
center of the newly constructed parlor, her hands on he
hips in irritation. The room smelled of fresh paint an
sanded hardwood floors. Through the open windows, sh
could hear her sons' laughter and smell a hint of lilac o
the breeze. "Down." She waved to the carpenter. "That en
still has to go lower. Haven't you a level, man? Surely
carpenter would possess a level."

"Have to go out to my wagon," answered the towhea
sheepishly. He came down off the timber scaffold and mad
a fast exit.

Jillian rolled her eyes. The new wing had been unde
construction all winter and she was anxious to see it com
pleted. She crossed the room to the scaffold.

"I don't understand why he can't see it," she muttere
to herself. She stepped onto a stool, lifted her petticoat an
hoisted herself onto the scaffold. "It's clear to me that th
side needs to be lowered." She adjusted the molding tha
was only tacked up with a nail in the center. "That's better.

"Jillian!"

She spun around. "You startled me."

Duncan strode toward her, one hand tucked behind hi
back. "You shouldn't be up there on the scaffold."

"The molding wasn't straight. I'll not pay these men fo

shoddy work. As it is, this addition is going to set us back two years."

"And what was that my lady-wife told me?" He cocked his head. "Something about the improvements being inexpensive?" He looked up into the vaulted ceiling. "This is beginning to resemble the Sistine." He looked at her, his eye narrowing. "And then there was the promise that the workmen would be in and out in six weeks time."

"You want it to be nice, don't you? Now, not only will the boys have more room, but we'll have a place to entertain our friends. When Bea and Indigo and their two children come next spring, we'll have room for them."

Duncan offered his hand to her, and she sat down on the edge of the scaffold. But instead of climbing down, she rested her hand on his broad shoulders. "What?" she asked. "Why are you looking at me like that?"

"No reason." He was still smiling at her. "Only because I love you."

She smiled in return, reaching out to stroke his tattooed cheek. "I never would have thought we could be this happy. Your grandmother, God rest her soul, was right. We do belong together, don't we?"

"Forever and always," he answered, brushings his lips against hers.

"Did you need something?" She was curious about whatever it was that he held behind his back. "You usually stay as far from the construction as possible."

"Will wants you to come out to the pasture to see him on his new horse." He chuckled. "Ian and Alexander are already fighting over who will get his pony now that he has no need of it."

She laughed with him. "I'm only surprised Lincoln isn't in the pasture with you."

"Oh, he would be, if he could escape Mary's watchful eye. As bullheaded as he is, that boy will be riding by spring."

"That's all you wanted me for? So, what have you got

behind your back?" She tried to catch his arm, but he pulled it away.

"Nothing."

She knew he was teasing her. "Nothing? Then let me see your hand."

"This hand?" He held up the one he was resting on her hip.

"No. I swear, Duncan, you can be worse than the children!"

He made a slight motion with his hand behind his back and then brought it around. "Nothing here, either."

She laughed, knowing he was toying with her. But she'd play his little game. "All right, you have nothing for your dear, devoted wife. Help me down, and I'll come see Will and his horse. I fear if I remain here whilst that carpenter tries to fix the molding, he and I'll have words again."

Duncan caught her around the waist and lowered her carefully to the ground. "There you go."

"I'm pregnant, not ill," she reminded him.

Duncan gave a sigh. "This one must be a girl." He turned away. "I swear you're more contrary than you've ever been. It's got to be a female child."

The moment he turned, Jillian spotted a silken green bundle thrust into the rear waistband of his breeches. She ran past him, snatching the surprise.

"What are you doing?"

"Is this for me?" She fingered the precious wrapping.

"Mayhap. If you've been good."

"Oh, I have," she answered in a sultry voice. "I seem to recall your remarking so just last night."

"So open it." He leaned against a sanded doorjamb, crossing his arms over his chest, obviously pleased that she was pleased.

She stared at the silken bundle in her hands, enjoying the anticipation. "Where did it come from?"

"Just came in on a ship. Indigo got it for me."

Jillian lifted an eyebrow.

"Legitimately, Bea assures me in her letter."

Laughing, she walked to a sawhorse and put her gift down so that she could open it. When she pulled on the gold cord, inside she found yet more silky material, this time purple. She look at him questioningly.

"You'll see."

Jillian lifted the first piece of rich purple fabric. It was a square of semi-opaque silk with two small ribbons running from the top corners. She knew what it was in a second. Laughing, she lifted the veil to her face. "Is this for me, or you?" she teased, remembering all too well the scarf Duncan had once worn to hide his tattoo.

"It's for you." He came to her. "And look what else. I ordered it especially for you nearly a year ago."

Jillian watched in fascination as Duncan lifted a pair of filmy, transparent harem pants from the bundle. Still left was a sequined bodice of modest proportion. She took the pants from him, watching them flutter in the breeze that blew through the window. "For me?" Then she looked up at him, playing innocent. "But won't I be chilly, my lord?"

Duncan came up behind her, wrapping his arms around her waist. "They're for our bedchamber, sweet." He nibbled her earlobe. "So, I can assure you, you'll not be chilled."

She turned in his arms so that she faced him, her laughter bubbling up. "Could I try them on now?" She pulled the veil over his shoulder in a slow, seductive way.

"Now?" He pretended to be shocked. "In broad daylight?"

She pressed her lips to his, whispering, "How better to see it on me than in broad daylight?"

Duncan lifted her into his arms, their laughter mingling. With her bundle in her lap, he carried her out of the parlor toward their own private chambers . . . and years of happiness.

Please turn the page for an
exciting sneak preview of
Colleen Faulkner's
newest historical romance,

TO LOVE A DARK STRANGER,

coming soon
from Zebra Books

One

January, 1661
Rutledge Castle
Kent County, England

The knife fell from Margaret's hand, hit the wood floor, and slid under the tapestry-draped bed. She stared in shock at her blood stained palms. The heat of the bedchamber was unbearable. The scent of the blood, his and hers, cloistering. Slowly, her gaze drifted to the dead man at her feet . . . her husband.

"Baby . . ." she whispered. "My baby . . ." Margaret reached out with her bloody hands to lift the infant from the edge of the bed. Swaddled in linens, he, too, was covered with blood.

Tears ran down Margaret's cheeks as she lifted the babe to her breast as if she could comfort him. He was dead, of course. She knew he was dead—the poor wee thing with his misshapen little mouth and slit throat.

A sob wracked Margaret's body as she sank to her knees, hugging the lifeless infant, wishing desperately that she could have saved him. She knew she should pray, but no words came. She was filled with nothing but regret for that which she could not change.

"M'lady Surrey . . ." A voice came from behind her, barely audible, yet insistent. "Lady Surrey!"

Margaret looked up to see the midwife. She held out her newborn son. "Can . . . can you help him?"

Gently, the old hag took Margaret's first-born from her arms and laid him on the great bed. She stepped over the body of Lord Randall as if dead men commonly attended lying-ins.

The midwife, who smelled of cloves, leaned over the tiny, still body. She listened for breath. She felt for a pulse.

A sob rose up in Margaret's throat as she came to her feet, reaching for her infant. "No . . ."

The midwife covered the child's sweet deformed face with the corner of the bloody blanket. "You must run, m'lady," she insisted in her crackly voice. "Run before I have to summon the earl."

Margaret's gaze fell to her husband's body. He was an ugly man with a flared pig's nose and bristly blond hair. Sprawled unnaturally on the floor as he was, his club foot lay exposed, its linen wrapping come undone. It was said that a sense of peace came over a man at his deathbed, but she saw no such peace. All she saw was years of bitterness and hatred. How odd it was that a man's cruel deeds had a way of showing on his wrinkled face.

"But why must I run?" Margaret whispered, too numb for comprehension. "He killed my child."

"A father's right . . ." the old woman hissed. She was moving about the bedchamber now with the same efficiency with which she had attended the birth only hours before.

"He . . . he turned on me. First, my child; then me when I tried to defend my son. It . . . it was self-defense." Margaret wrung her blood-sticky hands. "Surely no man would condemn me for—"

"No man?" The old woman yanked Margaret's bloody sleeping robe from her shoulders and dropped a clean day gown over her shivering, naked body. "Ha! *Any* man would condemn ye! Yer husband sought to rid himself of an abomination, and you killed him for it!"

"No. Not an abomination. A child . . . my child."

"I only say what they'll say, m'lady."

Margaret accepted the rough leather shoes and patched stockings the old woman thrust into her arms. "Surely the courts will—"

The midwife gave her a push. "Don't ye hear my words? No one will believe ye! Ye just killed the Earl of Rutledge's younger brother! Run, child! Run into the night and let it swallow ye up!"

Margaret took a stumbling step backward, clutching the shoes and stockings to her aching, milk-swollen breasts. "Run? Run where?"

"London! London is the only place to hide!"

"But my baby. He must be buried." Margaret reached out with one hand toward the bundle on the bed. "He must have a decent burial!"

The midwife ushered Margaret to the door, pinning a maid's cap to her dark, tumbled hair. "I'll see 'im buried in the churchyard, same as I seen all the others."

Margaret stared at the woman's wrinkled face. "I cannot run," she whispered desperately. "I'm too afraid. I haven't the courage."

"Ha! Men's words!" The old woman's gray eyes narrowed. "Ye had the courage to kill the bastard to save yerself, didn't ye?"

Margaret leaned against the door and slipped her feet into the stockings, not bothering to pull them up. "Which way shall I go?" She stepped into the leather shoes. "I . . . I've never even been to London."

"Take the road north, only stay to the woods' line." The midwife removed the mended woolen cloak from her own shoulders and covered Margaret's. "Flag down the first coach ye see, and say you're Lady Surrey's handmaid. Claim yer headed to London to see yer dyin' mother. By the time the earl notifies the sheriff, you'll be lost to 'im in Londontown."

Margaret rested her hand on the doorknob. She was so numb that all she could do was follow the woman's orders. "Say I'm Lady Surrey's maid, gone to London . . . dying mother," she repeated. Then her gaze came to rest on the bloody bundle at the end of the bed she had shared with her husband.

The midwife reached out to stop her, but Margaret couldn't leave her son without saying goodbye. She stepped around Philip's body and leaned over the bed. She lifted the corner of the fleece blanket; and with the love born of a mother, she kissed her infant's not-so-perfect little mouth. "Goodbye, my love," she whispered, letting the blanket fall. Then, with resignation, she turned to go.

"Wait!" The midwife grabbed her arm. "You'll not get a mile looking like that." She hurried across the room and came back with a clean rag dipped in the wash basin. She wiped Margaret's teary cheeks. Then she took Margaret's hands and scrubbed them vigorously.

The wash rag turned crimson.

"Go, now . . ." the midwife hissed, finished with her. "Run from the Randall curse! Run for your life!"

Margaret took one last look at the little bundle on the bed and then stumbled out of her bedchamber and into the cold, drafty hallway. No light illuminated the narrow stone corridor, but she knew it all too well. For fifteen years she had walked these hallways, alone in the darkness. For fifteen years she had been imprisoned.

Margaret followed the corridor from the east wing into the main house. All was silent, but for her own muffled footsteps. In the main hall, she caught a glimpse of pale light falling from a doorway. The earl's private office . . .

Her breath caught in her throat as she pressed her back to the wall. She had to pass the earl's library to escape the castle, that or retrace her steps back to the east wing and flee in a different direction.

She stole a glance into the lit room. There was the earl,

her dead husband's elder brother, seated at his desk. He was sipping a glass of claret, making that odd sucking sound that he did. Seeing the earl's deformed mouth brought tears to her eyes. It was the same mouth her son had been born with. It was strange, though, that looking at the Earl of Rutledge, she was revolted by his deformity, and yet the first glance at her newborn son had brought about none of the same feelings of repulsion. Then Margaret knew that it was not the deformity of the earl's palate that disgusted her, but the deformity of his cruel heart.

As Margaret stared at the earl in the feeble light, she came to the practical realization of what the murder she had just committed meant. If she could escape, it meant freedom. Freedom from her cruel husband, Philip. Freedom from the earl's twisted words and sexual innuendoes. Freedom from his threats. Freedom from her fear.

How ironic it was that the death of her son could bring her the release she had lost hope of so many years ago. But then, her grandmother had always said that even in the darkest moments, God shed light upon his children.

Suddenly feeling stronger, Margaret reached down and slipped out of her shoes. Picking them up, she tiptoed past the earl's open door. She walked down the corridor and out the front hallway. She stepped into the dark, cold night and into freedom.

Captain Kincaid Scarlet rode low in his saddle, fighting the bitter wind in his face. It was a damned dreary night to be about business. He'd have preferred to spend the hours at the Cock and Crow Ordinary with a jack of ale in one hand and a piece of the seductive Mrs. Caine in the other. He almost wished he'd let his friend Monti talk him into remaining in London tonight, but a man had a duty to his work and Kincaid understood that duty, even if Monti didn't.

Monti pulled in his mount to ride beside Kincaid. He

was a short man, with a broad face like a shovel and protruding ears. He wasn't a handsome fellow, but he was as devoted to their friendship as any man could be. "I don't like the looks of this, Captain," he hollered against the wind. "I told you I should have checked with my astrologer first. The snow's a bad omen. I can feel it in my bones."

What now? Kincaid scoffed, amused by Monti's usual litany. He was a superstitious man who saw ill-luck at every turn. "I see no snow, and your bones are always telling you to stay home when it's cold out." His words were no sooner out of his mouth, then the first wet snowflakes hit his cheekbones. By the light of the pale, slivered moon he could see the I-told-you-so look on his companion's face.

"There's still time to turn back," Monti offered. "No one would be the wiser." He wiped his runny nose with a green handkerchief he extracted from inside his cloak. "We can catch this stinking cuttlefish another night."

Kincaid frowned. No. He'd not turn back, not tonight. He wanted this one, and he wanted him badly. Nearly six months he'd waited for dear Edmund Tolliger to depart the city at a convenient time and circumstance. "Excellent try," he called good-naturedly to Monti. "But I'll not bite."

Both men ducked to avoid a low-hanging branch as the road, barely more than a trail in places, made a sharp bend to the right. The horses' hooves sank in the rutted road, splattering horse and rider with mud.

Just as Kincaid rounded the bend, he spotted something beside the road. He immediately whirled his mount around to go back.

"What are you doing?" The brutal wind tore at Monti's cloak as he attempted to turn his mount. "You know it's imperative that we stick to our schedule!"

Kincaid held up one gloved finger, signaling to his friend to wait but a moment. He rode his horse back to the spot where he had seen the bundle. Sure enough, there it was, a heap of blankets lying in the dead grass. No . . . a cloak.

Kincaid dismounted, turning his back to the wind to see what he'd found. He pulled at the edge of the wet, mud-caked cloak and, to his surprise, found a tumble of curls.

A dead woman lying beside the road? He thrust his hand beneath the cloak and felt warmth. No, not dead at all.

"Madame?" Kincaid crouched beside her. "Madame, could I assist you?" He tugged back a bit more of the wool cape. She was a tearing beauty, whoever she was. Not a beauty like the ladies of the court with their bleached hair and moleskin face patches, but a natural beauty . . . an innocent.

She was as pale as milk glass. "Madame?" He touched her shoulder.

She stirred, her dark lashes fluttering open. The moment her eyes focused, she sought to fight him off. "No!" she screamed, hitting him with surprising force. She kicked him in the shin, knocking him into the mud, and then scrambled up the wet bank off the road. "You'll not take me alive! I'll not go back!"

"I mean you no harm," Kincaid hollered, fascinated by the sound of the woman's voice, by her haunting eyes. He didn't know what color they were, though. *He couldn't let her go without knowing what color they were.*

He chased her up the grassy bank, taking care of his footing. The falling snow made it slippery. "Stop! I only want to aid you!"

She nearly reached the top of the bank before she skidded in the wet snow that was fast turning to sleet. "No!" she called one last time before she slid into him.

"God's bowels, what have you found? A woman?" Monti called from the road where his mount pranced back and forth nervously. "We've no time for wenches tonight, man! Come along!"

Kincaid reached down and picked her up. This time she didn't fight him. "Where are you taking me?" she whispered, her head rolling onto his shoulder. "Not Newgate."

Kincaid carefully placed one boot in front of the other, fearful he would stumble carrying her down the bank to the road. "I sure as hell hope not, sweetheart," he crooned.

"What are you doing?" Monti demanded as Kincaid reached the road and pursed his cold lips to whistle for his horse.

"Taking her with us."

"Bloody hell you are!"

How could Kincaid explain this to his friend? Yes, he'd always had a weakness for females; but the moment he had seen this woman's face, he had known she was different from the others. He knew he had to protect her, shield her, though from what, he was unsure. "She'll freeze to death on a night like this."

"Who is she?" Monti badgered. "Where did she come from? Whose wife do you carry off tonight, *Captain Scarlet?"*

Kincaid attempted to sit her on his horse, ignoring Monti. "Come on, sweetheart," he murmured into her muddy, tangled hair. "You're going to have to help me a little here. I have to mount behind you."

Either she heard him or in her state of unconsciousness she merely reacted. She grabbed the silver pummel of his saddle and leaned forward to rest her head on his horse's braided mane.

Kincaid swung into the saddle behind her and, opening his cloak, pulled her close to his own body for warmth.

Monti reined in beside him. "So, now we go home at last?"

Kincaid took up the reins in his gloved hands. "No. Our plans stand."

"Are you mad?" Monti urged his mount forward to keep up with Kincaid. "You can't bring a woman along! She'd surely vex our luck and we'd be hanging from the triple tree of Tyburn before the month's end."

"Nonsense. We're invincible, and luck has nothing to do

with it." Kincaid slid one hand inside his cloak to wrap his arm around her waist. She was dirty and shivering, but, sweet heaven, she smelled good. "Skill. Skill and charm is all it is." Then he sank his heels into his mount's flanks and the horse leaped forward, breaking into a run. Kincaid knew he'd have to make up for lost time now, or miss Tolliger. He'd waited too long for the Puritan bastard to let him go.

Captain Scarlet and his companion, Montigue Kern, thundered down the center of the road from Kent to London. Ahead lay a copse of trees and, if Kincaid were as correct in his mathematical calculation as he usually was, Tolliger and his mistress would be passing through in a matter of moments.

As the men grew closer to their destination, Kincaid was forced to remove his arm from the warmth of the woman's body to draw his blunderbuss. Out of the corner of his eye, he spotted Monti unsheathing his musket. Firepower was Monti's trademark. Every man on the highway had a trademark these days.

"What's your fancy this fine night?" Kincaid asked, wiping the freezing rain from his mouth. "The fallen log or the drunken jig? Your choice, my friend."

Monti scowled. "If you think I'm dismounting "

Kincaid hushed him with a wave of his broad hand. "The fallen log it is."

In a matter of minutes, they reached the designated spot. Kincaid dismounted and led his horse behind a giant leaning oak. He tucked the woman's cloak tighter around her. "Listen, sweetheart," he whispered, trying to better shield her from the driving snow and sleet. "This will take but a few moments, and then we can be on our way. A warm bed and a bit of hot porridge is all you need."

When he touched her, the woman lifted her head from the saddle's pummel. She looked at him, dull-eyed, as if she saw him but did not see.

He couldn't resist reaching out to catch a lock of hair

between his gloved fingers. "What's your name, sweet? Can you tell me that?"

"Lady S— . . . M—Meg," she whispered in the same haunting voice. Then she laid her head down again.

"Meg," Kincaid repeated, pulling a second pistol from his saddlebag. "Meg." He liked the name. It suited her heart-shaped face, rosy lips, and nut-brown hair.

"Captain!"

"Coming," Kincaid answered in a carefree tone.

"I hear the coach," came Monti's anxious voice.

"I'm coming; I'm coming." Kincaid secured his horse's reins to a tree limb and then walked back to the road. Tucking his pistols into his breeches, he caught the line Monti tossed him. The two had followed the routine so often that there was no need to speak as they worked.

Kincaid tied one end of the rope to a decent-sized fallen tree, and Monti used his horse to drag the log into the middle of the roadway.

"Approaching," Monti warned as he backed his horse into the cover of the tree line.

Kincaid stepped behind a tree just as he spotted the coach rounding the bend. It was snowing harder now, the snow mixing with sleet, driving sideways. It was a crappy night for business. Dangerous. He wiped the wet snow from his eyes and drew his primed pistol. In the dim light of the moon, his gaze met Monti's worried one and he winked. Then he swathed his face in a scarf of red silk drawn from his cloak and turned to face the approaching vehicle.

The coach rolled down the center of the guttered road and came to a halt at the log that blocked its advance. In the sleet, Kincaid couldn't make out the crest on the coach door, but it had be Tolliger. What other fool would be out on such a dreary night?

Kincaid took a deep breath, drew a cocky smile, and stepped out of the trees. Rumor had it, it was his laughing eyes that made the ladies swoon. "Stand and Deliver!" he boomed in his best highwayman's voice.

But the moment the words passed his lips, he knew something was wrong. The driver leaped to his feet, swinging a musket from beneath his cloak.

A trap.

The coach door burst open, and Kincaid found himself staring down the flared barrel of another musket.

Behind him, Monti gave a cry. Musket-fire exploded into the night, and the driver fell from his perch into the mud. The coach horses shied, and the vehicle began to roll backwards as more men poured from its door.

Soldiers. Blast them to hell!

Kincaid spun on the balls of his feet.

"Coming for you!" Monti shouted, barreling at a full gallop toward him

"Alive! I want them alive!" ordered one of the king's soldiers.

Everything was happening so quickly. In the wink of an eye. Yet in Kincaid's head, all seemed to move at quarter-speed. He saw the frightened whites of the solder's eyes as they lunged for the infamous highwayman known as Captain Scarlet. He heard the pounding of hoofbeats as Monti approached.

Kincaid knew all he need do was reach up as his companion rode by and they would be able to escape two astride.

But then he remembered the woman hidden in the trees. He couldn't abandon her. The soldiers would surely arrest her as an accomplice. It would be his fault. She'd be in Newgate, and he'd be drinking in the Ordinary by dawn.

"Go on without me!" Kincaid shouted to Monti, turning to run in the opposite direction.

"Captain!"

"Go!" Kincaid signaled as Monti galloped by.

Kincaid fired in the direction of the oncoming soldiers as he rushed into the woods, heading straight for Meg. Out of the corner of his eye, he saw the stock of the musket as it swung down and cracked him soundly in the head.

The ground rushed up, and Kincaid sank in darkness.

About the Author

Colleen Faulkner lives with her family in southern Delaware. She is the author of fifteen historical romances, all published by Zebra Books. Colleen is currently working on her next historical romance and will also have a short story in Zebra's Christmas collection, CHRISTMAS ENCHANTMENT, to be published in December 1996. Colleen loves hearing from her readers, and you may write to her c/o Zebra Books. Please include a self-addressed stamped envelope if you wish a response.

DON'T MISS THESE OTHER THRILLING ROMANCES BY BEST-SELLING AUTHOR COLLEEN FAULKNER!

O'BRIAN'S BRIDE (0-8217-4895-5, $4.99)

Elizabeth Lawrence left her pampered English childhood behind to journey to the far-off Colonies . . . and marry a man she'd never met. But her dreams turned to dust when an explosion killed her new husband at his powder mill, leaving her alone to run his business . . . and face a perilous life on the untamed frontier. After a desperate engagement to her husband's brother, yet another man, strong, sensual and secretive Michael Patrick O'Brian, enters her life and it will never be the same.

CAPTIVE (0-8217-4683-1, $4.99)

Tess Morgan had journeyed across the sea to Maryland colony in search of a better life. Instead, the brave British innocent finds a battle-torn land . . . and passion in the arms of Raven, the gentle Lenape warrior who saves her from a savage fate. But Tess is bound by another. And Raven dares not trust this woman whose touch has enslaved him, yet whose blood vow to his people has set him on a path of rage and vengeance. Now, as cruel destiny forces her to become Raven's prisoner, Tess must make a choice: to fight for her freedom . . . or for the tender captor she has come to cherish with a love that will hold her forever. .